Angel Flights

BAER CHARLTON

Angel Flights
Copyright © 2015 by Baer Charlton

All rights reserved. Printed in the United States of America. No part of this book may be used or reproduced in any manner whatsoever without written permission except in the case of brief quotations embodied in critical articles or reviews.

This book is a work of fiction. Names, characters, businesses, organizations, places, events and incidents either are the product of the author's imagination or are used fictitiously. Any resemblance to actual persons, living or dead, events, or locales is entirely coincidental.

Rogena Mitchell-Jones, Literary Editor
Mar Penner-Griswold, Content Editor
Book and Cover design by David L'Bearz

First Edition: October 2015

Publisher Mordant Media—A Division of Charlton Productions

MORDANT MEDIA ™©®
A Division of Charlton Productions

10 9 8 7 6 5 4 3 2 1

Contents

Summer 1974 1
Seven Years Earlier 11
Getting the Right Job 31
Training Day 35
Justice and Injustice 51
Ground Rules 77
Meet the Neighbors 105
Work Wrong Do Right 111
Where Were You This Weekend? 129
I Need You To Do Something For Me 143
Angel Meet Sleepy 155
Crossing to the Hacienda 167
How Did It Go? 181
Same Old Same Old 191
The Bad Side of Work 201
New Door? 213
Change of Plans 217
Winter Plans 231
Through the Door 239
The Work is the Work 247
Happy Birthday, Maria 257
Mexico to Study 265
No, What Are You Really Doing 273

Back to Work	281
Shutting the Fat Man Down	291
Getting Ready Down Mexico Way	315
Fat Man is Dead	327
Deliver As If Your Life Depends On It	343
Romeo and Juliet	357
Cricket	367
Run	383
Stay	393
Students	413
I'm Leaving—But First	427
We're Out of a Job Anyway	433
The Game Remains The Same	443
Saving Cricket	449
Where To Now?	467
What Do You Want?	475
Will You?	493
Well?	501
The Necklace	511
Rio	521
Other Books by Baer Charlton	523
About the Author	525

To an amazing friend—and a ride I will never forget.

Terrance 'Rabbit' Roberts
6/1946 — 3/5/2015

01

SUMMER 1974

THE DARK OF night in Los Angeles is never black. The city lights had long turned the black to dark shades of gray. The city never slept entirely, and the best the night sky could do was temper the glowing ember of the city. The shades of gray in the night were much like the searing sunset turned to shades of fool's gold instead of the purity of golden light.

Night or day, Los Angeles was not a city of black and white, but shades of gray—some darker, some lighter, and not all was what it seemed to be.

The late June heat didn't help. The city's concrete and asphalt held the heat of the summer sun.

The curtains hung lifelessly in the front bedroom of the small pink stucco bungalow. *Only a nod to privacy or dark.* Even they were slightly parted— hoping for air movement if a faint breeze was possible. The night air hung—dead.

The cast metal phone on the nightstand mum-

ANGEL FLIGHTS

bled through the cotton balls stuffed between the bell and the casing. Both the wall phone in the kitchen and the desk phone in the office rang a half-heartbeat after.

The large mass of bodies moved under the sheet. The thick outsized shoulder started to roll but was stopped. The phone rang again. Gabe growled. "Damn it, Gertie—get off me." The shape slithered off the large man and retreated to the other side of the bed.

Gabe rolled over at the third ring and looked at the softly lit numbers on the clock. The two flipped over to a three. "Three twenty-three... already arrested." He grabbed the hand piece off the cradle. "Hello?"

The cheery voice of an operator twittered in his ear. "I have a collect call from Amelia Burns. Do you wish to accept the charges?"

"Which precinct is she calling from?"

"I'm sorry, sir... what did you say?"

Gabe growled to clear his throat. "I said which precinct is she calling from? Which jail?"

"Oh... Oh, she's not in jail..."

Gabe heard a small voice he hadn't heard in four years... and never expected to hear again.

"Angel...? Angel... it... it's Cricket. I need your help." The last word broke into a wailing cry.

"Sir?"

Gabe's mind was instantly clear. His legs swung

over the edge of the bed as his left hand reached out for the chain on the lamp. "Operator, I'll accept the charges, but I need you to stay on the line a moment." He had not heard that voice in four years, but the code name of Angel galvanized his heart.

"Yes, sir?"

"I know you can tell me the address where she is. I need that information."

"Sir, I'm not at liberty—"

Gabe cut her off. "I'm a former LAPD, and now an officer of the court. This is one of my street informants that we lost a while back. Her life is in danger and I need your help. If you need to kick this up to your supervisor... then I suggest you get them right now—because I also know that even at three in the morning, they are standing right behind you."

A deeper, huskier woman's voice cut in. "Sir, I have you listed as Gabriel Street at 471 Stockton Street."

"Yes, ma'am. I'm a Special Investigator attached to the US Attorney General's office here in LA."

"Yes, sir. I would like to give you an exact location, but unfortunately, she is in Artesia. The best I can tell you is that she is about a half mile southwest of the 405 freeway. From the phone number series, I would say she is on Artesia Boulevard. Does that help?"

"You have the phone number?"

ANGEL FLIGHTS

"Yes, sir. 555-7812."

"Thank you. I'll take it from here." He could hear that the crying had subsided.

"Good luck, sir." He could hear the audible click of the operator disconnecting.

"Cricket?"

"Angel?"

"Sweetie, I need you to tell me exactly where you are. Where is the phone booth?"

"It's a Shell gas station. I'm on a big street."

"Can you see a street sign?"

"Not here, but let me go look…"

"Cricket…no. Do not leave the phone booth."

"Okay."

"Listen, I'm coming to get you… but it's going to take a while. So there's some stuff I need you to do first." He grabbed his jeans off the end of the bed and pulled them up one leg.

"Okay… what?" Her voice was starting to become more stable.

"What shoes are you wearing?"

"Penny loafers… We were just coming down to hang out on the pier…"

"The light in the phone booth, can you see the light, or is it in a plastic shield?

Her voice strained. He imagined her neck stretching as she looked up. "There is a plastic thing, but it's broken… I can see the light bulb."

"Okay. Do you have anything you can use to

break the light bulb?"

"The phone..."

He pulled a sock on as he cradled the phone on his shoulder. "Nah, the cord is purposely cut too short to..." He heard the phone being used as a club and glass shattering. *My mistake.*

"Now what?"

"Good girl. Now comes the hard part. I have to hang up for a few minutes, but I'm going to call you right back. Okay?"

"Angel?"

"Baby, I'll call you back in less than ten minutes. Wait... how many lanes does the street have?"

"Six..."

"Artesia. What is across the street?"

"A bunch of small stores."

"What are they?"

"A barber, a locksmith, a picture framer, and a dog grooming place—"

"What is the name of the dog groomer?" He reached to the bottom shelf of the nightstand and pulled up the yellow page book.

"It says Katie's Pampered Puppy Palace."

Gabe scanned the listings. He underlined the small listing on Artesia Boulevard. "Got it—Cricket, you're my hero. If you have a watch, I will call you back in five minutes, ten tops."

Her voice started to crack. "Okay, Angel."

ANGEL FLIGHTS

"Baby, it's going to be just fine. We made it through a worse time before—this is just a piece of cake. Now when we hang up, I need you to squat down and hide in the dark until I call. Okay?"

"Okay."

"Great... Oh, are you wearing pants?"

"No... a skirt and blouse."

"Okay. I'll call you right back."

The click on the other end made Gabe's stomach lurch. He dialed a number he had known by heart since he moved into the little house in El Sereno—three months after leaving the Marine Corps.

"Desk."

"Stan, it's Gabe."

"Hey, Gabe. How's the meat grind downtown?"

"I'll let you know the day I actually have to go there. Listen, I need two huge favors. First, I need a jumpsuit for a trustee or if you have a regular one even better. If it your wife's size—that would be perfect."

"You don't know my wife... she's almost the size of you."

"Wrong, Stan. I met her at the funeral last fall. I need to have someone run it over while I pull out my bike."

Gabe could hear the watch commander yell at one of the cops hanging around the station. "Gabe, it's coming, what's the second thing?"

"I need you to call the precinct that handles this

address in Artesia." He gave the sergeant the address. "That is across from a Shell station. There is a young girl in the phone booth at the gas station. She is waiting for me. I need one car to go and sit where she can see them, but to not approach her. She won't open the door until she sees me."

The man was thinking and the silence stretched. "Got it. Are you going to hang on while I make the call?"

"I've gotta run as soon as the jumpsuit gets here. Stan—we go way back... I know I can trust you."

"Should I warn them what you look like?"

Gabe ran his hand through his curls that flowed down to his massive shoulders. "Yeah, I guess you better. Warn them about the bike, too... Artesia is a touchy area when it comes to bikers."

"I get off in thirty. Is the kitchen light on?"

"The coffee is never off, and there is always too much food in the fridge—but if you stick around for a second cup, you won't be sleeping this morning."

"Can I bring you anything?"

"A whole chicken for Gertie; I haven't cooked anything for three days."

"How does she like it?"

"Raw—but I've only seen her take it from a few people other than me."

"I'll just bring some stuff and when you get back with the girl, we can have breakfast. I'm sure this is going to be a good story."

ANGEL FLIGHTS

"Thanks, man. I owe you." Gabe hung up and slipped his feet into the tall engineer boots. Grabbing his leather jacket, he went to the closet and pulled out a smaller one as well.

Walking through the kitchen, he smiled at the famous light over the kitchen sink. The commercial coffee maker showed half-full. He slipped out the back door and stepped over to the old garage that was sized for a Model A.

In the garage was his mass of black and chrome. Only in the light did the dark paint show the red flames that were there in the clear coat. Under the fluorescent lights of the boulevards, the mother of pearl radiated in the reds and pinks, making the flames dance. The oversized 1968 Shovelhead Harley was his latest bike—the fifth since he had left the Marines.

The bike rumbled to life. The neighbors were used to the quiet man coming and going at odd hours. His doings were his own, and nobody got nosey—they were positive they did not want to know the answers.

As Gabe closed the door to the garage, a police cruiser slid to a stop at the end of the driveway. Gabe walked down as he let the bike warm up. He retrieved the jumpsuit and reminded the cop that the coffee was brewed. The car moved back and the light went off as Gabe rode the bike down the drive. At the street, Gabe pulled on his gloves and slid the green tinted glasses down onto his face. He nodded thanks as the officer closed his car door. The cop's hand held his paperwork.

Gabe turned down the street and headed for Mission Boulevard. The freeway entrance was three miles away. Cricket was only fifty-three miles away.

But where their story began was a lifetime ago.

02

SEVEN YEARS EARLIER

HIS LAST FEW years had been spent mostly in a Marine gymnasium in the frozen asshole of humanity that America claimed as a state. Now Gabe sat hulking at the end of a grim bar.

The inside of the bar was no better than the outside that Gabe had walked past for years on his way to school as a kid. He was sure the barflies from his youth had long since died and were replaced by younger ones—but the men along the bar that afternoon looked just as old as the last set he had seen about four years before.

The bartender quietly polished a line of beer glasses before storing them in the cooler. The painted blue letters of the sign on the front window were snow covered—*ICE COLD BEER*. Even for a kid who didn't shave yet, the words seemed inviting when the concrete felt like molten lava through a pair of worn out, cast off flip-flops.

ANGEL FLIGHTS

The bartender flipped the towel over his shoulder and made his way down the bar. The man's movements spoke of physical agility years before his middle turned to gut and the rest had settled.

The bartender leaned on the bar with his arms at spread angles. He took in the haircut and the heavy load of upper-body muscle. From personal experience, he knew that kind of muscle mass came from only a few places. "Where did you just get out of?"

Gabe hated being transparent, but he also recognized someone who made their living sizing people up. "Marine Corps."

The man smiled softly and straightened up a little. He stuck his hand out. "Squid. Gunner's Mate on the Mighty Mo. The name is Chet. Let me buy you a beer, leatherneck."

They shook. There was no animosity so fabled in bars between the two branches. "Gabriel, Gabe—Master at Arms. My last base was Adak."

Chet laughed. His large belly bounced like a giant yo-yo. "From the frozen asshole of the world to the stinking armpit—what brings you to Alhambra?"

"I grew up about four blocks from here. I walked past here on my way to school every day."

"Folks still here?" The man shaved the head off the beer with a knife. Gabe smiled that the knife was a military KA-BAR.

"Mom is. Dad passed away a couple of years ago."

Chet put down a coaster and placed the beer on it. "Sorry to hear that."

"It was a blessing really. He was in Luzon during the second. He came home pretty messed up and never was really healthy after that. Mom carried the load mostly. She's a librarian and tutors kids how to read—every night. The survivor benefits are more now than he ever scratched out in a paycheck as a sweep or night guard somewhere he could sleep. Most of my memories of my father were of him sleeping."

"A lot of bodies came home, but not the men."

Chet leaned against the back bar and crossed his arms against the horror of old buddies long gone. He turned and looked at the future. "So what are you going to do now?"

Gabe shrugged. "I got home last night..."

"And decided to immediately hit the local watering hole." Chet rolled his body to face straighter and his voice dropped. "If your ambition is to be one of these alcoholics who spend their lives here... I don't need your business.

Gabe nodded at the honesty of the man whose living he made off the regulars. Then he laughed lightly.

"Actually, I came in because I had heard you have good homemade soup." He looked at his untouched beer and then looked up shyly. "I don't really drink beer... I'm more of a coffee kind of guy."

ANGEL FLIGHTS

The bartender smiled and picked up the beer. He carried it down to one of the rummies at the other end. He strolled back to the Crock Pot. Taking a large bowl, he ladled out some beef stew.

Stopping, Chet poured a tall mug of coffee and held up the creamer towards Gabe. With a shake of the head, he returned the cream to the cooler and brought the meal and coffee.

"Corned beef stew—my grandmother's recipe. I only get the best beef. The stew is only free three times—your first bowl, the day you get an honest, respectable job, and at your wake. For you, the coffee is always on the house."

"Thanks, Chet. Hopefully, I'll be back for the next bowl soon." He ran his face with closed eyes as he took a long sniff dramatically.

"Just like your mama made."

Gabe laughed. "Fat chance there. Mom never had time to cook like this. Our soup was Mrs. Campbells."

"There are worse ways to grow up…"

"Very true, Chet… very true."

Chet tended to the others as Gabe enjoyed the stew. True to his word, the beef was lean and tender. Gabe thought he needed to find a good job.

The job landed in front of him. The want ads from the day's Times. Chet had circled the ad. Gabe looked up.

Chet leaned in. "I know people in a lot of precincts. You can go see them or I'll bring them here. You meet them, they get to know you, and they put in the word."

Gabe read the ad again as he chewed. He wiped his mouth. "This is a general hiring call for the LAPD. They'll have a thousand guys lined up down there."

Chet stabbed his finger at the ad. "Either you aren't as smart as I thought you were, or you don't know shit about ads and how things work. That ad there—is nothing more than a billboard that says they have the money to hire new officers. It doesn't say where. I know Alhambra and Pasadena are both hurting for good officers. South Pasadena may also have openings, but they are so tight lipped a mouse can't find even a whisper of cheese in the deli aisle."

Gabe laughed. The man was warming up and Gabe liked his style. They talked about the military, policing in the coldest place on earth, and growing up in two very different generations, but in the same town. Chet even knew the house where Gabe had grown up.

Most of the old men along the bar stayed in place, nursed their drinks, and stared at the air or the television. A couple left and was soon replaced by the later shift of three. Gabe watched Chet's spare movements up and down the bar. The customers varied, but basically, it was a fifty-cent draft beer here and a buck shot there.

ANGEL FLIGHTS

Over the course of the day, Gabe figured, it all added up.

As Chet was looking after one of the men, the door opened for just a brief moment. The spry older man was rail thin but a lot more limber. He gained his vision and headed for the bar.

"Hey, Willie. What are you doing in the bottom lands?"

As the man came closer, Gabe could see a large scar that covered most of the man's throat. "Dropping an old bike and maybe picking up another car. How have you been?" The man took a seat as he nodded at Gabe. At that moment, Gabe could see the jagged scar ripped its way up the side of the man's neck to the left ear.

Chet stopped for another cup of coffee on his way down the bar. He put it down and nodded at Gabe. "Captain William Knight, retired—meet Marine MP Gabe Street—newly retired."

The slender man leaned along the bar and extended his hand. "Good to meet another enforcement person."

Gabe shook but frowned. "You don't look like Shore Patrol."

The man chuckled sardonically, "Not patrol, Naval Intelligence after the Seals wouldn't let me go play anymore." He ran the back of his finger along his neck.

"Can I ask?"

"Sure, we're among friends. My squad was a bit north of where we were supposed to be. I put up with hanging around for four days, took care of the problem and seventeen days later, my boys were home where we belonged."

Chet harrumphed. "With most of the old guys around here, the story gets grander with each telling." He turned to Gabe. "After getting off the meat hook he had been hung on, and killing all of the camp guards, he led his men and a bunch more into the jungle. It was a hundred twenty miles to the DMZ. He got them there in seventeen days."

Willie grumped. "Kilometers. It was only hundred and eighteen kilometers. Them klicks are a lot shorter than miles."

"They still put you in for a commendation."

Willie fluffed his hand at the air. "Whatever floats their boat—that puffy blue ribbon looks better on their record behind a desk than around my neck. I've got my glory scarf."

Gabe looked at the man who had just dismissed the greatest honor that could be handed to a soldier. He knew the man ran a lot deeper than his keel was showing.

Chet looked at his friend, "So what are you buying now?"

"I'm looking for something around a 1963 Dodge Dart GT. I want to stick a 340 or at least a 318 in it. Maddie wants to see what we can do up in the north counties. We think we can bracket it about nine flat or just above."

"Have you talked to Manny's kid?"

"I called over there. He's serving in Germany right now, and Manny only knew of a couple of guys. So I'll be around and looking for a while." He looked over at the empty bowl in front of Gabe. "Looks like the jarhead hated the soup today—I'll have the same."

"Coming right up." He called back over his shoulder, "Hey, Gabe, how are you getting around?"

"Thumb or a bus—until I can find something cheap."

Willie looked at him. "Know how to ride a motorcycle?"

"We had some Harleys down at Pendleton, and a Jap 200 with ice tires up in Adak."

"I know where a 1937 Knucklehead is... that nobody will touch because it was converted to a Panhead bottom end with foot shift."

"Why would that bother anyone?"

"It shouldn't—it's the fact that the thing is blown out to ninety-two inches and has a high lope cam. The bike will hit about one-forty in a quarter mile."

"Why are they selling it?"

"It's too slow." Willie buried his smile in the first spoon of stew.

Chet leaned in. "I heard that, you old bastard.

You are evil. The man survived the Corps, and now you want to put him on a killing machine?"

"Who is selling it?"

"My girlfriend."

Chet barked a laugh. "She's nothing but a young girl, but she is a piece of work. She and your mama have something in common."

"What's that?"

"They both know crazy people, and they both are librarians."

Gabe smiled. He wanted to meet this librarian who owned a fast motorcycle.

"Where do I go to see the bike?"

Willie jerked his thumb back over his shoulder towards the street.

The bike was strapped down in the back of an old Studebaker truck. The un-muffled exhaust pipe Gabe was used to seeing around the military bases. The bike looked basically stock—just stripped of everything that made it street legal.

"Do you have the rest of the parts?"

The three laughed. The bike was not much—other than a tiny seat on an engine with wheels and a gas tank.

Willie looked at Chet. "You think Roscoe is home?"

Chet nodded like he was drifting off to sleep. Gabe had the impression the man was not only conveying the affirmative but was also evaluating the

ANGEL FLIGHTS

idea of the man as a choice. "He probably could get it street legal by midnight."

Willie turned to Gabe and asked if he wanted to ride along.

The fence was eight-foot tall chain link, but by the look of the four dogs, Gabe wasn't sure if the fence was tall enough.

Willie leaned over at the nervous Gabe and stage whispered, "It's not the dogs you need to worry about, it's his wife. She will bite or cut off anything she thinks you might not need in a heartbeat. Oh, shit... here she comes."

Gabe looked up toward the deep front porch. A small woman pushed open the screen door. Gabe wondered if the woman was as tall as his bellybutton. He leaned over. "She really does look scary."

Willie deadpanned and whispered back. "If she sticks either hand in a pocket... run, because she probably has a gun."

She put her hand up above her eyes and looked at the truck, the bike, and the two men.

"If that asshole is filling your head with lies about me killing seven people, then it is pure bullshit. It was nine and they were all bigger than me. Now, you can either come in the gate like polite folk, or you can stand out there like that chicken coward Willie. Either way, I have fresh apple pie that is almost cool enough to be eaten with some ice cream."

Willie grabbed the gate and swung it open. Four

dogs raced at the two men. Willie put both arms out with palms down. The dogs came to a halt and sat in range of getting petted. Willie waited for the count of five and then squatted down and was massed by fur. "Woman, you know I hate animals..."

The woman turned. "You're on your own, Willie. Come on in, sonny. Chet done called ahead. We gots pie to eat before any work can get done."

As Gabe stepped into the house, they could hear Willie protesting about being mauled and licked by slobbering beasts.

She closed her eyes and slowly wagged her head. "The man is a conundrum. One day he hates animals, then he walks in the gate, and they jump him and he's like a little boy. We had a couple of dogs back when they—my Chester and him, were serving together. That man and the dogs liked to have a staring and growling contests. They never took to him, and he never could stand them. Refused to sleep in the same house—rather pay for a motor lodge somewhere."

She took Gabe's elbow and guided him deeper into the house. "Come on in the kitchen. Chester will be up in a minute."

"I thought your husband's name was Roscoe?"

She cackled. "Oh, heavens no... that was what they called him. It was on account of the 44 snubnose he carried. The gangsters used to call it a Roscoe... so the name stuck."

ANGEL FLIGHTS

She leaned over and yelled in a doorway that led down into a basement. "Roscoe, you have a new toy to play with." She turned and smiled. Gabe heard the pounding of boots on wooden stairs.

"What the hell you yelling about…" He came through the door and saw the size of Gabe. "Oh, my." He stuck out his hand. "Chester P. Coltrain—friends call me Roscoe. What can I do for you?"

His wife backslapped his chest as she moved about the table with a large slice of pie and ice cream on a plate. "Let the man sit and eat. Willie done bringed him… and that fool is out in the yard with the kids."

"Oh, cripes. Willie brung you…? Oh, there must be hell to pay in some place on this earth."

"I'm not in the military anymore."

The woman hauled off and slugged the man in the shoulder. "Damn it, Chester. For the last time, sit and let the man enjoy my cooking in peace—before Willie gets in here and disturbs everything."

"Yes, Honey." The man sat and a plate with a small piece of pie and ice cream appeared. The old man stuck his lower lip out and looked at his piece and then at Gabe's.

Honey came over and draped her arm around his head and shoulders. "Oh, snookum bear, I done gave you Willie's slice. Here is yours." She put down an even smaller piece and no ice cream.

The man's smile resolved. He leaned towards

Gabe. "You have now met the real Honey—she'll take your balls and you'll thank her for doing it."

Gabe looked at the woman sitting down with a plate as loaded as his was. "So if they call you Honey... what is your real name?"

She forked a bite into her mouth and shoved it over to one cheek. "Honey." She chewed slowly. "It used to be Honey Crackeneary, but Chester done gave me a much finer last name."

The front screen door squealed and four dogs raced into the house but bunched up at the linoleum of the kitchen and eating area. Willie's voice was clear and harsh. "Boys! Come! Lay down." His footsteps were light. "Honey, I could smell that apple pie all the way out on the grass." As Willie sat in front of the last plate of pie and ice cream, he blew a kiss at Honey. She snuck a hand over and slapped his hand. They both smiled. Gabe guessed it was an old game with them.

"I saw that old Knucklehead out in the truck... How is Maddie, and why didn't y'all bring her?"

Willie took a bite and moaned his approval, and then through his full mouth, he explained. "Maddie is done racing that under-powered heap. I thought maybe Gabe here might want it if you can make it street legal and the price is right."

Roscoe looked at Gabe. "What's the right price?"

Willie coughed. "He just got out of the jarhead

church… talk slowly and don't expect much."

Roscoe stared at Gabe. Gabe shied a bit, but he knew this was the time to step up and trust. "I have three-hundred and some that can go to transportation. I have four-fifty total to live on until I can find a job."

"What did you do in Uncle Sam's Marching Boys' Choir?" Roscoe was taking very small bites. Gabe figured he was probably diabetic. The bulbous nose with the exploded capillaries that spread across his face could speak to alcohol abuse, or not.

"I was a cop."

"So get a cop job."

Gabe snapped his fingers. "Just like that."

Roscoe softly put his fork down. Gabe worried he had just pushed too far. Roscoe deliberately wiped his mouth as he watched the young man. "How long were you at Chet's place?"

"A couple of hours." Gabe put his napkin on the table.

"What were you drinking?"

"Some of the best coffee I have ever had."

Roscoe looked down the table to Willie, who was still eating. Willie noticed the silence and looked up. He thought a moment and nodded.

Roscoe turned back to Gabe. "What did you have to eat?"

"Something he called corned beef stew."

"He pulled it out of that old crock pot?"

Gabe frowned at the strange questions. "Yes... but why is that important?"

"Did you like the man?"

"Enough that I want to go back more than a few times, sure."

"Where did he suggest you think about working?"

"He showed me an ad for Pasadena and LAPD and mentioned Alhambra... so I guess he was talking around here. Why?"

Roscoe smiled. "Because that means you have whichever job you want. He sits on the civilian boards for all of them. We're not supposed to know about it but also the South Pasadena."

"And he's just a bar owner?"

"Not really. His mother and he own about six or seven square blocks of that area—maybe more. All commercial. He is the biggest taxpayer in the valley."

Gabe gave a low whistle. "So why do you think he liked me?"

"Did you see anyone else drinking coffee?"

"Willie had a cup..."

"Anyone else would get Nescafe instant. And food... he has stale sandwiches." Roscoe looked at Willie. "How was the stew?"

"It wasn't road kill. Remember that cook Brooks something?" The man nodded. "That good."

Roscoe looked at Honey. Honey smiled—she

knew where they would be eating that night.

Gabe pushed his empty plate an inch. "Ma'am, that was very good, thank you." Honey nodded and pushed at her tangle of puffed up gray hair.

Gabe looked at Willie. "So what did you want for the motorcycle?"

Willie pushed his finger along the tabletop as he thought. He knew the motorcycle was a lot more valuable than a few hundred dollars, but he also knew it had made Maddie a lot of money in winnings at the drag races. Money wasn't the real object here. He had hauled it down to give back to Roscoe to do what Roscoe did—find a buyer or part it out. "I think you need to take it for a spin first."

"Okay, let's get it unloaded."

"Not here." Willie looked to Roscoe.

"How about the river bed through Glendale and Burbank… they're dry right now."

Willie raised one eyebrow. "Then maybe I might want to go for a ride."

About an hour later, in the dying light, the bike was on the dry concrete bed of the greater Los Angeles river system that moved millions of acre-feet of rainwater through the city.

The rest of the year there was only a trickle down the middle—or none at all.

"Okay, you have about ten miles of open shot from here to Sylmar. If I were you, I'd keep it cool on the way up. Then you know if there is anything dangerous on the way back."

Gabe thought about the logic. "How do I know when I get to Sylmar?"

"River bed is going to change and you can't drive up those stairs. There is an access ramp to the right just before the stairs. That's in case you want to just loaf it back down here on the city streets."

"Got it." Gabe hit the starter button and the large oversized starter fired the engine. He waited for the engine to warm up and settle down and run smooth.

Willie leaned over and yelled near his ear. "If you think it will smooth out by warming up, you're wrong. As she gets warmer, the high lope cam will run more erratic."

Gabe nodded and pulled in the clutch. With his toe, he dropped into first and slowly let the clutch out. He found that the engine wouldn't stall, and the clutch engaged in the first quarter of the lever. He was gone in a shot.

Roscoe chuckled. "What's the starter from?"

"A dead Ford Falcon—Maddie got tired trying to kick that monster over. Harley has been robbing parts from Ford since the twenties. The main brake plunger is off a Falcon too, but that is considered Harley stock."

They sat on the tailgate of the truck. "How long do you give him?"

"He said he had ridden bikes before, so I think he's going to get used to the bike about early

Burbank. He'll get up to Sylmar and sit for a few minutes to think about it. I think he'll make up the time on the way back... so if he's like me, I'd say about seventeen minutes."

"And if he's more like Maddie?"

"Twelve."

He was off by two minutes. But Gabe was approaching from the south.

Gabe smiled. "The concrete has those obnoxious expansion joints, so every twenty feet is a tiny ridge. So I circled out in Sylmar and took the freeway back... I think I passed a CHP, but he never knew what happened."

"So what do you think of a little woman's play toy?"

"I think it needs better tires and the back brakes seem to grab off and on." He smiled up at Willie. "How little is little?"

"About five-seven and maybe a hundred pounds."

"This must float on her at about hundred-forty."

"We have a solid lead seat that weighs about seventy pounds, and then there are the extra thick fenders, all in all, it adds about one-ten."

Gabe ran his hand over the tank. "So what did you work out for the price?"

Roscoe cleared his throat.

"You go follow Chet's lead. He'll put you where he wants you, but it will also be a good fit for you. I get your first paycheck and Willie gets the third and fifth. If you ever want to get rid of it, it comes back to me."

Gabe knew that any check he would get wasn't going to pay for this kind of motorcycle or motor. He reached over and shook the hands of his two new friends.

03

GETTING THE RIGHT JOB

GABE LEANED FORWARD on the bar studying the map. Chet had drawn orange marker on the precinct boundaries. He had numbered them in preference and then placed a letter code where Gabe could transfer into the openings. Chet stressed that need and Gabe's experience in law enforcement would allow the precincts to walk Gabe in as a transferring cop instead of a recruit.

This fact was weighing on Gabe as the one place Chet underlined had a letter code of UNG. The fact that the area was in the barrios of Boyle and Lincoln Heights didn't make Gabe any more comfortable—he had guessed the code stood for Undercover Narcotics and Gangs. The Mexican gangs had been notorious even to a kid growing up in the late 1950s in a fairly white area of Alhambra. Even mostly lily-white Alhambra High had experienced some conflicts from the factions of Zoot Suits and street gangs. Gabe reached back and felt the flat scar on his lower back where a knife had almost ended his high school career of football. Luckily, it had gone in below his kidney.

"How's it coming?" Chet flipped the towel over his shoulder.

Gabe sat back studying the man. Chet was the quintessential bartender, maybe even owner. But Gabe now knew just who the man really was—one of the more powerful men in the police network—a retired detective captain with his finger still in the pie.

"I think I like the horse patrol out in Chatsworth, maybe even Devonshire." He watched deadpan at the older man.

Chet smiled. Then he gave a small chuckle. "You're afraid that I want you to be my eyes and ears in some precinct. You think I want a beat boy to do my dirty work." He slowly moved in and stuck his arms out into a spread as he braced along the bar. "First of all, I get more than enough cops coming in here and letting me know what is going on. Second, I have too many of them that want to be my *boy in my pocket*. I hated spying when I was on beat. I hated it as a detective. I never even had any snitches on the street. Those sneaky little bastards you have to pay and they still lie to you—tell you what they think you want to hear.

"What I don't have is a friend who is young.

BAER CHARLTON

Someone who is new on the job—someone who still gets excited about helping people. All of the guys I know still on the job are desk weenies who are so old they shouldn't be put out to pasture—they should just be shot and put out of my misery."

He pulled the towel off his shoulder and stood. "Look, you just got out of one job a week ago. Maybe you should look around and think about what you really want to do. Maybe being a cop isn't for you… Maybe you want to go sell shoes or drive a taxi. Maybe you should just go back to being a Marine."

Gabe pushed his coffee cup around. "I still have eighty-two days to think about that. They would probably send me somewhere nice like Washington, DC."

Chet went to the cash register and took out some money. He returned and fanned out the five twenties on the bar. "Look, you have some time. You have a bike. Take this and take a ride up or down the coast for a few days. Come back when your head is clear and we'll talk. One way or another, we are still friends, and we will figure this out." He took up the map and started folding it.

"I have some money."

"I know. Now you have a little cushion. Don't stay in fancy motels. Santa Barbara has a nice YMCA right near the beach. So does Santa Maria. If you make it to Monterey, you can eat where Steinbeck wrote Grapes of Wrath. Go find a little quiet and time to think… I know… it helps."

Gabe put his right hand at the side of the fan of bills. He hesitated for a couple of heartbeats, and then scooped them up. He shoved them in his pocket.

Standing, he stuck his hand out. They shook. "Thanks, Chet. You're not my father, but you make a great uncle. I appreciate… well, let's just say I appreciate it."

The man waved his hand about in the air as his face was in the cash drawer. "I'll see you when you get back."

04

TRAINING DAY

"SO YOU WERE an MP in Alaska...?" The short sergeant walked fast but kept looking back at the much larger Gabe.

"Yes, sir. Adak, sir."

"I thought that was an Air Force base."

"Yes, sir, but they have several different groups. Most of the medical are Navy, and they don't like to knock their own heads, so they get Marines to keep them all in line. When they need to restock the meat locker, they import some Army guys and stick them out for bait."

The man frowned, as he turned and twisted around. "Stick them where?"

"Usually out on a small ice flow."

"And they just sit out there—what are they bait for?"

"Usually, killer whales or polar bears. Those Army guys are kind of tough, so they still move around good after you cut a bleed line on them. They can put a good quart of blood in the water, and of course, the screaming is what gets the bear's attention."

The sergeant stopped but didn't turn around. "Tell me, does it snow as deep as the bullshit?"

Gabe chuckled. "Oh, hell no, sir. It's cold as hell, but it's too cold to really snow. But all winter long the bullshit just keeps building."

The man turned around with a quirky smile. "Oh yeah, you're going to fit right in."

After meeting with the lieutenant, he introduced Gabe to his training officer, Don Diego. The large scar on the man's face that shot across the forehead, and slashed back through the eyebrow, across the nose to stop at the edge of his thin-lipped mouth, didn't help with the nickname of Zorro.

In the car, as they pulled out on Mission Boulevard, the man was quick to settle the thoughts.

"The last name is actually Diego y Esperanza de Garcia... also naming the love interest and the sergeant of the movies doesn't help get Zorro out of people's minds. As you get to know me, your nickname for me will move from asshole to just grumpy. If we become friends, you can call me Snow White or any other dwarf and I won't care."

Gabe looked across at the man who could barely see over the steering wheel.

"How did you get into the police force, or, uh,

well, in undercover?"

The man snapped a fast glare at Gabe as he jerked the car into a fast U-turn. "Is that a short joke?"

"No."

"Good, because the last training monkey started making short jokes and he got shot."

"So the answer is…?"

"My whole family has always been cops. Even my great uncle down in Mexico was a Federale, who was once shot by Pancho Villa himself."

"And he lived?"

"Pancho was a great man, a great horseman, but a piss poor gunman. Uncle Manny got hit in the leg. They chased Pancho for three more days until his horse wore out."

"Pancho or your uncle?"

"Who knows… That is usually when my great uncle would drift off into his own world or fall asleep." The two laughed at the joke of real life as Don hit the lights and blipped the siren. They were pulling over a big car with a lot of young men in it.

"Have you ever done a traffic stop before?"

"A few times—not much moving on the base in the long winters."

"Stay on the sidewalk, keep your hand on your weapon, don't move past the rear door, and watch all of the hands. If I pull anyone out… watch the others. There are at least four guns in this car."

ANGEL FLIGHTS

They slid out of the patrol car as they watched every head and shoulder in the car before them. The two officers took their time moving forward. Every movement, every turn of the head was registered.

Don stopped. "Driver, put both hands out your window where I can see them."

As the driver turned, Gabe noticed the shotgun rider also moved. Gabe took two quick steps and stuck his revolver into the guy's ear. "I wouldn't do that if I were you." The sawed-off shotgun was halfway up out of the foot well.

Gabe started to reach in for the shotgun and noticed small movements in the back. "You three in the back, if you twitch or even think about your girlfriend from last Saturday night, I will have to explain how you got a 357 hole through your pecker. Comprende?"

The three nodded.

"Now, grab the shotgun by the barrel and pass it out to me. You three in the back, stick your baby fingers in the barrels of your guns and hold them up."

The three hesitated until Gabe cocked his revolver and pushed it harder into the front guy's ear.

"Do what the man says, pendejos."

Two pistols and one zip gun showed handles up. The shotgun was coming out of the window pistol grip first.

Gabe took the shotgun and laid it on the top of the car. "You know when you chop both ends off a

12-gauge, it either blows up in your face or shatters your hand where you can never jerk off or wipe yourself again. It's really hard to impress a girl enough—to get her to jerk you off and then clean your asshole when you shit yourself every morning."

The young man blanched.

He took the closest pistol and had the kid in the middle pass the zip gun. Don took the other pistol, then they had the five slowly climb out one at a time and lay down on the sidewalk with their arms and legs spread out.

A thorough pat-down produced four switchblades, a standard pocket knife, and two more pistols hidden in socks, but what they found in the car was far more interesting. There were more places in the doors alone than would be found in some baggy pants and an oversized flannel shirt over a white t-shirt.

Gabe had never seen a human tear a car apart like a bear or rabid dogs would have. While the street toughs moaned about their car, Don methodically tore out the seats, door panels, carpets, and headliner. The trunk lining was on the street when Don used one of the huskier knives to go to town on the extra spare tire.

Soon, about twenty large plastic bags were on the roof with the weapons.

The four doors contained more where the window should have been when rolled down. Under where the back seat had been was stacked with a well of bags. Gabe estimated about fifty more pounds of marijuana. What had looked like some low-level street toughs riding in a more upscale car was something more—much more.

As Don and Gabe sat chewing on bad sandwiches as they filled out the paperwork, Gabe asked, "How did you know?"

Don leaned back. "Where to begin? There is a lot you will learn just by being on the street. The guy wearing a red shirt, but he's walking into a café that is the hangout for a bunch that wears blue. You just know either he is stupid or he is there to shoot someone. Either way, someone is going to die.

"But those guys were wearing different colored shirts…"

"It wasn't the shirts. It was the wrong car. If they were just riding, it would have been a DeSoto or maybe a 56 or 57 Chevy, something cheap but with no window post. This had no window post, but a four-year-old Belvedere is too expensive. It had the wheel covers your mother would want, but not a gang member—they want to blend in, but with a certain style."

"So why the Plymouth?"

"Faster engine."

"So you pulled them over because they had a faster car?"

"No, I pulled them over for two reasons. First,

the car had come up on the stolen list about a week ago. It was stolen up in Pasadena. The minute I saw it was cream or tan, I knew it would show up down here. The second was the size of the guys. Everyone was full grown, except the little guy in the middle in the back. When we finally find out who he is, I'll bet he's missing from one of the middle schools. This was his test to see if he could shoot someone if they got jumped. But at a minimum, he was involved in a serious crime and was packing a gun."

"What the hell was he doing in the back seat of that car?"

"He wants to be a member of the gang. The gang wants him, but he has to prove himself."

"Why would they want him?"

"Because they will have him carry drugs or even kill someone—if he gets caught, the worst the courts will do is send him to juvenile hall until he's eighteen. Then they seal the records. Meanwhile the big guys, who would do twenty to life, go scot free and round up some more peepers."

"Peepers?"

"Peep peep... like little chicks."

"That is sick."

"Welcome to East LA, my friend."

As the weeks rolled by, the two became friends and the grumpy side only showed towards the street that deserved that side. Their patrolling took them all over the west end of the San Gabriel Valley and into parts of eastern Los Angeles. The weathered cop rattled off history of who was who and where and how things had changed over the years since he had been a real beat cop. The patrol car gave them a presence that settled much of the activities that as undercover they would have to deal with or turn a blind eye to.

The heat of the day was reaching an obstacle to staying alert. The car moved quietly up the hill. Boyle Heights had been quiet for months. One of the big guys in crime had taken a large fall and was now living in central California at a house known for its solitary confinement—Soledad.

Don nodded at the young man with the long shirt and chino pants just going into the Mexican restaurant. "I think it's lunch break."

They parked the car across the street and Gabe grabbed for the shotgun. Don waved him off. "I think I know what's going on, but let's see if talking can solve this first." The two crossed the street with a car length or more between them. Don didn't turn his head as he quietly asked Gabe if he was ready for the front door.

Gabe nodded and headed for the front as Don jogged down the driveway towards the back.

Just before Gabe reached for the screen door, it exploded with the street tough busting out in a full run—Gabe stuck his foot out. The kid went sprawling, the small handgun flipped out of his pants and skidded, spinning across the front patio.

A second later, a short young girl with a large chest hit the door and stepped between the kid's legs. Just as he was rising up, she kicked him—hard. The pain must have been great because he passed out.

She turned and rattled something off in Spanish. Gabe only caught one of every third word—but it was enough. The boy was her brother, and he was dumb enough to try and rob the place where she worked. Gabe tried not to laugh.

Don stepped through the door and put his arm around her shoulder. His Spanish was perfect, and his soothing words had their effect.

Finally, Don nodded to Gabe. "Get his pistol and if you want, you can kick him, also." Then he reassessed the size of Gabe. "Better just make it the ribs, and only hard enough to crack one or two.

Gabe grabbed the gun, which had the words *Tom Mix* cast into the toy's barrel. He looked at the kid who was just starting to come to. He reached down and grabbed a wad of hair and pulled the head up so the ear was close to his mouth.

"Pendejo, you really need to stay in school. If I see you on the street again during a school day, I'm going to hold you down and let your sister kick you a lot more. You understand."

"Si."

"Good." As he let the kid drop, he booted him several feet across the patio and into one of the table legs. Gabe knew he didn't do any damage, but the

ANGEL FLIGHTS

kid would remember that, too.

"Hey." The kid groaned.

Gabe turned at the door.

"It's summer, asshole."

"So go to summer school, genius."

The burritos were as big as both of Don's fists. The meat was succulent and well-seasoned. The waitress, Maria, was bustling about cleaning and pouring more water or coffee.

Finally, she sat down next to Gabe. "Thank you for not hurting my brother. Most of the time he is smart, but some days, he can be so stupid."

"De nada, senorita."

"Oh," Maria gushed, but in a teasing way, "you speak Spanish."

"Very little."

"You have mi Tio El Senor Grumpy bring you every day, and I teach you muchas."

Gabe scowled at his partner. "Tio?" Uncle?

The older cop blushed. "Their mother is my baby sister."

"So you knew who the peeper was storming the other gang headquarters."

"I had my suspicions." Zorro closed his eyes as he started to chuckle.

Maria put her hand on Gabe's arm. "Esta bien. He does that to all of his newbies. It's how he knows when they can handle themselves."

"So you knew what was going on?"

She nodded with a small snicker.

"So that kick wasn't real… and neither was the gun."

Her face opened up in anger. "Oh, no—that kick was real all right. He stuck that old dirty pistola in my chichis. You damn right I kicked him." She leaned in with a smirk. "Is okay—is not his first time he gets kicked."

Gabe looked over to find the uncle pinching the bridge of his nose and shaking his head. The man looked up. "This is why I never worried about any of the gangs that come here. They would be stupid to tangle with either one."

"So how is the kid in school?"

Maria buzzed her lips. "School is a waste of time for him."

"He's dumb?"

Don leaned back. "Just the opposite. He gets straight A's. She's right—if we knew what to do with him, we'd let him challenge the four years of high school and move on to college."

"What about scholarships?"

Maria leaned in and put her hand gently back on his shoulder as she looked at her uncle. "I think he is special."

Don chuffed a laugh. "She means you're special as in stupid. You have to graduate from high school to get a scholarship. For really smart kids, there is no money to take a shortcut."

ANGEL FLIGHTS

"So he has to be bored for four more years—just to get a scholarship to move on in his life?"

They both nodded. Gabe wondered otherwise.

****

The large bowl was empty as he thought about the kid. Gabe knew he hadn't had the smarts to get any kind of scholarship, but he knew if he didn't do something after high school, he would soon end up in trouble—so he joined the Marines at seventeen instead.

"So you hated the chicken stuff too, I see."

"Chet, it was as great as every other soup. I don't know why you don't just open up a soup diner."

"Because cops don't eat in a soup diner, and when they get off work, they want a drink—except you."

"I tried drinking, but nothing ever tasted as good—as it felt bad the next morning. With coffee, I can drink a whole pot, go home to bed, and wake up feeling great the next morning."

"You're a smart guy to figure that out while you're still young."

"Speaking of figuring things out, Chet—I have a problem I'm working on."

The man put the bowl in the sink and ran some hot water. "With the job?"

"It's connected. My partner's nephew is going into the ninth grade. Straight A's the whole way. He's bored, but he can't challenge the high school courses because they said he has to graduate from high school to be eligible for any scholarships."

"So what's the problem?" He washed the bowl, wiped his hands on the rag, and flipped it over his shoulder. He stood with his hip against the back bar.

Gabe kept thinking. "It just doesn't seem right. The kid can do college work, but he has to muck around for four years because someone says he has to be a certain age."

"There is more on your mind than just that…"

"I graduated from school when I was seventeen. The folks signed off so I could join the Marines. There was a way around for me, so there should be something for this kid."

Chet looked out the open door at the street. A car drove by. "Life isn't always fair. You were a Marine—they could have sent you anywhere. You didn't have a choice. You were trained to kill for your country, and if it came to it, die for that country."

"Your point being?"

"But you couldn't vote for the man who could send you there."

"Still can't until this fall."

Chet realized what Gabe had just said. He wasn't twenty-one yet, and yet he was in a bar and was a cop. "When?"

"October."

"Crap..."

"Chet, you never asked. Nobody ever does. I've never been asked... ever."

"So that is why you want to help this kid."

"Maybe part of it, but mostly because he lives in a bad area, and I'd like to see him make something of his potential instead of having to go to his funeral."

"Who's your training officer?"

"My Field TO is Don Diego."

The man laughed. "Oh, crap. You got Zorro."

"He's a little sensitive about that name."

"Well, then he shouldn't have been in that bed when he got his face cut up like that."

"Jealous husband?"

"Jealous mother. He had been dating the mother for several months, but one night ended up in bed with the daughter. The mother wasn't amused when she came home early and found him in her daughter's bed."

"How old was the daughter?"

"A student at City College—so maybe she was nineteen or twenty?"

"I wasn't going to ever ask him."

"Yeah, probably best not to ask about his mother-in-law. Just let sleeping dogs lie and all of that." The man continued to chuckle.

"He married the daughter?"

"Sure, she was only about five or six years younger than him, and when she said she was pregnant, he jumped in with both feet."

"He never mentioned he had a kid."

"He doesn't. She wasn't, and rumor has it he can't. I don't know if that's true, but I do know he never had any kids. But his two sisters kept him with plenty of kids to spoil and dote on."

Gabe ran his finger forward along the bar top, feeling the grain of the wood that was barely there. "So what about scholarships?"

"I'll ask around."

Gabe looked up and blinked.

"I'd really appreciate that, Chet. I really would. Thanks."

"But…"

"Oh, crap. What?" Gabe slumped in his seat.

"A few months ago, I gave you a hundred dollars to go up north. You came back two weeks later with a great tan and gave me two hundred, and then paid off Roscoe and Willie, and moved into that tiny apartment. Where did you get the money?"

Gabe blushed.

"I'm serious. Spill the beans or it's no deal."

"You'll work on something for the kid?"

"Where?"

"Reno." Gabe shied his head and his voice lowered, "…and Carson City, and Tahoe."

ANGEL FLIGHTS

"Are you really that good?"

"Good enough, I reckon."

"Damn… damn it all to hell." Chet just leaned back and roared with laughter.

It made Gabe feel good to see his friend this happy.

05

JUSTICE AND INJUSTICE

"SO WHAT HAPPENS now?"

Zorro shrugged, but his face was dark. "For us? Nothing. The father goes away for about six of his twenty, but because his daughter is only thirteen, he will probably get a shiv in the heart or kidney sometime soon. Inmates tolerate some really nasty stuff, but child molesting isn't one of them—especially when it's your own daughter. "

Gabe slid out of the unmarked car they were using that day. "Actually, I was talking about the daughter—after all, she's the one who's pregnant, and her father is the father of her child."

They crossed the street to the restaurant. The young girl with her fists on her hips was glaring at them.

Gabe studied the young girl who was only a few years younger than he was. "She looks grumpier than you, Grumpy."

ANGEL FLIGHTS

"She's not looking at me, Jefe."

"Hey, when did I become the boss, boss?"

They stepped into the confines of the front patio. The older cop leaned over and kissed her on the cheek. "When she looks like her mother. Te amo hija." He kept walking into the café. "I'd run while you have a chance, Gabe."

Gabe stood his ground in front of the much smaller girl. He liked how she looked with her hair pulled back in the long ponytail. The tightness of the shirt across her large chest didn't hurt. Gabe opened his mouth in a smile…

Maria's finger came up and pounded into his chest with each word. "What? Did? You? Do?" Four words and she had walked him backward onto the sidewalk.

Gabe threw up his arms. "I've been working. What are you talking—"

"Yesterday Lito got a call from the school. He was there until dinner. He is there again right now. He is taking every test that they can find. He is challenging the entire high school curriculum in four or five days. If he can do fifty sit-ups, ten pull-ups, and run a mile in less than ten minutes, he passes."

"That's a good thing. No?"

"NO! Then what? He just hangs out in the neighborhood for the next four years. Maybe he washes dishes here? That kid is only thirteen… he can't go to college yet. We don't have that kind of money and he can't get a scholarship. We told you that, pendejo."

"Maybe someone found a way." Gabe softened his tone in hopes that it would calm her.

"What part of thirteen did you not understand?" She spun on her heel and started to walk away. "El Fregon."

Gabe grabbed her arm and spun her around. "Meda, you had your say, now I get mine." She crossed her arms over her chest.

Gabe slumped. "Yes, I meddled… and if that makes me *The Irritant*… so be it. But that kid has more brains than most of this street combined. Grumpy has shown me some of the kid's work. He wants to be a doctor and help people. Other kids his age wants to pack a gun and kill people instead—both are coming from the same neighborhood. One we arrest, and the other I want to help him stay away from…" Gabe put his hand on her shoulder. The shoulder all but disappeared under his large paw.

"Look, I spoke to an old cop your uncle used to work with when he was young. The guy knows people, and they all want to help. The first year we can get him to City College, and he can do his magic there. After that, he may have opportunities that aren't available right now. A year is a long time and a lot can happen. But he needs to take this chance."

She grumped as she turned to go in. Gabe stepped alongside and draped his arm on her shoulders. "Can we just call a truce here and be friends?"

"Mmm... maybe... but you are still a fregon." She slapped his butt.

"Oh, great. I'm a pest to you and stupid to your uncle. Can't you two get together on something?" They laughed as Gabe grabbed the screen door.

The dishes were all but wiped clean. Maria told Gabe he couldn't lick the plate, and if he needed another burrito, she would get him one. He had been tempted, but he settled for more coffee.

"So, back to the young girl..."

Grumpy glanced sideways at Maria. Gabe could tell he was stalling... something the man almost never did.

Maria came over—she had been listening in the small confines of the café. "What about a young girl?" She gave her uncle a hard look. "Tio?" Her voice was menacing.

"We arrested her father today. That is all, hija."

"That is so much bullshit." She turned on Gabe. "Now."

Grumpy scowled and Gabe shied. "She's pregnant."

"Who is the father?"

The men looked at each other. One was clamping down—the other seeking guidance.

She stood. "Mierda..." Her face turned dark and ugly. 'Why didn't you just shoot the bastard?"

Both men were wondering the same thing.

"Quién es ella?"

"You don't know her... she's Rafalito's age."

Her face looked like her uncle had just slapped her. "She's thirteen and her father is..." She took up one of the saltshakers and threw it against the back wall. The old glass exploded and the cook stepped out of the kitchen door to look around. She pointed him back into the kitchen. With her face—nobody would argue.

She turned back to her uncle as she collapsed in the chair. Exhausted, she asked again. "Who is she?"

The man showed his age as he looked at his niece. "I'm telling you—you cannot help."

"Tio, she needs amigas." Her hand was on his arm pleading.

"There was no mother. She and her little sister were taken away by child services."

Maria's face turned to horror and she exploded. "So some other asshole can fuck her some more until she runs away or kills herself?"

Grumpy snapped his head. "You don't know that. And watch your language."

"I know plenty, and I don't care about my language." She leaned in, angry and combative. "At best, she ends up like me. That is if she is *very* lucky and has friends or family. You know how it is. tio. They no let you ever forget."

Gabe frowned. "What do you mean like you?"

Maria's head snapped around as if Gabe had just

ANGEL FLIGHTS

appeared. She thought a moment then stood and walked into the back rooms. Zorro's head fell into his hands.

A few moments later, she reappeared with a small child in her arms. The baby was cooing and gurgling as any happy baby in their mother's arms. Maria had transformed. She was all glowing smile as she poked and talked back to the baby.

She retook her seat. "This is Lincoln."

Gabe guessed at the story as he studied the handful of sandy colored wavy hair. The skin was pinker than the olive of its mother. "The father?"

Grumpy growled. "Levinworth."

She was more forthcoming. "I was on a class tour of a ship in the Navy yards in San Pedro. I got lost and when they finally found me…"

"She had just turned fifteen."

Gabe sighed. "But looked much older…" *thinking of her large breasts.*

She nodded. "Since I was twelve."

"So what happened? I mean… now you are a family. But what…?"

"Girls in my condition?" She lowered her one eyelid in a challenge. Gabe didn't flinch. "In the barrio, we have three choices… other than suicide. The first is you have your friends at school start slugging you in the stomach, very hard." She watched Gabe's face for horror—it was very slight, but she noticed. "The second is you go visit relatives in Mexico…

And after you are okay again, you come home with your cousin's baby—or none at all." She cooed at the baby on her lap.

Gabe put his hands out. She hesitated. He nodded and the child was passed. "Hola Senor Lincoln." But then he looked up at Maria about the third.

"The other is the Saint Anne's program. They put you in a home with a good Catholic family where you work as a mother's helper—kind of like a nanny. The pressure to give up the baby is not strong, but it is there. They make sure you see what kind of family and home you won't have if you keep the baby. In a lot of ways, it is nice—but in others..."

Grumpy growled softly. "And then there are too many that take the other ways."

Gabe frowned and looked at Maria, not Grumpy, who he knew did not want anything to do with this conversation. The whole situation was too close, and as Gabe would discover over the years, too often.

Maria's hands played with the edge of her apron. Her gaze was on the hot street but far away. "Some... some... morta."

Gabe understood. They take their lives. "And others?"

Maria took in a deep sighing breath and looked back at him. "There are men... with rusty coat hangers... in dark alleys... the kind of men who make you wish you had just died."

"So the choices are never good?"

ANGEL FLIGHTS

Both looked at the table and shook their heads. Zorro pushed the pepper shaker and hot sauce bottles around. "Maybe for the rich people. Maybe they can pay a doctor to do something and not call it what it is… but in the barrio…"

Gabe wondered why his partner hadn't shot the man that morning. They could have made it look like a righteous shooting. His attention moved from the happy little boy on his lap to the partner who he was still getting to know. Unlike the concrete canals of the Los Angeles River system, this man's rivers ran very deep.

Grumpy glanced at his watch and stood. Gabe handed back the baby after he had kissed the head. Maria smiled at the familiar touch. She slid Lincoln into her left arm and put out her right hand to Gabe's arm and mouthed *gracias*. He put his arm around her shoulders and squeezed. "De nada."

The late afternoon heat hit them as they emerged from the shade and ceiling fans. Maria with the baby on her hip stood in the screened doorway. She called out a goodbye. "You two need haircuts." They waved. She didn't have to see their unmarked car to know they were preparing to go undercover.

With her uncle, it was an on-again-off-again thing. From the first day she met Gabe, she guessed he wouldn't be on patrol duty long—he just didn't seem to fit the profile. He was too tall, too much muscle. With longer hair, he would look more like the bikers that occasionally came up the hill to Dos Palmas. The ones that wore leather jackets under jean jackets with the sleeves cut off and patches of this gang or that gang sewn on the back.

The leather jacket slid over his large frame six hours later. Gabe put on his shades and pulled the short leather gloves out of the jacket pockets. The large engine chuffed as he contemplated and pulled the gloves on.

"Hey, Street."

Gabe's head snapped around. The desk officer was standing in the door. His right forefinger slid across his throat and then he waved him in. Gabe turned off the bike and followed the other officer with the quirky limp back into the precinct.

"Captain wants to see you."

"Thanks, Stan." Gabe turned off down the ancillary hallway as the wiry sergeant returned to the front desk. Gabe noted the slight limp as well as the way the man held his shoulders stiff. The bank shoot-out was famous around the precinct. Shot-up, the officer had dragged himself to the only living robber, slapped handcuffs on him and the handle of the front door. He had thrown his service revolver to one of the bank tellers before passing out. He had wanted to make sure the robber couldn't get away or shoot him with his own gun. The robber died before he made it to the hospital and Stan had spent a month recovering before being moved to a rehab home. The

ANGEL FLIGHTS

captain was told to retire the officer, but he told Parker Center the officer was more valuable than any given floor full of workers. Stan had a desk job for life.

Gabe stopped at the captain's open door. A large biker slouched in one of the chairs. From the haircut, Gabe guessed the man had gotten out of prison that week.

Gabe knocked on the doorframe. "You wanted to see me, Captain?"

The man turned around from the large map that covered one wall of his office. Gabe liked him from the first day—the man shunned the desk and was constantly pinning and re-pinning the trouble spots in his precinct and the surrounding area. "Come on in, Street. I'll be with you in a minute."

Gabe stepped in but did not sit. The only chair was next to the biker. The man watched him with a low level of interest. He was obviously bored with why he was there.

"How many inches over is that Knucklehead?"

Gabe frowned and looked around. The biker hadn't moved. Gabe turned back around.

"I figure you have at least eight-six inches in that engine of yours. Otherwise you wouldn't need such a big ass starter."

Gabe turned. "Are you talking to me?"

The biker looked up and pointed toward the captain. The captain turned around. "Stuffing a Knucklehead top on a Panhead body is a nice way to make room for some custom jugs and better oiling. What's the top end?"

"I hit about one-thirty between Reno and Carson City, but the morning was cool so the air was fat."

The captain looked at the slouched biker. The biker screwed up his mouth and then answered. "About six-thousand-foot elevation. Ever run it down here?"

"Once—in the river basin between Glendale and Sylmar."

"How fast?"

"A little over five minutes—it was my first time on the bike."

The biker snorted. "How did you like the expansion joints?"

"I didn't. I came back on the freeway."

"How long?"

"About the same, maybe faster."

The captain raised an eyebrow and turned to another map. "That makes it in the neighborhood of one-fifty."

The biker coughed as he sat up. "More like one-seventy or eighty. Who built that monster?"

"A guy named Roscoe."

The captain sat down on the corner of his desk and frowned. "How do you know Roscoe?"

"Sorry, sir, but I can't divulge my sources."

The biker chuckled. "It's okay. I've seen the

bike out in front of Chet's place enough to know you're already connected."

The captain offered up a half-smile. "Street, this is going to be your new brother, Rabbit."

Gabe turned and took in the idea that this man was actually an undercover officer. He stuck his hand out. "You need a haircut."

The man laughed. "You need to grow a beard—fast."

The captain shuffled through some papers. "As of tonight, you are no longer a cop. You don't ever want to come here. You can still drink at Chet's place. We'll use that as another dead drop. Roscoe is a good out of the way wrench for your bike—keep using him. I know you like Zorro's little niece, but no more than about once a week for lunch or something—but only if you two are together. You can't afford to have a girlfriend or anyone that may look like they could be used against you. You understand?"

"Yes, sir."

"I'll let Zorro know he needs to clue his niece in that she knows nothing about you if you show up. You can build a friendship from there—but not past her being a waitress—understand?"

"Yes, sir—besides, she's not eighteen yet."

The captain's reaction told Gabe the man had thought she was older also. The fact she was a mother was probably a closely guarded secret as well.

Rabbit took over. "Where do you live?"

"Alhambra."

"You're going to need to move—somewhere in East LA. We'll find you a quiet neighborhood. Usually, the older neighborhoods are best. If you're the only biker, people aren't nosey beyond the occasional Mrs. Kravitz, and there is nothing there for the gangs because usually there are no rentals."

"You're talking about buying a house?"

"Sure, why not? You're a respectable adult who just happens to drive a different kind of vehicle and, well… have a different kind of job."

The captain cleared his throat. "Um… maybe you two scofflaws might want to take your criminal activities elsewhere. Rabbit, you weren't the guy we were looking for and your buddy just came to pick you up. He can take you back to your bike."

Rabbit shot him a finger and the captain laughed.

They rode towards County General Hospital. Gabe wasn't sure about what had just transpired, but he was sure it happened that way so Zorro was not involved. Any police response from now on would be as clean as any cop confronting a biker could get.

"The captain likes you."

"I think he likes what I represent—connections."

"If you had Zorro for your field training officer—you were connected enough. You're going to need every one you have, and you also need to protect every single one you have. You have to stop being who you are and start being who you have to be."

Gabe eased the bike into the hospital parking lot. "For how long?"

"Not counting the jail time, I've been at this for five years."

Gabe's mind went back to the landing field in Alaska. Some days, the temperature would get so cold the airplanes could not land. Even the hot rubber of a landing plane would freeze and then it would be ice on ice and there was no stopping. The tires would stop rolling and the plane would slew all over the runway.

The idea of an officer being in deep cover for years slewed his mind like those planes in Alaska. Even with his limited knowledge of civilian police work, he knew more than a year was a risk.

"How long were you in jail?"

The man pulled his leg off the motorcycle and chuckled with a shrug. "This last time was short. The public defender had me out in six days. If I take the fall, and I won't, I'll go away for maybe a few months in downtown."

"Charges?"

"Stabbed a guy with a bottle—it was a bar fight."

"Self-defense?"

"We had to make it look that way. But the guy's cover is solid now or will be when he gets out of here." Rabbit nodded at the hospital.

"FBI?"

"Treasury—drugs and weapons." Gabe nodded in understanding

"So, where to now?"

"Now, my long lost friend, we go run the circuit."

"Circuit?"

"By midnight, you will be an old hand at it."

The taillights of the two motorcycles were bleached out as they rode towards the big ball in the sky that hovered somewhere over Santa Monica. The sound of the two big Harley engines pounded off the concrete of the large I-5 overpass as they raced down Mission Boulevard toward downtown LA and dinner at the Far East Café. It was the perfect place to start plotting any clandestine endeavor—had been for more than half a century.

"When did you find this place?" Gabe shoved more noodles into his mouth.

"I didn't. My father did. He was FBI and tasked to help round up the Japanese during World War Two. The buses parked right out there. Some of the waiters back then were Japanese, but the whites looked at the Chinese restaurant and just assumed that everyone was Chinese."

Gabe rolled his eyes. "Because they all look so much alike…"

Rabbit nodded with the chopsticks in his mouth

full of noodles. He chewed and swallowed. "We, you and I, are just the same. Radical dress, hair, and motorcycles—we must be outlaws. The money leaching bankers and crooked lawyers are out there meeting the nicest people on their Hondas."

"What about the real outlaws? I mean Chinese know when someone is Japanese or Korean and not Chinese..."

"Same rules... but they don't apply. Ethnicity is ingrained. With the outlaws, they become outlaws because they want to belong to something. If we come along and make that something bigger, then we're welcomed."

Gabe thought about the lack of the usual police equipment and marks of authority. "So without badges and such, how do we make arrests?"

Rabbit shoved a pot sticker in his mouth and talked through it. "We don't. That's something cops do. We're not cops, nor do we care about what they do. We're outlaws, and small-time criminals, who ride scooters, get drunk in certain bars, hang out with other criminal sorts, and get laid by girls you wouldn't even mention to Mom—much less take home for Sunday dinner." He shoved another dumpling into his mouth and wiped his mouth with the back of his hand. "Ever smoke marijuana?"

"No."

"You will."

They had stopped in at a bar in Santa Monica,

looked around, and left. The man Rabbit was looking for wasn't at the second bar either. The sun was going down and so they gave up and headed up over the pass toward Van Nuys.

Gabe liked the wide freeway that wound in lazy curves through the low hills that separated the San Fernando Valley from the greater Los Angeles area. The valley was still part of the large metropolis, but the people in the Valley would tell you there is the Valley and there is LA—even though they would tell someone elsewhere they lived in LA. It was the cachet of the only place that went by its initials, without acknowledgment of the state—New York City didn't even come close—they were just another fruit.

The two found space among the many other bikes parked in front of the donut shop. Nobody actually bought donuts there, but on a cold night, the coffee was at least warm. The amount of leather and denim that stood or squatted around the north end of the parking lot would be considered a small herd and a medium-sized cotton farm. Most of the men were clean-shaven, but some were sporting some kind of facial hair. Gabe looked about as to what might look good on his face.

"You're an asshole, Rabbit."

Gabe looked at the large man slowly rising from his leaning squat against the tiled wall. The man kept rising and rising. Gabe was starting to feel short. The mountain of a man stopped growing just short of maybe seven feet tall—but the shoulders looked like he was hiding football pads under the acre of leather.

Gabe hoped that the man was a friend of Rabbit.

"Oh, crap." Rabbit hung his head. "Bob, I just forgot my manners. When they arrested me the other night, I should have made them run your sister in as well."

"She told me... when she woke me up at one in the morning to come get her." The man growled and then laughed. "She said you were the most entertaining date she had gone out on in years."

"She's not bad in a bar fight. I think she even hit some guy with a pool cue." They both laughed as Rabbit turned toward Gabe. "Gabe, this is Crazy Bob. We really call him Tiny Dick, but then he just goes and does something to prove he is crazy and we have to go back to calling him Bob."

The two large men shook.

"Gabe and I go way back. He was in high school when I was dating his sister. I might have married her... except for the drunk who jumped the curb..."

The large man frowned at Gabe. "Hurt bad?"

Gabe played along. "Killed her outright—she had just walked out of the Frosty Freeze. They found the cone stuck to the asshole's windshield."

"Oh, shit. I'm sorry."

Gabe shrugged. "It's been a while... but I still miss her."

The conversation bumped along about mishaps,

mayhem, and then finally, motorcycles. The evening was filled with bikes leaving to cruise Van Nuys Boulevard slowly up to Sherman Way and back. It was all about looking and being looked at. As the three joined the evening's dance card, Gabe noted the occasional hot rod and a lot of kids driving mommy's or if they were good looking girls—daddy's car. The idea being that the lesser boys would feel inferior and not try to talk up daddy's little girl. Of course, daddy's little girl was there specifically looking for the bad boy to play with—the better car just provided the superior sorting tool.

Rabbit yelled over to Gabe as they approached the Ventura Freeway. "It's dead here. Let's see what's happening over in Hollywood." They nodded at Bob, who continued back to June Ellen's donut shop and probably a sale or two of marijuana.

The two bikes howled their way up the on-ramp and then settled down on the freeway. Gabe could sense by the slower speed that Rabbit wanted to talk.

"Bob is a small time drug seller. You can get some Mary Jane or uppers from him—but that's about it. Never get him busted. He has a few people to support, and he isn't one to really keep a secret. If something is happening, Bob usually knows a little about what is going on and who."

"So he's an informant?"

"Not that he knows. He's just friendly. He used to have a drinking problem—so he just doesn't go into bars anymore. I've never heard him mention drinking in the last few years. I'm not even sure if he even smokes anything he sells. He just hangs out on cruise nights and talks or cruises."

"Does he come over to Hollywood?" The bikes bounced as the freeway transitioned to the Hollywood Freeway.

"I've never seen him here."

Gabe digested the new information as they wound through the Cahuenga Pass to Hollywood. The traffic had seemed light but got busier as they neared the Sunset exit. As they pulled off the freeway, Rabbit pointed at his gas tank. They pulled into a cut-rate station, but Rabbit nosed his bike towards the back and Gabe followed.

As they shut down the two Harleys, Gabe frowned at Rabbit. The other man held up one finger. A moment later, the attendant came around the corner with a pair of five-gallon gas cans. Without saying a word, he rigged the nozzle in each. Rabbit slipped him a couple of ones and the kid left.

Rabbit turned to Gabe with a smirk. "Ever run aviation fuel in a motorcycle?"

"No... why?"

"It's one-hundred-ten octane. Just don't run it all of the time... you'll burn your valves. But at least your engine runs hard when you do." He gave Gabe a goofy smile like they were a couple of young teens sneaking a cigarette out behind the school gym. "If something starts tonight about a race, we don't want to risk running on regular gas.

Gabe opened the cap on his tank and took up the other gas can. *In for a quart—in for a few gallons... or something like that.*

As it was, the opportunity didn't take long to appear. As they pulled up in front of the pancake house and backed their bikes to the curb, three men rose from squatting against the wall. They circled around Gabe's bike—eyeing the hybrid of two engines and the strange starter. The Panhead motor had been around for a decade and the knuckle was old time—1930s, but using a car starter was new to everyone. The idea of an electric start on a Harley was only a couple of years old—starting with the Electra Glide.

"Why not just use a stock Electra Glide starter?"

Gabe shrugged, "It was built before Electra Glide came out."

"What's it off of?"

"1962 Falcon."

"Don't look like no stock set of jugs..."

Gabe gave Rabbit a bored look. "They aren't."

"How fast is it?"

Gabe's head swiveled around as Rabbit's matched. The newcomer looked a little cleaner, a little neater, a lot more intelligent, and respectable. Gabe took a run at the real question. "What color is your money?" *The man was looking for a race.*

ANGEL FLIGHTS

"Pink slips."

Gabe snorted. "Only an idiot would give away his scooter."

Gabe turned back to Rabbit. "Come on. This is worse than the Valley." He started to swing his leg back over the bike.

"I'd wager old ladies for the night... but you don't seem to have one."

Gabe slowly ground his head back around. He looked both ways along the sidewalk. There were a few women, but they appeared to be with other guys. "All I see that you brought to the game was an empty hand was a penis might go... if you had one." He turned back around and started to pull his gloves on. Out of the corner of his eye, he noticed Rabbit wasn't moving.

"Twenty bucks."

Gabe looked out at Hollywood Boulevard. The traffic was heavy for a Wednesday night—even for Hollywood. He ignored the man and pulled on his second glove. Turning the key, he reached forward for the starter button.

"A hundred."

Gabe looked at Rabbit. There was a small smirk. Rabbit nodded a small drop of the head and then looked at his watch. "River to Sylmar and back on the freeway."

"Done."

The crowded sidewalk emptied and the air filled

with noise and exhaust. Rabbit and Gabe made the yellow light, and no car moved as a steady flow of motorcycles streamed through the red light onto the eastbound Hollywood Boulevard.

The few tourists watched with their hands over their ears. The herd of choppers thundered down both lanes then split between the cars and along the center yellow line. Quarter tons of hot steel and foreboding visages flowed through the traffic like water around rocks in a stream.

Other bikers on the strip sensed something going down. Choppers and stockers made U-turns, left curbs, and emptied parking areas—as the stream became a river.

Rabbit laughed maniacally in the night air. "Now do you see why I gassed up beforehand?"

"What's the guy riding?"

"I didn't see—but if Roscoe didn't build it—it won't matter." Rabbit shot Gabe a large toothy smile. It glowed hauntingly in the neon lights of the car lot as they raced by.

At the bottom of the river, Rabbit dismounted and came over. He hunched in. "Listen, stay with this guy until Burbank starts to thin out. There are four places between here and Lockheed that he can get out and cheat. We'll send some bikes up the river to watch, but you never know… so toy with him until you see the fire on top of the big pipe on your left—then let her rip."

ANGEL FLIGHTS

The crowd gathered and the rules were laid down—standard outlaw race—safe the first half, dangerous and breaking the law the second half. Rabbit sent about a half dozen bikers up the river to watch the exits. The last exit was in Sylmar and the one the racers would use—the same as Gabe had used the first time.

Taking both men's money, he handed it to a woman who was spilling out of her blouse and jean jacket. With a great show, she rubbed each bill on her bulging breasts and then stuck it down deep in her cleavage. The smile on her face was purely sexual.

"Okay, the exit in Sylmar is this side of the gravel pit. From there, you can take whatever way you want back to the slide down there, and then come back here. There is a bunch of construction on San Fernando Road, so I would suggest you not take it. The one way back you cannot use—is the river. Use the river and you forfeit. Take any exit out of the river this side of Sylmar and you forfeit. Try to do any bodily harm to the other racer, and if you are still alive tomorrow morning—you are going to wish you weren't. Are you both clear?"

They nodded.

"Then you are free to go when you want."

Both men grabbed at their clutches, kicked their shifters and there was nothing but two red glowing dots in the dark—getting smaller—fast.

The woman with the large breasts was named Tina. She wasn't the smartest fox in the den, but she did take a liking to Rabbit. As the three ate a midnight dinner at the Pantry, Tina snuggled into Rabbit's arm with her legs pulled up and bent on the booth seat. Her eyes were in a war with the heavy false eyelashes packed with mascara, and staying awake. Gabe didn't blame her. He too had been up since before dawn.

"So when did he know he had lost?"

"I remembered the large tower of the Lockheed building. When it came into view, I knew he had one exit left before he would have to go the distance." Gabe took another sip of his coffee.

"But how did he know?"

"We were neck and neck. Both bikes were wound tight. But… can you tell the difference between twenty-eight hundred RPMs in fourth and thirty-nine hundred RPMs in third?"

"No."

"Neither could he. He thought I was already in fourth gear like he was."

Rabbit did some fast math. "Are you saying you were running over a hundred in third gear?"

Gabe smiled as evil as he could. "He knew he'd been had when I shifted. The look on his face was beautiful."

Tina giggled. "I bet his pants don't smell good

now either."

Gabe smiled and looked at the young woman. He realized the soft gurgling was her snoring. He took the last swallow of his coffee and slid out of the booth. Quietly, he nodded at the woman with one breast now sagging out of the half-buttoned shirt. "Good luck with that. I'll meet you at Roscoe's in the morning or Chet's after about three."

Rabbit nodded and looked at the top of the head leaning on his arm. He raised his eyebrows with one eye closed. He leaned forward and took in the large breast. He looked up. "Chet's."

Gabe smiled and walked out from the oldest diner in LA. The waiters were dressed in tuxedos, but the customers were from all walks of life. There were fur coats and tuxedos standing next to the garbage collector taking a lunch break—the line to get in was always interesting.

06

GROUND RULES

"RABBIT'S A GOOD man. Just don't let him talk you into using that damn jet fuel too often."

Roscoe was bent over fiddling with the massive carburetor. The large SU side-draft carburetor was off a European touring car—but it allowed Gabe's oversized engine to breathe fully.

Gabe leaned his hip against the grease-stained workbench. His arms were crossed so he didn't inadvertently place them where they could do damage. "What do you know about him lately?"

Roscoe looked up at the pegboard as if he was searching for a tool—but Gabe had seen him grab most of the tools off it without looking. His foot reached back and pulled the metal stool toward his butt as he sat down with weight.

"Is this about him smoking that weed or the other drugs?"

Gabe shrugged unsure. "Probably a lot of both—

and all of it. Five years is a very long time to be undercover."

Roscoe weighed his answer for a few moments. He stood as he looked in an old chipped coffee mug. The mug said 'Chief' on the side. "I need some coffee for this."

Gabe walked straight into a warm hug in the kitchen. "Hello, Honey. How's my girl?"

Honey laughed. "I don't know who your girl is, but I'm doing just fine for an old woman." She pushed back and looked up at the man. "Other than you need a shave and a haircut, how are things going with you?"

Gabe washed his hand over his hair and unshaved face. "It's my new look."

She sagged. "Then I don't want to know. You're starting to look like another guy named Rabbit." She poked at his chest with a curled knuckle. "Just don't get to a place where it scares the dogs. And if you need to get sewn up—I used to be a nurse." She pulled the newspaper off the table along with her coffee mug and went into the back sunroom. She knew when to leave the men alone.

Roscoe held out the coffee pot.

"Yes, please."

The two men settled at the table—sipping their coffee. Finally, Roscoe started, but Gabe wasn't sure where.

"It's been so long that I'm not even sure he

knows where his paycheck comes from. If I didn't know better, I would think someone just mails some money straight to his bank. Maybe they just stuff cash in an envelope and stick it in the crotch of a tree or something. I try not to think of those things. I wrench on his bike and he hands me a handful of cash. Sometimes, there is a hundred dollar bill in the stack—most times it's just fives, tens, and twenties with the occasional fifty."

His head still hanging, his body harrumphed. "First time I saw one of them fifties with Grant on it—it took me a minute to remember that it was real money."

The older man looked up at Gabe. Gabe could tell he was drawing up what was next from a very deep well.

Roscoe licked his lips. "What I can tell you is the man has a strong compass for what is right and wrong in the world. You have been very lucky. You worked with Zorro, and now you have the wild one. Both are basically the same man in a lot of ways. They don't kick dogs, they help little ladies across the street, and they open doors for everyone including other men. Rabbit is scruffy, but he is a gentleman—a man with a lot of honor. You just need to be with him for a while before you judge.

"I don't know what his job really is—but whatever he does—there is a purpose. If he smokes some of that killer weed—there is a reason. If he actually

ANGEL FLIGHTS

takes some drug—there is a reason. He thinks a lot more than he shows. If he trusts you, then he will tell you what's going on. If he finds a reason to not trust you—you'll find yourself back in a patrol car driving a midnight beat in Covina."

Gabe sat staring at the colored flecks in the Formica tabletop. His head gently nodded. Everything Roscoe was saying was what his gut had been telling him. *Just drift with the river—and watch where it takes you.*

"Has he told you anything?"

"We only met yesterday. We went over to Van Nuys and down to Hollywood... then had the race."

"The circuit."

Gabe scrunched up his face in question.

"It was Wednesday night. The kids get in daddy's car and drive up and down the boulevards. Over here, they do it on Valley Boulevard in Alhambra and a little on Colorado up in Pasadena. I think kids everywhere do something like it—it's part of growing up. It's a peacock thing. The boys show off their pretty feathers, and the girls fluff their sweaters—so to speak. It's the dance."

"And the bikers?"

Roscoe leaned back. "Ah, now there is the question. I think a bunch still want to be those young kids again or still. But for others, it's about belonging to something. Even if it's just that you go ride the same street or sit in the same parking lot—you are doing it with people you recognize, and more importantly—they recognize you."

"Personal experience?"

"Hot rods and hopped up cars, and sitting in the A&W in Covina, or taking a drive to The Hat in Alhambra for a pastrami sandwich."

"Not motorcycles?"

"Nah, my first love was a Lincoln straight-eight in a 1932 deuce coupe. The second was Honey, and then the war hit and I learned about motorcycles from Uncle Sam. After the war, they still needed a monkey on the wrench and I stayed on until we came home from Korea. That was where I met that crazy guy, Willie."

"Who's the woman who used to race my bike?"

"Maddie? She's his best friend. Her family brews moonshine and builds very fast cars—she races them. She was the first woman to break the two-hundred miles per hour speed at Bonneville—took her two tries and four years to do it."

Gabe frowned.

Roscoe got up for more coffee. "She stepped off the motorcycle before it came to a complete stop the first year."

"How fast was *not a complete stop?*"

Roscoe turned and leaned against the counter. Holding the mug with both hands close to his lips, he blew on the hot coffee, "Somewhere shy of one-eighty."

ANGEL FLIGHTS

"But that is nuts…"

Roscoe nodded. "A person has to be at least a little nuts to be a librarian."

"Wait… so you weren't joking about her being a librarian?"

Honey wandered in with her empty mug. "Are you two talking about Maddie?" She looked over her shoulder at the two. "She's nuts, all right. But one of the nicest people you will ever meet. And she keeps that crazy Willie in line—now there is someone who is not wired to both legs of the power line."

Roscoe gave her a stern look and cleared his throat. Turning back to Gabe. "What else did you and Rabbit talk about?"

"That I need to buy a house somewhere in East LA."

"Any place in particular?" Honey leaned back against the counter next to her husband.

"Boyle, Lincoln, or Sereno or something—just not Alhambra or South Pasadena."

Honey thought a moment with her finger on Roscoe's arm. "Who was that guy who worked for DWP… Mexican guy or something. He had that funny limp like he was missing his foot or something."

Roscoe pinched the bridge of his nose and scrunched his face. Looking up at Honey, he searched. "Manny… Manny something…"

"Garcia?"

"Noo… but close." He snapped his fingers three

times to a hidden beat of remembrance. "Gonza…"

She slapped his arm gently. "Gonza y Estrella. Manual Gonza y Estrella."

"Right… and he moved his mother into a home just a few months ago."

Honey turned and rested her hand on Gabe's shoulder as she walked past. "I'll have the information for you in a few minutes. He grew up in El Sereno and would know of anything else of interest, too."

Roscoe watched his wife disappear into the other room. "I think the FBI calls her to ask what she has on people. No bit of information escapes her."

"What did she do before?"

"She was a snoop."

Gabe laughed but the older man didn't. "No seriously, what did she do?"

"She was an investigator for the District Attorney's office. That's how I got to know all of you cops—through her."

"So you were never a cop?"

Roscoe sat down and pulled up his pant leg and exposed the short prosthetic leg and foot. "Last day before my company pulled out of Korea." He pushed the pants back down. "I came home about four months late. I was worried how I was going to break it to that woman in there."

"What happened?"

"She walked up to me at the train station. Told

me I was nicknamed after the snub-nose in my pocket, and she would never call me stumpy or snub-toes. I had to laugh. We never mentioned it again until that night when I stepped on her toes as we danced."

"Where were you?"

"There is a food joint... downtown LA... been around forever..."

"The Pantry...?"

"Bingo. It was a Friday night and some guy was playing a violin on the sidewalk entertaining the people waiting in line. I asked him if he knew the two-step. He said he only knew the short version. I told him perfect."

Gabe roared with laughter. "This is such a crock of bull. You did not."

Honey walked in. "We did, and he broke three of my toes that night. And I still took him home after—and I'd do it all again."

Gabe's mouth hung open. She stuck a small piece of paper in it.

"He'll meet you over there in about twenty minutes."

The house was small with an overgrown back lawn and a few dozen rose bushes that were on the list of dead or dying. The garage had been built for a Model A and a few garden tools.

The older man moped his way around the small house. "The folks built it in 1921. They bought the furniture up in Pasadena at a used furnishings store. It all goes with the house—I don't want any of it. I grew up with it all, and it wasn't very fond memories. All three of us kids lived in that front room—me and two sisters."

Gabe winced. "Ouch." He peeked in the bedroom at the one bed, one nightstand, and one tall dresser of seven drawers. He didn't have to look around the corner to know the closet would be about one yard square.

The man nodded. "My oldest sister is seven years older than me. She did most of her dating with her boyfriends sneaking through that window. Not long after she started, she was married. My middle sister and I were afraid her husband would just move in with us."

"I take it that didn't happen."

"Nah, they moved in with his family." He laughed sadly.

"Anything I should know about the roof or furnace or something?"

"Nah, it's all well maintained... except the yards. I hate yard work. If you need someone to help you with the yard, the neighbor on this side is Japanese. The boy can mow the lawn, but his father is the gardener. Let him come over and show you what to do with those roses. They used to be pretty amazing, and they would grow award-winning flowers all year."

ANGEL FLIGHTS

"Any suggestions about how I can get financing?"

The guy looked at him for a long moment. "Personally, you look like a thug—no offense. But I've known Honey and Roscoe sort of from a distance for years. She mentioned that I should call Chet and he vouched for you. I can't imagine a bank giving you anything but grief. But Chet said he would co-sign if that's what I needed." He pulled out a slip of paper. "This is my brother-in-law that got my oldest sister pregnant and married her. He's my lawyer, and he can run the escrow and financial papers. Other than that, I guess we have a deal."

Gabe looked around. "It really is a nice little place. I want to thank you for doing this."

"Think nothing of it. I grew up here, and I damn sure wouldn't want to have to be a landlord of it. It was hard enough to just come over and fix things when mama was here. I'm just glad to get rid of it."

"What about your sisters?"

"Neither one has been here in the last five or ten years. They hated it here."

"Well, I think I'm going to love it."

"The neighborhood is pretty quiet. It's starting over, and there are several little kids on the block. Across the street, the plumber's wife is … well, you'll get to know everyone soon enough."

As Gabe left, the neighborhood kids on their tricycles waved shyly at him. When he started the motorcycle, they all smiled and twisted their hands on their handlebars. Gabe took the hint and revved the large loud engine a few times before he left. The kids were small but all smiles and waved as he rode off. *Some of the neighbors are going to like me...*

The coffee mug was waiting as Gabe walked into the bar. Chet was serving up a bowl of stew. He grabbed a few packs of crackers and shoved them alongside the bowl on the plate. 'How's your new house?"

"The lawn needs mowing... but the house is nice. It has two small bedrooms, but a very comfortable size. I don't even have to buy any furniture... and it looked like sheets and blankets are even covered. I'll move my two pairs of jeans and shirts in and call it home."

Chet nodded. "Perfect for you, but I remember what it was like with four teenagers in that front room."

"I thought he only had two sisters?" Gabe took a mouthful of stew and closed his eyes.

"I take it from your face that you like venison stew. A CHP buddy works the Angeles Crest. Occasionally, he brings me some of the fresh road kill. In the fall, I can fill the big deep freeze."

Gabe took another mouthful and held up his four fingers spread.

"Yeah, well, I had to try out the goods before I bought the farm." Chet laughed. "I married his

ANGEL FLIGHTS

younger sister. That window was like a revolving door—probably still has my handprints on the windowsill. There were nights when there were six of us in that room. We just knew the folks could hear us, but they never said anything."

"So you and Manual go back a long time."

"Gonzo? Sure. Until I had to put mom in a home, she still lived in that white house on the other side of the Japanese family. She and Mrs. Giovanni across the street were the neighborhood snoops. They knew everything. If we thought Mrs. Giovanni was still awake and sitting near her front curtains, we would sneak along the back fence. That fence runs the whole length of that long block."

"So you kids were naughty, but being good."

Chet snorted and nodded as he moved back down the bar to wash some glasses. "Where's your buddy?"

"He said about three."

Chet looked up and listened. "I think he's a little early, and in a hurry. You better eat up."

Gabe heard the motorcycle and the sharp chirp of a skidding stop. As he slurped down the last of the stew, Rabbit walked through the door still wearing his gloves.

"We have to go now." He turned back for the door.

Gabe looked up to Chet who only nodded. *Lunch was on his tab.*

Rabbit's engine was already running and his left hand was holding in the clutch. Gabe rushed to catch up. A mile down Huntington Drive, Gabe moved along side.

"What's up?"

"We have to save a guy. He's going to prison anyway, but I need him alive, not dead."

"Informant?"

"Little brother."

Rabbit leaned his bike over hard as he wound the throttle hard turning onto the freeway on-ramp. Gabe followed as they wove in and out of the afternoon traffic. The two dark figures were like demonic wraiths in the hot sunshine. As they ran down the slow lane, it didn't pass Gabe's notice in the corner of his eye, he saw a mom with a child risk crashing as she leaned across the entire front seat to push down the door lock. Gabe chuckled to think how dumb of her to think he would get off his motorcycle at seventy to climb through her door and rape her.

He became sober when he thought about how many irrational fears drive people to do stupid things. As he glanced in the rearview mirror, he saw the scruffy unshaven face and black glasses—not the reassuring look of a cop.

A few minutes later, they crept the bikes down a back alley. Parking, Rabbit indicated they would leave them there. The neighborhood had seen better times—probably during World War II. The paint was

ANGEL FLIGHTS

peeling where the boards of the fences hadn't rotted yet. The rubbish cans were rusted and dented.

Rabbit put his finger to his lips as he pushed open a back gate. The exposed yard had a rusted swing set where empty chains hung. The lawn had long been beaten to death and was just a sparse brown thatched padding over the hard pan of clay dirt.

Rabbit lead along the one side of the house and through a gap where the small chain-link fence used to have a gate. He looked about and found a few rocks about the size of golf balls. As they got near the corner of the house, he stopped.

"How is your throwing arm?"

"What do you want me to hit?"

"Break that bedroom window over there." He pointed at the house across the narrow street.

Gabe wasn't sure he could hit the window, much less break it. "I'll try," he whispered back.

"Throw it like a man's life depends on it."

"Why don't you do it—it's your brother."

Rabbit gave him a hard stare. Turning, Gabe watched as he wound up—the rock barely made it to the street but three cars down. Gabe wanted to laugh, and maybe say something about throwing like a girl—but he knew that a girl could throw better.

Gabe grabbed the rocks and lobbed them one by one. The first hit somewhere down the side of the house. The second was on the roof above the window, but the third went through the now open window—hitting the large black man in the face.

Gabe saw a flash of the giant hand come up to the face then the whole disappeared. A moment later, a giant of a man exploded out through the front door. His body was covered by a pair of white boxers with tiny hearts on them. His top was draped with something large and green. Even barefoot, the man was moving fast. His face was pure anger.

He crossed between the two parked cars and onto the lawn Gabe and Rabbit were standing on. At the end of the street two cars squealed skidding around the corner. All three looked. The black man moved faster as he saw Rabbit.

Rabbit grabbed Gabe's jacket and turned him so that all three were headed into the sanctuary of the back yard and the gate beyond. Rabbit glanced back at the large green snake churning around the almost naked man.

"Oh, shit. Oh, hell no, Michael. Get rid of that thing. You are not getting on my bike with that monster."

They all glanced back as the two large cars screeched to a halt in front of the small house. The neighborhood erupted in a cacophony of varied gunfire. The front of the small house began to disintegrate where Gabe had only worried about breaking a small piece of glass.

Gabe took in the situation. "He can ride with

ANGEL FLIGHTS

me." The fact that there was almost no seat covering the rear fender never dawned on him.

As they turned out of the alley, Gabe knew the man's butt cheeks were draped over both sides of his rear fender—he didn't even want to think about where the pillion pad was stuffed. The fact that eighty pounds of boa constrictor was on the back as well—never entered his mind until the snakehead—the size of a medium dog—came snuggling along his neck as they climbed up onto the freeway. Before he could stop, all ten feet of the snake was wrapped around him—inside of the leather jacket.

Michael leaned forward laughing. "She must like your smell. She goes nuts for women—I think she's a queer or something. Her name is Gertie. She don't squeeze or nuttin'. She jus' like to ride bikes from in da jacket."

Gabe rolled his eyes. "Good to know." He could feel the football shaped head nodding just below his chin.

Rabbit took the exit down into south central LA. If the neighborhood before was poor, this was destitute. Gabe followed with the large man hunkered against his back like a large blob. The stares would have been funny, but none of the three had time for paying attention.

As they parked at the curb, an older woman came out the front door. "Michael Thomas Alexander Washington, where are your pants?"

The man stood up with a huge smile as he gathered in the fair-sized woman into his hug. "Momma, this motorcycle be so fast, they done blowed off."

She slapped at him until he opened his arms. "Don't you be telling those kind of fibs, young man. And by the way—you stink. You smell like that damn snake of yours." She looked about and then grabbed at the front band of his boxers. "Speaking of which... where be that she-devil?"

She noticed Gabe—with a second head. The snake licked its tongue out and tasted the air.

"If'n you be comin' in my house, young man—you keep zipped up." She turned and stalked off, dragging the large naked man by the ear. "Rabbit, you take care'o yo guest."

"Yes, momma."

Gabe looked at his partner. Other than the windblown tan from riding a motorcycle, Gabe could guess that the covered parts were milk white.

Rabbit deadpanned. Then gave up. "She was a nurse's assistant at County General when my mother gave up her fight with heroin. She knew what Child Services was like. I was about three. When I was seven, she brought Michael home to keep me company. She showed me just once how to change a diaper, how to warm his bottle, and the right temperature for his bath water.

"She told me it was her job to keep a roof over our heads, it was mine to take care of my little brother. We've been family ever since."

"Just the three of you…"

"Didn't need nobody else. When I needed to go to school, I took Michael across to the widow." He pointed across the street. "When I got home, she made me do my homework before I could bring Michael home. Momma got home about ten o'clock to kiss me goodnight. In the morning, she got up to kiss me at the door."

Gabe thought about growing up that way. He kicked at the dirt that passed for the front yard. "Hard life."

"Not really. I had a mother and brother. We ate almost regular, and the house is hers."

Gabe thought about saying something about love winning overall, but the large snake started to move like it wanted out. Rabbit pointed at the neighbor's lawn. The man had just finished mowing it and Gabe could smell the rich scent.

"She likes to lie out on freshly mowed lawns. Just go lean over and she'll get out." He laughed at the face Gabe made of pure *help me*.

True to Rabbit's word, the large snake oozed out of Gabe's jacket onto the lawn. As all ten feet stretched out, she straightened and relaxed in the sun.

"So she likes the grass and sunbathing?" Gabe looked at Rabbit who was nodding his head back over his shoulder.

Gabe looked down the block as a line of kids on

tricycles and small bicycles raced down the sidewalk toward the two men and snake. Rabbit pulled Gabe out of the way as two tricycles almost ran over his feet.

Gabe turned to watch the controlled crashes of every mode of transportation as the kids hit the lawn and skidded to a stop on their knees next to the stretched-out snake. Tiny hands looked even smaller as they began gently petting the snake that probably could swallow some of the small children whole.

The man came out of his house holding two large glasses of lemonade. As he crossed the lawn, he was chuckling softly. "I was wondering where she was hiding. Michael didn't look like he had any place to hide her." He handed Rabbit and Gabe the two glasses.

"Hello, Mr. Svetlick. Thank you." Rabbit hefted the glass. "Mr. Svetlick, this is Gabe, a good friend of mine. Gabe, Mr. Svetlick."

Gabe noticed the accent as the man stuck out his hand. "Please, we are among friends. Call me Vasiliy Fyodor Alexander Nikolaevich Svetlick." The man nodded as they shook. "But, if you vish to be more formal, Nick is good, dah?"

Gabe chuckled at the man's deprecating humor about his heritage. "Nick it is." He nodded at the kids and snake.

"Ah, da monster? Yah, dees kids, day love her. She love my lawn because I cut it longer and soft for her. She also love the kids—dat is vhy she stretch out dat vay—she make room for more hands."

Rabbit leaned in. "The moms used to freak out when she was only five or six feet long, now they won't even come out of their houses. The kids don't have that fear—so they get the love."

"But I thought you hated her...?"

"Eah, she's okay. Michael used to torment us both by sticking her in my bed when I had a girl over. She really is in love with the smell or taste of women. In bed, she might lay next to you for warmth, but she will smother a woman. She just can't get close enough to them."

"What about your mother?"

"Oh, she was serious about not letting her loose in the house. Besides, she has a new dog—one of those little squeaky toy kinds of dog. One bite and it would be only the dog license that came out the other end in a week or two."

Svetlick stopped watching the kids and turned with a smile. The contented look on his lips was not what Gabe saw in his eyes. "You come and bring Michael. Dis makes dem very happy. It is a good thingk." His voice lowered. "But if you are here, and Michael is here, dis is not such a good thingk, dah?"

"No, Mr. Svetlick. It is not a good thing. I'm afraid that Michael will still have to go away for a few years."

"This is a sad thingk. You two make your mother happy. Dis will not."

Rabbit nodded. "I'll stop in once in a while when I can, but... well, you know how it is."

The man screwed his face up into a quirky mass as he turned his head and smiled at Rabbit. "You know, I build up a very nice hamster here. First the widow, now your mother."

"You mean a harem?"

"No," he poked at his own chest, "this hamster. Run here, run there, run in circles... hamster." He laughed and the two other men laughed.

"Vell, I go now." He took the glasses. "I have other hamster shit to do." He winked. "I no show up at the coffee shop, the young waitress die of heartbreak." He turned and went back inside.

They both turned at the sound of the other screen door snapping against the door jam. Michael was dressed more for a school run by nuns than a small-time hoodlum.

"I can't believe I still fit in these."

"Why not, you only got out a year ago."

"Three—asshole. What did old man Svetlick want?"

Rabbit rubbed his brother's head. "Show some respect. You know what he wanted—he wanted mom to come out and ask him to dinner."

"Do you think they ever....?"

"Hey! Show some respect."

"Well?"

ANGEL FLIGHTS

"No. I mean no. God, I don't even want to think about that. You're talking about our mother."

"Well, she isn't really..."

Rabbit slugged him hard in the shoulder. The younger brother didn't even flinch—his face just broke into a large smile.

Rabbit hated that he couldn't even affect his little brother who was about twice his size. "Fuck you. And don't be talking like that about Mom. You hear?"

Michael nodded.

"And don't be a smart-ass in prison either. They will find someone bigger than you and turn you out like a cheap suit. You hear me?"

"Yah."

"Yah, what?"

"Yes, big brother Teddy."

"That's better. Now go get your snake. We need to talk."

"I don't have my jacket. I left it in the other house when I ran out."

Rabbit stared at him for the count of five. The younger just shrugged his arms and smiled. Rabbit's head ground around toward Gabe, but his eyes were still on his brother.

Gabe got the point. "I'll get her." He walked over to the snake and the kids took one last pet each and got back. "How do I get her up?"

Michael snorted. "Bend over and show her your

crack."

Rabbit slapped the back of his head.

Michael leaned forward and spread his shirt open. Gabe did the same and eighty pounds of snake shrunk up into a large ball, then the head rose and everything began to disappear into the jacket as the body convulsed and curled its way around Gabe.

Gabe took one stumble step. "That is one neat trick."

Michael looked at Rabbit. "Can we have a barbecue?"

"I threw it away. The bottom rusted out."

Gabe pursed his lips. "I have a small hibachi at my new house."

"When did you buy a house?"

"This morning." He held up a red die connected to two gold keys by a chain.

"This I've got to see."

Two hours and forty miles east, the three sat at the dinner table cutting up their steaks. Rabbit looked around the small bungalow. "Nice place."

"I kind of liked it the minute I walked in. It felt like a 'grandma lives here' but without all of the trinket stuff." Gabe ran his hand along the walnut table. "I really like the old furniture."

Michael slowly cut his steak. "This table is Queen Anne, the dressers are Georgian revival, and the beds are Edwardian. The bed in the front was extended to fit the longer modern mattress. But the one

ANGEL FLIGHTS

in the back is worth more than the rest of the furniture combined. It is actually from England. The Settle in the front here, as well as the Morse chair, is from the late nineteenth century, but they are out of favor right now." He took a bite and looked up at Gabe. He shoved the piece of meat to the side of his mouth. "What?"

Rabbit put down his fork and wiped his mouth. "Michael worked in the furniture district for a couple of years—until his boss went away to prison for forging antiques. Michael can spot a fake from across the room, and as for value, he is better than his boss ever was."

Michael chewed slowly behind his self-satisfied smile.

"So, if you're so great—what are you going to prison for?"

Rabbit jumped in. "Stupidity. That—and not listening to his big brother."

Gabe weighed the brotherly rivalry. But as he watched, the younger dissolved and finally nodded.

Michael put down his fork and glanced down at the floor. He smiled. "Now we find out who loves who."

Gabe frowned until the large football of a green head appeared at his elbow.

Rabbit howled with laughter. "Ow, little brother—you are his-tor-y."

Gabe watched as the snake threw its head back

and forward as its mouth opened wider and wider. "What the hell is she doing?"

"She's opening her mouth for you to feed her." Michael stared in amazement as his snake was performing what heretofore had been only his special domain.

With the head cocked open, the snake rested with the mouth looking more like a large funnel. Michael shoved the A-1 sauce across the table. "Put some on your plate and dip a chunk in it. Then push it down her throat until you start feeling the throat contract around your finger."

Gabe stuck the dripping chunk into the throat as directed. He quickly withdrew his finger. "Damn... that felt weird."

Rabbit laughed. "You'll get used to it. She's your girlfriend now."

Gabe looked at his partner and then at the brother. Both were nodding. He realized the woman in the room had made her choice. He could only imagine what kind of damper it would put on his love life. He was just beginning to understand how demanding she could be... As he shoved the fourth piece of steak down her throat, he realized she was eating more than he was. He hoped she didn't like baked potatoes.

"What else do I feed her? I mean, is there like some Purina Python Chow?"

Michael stared at his ex-snake. "Got any small

dogs in the neighborhood?" He looked up at the silence. "I was kidding. She will take a fresh whole chicken... she doesn't like the skin so just take it off. And you can get small bunnies or chicks from a feed store."

Gabe put down his fork. He was done at the thought of feeding live bunnies to a large snake. "How often do I feed her a chicken?"

"One a week will be enough for her to grow, but not get fat. Oh, and keep the steak to about three bites. Tap her top lip with your finger... just once is enough."

Gabe watched as Gertie ratcheted her jaw closed and unwound from the table leg. He watched under the table as she moved across the hardwood floors toward the bedrooms to explore.

He sat up with a frown. "Where does she shit?"

"Leave the lid up."

"No, really..."

"No, actually you will find it in the bathtub. You can either pick it up with some toilet paper, or just wash it down with the shower. Other than that... just let her roam. But you have to warn any women you bring home."

Rabbit snorted and then belly laughed. "Remember that little blonde I brought home...?"

Michael joined in the laughing. "She met Gertie about the time she climbs on top... she came off and liked to hit the ceiling. For a little thing—she sure had some lungs."

Rabbit snorted. "She slowed down after the first mile and figured out she had forgotten her car, clothes, and even where she was."

Michael laughed and pointed at Rabbit. "Them six niggers down at the Chevron thought they had died and gone to heaven… blonde white pussy was running wild in the street… until you came along naked on the motorcycle and swoosh—she be like last night's wet dream—gone, but fo-ever dried in the sheets."

Rabbit's shoulders were still shaking as he looked at Gabe. "So remember—always warn them first so you can shut her up in the bedroom you are not going to be busy in."

As Gabe sat on the front porch with his new roommate nuzzling his neck, he watched the tail light disappear up the long street. He remembered they hadn't discussed what Michael was going to prison for… but with the long day's business, his tired brain didn't care. His eyes fell on the long grass of the yard. He looked around at Gertie. "I'll mow the lawn this weekend. Then maybe you can meet some new kids to pet you… and some moms to scare."

The big head nuzzled in harder.

07

MEET THE NEIGHBORS

BY THE TIME Gabe had transferred all of his clothes to his house, the grocery store was closed. Gertie would have to wait. The lawn mower was still where he had left it at the end of six feet of mowing.

Gabe looked out at the lawn. He wasn't tired, and the coffee pot was still on. Gertie lay curled next to him like an obedient dog. Her large head lay in his lap. A neighbor walked past and waved—Gabe waved back. "You can lie out on the lawn tomorrow girl." Her head moved. He could feel the weight of the large head. She then raised it and curled in on herself. It broke his heart. He looked at the reel mower. It was pretty quiet. The street light was right overhead…

Gabe was about half done when the spotlight lit up the front yard. Gabe hadn't heard the cruiser pull up. The two officers walked into the light and Gabe recognized the two from El Sereno precinct. He stood the reel mower upright and took off his gloves.

"Howdy, Mike, Pete. Are you rousting the quiet neighborhood?"

"Gabe? Is that you under all that fuzz?"

"Fuck you, Mike." The three laughed as they shook hands.

"We didn't know you lived here."

"I bought the house last week." He pointed up the narrow driveway. "If the kitchen light is on—so is the coffee. The back door doesn't even have a lock, so you guys are welcome anytime. Just don't let the snake out."

Pete stood up straighter. "Snake?" He looked around.

Gabe pointed at the dark mass on the front porch. "She's waiting for me to finish mowing the lawn. She likes the feel and smell, I guess."

"Yeah, right… what kind of dog is tha…?" The officer pulled up his large flashlight and turned it on the green mass. Gertie raised her head. The eyes glowed like burning embers from the light. "Oh, holy shit!"

Gabe snorted. "Why don't you guys head for the coffee, and I'll join you in a few minutes. I just want to finish this and put the mower away.'

Gabe came in the back door. "How's the coffee?"

The two officers turned. "You need a new pot."

"I just made a fresh pot."

"No, you can taste the rust. You need to buy a new pot. Also, this one is a little on the small side."

Pete looked around the floor behind Gabe.

Gabe rolled his eyes. "Relax, Pete—she's out front on the lawn. Besides—she likes girls—so you are almost safe."

"Fuck you, Street." They laughed at the old verbal horseplay from the precinct.

"So what are you doing now? You just disappeared one day, nobody knew anything."

Gabe looked at the older officer. He knew that the man would never make sergeant. He would finish his forty, take his pension and either grow old with lots of grandchildren—or eat his service revolver before he got his tenth pension check. There was no light for life in the man's eyes. He had taken a job, not a career, not a calling—just a very long job.

Gabe looked down at the mug of bad coffee. "You're right—I need a new pot." *The conversation was over. They all knew it. The light was on, the coffee would be hot— no other questions.*

The weeks drifted by as Gabe got used to the house and yard, and the neighbors settled down about the biker who mowed his lawn and then turned his snake loose among the band of small kids who loved petting the big monster. Gabe even convinced a few of the moms to actually touch the 'slimy' thing—only to discover she was dry, warm, and felt like high-priced stockings on well shaved legs. But none were willing to snuggle closer—or let Gertie snuggle, either.

During the workdays, Rabbit would usually come by for morning coffee and some kind of thrown together breakfast—or they would grab something on the run. The fastest was a chorizo and egg burrito from one of the drive-thru shacks open for the early shift workers headed for the Chevy plant in Van Nuys.

"Gabe!" The back door banged shut in the dark. The sound of heavy boots on the linoleum kitchen floor was short lived before they became thuds on the hardwood. *Rabbit.*

"Fuck you. It's too early." Gabe stared at the dimly lit clock. The little number card fell over. The three was now a four—*two-twenty-four in the freaking morning. Who the hell gets up this early?*

"You have ten minutes to shower, shit and sh— well, in your case shower and shit. We have to catch an early delivery."

Gabe moaned, and then realized he couldn't move his hips or legs.

He reached under the covers and found Gertie's head. Patting it a few times woke her up, and she moved enough to let him get his legs out. She shifted into the larger warm spot. He pulled the covers back over her and stood with a sour look at Rabbit.

"Good morning, sunshine." Rabbit was way too

chipper for the hour.

"Fuck you." Gabe stumbled into the bathroom. "Reheat some coffee in a pan."

He turned on the shower and sat down on the toilet while the water warmed up.

"Your new big ass pot is still on. Or at least the red light is on. When did you get that?"

"What big pot?"

"Looks like it holds enough for a church dinner." Rabbit leaned against the door with two large mugs that Gabe had never seen before. The mugs were steaming. Rabbit offered one mug out as he sipped on the other.

Gabe looked at the strange mug, took a sip, stood, and flushed. "Damned if I know where it all came from. I had a lady over last night…" He took one more sip and setting the mug on the windowsill, stepped into the shower. "Gertie was locked in the back bedroom, and I hadn't made any coffee in the old pot."

"Well, your kitchen light was on. Gertie was humping your ass like a rabid, horny dog, and there ain't no woman to be seen. Maybe Gertie ate her."

Gabe chortled. "Gertie is my girl who likes girls." An empty plastic shampoo bottle sailed over the shower curtain and landed at Rabbit's feet.

He picked up the bottle and slam-dunked the garbage can. "You are down to four minutes."

The water shut off as the curtain was swept

back. Grabbing the towel from the rack, Gabe started toweling down. As his backside came into view, Rabbit laughed.

"Damn dude. You said a woman—not a lion and lamprey."

Gabe looked around with a large toothy smile.
On the way out, Gabe noted the size of the industrial sized coffee urn. The cabinet door above was ajar. He opened it to find the upper cabinets filled with large cans of coffee. *Cops love their coffee—and a quiet, safe place to hang out and do paperwork.*

Gabe rolled the bike out of the garage and softly bump started it as he neared the street. The two bikes chuffed their way down the still neighborhood street. The time was 2:36 a.m.

08

WORK WRONG DO RIGHT

THE BEAN BURRITO and coffee was not helping Gabe's head. The sunrise being over an hour away was his only hope. The fumes from the truck somewhere up ahead weren't helping. *Fuck this loafing behind this asshole.* He pulled on the throttle and shot forward into the fast lane. Rabbit was slow to respond, but eventually, caught up with him. He indicated to take the off-ramp.

As they pulled to the bottom of the ramp, Rabbit's face was almost purple. "What the fuck was that?"

"Some truck with a bad engine ahead of us was making me sick. I wanted clean air."

"That truck was our target, asshole. Stick with the program unless you drew up the plans." He shot across the street and headed up the on-ramp. Gabe followed.

Gabe settled in at the far edge of the fast lane

where the fumes were much lighter. Rabbit nodded that he understood. They closed cautiously on each truck until they found the one leaking uncombusted diesel through a rusted-out exhaust. The informant had only said it was a big rig that stunk to high heaven and sounded like small grenades going off. Rabbit had figured out the problem that would let them follow the truck and only have to watch for when it turned off the freeway. They had picked up the truck just south of the nuclear plant at about four that morning. The lack of traffic and the wide-open space had been their best weapon, but also their biggest danger of being noticed. They had stayed back over a mile until there was more traffic.

As they moved through the dark, Rabbit had fallen back a ways and then hid behind another truck as if he had turned off. He reached forward and turned his headlight off. Combined with the black painted Springer front end, instead of a mass of pretty chrome, the bike was close to invisible.

Rabbit rolled out and up alongside Gabe. He nodded for him to do the same. "Slowly make your way across as to not spook the guy."

Gabe took the better part of a mile slowly crossing the lanes. As he returned, he noticed Rabbit's tail light was still on. He made a mental note to have Roscoe rig his that way too—maybe have a back cutout only as well.

The truck continued through the night.

As they crossed downtown LA, the freeway had more light and the two bikers played a game of hiding behind or moving in the shadows of larger trucks. The early morning was still more on the warm side than chill, and the ride was comfortable. Gabe wondered what they would do in the middle of winter when the LA rains were more like monsoons or open fire hydrants.

The three of them rounded Hollywood and the truck strained as he climbed the pass through Hollywood Hills toward the San Fernando Valley. If Gabe had thought the truck obnoxious before, he now had a whole new meaning of the word. He stuck to the center break down lane but close enough to be in the truck's blind spot.

The truck slowed as it approached Barham. A weak glow showed dully from the old indicator light hanging by its wires. The truck shuddered as the driver downshifted. Gabe was pretty sure this would be the truck's last effort as a wheeled vehicle. It turned right toward Burbank. The dark streets were a grace because there was no other traffic on the four-lane street. The two cops fell back and followed more by smell.

As they entered the industrial area on the edge of Burbank, they moved to within a block of the truck but with their lights off. Anything that happened now would be quick and soon.

The truck slowed and turned left onto a short

cul-de-sac, and then into a fenced yard. It stopped at the gate for a moment, and then moved through. Rabbit pulled up into a large parking lot that was the backside of Lockheed Martin. There were cars and trucks of workers on the graveyard shift. He slid behind a low profiled Fairlane. Gabe followed and they shut off their engines.

Rabbit pulled a small set of binoculars out of his jacket's inner pocket. He watched as the truck laboriously turned and backed up to a loading dock. With the truck in place, the roll-up door slid open. Rabbit handed the binoculars to Gabe.

Rabbit's whisper was a rumble. "The tables with all the lights—they are processing the tar into heroin." He leaned back exhausted. "There are probably twenty or thirty Mexican girls they smuggled up… they thought they were coming to the land of opportunity. Instead, they will be in there wearing only their panties and maybe a bra. The whole process will take a few days. They will be fed almost nothing and will get only a few hours of sleep. If they are lucky, they will be taken up to a farm in the Central Valley afterward."

"And if they are not lucky?"

Rabbit took the binoculars. "There will be a warehouse fire where the seamstresses died. Or they will be taken out into the desert where a shallow grave is waiting."

"You've seen this before."

Rabbit nodded. "You asked once why I've been undercover for so long… things like this—and they take a long time to find them."

"So what do we do now?"

"Nothing. We're just two bikers who don't give a damn about what other people do." The man glanced at his watch. "Besides, it's time for breakfast." Rabbit closed his eyes and then opened them with the smile that Gabe had come to know as his *Let's Go Fuck Someone* smile. The cop was showing through.

"Any suggestions?"

The large man fluffed at his long hair. "I'm feeling like some pancakes and eggs at the Long Green." He turned the key and jumped on the kick arm. The bike farted and roared to life just as the shift whistle blew at the aircraft plant. He looked over at Gabe and smiled with a self-satisfied grin. They would exit with the cover of many others.

Rabbit shot out and stopped on a section of asphalt that was still damp from the night air. He revved the bike and dumped the clutch. The rear tire smoked and he spun the bike in a few circles celebrating the end of the shift day—time to party.

As they loafed up the San Fernando Road, Rabbit slowed and pulled into the Atomic Gas Station. They filled their tanks as the attendant sauntered over. The kid had a sea of zits over his face and neck. His hair was an inch or so long on top and

ANGEL FLIGHTS

shaved white sidewall on the side. Gabe figured he was either a hayseed, recently drummed out of the Army but still holding onto hope, or not all right in the head. He was wrong on all accounts. Rabbit told him to call his dad and tell him to come up to the Long Green. The kid was a drop for his dad.

Rabbit nosed his chopper off the road and into the gravel parking lot in front of the long, low white building. What looked like it could have once been a commercial chicken coop was a restaurant like a rail car diner but twice as long. The cook's station ran the entire back wall and faced the long counter. The two cooks walked in the three-foot alley between the counter and stoves. They were cook, waiter, and busboy to the counter. Four mismatched chairs bracketed the center door for customers waiting to pick up a to-go order.

Rabbit and Gabe sat at the counter. The thinner of the two cooks turned and took their orders. There was no menu—just tell the man what you want. Time was money, and someone was waiting for your seat.

It wasn't long before the Treasury agent slid up to the long counter next to Rabbit. His partner slid onto the stool the other side of Gabe.

The cook turned from the grill. He stepped over to the giant coffee urn and filled two Navy-style mugs. Putting them down, he looked at the older agent. "Usual short stack with two over easy and bacon?" The agent nodded. The cook ignored the younger agent next to Gabe and turned back to the grill and shot out a line of pancake dough. "Pair of double cackleberries loose."

The taller and heavier-set cook at the south end of the diner answered, "Full hand of dead chicks with runny noses."

Gabe marveled at the two men. They had been cooks in the Navy, and after Japan had given up, they gave up the Navy and bought the diner. There had never been a menu, nor had there ever been any little pieces of paper. Both men remembered every made-up order of each of the thirty people lining the long counter. Most were laboring men in a hurry. The breakfast ran for four hours and the stools turned over about two to three times in each hour.

Rabbit told Gabe he had been there one day when the IRS had showed up. They couldn't prove what they made and settled for everything they had in the drawer. They did it every quarter. The IRS agent had written them a receipt, and as they walked out the door, the larger cook wadded the piece of paper up and stuck it on the burner. As the official paper had burned up, he stuck a pan on it and chopped in a couple of eggs to fry. Gabe was sure the two men paid their bills the same way—cash on the barrelhead.

There was very little talking as Rabbit took a piece of paper out and borrowed a pen from the older agent. He wrote an address and muttered, *"Give it until tonight."* The man nodded and continued eating his breakfast. The younger agent never said a word, never looked over, and never acknowledged their existence.

When they finished, the larger cook started clearing the plates. The older agent waved his finger at the line of the four seats. The cook stood up straight and performed what Gabe thought of as creative math. It sounded like he actually remembered everything and pricing it out, but the numbers didn't really add up right. The final tally sounded good enough and the agent dropped a five and a couple of ones down on the counter. They stood as the cook scooped the bills into his pocket, and they left separate ways as if they had never met.

Cops for a couple of minutes—bikers always.

Rabbit stood by his bike and glanced at his watch. He thought and then nodded at his internal conversation. He looked at Gabe. "Let's go move some product." They mounted and roared off up San Fernando. They horsed back and forth, surging and falling back. It was an old game practiced by motorcycle officers who have to read each other's body cues and minds so that they move as one unit.

As they sat at a light, Rabbit thought and then asked as he watched the light. "Do you think you could handle that bike on a dirt trail?"

"What did you have in mind?"

"I think we need to see about having you learn the motorcycle course the LAPD puts their officers through. A lot of it is about riding in bad situations like rain and back trails. It would make a better rider out of you."

"Did you do it?"

As the light turned green, "No—just always wanted to—this would be a great excuse."

They rolled through the light and veered left onto a diagonal side street. The houses were mean and squat. The cheap stucco homes had cracked veins and dark patches like the shadows of dead trees. Some showed signs of earlier prosperity with a car in the front yard—until you noticed the concrete blocks where wheels and tires should have been. Some had hoods up. Others had no hoods. The lack of radiators and engines were obvious. One shot at prosperity and then it was back to the city bus.

The street had cracks and potholes that multiplied as they ended one block and rolled down the next. More cars with no engines, yards with nothing growing but the occasional heat-stunted tree. Young men sprawled in a state of torpor in the morning sun—recovering or just enduring from a night or from years before.

The house was once a pink tan adobe. Now it was as sun-blasted as the rest of the neighborhood. The day was threatening to be no less harsh as Rabbit set his hand out palm down. They sat, waiting.

ANGEL FLIGHTS

Gabe faced down the street, but under the plastic wraparound shades, his vision danced all over the house. As one curtain drew back a half inch, his eyes snapped on the movement. He didn't have to think—he already knew Rabbit had seen it, too. Both looked about bored and resolved. *Waiting.*

The door cracked open. Nobody came out. Rabbit nodded and rose up off the chopper and was followed by Gabe. Looking both ways down the neighborhood, they crossed the sparse front yard and entered the front door. An emaciated woman sat on the couch with a nearly skeletal baby at her small narrow breast. She jerked her head towards the hall leading back into the house.

The tall fat Mexican sat at a kitchen table. The skinny Mexican leaned his chair against the wall. The 12-gauge pump shotgun was across his lap. His right hand gripped the handle with a finger on the trigger—ready.

The big Mexican smiled with three teeth capped in gold as he unscrewed the top on a bottle of Pepto-Bismol. "Rabbit, you're up early." He chugged a quarter of the bottle in one gulp, and then took one last sip of the pink goo.

"I have to be somewhere else later, and I need the money."

"You know how this works." He took another quick sip and slowly screwed the top back on the bottle and slid it into the large case of unopened bottles.

Rabbit held his arms up on his head. The shotgun guard stood and carefully stepped forward. Rabbit nodded to his front left. The man reached into the leather jacket and took out a fat tan envelope and handed it to the big man. The fact that Rabbit and Gabe both had guns down the back of their pants was assumed and of no concern. The shotgun retreated and took back his position. Rabbit lowered his arms and stuck the first knuckles of his hands in his pockets. *Bored and waiting—but with hands that were instantly ready.*

The big Mexican counted the three stacks of bills. He nodded to the guard.

As the big Mexican placed the money back in the envelope and opened a small cabinet behind him, the small guy opened a cooler beside him and took out four large square packages wrapped in aluminum foil and taped plastic wrap. The tape was the same silver tape used on heating ductwork—very sticky and tough. The shotgun placed the packages on the table as the big man turned from closing the safe.

The big man eyed Rabbit. "Next time call first—and come alone."

Rabbit stared him down. "I don't have a phone, and this is my new partner."

The man took in the information. He was used to dealing with nothing but losers at the bottom of society—it was his stock in trade for customers. He was

ANGEL FLIGHTS

also used to constant change, whether he liked it or not. It made him uncomfortable, but it was what buying the pink drink by the case was all about. He nodded.

Rabbit picked up two of the packets and handed them to Gabe. He shoved the other two in his jacket.

"Does your partner have a name?"

Rabbit thought a moment about what he knew about the man, "Snake." He didn't blink.

The Mexican stared for a few seconds—weighing the idea. Finally, his eyes blinked lazily as he nodded to Gabe. "Pleasure meeting you, Snake."

Gabe only nodded slightly and turned. As they walked back out through the living room, Gabe noticed what looked like a 44 Magnum half buried under the woman's leg. The grip was turned out. *She was the backup.* He wondered if the recoil would snap what little she had of bones in her arm.

Gabe didn't ask until they were back on the rapidly moving San Fernando Road. "What the hell are we doing?"

"Moving four keys of meth. And... making some money."

"We get paid to bust people like that... not help their business."

Rabbit rolled for three blocks in silence. "Do you want to wear a scratchy uniform, drive around in a car that smells like the dinner the drunk puked up last night and go home to beat your wife, kick the dog and drink beer until you pass out—and then get up to do it all over again?"

"No."

"Then learn my way of doing a better job." He looked over his shoulder and took the right over to the on-ramp. As they settled onto the freeway, he looked over at Gabe. "You've questioned my way of doing things twice now. Once more and I either give you back to the captain or take you for a ride out into the desert.

"The life out here has no rules. Things don't fit like that book you read about being a cop. The only way you will survive is ask questions—don't tell me what is wrong. Keep quiet until you understand what is going on, and follow my lead. With luck, you will make it through the year."

"What happens then?"

"That is up to you."

The industrial complex was new. The buildings all had fresh signs and the cars were less than five years old. They pulled up behind one of the buildings and walked into a machine shop. "Hey Werner, vas is los?"

The machinist looked up and registered who was in his shop. He turned off the lathe and walked over. "Nada, Rabbit… "

"Nada fucking thing," Rabbit and the man finish in unison.

"Werner, Snake—Snake, Werner." The man

stuck out his hand and they shook. "He's my new partner."

"Treasury or LAPD?"

"PD." Rabbit turned to Gabe. "Werner is our drug cutter. He also keeps track of all the movements, and does the reports for us. He is also…" He turned to look questioning at Werner, "what, FBI?"

Werner wobbled his hand with a smirk for a smile, "FBI, Treasury, ATF… some of that alphabet… Someone is writing me a paycheck… somewhere."

Gabe frowned, "Us?"

"We're not alone. There are others we will never know about unless Werner talks."

The slight German held his thumb and one finger to his upper lip and pulled it up exposing a strange looking tooth. "I don't talk."

Rabbit laughed at the joke. "Nah, he just has a funny looking tooth."

The machinist bobbed his head. "What do we have?"

Rabbit and Gabe pulled out the packets. "Four keys of meth from the Mexican in Panorama City. It looked like he was doing a lot more business now. Judging by the cooler his shotgun was sitting on, I'd say he had at least another twenty keys or more in there."

The man whistled. "That is a hell of a ramp up. We had him pegged for that much a month only last

Christmas."

"That's why I went in without calling ahead. I think if I call, he hides most of what he's sitting on."

"Okay, I'll get this cut down. Who is it going to, and how do you want it?"

"Two are going out to Redondo so they need to be stomped hard. I think he deals some of it straight through. Make them about forty-five pounds each. That will give him a hard burn in the nose, but won't kill anyone out on the street."

"The other two?"

"Break them to five each. I have a new guy in Artesia that wants to be a big pipe, so he's expecting some really high-grade shit. At forty pure, he can pound it about ten times and still come out a point or two higher than anyone else on the street."

"Okay, ninety and ten—give me about an hour to test, log, cut and pack."

"We only need the ten this morning. Sit on the ninety. That is too much to carry on the bikes all at one time. We'll come get the ninety this afternoon. We can blend with the herd."

"Thirty minutes then."

"We'll be up at Aunt Bee's having lunch."

They walked out the back and wandered up the alley of shops. Gabe walking in silence thought until they got to the small café that served the people who worked in the industrial park. The coffee was warm and felt good, and the place was all but empty.

ANGEL FLIGHTS

"Figured it out yet?" Rabbit studied his partner.

"Never tell anyone what you are really doing... even another cop."

"Even the Captain..." Rabbit nodded. "They might mention something that gets to the wrong person and you end up dead. They can know after you are finished—like this morning. But not until."

"So where are the ten pounds really going?"

"Werner is the one exception to the rule. He keeps the records. If I get killed, they know where things were going and to whom. That is my insurance—and yours, too. Werner is critical... whether he has cyanide in that tooth or not, I'm pretty sure he is responsible for at least a dozen or more undercover agents. Drugs are a big deal and they are getting even bigger.

"When I started, I thought a kilo of weed was a big thing. This morning, we followed a truck with two tons of heroin tar. Next year, a new Mack truck pulling a forty-ton load might replace that truck. It's our job to know that and try to stop it from happening."

Rabbit waited.

"You don't really sell the drugs, you only disseminate."

Rabbit nodded.

"That way, you know the players from the big to the small or almost small."

Rabbit put his coffee mug down with a one-sided smirk. "So... you're not just a dumb beat cop after all."

"So, why such a wide-ranging focus?"

"If I take a shotgun to your gut, do you live?"

"No."

"And we almost never see the head. But the feet—the little guy dealing dime bags on a street corner. That guy is nothing. We cut one dealer and the next day, three more will beat each other up to take over the corner. But cut out the middle guy, the guy supplying all of those dime bags, and the corners dry up.

"Sure, give it a month, and there is a new middle guy, and the corners are filling back up. So that's why we control the Fat Man and a few others. When things are getting too hot, we cool them down with a dropped shipment. If we really need to cool things down, we take out a big guy. But it's better to monitor and keep them going. It took me almost two years before I could call ahead and not get body searched by that scrawny bitch in the front room."

"I saw the Magnum under her leg."

"Oh, shit. That pistol is nothing. The thing you don't want her to do is search your crotch. She doesn't care if you are wearing tight jeans or leathers—she can slide that boney hand down your pants faster than a shiv through the heart in Soledad Prison. And once she's there..." The man shivered. "You don't want to know."

ANGEL FLIGHTS

Gabe didn't laugh. He knew what he was hearing was straight. This big man in front of him was scared and repulsed.

"So where now?"

"We go meet the neighbors in Artesia. Well... after we get some money in Redondo Beach."

"Who are the neighbors in Artesia?"

"A pair of identical twins from Sweden—Ingrid and Suki."

"That sounds nasty."

Rabbit got up with a lusty look on his face. "Oh, I hope so."

09

WHERE WERE YOU THIS WEEKEND?

GABE PUSHED THE mower, the reels cut the grass, the kids waited on their tricycles, and the large snake waited on the porch. The big biker in the pink stucco house had become a fixture in the neighborhood. If there were any single moms in the neighborhood, they weren't attempting to get past the large snake.

Some of the moms took Gabe aside to point out their kid after he asked one kid if she had finished her homework. The girl had stalled with her hand halfway to petting the snake. Her eyes got big. This was bigger than missing Gilligan's Island or even dessert. She and a couple of the other larger kids withdrew their hands. Word had gotten out. Homework first, then the snake—Gabe even took to checking the work over. A spelling bee along the ten-foot snake had become very usual with even the little ones getting words like cat and dog.

ANGEL FLIGHTS

Gabe lay on the grass with Gertie's head resting in the crook of his arm. The sun was more on her, as Gabe was sheltered by the shade of the large cottonwood.

"Hola, senor."

Gabe raised his head and looked at the older woman. He was thinking she was the grandmother who lived across the street and two down. It was the only family on the block with four generations living under one roof—or would be as soon as Yolanda gave birth to what was hiding under the large t-shirt.

Gabe had met the father who was stationed at Camp Pendleton. He was a nice boy—a little shy for a Marine—but from what Gabe had seen, loving and gentle. They were sweethearts in high school and waited until he had secured his position in the Marines before proceeding with marriage—or anything else, according to Yolanda.

Gabe sat up. "Buenas tardes, Senora."

She laughed. "No, no, speak Espanol?"

Gabe blushed, holding his thumb and finger a tiny bit apart. "Poco."

She waved at him to come. Then looked down at the snake and shook her finger back and forth.

Gabe stood with a laugh and began picking Gertie up. The woman suddenly stepped over and petted the head, then bent and kissed Gertie on the forehead. Gabe put the snake on the porch and followed the woman back to her house.

Yolanda was sitting at the kitchen table as they entered. She looked up and laughed upon seeing Gabe. "It took Nana long enough to make you come eat some of her tamales." She pushed a chair out with her foot. The older woman nodded and pointed.

"Am I a guinea pig?"

Yolanda snorted. "Not hardly—Nana has been cooking tamales for over seventy years."

Gabe bit into the warm tamale. "Oh, my gosh. I've been here for seven months—why didn't she come and get me before?"

Yolanda laughed with her grandmother. "She was—several times. Either it was in the middle of the night, or you were on your way out the door. You come and go at odd hours, senor." She studied him for justification. The subject of the cop cars parked in front at odd hours was a silent gorilla in the room. Everybody was curious, but nobody was going to ask.

Gabe chewed and held her gaze. "She can come across any time she wants. If the kitchen light is on, the coffee is on. The back door doesn't have a lock. If I'm not home, she can leave anything in the fridge. If I'm home, she can get a hug from me. If I'm not home—she might get a hug from my snake—which doesn't seem to bother her."

Yolanda struggled as she stood up and waddled out of the room. Gabe frowned at the retreating large t-shirt and shorts. He looked back at the older woman who just shrugged.

A moment later, the young girl came walking down the dark hall cooing and talking baby talk to something in her arms. As the light of the kitchen fell on her, Gabe realized it was a very large lizard. The tail hung to the girls knees.

"This is Poppy. He is Nana's, not mine. When my grandfather died, we bought him as a little companion for Nana." She poured him into Gabe's open arms.

He laughed. "Not such a little companion anymore."

The young woman grabbed the table and back of her chair as she eased down with a hand from her grandmother. "He's twelve now. But I still miss my real Poppy." She put her arm around her small grandmother's waist and hugged her. The woman stroked her head and mumbled a rat-a-tat of Spanish.

"She says she likes your snake, too."

"Gertie has a thing for females, also. That... and barbecue steaks with sauce."

The girl giggled. "She's a lesbian?"

Gabe nodded. "Maybe, but she also likes sleeping with me."

"You must make a lot of heat. They really like heat. During the winter, Poppy stays in Nana's bed. She leaves the electric blanket on very low all the time."

"Hmm, I'll remember that for Gertie next winter. She didn't complain, but I did find her curled around the floor furnace several times this last winter."

"They will find any heat they can."

Gabe picked up his empty plate as he stood. "Speaking of heat—I have a hot date I need to shower for. Thank you for the tamales."

"Nana had hesitated coming over until I told her you had a giant snake she would have to get past. Then I couldn't stop her unless I tied her up."

Gabe laid the plate in the sink and then leaned over and hugged the older woman. "She can come over and play with Gertie anytime. She's the first woman I have seen kiss my girl."

They laughed as he left and headed for his home and a shower. He had some things he wanted to talk over with Chet.

The bar was busy for a Sunday evening. Five other customers were scattered along the bar. Gabe was reading over some brochures Chet had gotten for him. The bowl of stew, although almost empty, sat unfinished. The coffee, on the other hand, was slowly draining and refilling as the stack of brochures was moved from one pile to another.

The large arm was reaching for the last brochure as Chet refilled the mug. Chet looked at the tightness of the T-shirt across the chest and as well as the bulging arms straining the sleeves. "You look like some of the guys in prison who spend the exercise period pushing weights."

"I missed the gym on the base, so I got some old weights and set them up in the garage. It's a little cold in the winter, but it's better than a front room full of iron when I bring home a date. The size kind of settles some questions in people's minds. If they want to think I've served some time, well, that's on them." He smiled at the old cop.

Chet nodded at the brochures. "So what do you think?"

"This is what you think I should do?"

"In a way, it's a natural progression for some. Roscoe, Honey, and I have all seen it. Some guys can see the people who are hurt, but there is no recourse or help. They are what in war are called collateral damage. Like what is going on over there in Vietnam. There are a bunch of those guys in black pajamas in a village. They are hiding there, and when night comes, they sneak out and mortar our guys, and then run back and hide. So we bomb the hell out of the whole valley.

"The twenty bad guys are killed, but what about the two hundred old people, mothers and their children? They're turned to rice-paddy sludge as well. It's not fair, but that's war. On the streets, hopefully the bad guys get justice, but it's the aftermath—the collateral damage—that's where you can help. The ones like Zorro's niece. She was lucky she had a loving supportive family. But what about those who don't have that safety net?"

Ever the bartender, Chet looked down the bar at the other four men leaning on the bar. His trained eye evaluated how long before he needed to go pour a refill.

He tossed the towel over his shoulder and turned back to Gabe. "A couple of months ago, you guys were talking about a drug lab that blew up. The guy was killed, but what about the little girl, and did she even have a mother who could take her in? Then there was the house next door that burnt down also—what about those people?"

Gabe wagged his head. "So prosecute? Who? The guy died."

Chet pulled the towel down, wiped a spot, and flipped the towel back over his shoulder. "Not everything is so black and white. There are many gray areas where a champion, for doing right by those that have nobody else, can happen. If that little girl ends up in the system, who will stand beside her and watch that she is taken care of, not just shoved off into some hole somewhere?"

"So you are not talking about prosecution…"

"Gabe, you are going to have to find your way. All I know is what I see. You are not the kind of guy who will be happy wearing the blue. It doesn't matter if it is a wool uniform or the jeans…" Chet leaned

ANGEL FLIGHTS

back against the counter. Gabe could feel the air current from the door opening.

Rabbit slid onto the stool next to Gabe.

Chet asked, "Coffee or beer?"

Rabbit looked up. "No thanks, Chet. We have to go." He reached over and took Gabe's gun out of the back of his pants. He pushed it across to Chet.

Gabe didn't flinch or ask. He gently pushed his coffee mug forward and grabbed his leather jacket as he stood. Chet noted the leather jacket was now inserted into a cut-off jean jacket. There were a few patches here and there, but no large one on the back—the same as Rabbit's jacket. He watched as the two left, and then wiped down the counter as he lifted the stack of brochures. *The seed was planted.*

The night air stank of something burning. As they headed toward downtown Los Angeles, Gabe was reminded of a few years before when it seemed like all of south central Los Angeles was on fire. He was on law enforcement exchange from Adak and posted at the Ramparts precinct. Large groups of police from all over the city were asked to respond to a massive riot in the Watts area. Almost three dozen people died during that week, and there were thousands of arrests that overflowed every jail cell in the greater Los Angeles area. Some prisoners were even bused as far away as San Diego.

"What's burning?"

Rabbit jerked his head towards the south. "Firestone… and if they don't get it under control soon, it's going to stink like burning rubber. If it gets to their main warehouse, that shit will burn for a month."

"So where are we going?"

"To a bar…"

"We just left a bar…"

"Was there a fight breaking out?" Rabbit motioned for the southbound ramp.

"Which bar?"

"The Lamppost." It was a bar which, for over a decade, had been considered neutral territory among the biker gangs. Gabe and Rabbit had been there many times. Nobody was allowed to wear their colors or club emblazoned jackets into the bar. The bikes that lined the street looked like someone had done the laundry. Five or six club territories came together in an eight-block radius that all considered neutral. It was a place to go and drink, shoot pool and relax. Only an idiot would start something there. And, if they did, it would probably be about a female—anything else would start a gang war.

They headed the back way to Artesia. Gabe always marveled how in the center of a huge metropolis, there was an area that was many square miles with nothing but oil derricks and grasshopper oil pumps slowly bobbing, rhythmically, year after year. The two taillights disappeared across the rolling plain of machines and dirt at well over a hundred.

ANGEL FLIGHTS

As they slowed coming into civilization, Gabe's curiosity got the better of him. "Are we stopping this fight?"

Rabbit ignored him. The clamped jaw told Gabe all he needed to know. Something was going down, and he was just back up. It would be up to Gabe to separate the fight from the rest of the Sunday crowd. He hoped it would be only a small evening.

From a few blocks away, Gabe could tell the large bar would be packed. The bikes lined both sides of the street. The overflow was parked randomly in the next block.

As they approached, four bikes took off from the curb near the entrance. Rabbit and Gabe slid forward and backed their bikes into the hole. They shut them down and pocketed their keys.

"No chance of talking you out of this, is there?"

Rabbit's eyes were stone cold and dark. His jaw was set.

Gabe knew the look and the intimidation factor of his height, heavy shoulders, and giant biceps from lifting a lot of weight over the years. He slid out of his leather jacket, and turned the cut-off jean jacket inside out and wore it like a vest. The exposed blank inside was acceptable in the bar. They waded in.

Rabbit didn't bother with getting a beer. He didn't need an excuse. Besides, the bar had long ago stopped selling the longnecks that made a useable weapon. Breaking a bottle bottom off was like setting off an alarm. And bringing any kind of weapon was something the general patronage frowned on. If you used a weapon, or even pulled one, you might not see the next morning. At least until the swelling went down.

Gabe kept within an arm's reach of his partner. Most in the bar knew or assumed they were almost connected at the hip. Usually, it meant the two large dudes were treated with respect and deference—even by those who were just as immense.

Rabbit stopped and then moved through the crowd, as his attention never left the man at the pool table watching the shooter. Rabbit jerked glimpses of the surrounding crowd watching the game. There were several bills on the edge of the table in many places. Rabbit looked at Gabe and nodded toward two guys standing near one end of the table. This is where the trouble would come from. Gabe shifted and eased left and behind them.

As he took position, he watched Rabbit ease up to the shooter and talk softly at his shoulder. Gabe watched as the man's eyes widened slightly and then he nodded. He turned and handed Rabbit the pool stick and blended into the crowd. Rabbit stood, and then spun the cue in a propeller move. The crowd moved back. The other shooter only had wall behind him.

"What's your problem, Rabbit?" The man was more pissed than curious. "You of all people know

ANGEL FLIGHTS

better than to make trouble in here."

Rabbit continued the propeller at a moderate pace. The 'swoosh' of air was becoming audible with the silence of the crowd. "You're right, Pepper, and I served that six-month banishment. I have also kept my nose clean for the last year. But this one? This one is all on you, Pepper. You're the screw-up this time."

"What the fuck you talking about, you crazy fuck?" The man was edging sideways trying to gain some moving room. The crowd was too solidly packed.

Gabe felt more than saw the movement of one guy's right hand reaching back for a knife or something. The preparation was short lived as Gabe gently placed his hand on the man's shoulder and started to squeeze the muscles that ran toward the neck. All movement stopped and Gabe eased up. *The discussion was over—for now.*

"Normally, Pepper, I would just wait for a numb-nuts like you to screw up big enough to go to jail. Then I would pass a word along how you have been banging your little sister—since she was six. That way, someone else would take care of you the way that is proper for scum like you."

"What the fuck are you talking about? I never touched my little sister—and I ought to gut you right here just for saying that." The words were said, but the quiver in the voice and the man's movements said otherwise.

Rabbit took a step. "It might have ended there—keeping it in the family and all. But, Pepper, you just couldn't control yourself, could you? You started in on your niece, too. What was wrong, Pepper? Was your sister getting too old at fourteen? You had to go and turn out a five year old? You think the doctor who saved her life wasn't going to talk to someone, you asshole? You left her bleeding from both holes, asshole. I don't care who is talking—but that is monster territory." With a large sweep of his hand holding the thin end of the cue, he smashed it down on the edge of the table. The cue shattered in the middle where it screwed together. The heavy fat end arced into the air and his other hand caught it. As he advanced, he traded the two ends in his hands. The left would be the whip, the right and dominate would be the bludgeon.

Pepper exploded and made his first mistake—he left his cue whole. He swung from the heavier end. Rabbit took the blow along his raised left arm and waded in with the smaller club for a close quarter beating. He swung over his head and smacked the man's head hard enough to ring his ears, but Rabbit wanted to hurt the man, not knock him out. The next arc raced overhand and swept directly and with a lot of body force to the man's left knee. The sound of the bone shattering was heard as a juicy wet snap.

The room exploded. Gabe's last memory was

cracking together the two heads in front of him. The sound was one he hadn't heard since his MP days in Adak. At least, there you could throw the combatants out into the cold to cool off. The temperature in the bar was heating up as fast as the fight was spreading. Even the women were taking part as saps and brass knuckles came out of boots and back pockets.

Gabe thought he heard a shotgun discharge—and then there were the sirens. After that, it was all dark.

10

I NEED YOU TO DO SOMETHING FOR ME

RABBIT OPENED ONE eye. The ceiling was white sound tiles so he knew he wasn't in jail. He tried to move. He rolled his head to the right. The door looked like a hospital. He raised his head a little. His right leg was elevated with what looked like several metal chopsticks in it.

He couldn't feel it, but then everything seemed to be kind of a dull ache.

"You should see the other guy."

Rabbit closed his eyes so he wouldn't get woozier as he turned his head. He opened his eye. For some reason the other wouldn't.

He wrinkled his forehead.

Tape.

"There's a patch taped over your left eye. The doctor said he might take it off in a couple of days—if you behave… and don't touch it."

Rabbit turned a little harder and finally found

ANGEL FLIGHTS

Gabe sitting in a chair by the window. The man had some butterfly strips on his cheek and forehead—surrounding a growing black eye.

"Wha...?"

"What happened? Good question. About the time I was finished with Pepper's two buddies, and you were finished rearranging Pepper, half the Redondo crew started rearranging you. That's probably when I got the split on the back of my head that took ten stitches."

"Where?"

"They had us at Central County, but Chet got us transported to Memorial in Pasadena. Our charts went to Long Beach. Yesterday I heard that Pepper was in Central, but after a few old friends of his had a party, they had to take him to lock-up in County General. They have an ICU there now and he's doing okay."

Gabe stood and moved to the bed. "My guess is that wherever you were this last weekend, was where you heard all of that about Pepper. So don't go wandering off. We'll talk tomorrow."

Rabbit tried to reach out but found his left arm was too heavy to move. "Gabe."

The man stopped and turned back. "Yeah?"

"What day is this?"

"Wednesday."

"Come back tomorrow."

"I'll be here." He turned.

"And Gabe?" He watched for the face. "Are the bikes okay?"

"Yeah... I got yours hauled over to my house."

"Good. You're going to need yours this weekend."

Gabe looked at the man in the bed. Whatever it was—it had almost gotten his buddy killed. He wasn't sure if he wanted to know what his plans were for the weekend. He turned and walked down the long hall.

It would wait for tomorrow.

Rabbit waited—listening to the hard footsteps with the chunks of steel buried in the soles and heels of the man's boots. Some people carry weapons in their pants—he knew his partner walked on his. He had watched what the man could do with his bare hands and feet before he put on the steel-edged boots.

Rabbit laid back. "Nurse... anybody?"

Gabe laughed softly as the elevator door closed. The two nurses looked sideways at the tall biker. They didn't want to know.

Being hungry and in need of a smiling face, Gabe broke down and headed for Boyle Heights. Rabbit and he hadn't had a Maria fix in a couple of months. The last time they pulled up, Zorro was there with a new trainee. Zorro took some malicious pleasure in writing them each a ticket for exhaust modification violations. It was a chicken shit fine,

ANGEL FLIGHTS

but it looked hard-ass for the smaller old man to terrorize the two towering bikers. The newbie was impressed, and Maria brought out Lincoln to make up for it—after Zorro and his trainee had left.

As Gabe walked in the door, the tiny man was standing in the doorway to the back. His right hand firmly grasped his mother's finger. There is standing up for yourself, and there is standing on your own—but standing while hanging on to mom is the best. As he saw Gabe, he squealed and the finger was forgotten as the shoes slapped on the concrete floor.

Gabe picked him up and swung him around. The two smiles were mirrors. Gabe's attempt at a matching high-pitched squeal was somewhere between a bull being castrated and a large truck locking its breaks on the freeway. The small boy didn't care—he loved how his favorite giant flew him up near the ceiling.

"I'm surprised he even remembers who you are." Maria grumped with her arms crossed and a sour frown on her face.

Gabe flew the little man to the other side of her pouting face and the two men mushed kisses on both cheeks before soaring back off to the ceiling. The smile was there, but she was upset that it was so easy to bust her pout. She turned to get the large Machaca burrito that was Gabe's favorite.

Gabe sat down at his favorite table and placed Lincoln on his one leg. The large platter placed in front of him had a few finger foods for Lincoln as well. The two men ate under the watchful eye of Maria.

"How is everything?"

The young woman shrugged. "The days are the days. Not much changes."

Gabe took a bite and nodded. When he could, he continued, "And your brother?"

"Oh, crap. Lito is kicking the doors open every chance he can. He is finished with all of his freshman work and more than half of the sophomore work. He didn't like his advisor who kept getting in his way, so he walked into the Chancellor's office and asked him if he would be his advisor."

"That takes a lot of—"

"Cojones?"

"I was going to say courage." He smiled and then laughed. He cooed at the child on his lap. "Your mommy is very funny. She likes cojones." The little man squealed and laughed.

Maria laughed as she got up with mock disgust. "You are horrible, Guapo." She turned as a crowd of five workmen came in.

Gabe confided in Lincoln. "Your mommy thinks Uncle Gabe is handsome. What chu tink, little man?"

Maria threw back a stern warning. "Don't you dare teach him Cholo talk."

Gabe nodded and finished his lunch. He knew he needed to go up to Sylmar and move some product. With Rabbit in the hospital, he would need to maintain their cover and the surveillance. Whatever Rabbit had planned for his weekend had to come after he took care of their real business.

****

Rabbit hadn't moved, but he was more awake. Gabe had pulled a chair over to the bedside to make it easier for the man to talk quietly. Gabe didn't like what he was hearing.

"How big of a problem is it?"

Rabbit closed his eyes. "Big enough that these doctors and nurses thought they needed to do something this big—even at the risk of everyone involved."

"It sounds like the underground railroad before the Civil War. This is the twentieth century, for cripes sakes. I don't know the law, but isn't there something legal and here?"

"If there was, do you think these doctors would have bought the hacienda in Mexico? Look, this is the reality, and this is how a few of us are handling it. As word gets around, I'm sure there will be more that need help."

"How many bikers?"

Rabbit relaxed—he knew Gabe was in. If not for the long haul, at least to cover Rabbit while he couldn't ride, but he hoped his partner would help even after. "Most Fridays, about sixteen or twenty show up. They see how many are needed. Sometimes a few just go along for the ride, and sometimes they pick up a girl or three on the way. But most of the girls are collected there at Hollywood."

"Are they from the Hollywood area?"

"Oh, hell no... They come from all over the LA area. We aren't supposed to talk to them, but young girls are young girls. They are scared and feel alone—even when they are with the other girls. They will talk. We try not to encourage them. It's not safe for them or us to know who they are—or them to know who we are—but I had a girl who found out about it and took the bus down from Buena Ventura one time.

"As you can guess this last weekend, I happened to know who the girl was. She knew who I was, and so she felt safe choosing me. I tried not to listen, but she just needed to spill her guts—not for her, but her cousin."

"The five year old."

Rabbit nodded. "Many of these girls have been molested since that age—or at least that's when they remember it started. My guess is it started with changing diapers." He paused. Gabe could see he was having a hard time.

"It's okay, man—take a rest."

"That's just it—it's not okay. None of it is. It makes me sick just thinking about it. Sunday I just wanted to kill Pepper..." The man rolled his head and looked out the window for a few minutes.

Gabe decided to give him some time. He got up and went looking for the cafeteria. The coffee was hot but didn't help. He was back at the bedside in fifteen minutes.

"When you get there, you are looking for a crusty old lady named Lois Lane. Don't laugh, I checked her out—that's her real name. She's the only one who knows my real name. If she doesn't trust you, use it. If she asks to see your badge, tell her you left it in your uniform pants but you would be more than happy to show her your balls."

Gabe started to laugh, but saw Rabbit was serious. "And that is code for...?"

"When I first showed up, she had asked if I had a problem with transporting underage girls across international borders for what both countries consider immoral purposes. Before she could say anything, I dropped my pants and held out my balls."

Gabe snorted. Having spent almost a year with his partner, he could easily picture the behavior. "No more proof needed?"

Rabbit harrumphed. "She stepped in, weighed them in her hand as she stared me in the eyes. She told me she had seen other bikers and cops with bigger ones that wouldn't make it to San Diego—that it took a lot of heart to cross the border week after week."

"Whew, tough broad!"

"She was letting me know she knew who and what I really was. I think it was a challenge on many different levels. We never talked about it again. It took me several months to remember which hospital I had seen her at—and she had seen me. She had been the one to cut away my last uniform... to save my life."

"I'll let her know where she can find you for a while."

"It would be good to see her face. She's a little prettier than you are."

"Speaking of pretty, Maria sends her best. If she can get Zorro to haul her up here, she'll come visit you while he does something else."

"She can't bring the kid. They won't let him in."

Gabe laughed. "He's walking now. I think by the time you're ready to get out, he might have to sign you out—or at least his uncle will."

"How does Lito like college?"

"I don't think his age is getting in his way. I think it's the adults who are the problem. But from what Maria says, he got the chancellor to sign on as his academic advisor. I don't think he's going to have any more problems challenging courses."

Rabbit nodded his head up. "Speaking of challenges..."

Gabe nodded. "I moved six keys from the Fat Man. Werner did a fast job for me and I got it all delivered last night. I think we might be getting a new heavy dealer in San Pedro. I got introduced to a dockworker... I think he's either a longshoreman or a supervisor. He did a lot of butt sniffing, and it sounds like he might move a few keys of medium cut a week."

"We've wanted to get an eye into the ports for a long time. This could be a very good thing."

"Joker asked if I wanted to handle a guy in Redondo, but he's a lightweight—a few ounces a week. I told him that he should take it and just step on it a small squeeze. It would up his count and he could move into a full key or more."

"Good thinking. Joker is a good one to help along. He wants to please so we can have eyes into things down there along the beach without being there."

"Werner showed me the new pill machine he built. He can fill the hopper with about fifty pounds of mix, and the thing just sits there and bangs out whites all day long. That guy is really smart—funny, too. Did you know that during Korea he was a long-range sniper? His longest shot was a mile and a half..."

Rabbit laid his head back. "Look, I need some sleep and some painkillers. You've got this tomorrow. Just show up at four-thirty and follow along. Stop in when you get back Sunday evening. Now go find me a nurse with a needle and get out of here."

Gabe patted the man on the arm and left. The nurse at the nurse's station nodded as she saw him walk up. "He's about an hour overdue. I didn't want to interrupt." She held up the syringe. "This is night-night until tomorrow morning."

Gabe smiled and left.

11

ANGEL MEET SLEEPY

GABE KIND OF knew where the address was. As he eased to the curb, he looked down the long industrial alley. There were a dozen choppers parked along one side. The bikers were milling around. He glanced at his watch—he was six minutes early. He nosed the bike into the alley. The big motor and straight pipes hammered off the brick walls.

The bike chuffed to silence, and he backed it into formation at the end of the others. A short-haired man with a neatly styled beard walked over. Gabe knew him from around the circuit. The voice was little more than a strained squeak. The patch on his jacket said Mike—everyone knew him as Deaf Mike.

Gabe smiled. "How you doing, Mike?" They shook.

"You need to trim your mustache so I can hear you." The man signed as he spoke. Gabe kept meaning to learn how to sign—even if it was just a few

ANGEL FLIGHTS

signs. He just didn't know where to take lessons. He didn't want to ask Mike—he wanted to surprise him.

The man shook his finger back and forth and looked around. "Where is Rabbit?"

"In the hospital. There was a fight." Gabe pantomimed hitting something.

"Bad thing." Gabe wasn't sure if he said thing or scene.

The whistle was low and quiet but had a galvanizing effect on the small crowd. Gabe noticed a couple of women who seemed connected to some bikers. He guessed they would act more like cover. They all filed into a large warehouse of a room.

The older woman at the door stopped Gabe. She looked at the faded name patch. "Sandpaper doesn't work as well as sewing it to a bag filled with rocks and dragging it for a few miles down a desert road—Snake." She looked behind him.

"Rabbit is out of the game for a while. He's in room 342 at Huntington—if you want to go check his balls." Gabe stared her in the eyes. The woman didn't flinch. He liked her right off. "Or I can drop my pants and let you check mine."

She smiled softly. "I take it you know what's going on."

Gabe nodded. "I'm here until I'm not needed."

"We'll see." She pushed him in and closed the door. "How bad is he?"

"He kept his balls—I assume. But his arms, a

few ribs, and his right leg are going to take a while. His leg looks like a pin cushion of metal chopsticks."

She turned. "Hmm, multiple fractures. That rig on his leg is called external fixation osteotomy. The slang term is called a halo. It makes sense that he got that instead of a cast—he's one of my oldest angels. A cast would have only lasted until he could break it off in the parking lot."

Gabe smiled and followed the woman into the middle of the room. He stopped at the one end of the loose half-circle.

She slowly turned and looked around. "Some of you have heard this speech a hundred times. And I want to thank you for the opportunity and for your help. Two of you... excuse me, three of you are hearing it for the first time. Thank you for coming, I hope you stay.

"A few years ago, some very special courageous doctors and nurses got tired of seeing young girls of all sorts of ages coming into their emergency rooms. The girls were usually hemorrhaging, bleeding, as a result of a visit to a butcher up a back alley. They were desperate to terminate what was growing inside of them. We make no judgments about why they come to us. They are in need, and we don't turn them away. If they found us, they are desperate.

"How desperate you may ask? They usually have no other avenue. There are no hard statistics as of yet, but the street numbers go like this. Eighty percent of the girls have been sexually assaulted by either their own fathers, brothers, or a trusted uncle. Usually, this has been going on for years. These girls come from poor families, middle-income families, and wealthy families. Child molestation, incest, and pedophilia have no defining boundaries. It happens in white, colored, Mexican, Asian, and every other kind of people you can think of. So, if you have any hint of judgment you might pass on these young girls, you can leave now… Any questions?"

She slowly turned as she looked everyone in the eye. All were solemn and quiet.

Lois turned toward one of the inside doors. She nodded and the woman standing there opened the door.

The parade was of hard-bitten biker women that looked between twenty-five and thirty—the kind Gabe was now used to seeing on the circuit and in the biker bars. The only thing missing in Gabe's evaluation was the broken slouch that came from the thousands of hours perched on the back of a bike—but that wouldn't matter as they sat on the back of the bikes going through the border. The girls filed in and formed a mirroring semicircle facing the bikers.

Lois looked at the woman by the door. "Is that all?" The woman nodded.

Lois looked at the young girls—who now looked like what was referred on the street as 'ol' lady' or 'biker bitch.' She sized up each girl. They were all playing the role of not only their own lives but also the man transporting her. Their safety was in each other's hands.

"Here are the rules. You will choose your Angel. No Angel will choose you. You will show them your name tattoo on your arm. By Sunday, the tattoo will have been washed off." She pointed over her shoulder at the men. "Every one of these men is named Angel—no matter what a patch on their chest may say. Their name is Angel. Go ahead, say hello now."

The line of girls chorused, "Hello, Angel."

"Great. In a few minutes, you will choose your Angel. This is your Angel for the duration of the weekend. If something was to happen, you only have to remember that one name. Every other Angel will help you.

"Now, just as your name isn't Mickey or Sneezy or Jiminy Cricket, their name isn't Angel. You will use these names and that is all you are to know about each other. DO NOT TALK about anything personal. You can enjoy the sunset, talk about how bad the traffic is, maybe even comment on how you can smell the ocean as you pass it. But you will not talk about anything personal. Do I make myself clear?"

She walked along the line of girls. They all nodded obediently. It wasn't a far stretch to picture Lois Lane as a nun or Mother Superior at a girls' school.

"After you choose your Angel, you will leave here. You will get on the motorcycles. Your next

ANGEL FLIGHTS

stop, other than for gas and the toilet, will be in Mexico. You will be let off in a courtyard of the home you will be at for the weekend.

"On Sunday afternoon, about this time, your Angels will return to pick you up. The border crossing will be busy with all of the tourists coming home. You will say nothing at any time. This is the most dangerous part of this whole weekend. You will literally have your Angel's life in your hands for this entire time. You must play your part to perfection. If you have any doubts, pretend to be very sleepy and just nod your way through the process. Any questions?"

There were none.

"Okay. Without talking, choose your Angel."

The girls had been making visual choices, and surprisingly, the process was smooth. The tall redhead with a smattering of freckles came to stand in front of Gabe. The leather jacket hung over her one shoulder as she pulled up the jean shirt. The dwarf was Sleepy. He wondered if she would sleep for any part of the trip.

He followed the cue from some of the others and put his arm around her shoulder and walked her out. Outside, the conversations were short and quiet. Gabe heard instructions about getting on a motorcycle and where your feet went.

As they got to his bike, Sleepy made a soft comment as she pulled on her jacket. "Nice Knucklehead." And then she passed her leg over the bike and sat back against the sissy bar. Gabe passed his leg over as she zipped her jacket up. The routine felt familiar—even though he had never really had anyone on the back before. She obviously had more than a passing smattering of experience. Gabe smiled as he lowered his wraparounds onto his face and started the motor.

Deaf Mike slid up with a small blonde on the back of his dull-red Indian Chief. He motioned that Gabe was to stay with him. As they turned and settled on Sunset Boulevard, Gabe noticed in his mirrors that the large group had broken up into smaller groups of five and six. Mike passed the on-ramp for the Hollywood Freeway, and Gabe figured he was going to continue to the I-5.

The evening commute had loaded the freeways, and the motorcycles were forced to split the lanes and pass through the slower traffic. It wasn't much faster, but at least they were moving. They transitioned onto the 60, which was an older freeway that ran all the way out to Pomona. It didn't make a straight shot toward where all the new housing was going in, so it had less traffic.

Gabe settled in behind Deaf Mike and next to a Panhead that was running upswept fishtail pipes. The noise was a warbling thrum that Gabe knew would cause hearing problems later. He signaled to the guy and pointed at the pipes and then his ears. The guy

ANGEL FLIGHTS

laughed and then fell out and slid back to take up the rear with his pipes facing nobody.

At the Brea Canyon, Mike led the pack off the freeway and to a gas station. For the bikes with smaller tanks, there would be one more stop just north of San Diego. For the bikes that were running the stock Harley tanks, they would make it all the way down to Mexico and cheaper gas.

Gabe had yet to hear one word come out of Sleepy's mouth during the ride. He watched Deaf Mike and wondered if Sleepy was also maybe deaf. Testing his theory, he asked if she wanted a candy bar or anything out of the vending machine. She only shook her head and leaned back against the sissy bar to close her eyes. *Scratch one—she's not deaf.*

The traffic was easing up as they dropped down out of the Brea Canyon into the upper section of Orange County. The late light would see them through to San Diego, and the strong sundown would confuse appearances enough that they should slide across the border without any close looks.

The bikers were feeling kind of frisky as the I-5 joined with the I-405 and some slow/fast horse play ensued. Gabe was thinking about the bikes being construed as breaking some law, but as he watched, it was actually legal and still under the speed limit. It was the usual blowing off steam that came from riding mind-numbing and butt-numbing mile after mile. They were all playing the part of bored bikers on the way to a weekend of hell-raising in Mexico.

As they finally came out of the landlocked freeway and started running along the ocean south of San Clemente and north of the nuclear plant, Gabe called back to Sleepy. "Hey, Sleepy, you sleeping back there?"

"We're not supposed to talk."

Gabe laughed. *She would make a great hall monitor or uniform cop.* "You can enjoy the ocean or the view or the evening, or even how nice my new haircut looks."

The silence was thick. Gabe gave up. *I think I'll just count the dots on the road...*

"The ocean is nice. I don't swim, so it also looks very frightening. On the way back, can I drive and you ride back here on this school eraser you call a seat?"

"So you don't like my new haircut?"

"Did you do it with some kindergarten scissors?"

"I paid four bucks for that hacked at look."

"Was the barber blind?"

"No. But he does have no arms."

There was silence as she thought. "So he uses his feet?"

Gabe nodded. *If you aren't willing to engage in a reasonable conversation—you get what you get.* The conversation turned to silence.

The group eased off the freeway at Pacific

ANGEL FLIGHTS

Beach. They clustered around the one group of pumps and just shared the bill. One of the other groups clustered around the other pump. This was the last chance at a bathroom as who knew what the line on a Friday night would be like. The girls used both bathrooms. The guys laughed as word leaked from one room to the other. *The men's bathroom was always cleaner.*

All of the guys and the older gals chuckled at the revelation on the young girl's faces. Education about reality—can come at the oddest times. There was silence as the guys repeated the same process. One of the guys commented that the girls must have cleaned up the women's side. This brought laughter to the men and a shocked look to the girls, as they looked for any of them that might have. The joke was that they thought it must usually be worse than it was. The guys knew they had seen it in worse condition—but they had also seen the guy's side in disgusting conditions as well.

As they rode through the downtown section of San Diego, Sleepy leaned forward. "We think that your barber sits on the chair, and you sit on the floor."

Gabe thought about the logic of that idea. He also realized the twenty or so minutes the girls were together, a lot had been shared. Earlier that day, they didn't even know each other. Now, a few hours and over a hundred miles of butt-numbing travel in basically forced silence—they had bonded in a sisterhood. He wondered how many of them would try to stay in touch after the weekend.

"How does she get to my beard?"

"She doesn't. You hack that up yourself. I saw the razor cut under your jaw."

He nodded. He wasn't about to tell her that the razor that cut him was more like a broken bottle in a bar fight less than a week earlier. Some education a girl doesn't need. Some are enough at one time while the others can come with time... or hopefully—never.

12

CROSSING TO THE HACIENDA

AT ANY GIVEN time, the border ranges from docile to almost stupefying in the slow creep of cars headed for the heat, beaches, or excitement of Tijuana. Friday evening is never one of the sleepy times. Cars were jammed for over a half mile. This is what the bikers were counting on.

The last thing a border guard of either side wanted was for anything that could cause the flow of the mass to snarl to a stop.

Sitting in your car with the border crossing in sight can be a frustrating anguish. Seeing someone else sailing cleanly past you towards that common destination can cause the blood to boil. Having that person within touching distance can provoke you to do stupid things—like open a door.

Mike was one of the oldest bikers at this game and took the lead between the far left lane and the next. Rolling at barely fast enough to stay upright, he eased his line of six motorcycles between the two lanes of cars. The loud rumble of the bikes turned to a window-rattling warning as they threaded down the line. The border patrols on both sides heard them coming and were prepared.

The last hundred feet of cars in the left line was held up by the patrol officer about two car lengths from the concrete divider that supported the cover over the entire border. Another line of five loaded choppers sat facing the border between the middle lanes of cars.

The Mexican Federales stepped up onto the curbing. One of the four American border officers held his right hand in front of the car—stopping it. His left hand was in the air. The pointing finger was circling in the air. A subtle signal, but one that servicemen, construction workers, and bikers all knew well—Mike hit second gear and the rest followed.

By the time they passed through the border, Gabe's speedometer was reading forty.

The thunder of the two groups of bikes was elevated by another group in the slow lane. The crossing was deafening, and then all sixteen bikes were absorbed into the constant sound of Tijuana on a Friday night.

The other two groups were either behind or ahead. Mike looked at the sun. They had some time to kill. Gabe looked at his watch.

Avenida Revolución isn't the largest street in Tijuana, but it is the most important. In the world of the city just south of the border, this is where it all happens—or at least starts. Whatever you came for, it was here. Bars, girls, gambling, food, and cheap products—everything was for sale. As the old joke goes—even your mother, and for a price, she can be a virgin.

The bright neon hadn't hit its point of gaudy yet. The strong golden light of the last part of the day washed the colors to pale attempts. The bands in the bars were just starting to warm up, and the girls were barely awake as they walked past the men who were there with their wives and maybe children—the last of the tourist shoppers.

The shoppers the whores were interested in were still on the other side of the border. Those men would show up after dark—when the lines on the face and the sag in the clothes were not so obvious.

Gabe watched the traffic and his mirrors. He was point with Mike. The others were stacked two-by-two behind. If they were trying to blend in—it wasn't working. They were the circus parade in town. The streetwalkers saw no sale, the bars saw trouble, and the family men saw it was time to take his wife's advice and take them home before the trouble started.

Should have stayed in Pasadena where you belong.

The grand Avenida grew into a standard four-lane boulevard, and then into a two-lane highway. The roadway ran down into an ancient wash. Low-lying cliffs ran along the right side. Shacks made of little more than rusted tin and pieces of scrap this or that clung to the edge of the cliff and provided the residents a view of the large valley if not anything else.

"They seem very poor."

Gabe almost jumped at the sudden sound. He had been lost in his own thoughts about the buildings, their construction, and what he had been learning from people like Zorro and Maria. With Rabbit—he saw a completely different side of poor or destitute. The people he saw were broken and didn't know it. The people on the cliff were broken but understood it.

The difference was a vast leap from thinking you are living—but just moving while dying and knowing you are living—and living each and every day until you have to die.

"They may not have money, but they may have more than money can buy. Look at the way the buildings cling to the edge." He pointed along the whole ridge. "It is as if they would die to not be able to see this view." He pointed out across the flat desert. "There is a subtle beauty in that landscape you have to sit still for a long time to appreciate. You can't buy that."

"So that is their wealth?"

"No. That is their bank account. Their wealth is that they find someone to sit with... who can also see that beauty."

"You sound like a philosophy teacher or something."

"No... I have nothing to teach. I learn. I was taught to sit and watch thousands of miles of ice and a little snow. It took days to see the real beauty."

"What did you see?"

"A seal."

"A seal? A stupid seal? That was it? You sat freezing your ass off and saw only a seal?"

"No. The seal was dinner." *Catching the Russian sub surfacing in American territorial waters was the beauty.* Gabe had always wondered if the thirty pictures of the polar bear feasting on the seal had ever been shown to the Russians in whatever diplomatic game of chess the photos had been used.

Mike waved his left hand at Gabe to get his attention. He pointed to a dilapidated building. The sign said *Gurls, Gurls, Gurls all gone loco*. Gabe assumed it had once been a strip club of some kind. But now, it was the signpost for a dozen other girls. There was only one building at the end of the mile long road into the desert.

They pulled directly into the large driveway that was paved with crushed seashells. The slight pink of the bleached white shells was highlighted by the last rays of the sunset. Most of the bikers knew the low-lying hills barely hid the Pacific Ocean and Rosarita Beach a few more miles south.

The walls surrounding the hacienda were high and arms of a dark wood stuck out of the upper reaches. The entire compound appeared to be larger than a city block, but as they rode through the gates, Gabe could see it was more like a small village lining the inside of the walls. They parked around a central fountain. The water looked clear and refreshing, but Gabe remembered the old saying about don't drink the water—only the beer.

A couple of the bikers stretched and cupped their hands bringing water to their faces, and then drinking the second handful.

"For those who are new, this water is safe to drink. They have their own well and purify it before you see it. Just don't drink the water out of the toilets. The seat might fall and explaining that bump on the head could prove to be embarrassing." The man grabbed Gabe's head and in play—pulled it forward. "Oh, I see you have been here before."

The crowd laughed and Gabe punched at the guy for his jest. They were both smiling.

As everyone stretched, the two legitimate biker bitches rounded up the girls. "Girls, this way please. Gentlemen, we will see you back here at four-thirty Sunday. Be on time. Enjoy yourselves, but safely." She shooed the last girl through the large door and followed as it shut.

BAER CHARLTON

Gabe looked at the two bikers they had ridden with. There was no telling if they were bonded or just drivers. Gabe figured it wasn't his business. He had something else on his mind. He turned to Mike.

He got the man's attention. "Do you know where I could get a new seat tomorrow?"

Mike laughed. "She no like the...?" He stood and hit the crack of his ass with the front edge of his hand—imitating what it must feel like to ride on the tiny square of padding—for two-hundred miles.

Gabe rolled his eyes. Mike got back off his bike and walked over to one of the other guys. They talked a moment and they came over. "Mike says that your bitch doesn't like the Kotex box." He was laughing.

"She asked if she could do the driving on the way back, and I could shove the pad up my butt."

"Smart girl... My ol' lady wouldn't even talk to me until I got a decent seat." He pointed to the seat that the biker's bitch had ridden on. The back seat was about twice as thick and was the width of the rear fender and a little more. It did look comfortable.

"Does she like it?"

"She was the one with the short red hair. She's picky as hell—more so than most nurses. Our only problem is on days like this. Her shift started at four this morning. She keeps falling asleep on the back. Watch her when she gets on. She slides her jacket down over the sissy bar." He laughed.

ANGEL FLIGHTS

"So she's one of the nurses. One of the originals?"

"Nah, we've only been doing this for about three years. Lois Lane was one of the originals. She roped Hotshot into doing this and then Hotshot met me. She's the one who found the guy who built this for me. He's down in Rosey." The man indicated the direction they were headed next.

"Do you think he could build me one this weekend?"

"Let's go ask him. We're all headed for Rosarita anyway. He lives only two blocks from the lobster shack."

"Lobster shack?"

"The place doesn't have a name. An old sailor owns it. The guy used to sail up and down these waters as a drag fisher. Then he found out about all the lobsters and settled down. Bikers, surfers, and old Bohemians have been coming here for years. Twenty clams and you can eat all the lobster you can get your gut around."

"Then, why are we talking here... while there are bugs to eat down the road?"

They laughed and fired up their motorcycles. Following the rest of the bikes was easy—as they were the only thing on the road to Rosarita. Gabe hoped the place wouldn't run out of lobster before he got his share.

As they arrived at the building with a large area

full of picnic tables, the other biker waved Gabe off. "Go get started. I'll go get Lupe and bring him back. He can look at your bike, and you might just get away with buying him dinner and some beer."

The group was settling in with pitchers of beer and bus trays filled with lobsters. Not just the tails, but the whole things. Gabe and another biker were the new guys and were looking for plates. One of the other bikers just coughed and pointed at the fire pit in the middle.

Gabe watched as a grenade of a lobster shell sailed over a table of other diners to land in the pit. The juices sizzled in the flames. A fast glance explained the lack of plates. The table was for holding the beers, and your hands were for holding the lobster until you were done with the shell.

Gabe thought about sitting in an igloo eating blubber. It was expected that when your hand was greasy, just rub it on your neighbor. By the end of that night, Gabe's uniform jacket was waterproof along the shoulders and upper arm. By the end of the 'sightseeing tour' hunting for Russians, Gabe looked like a native and was a lot warmer for it.

He mused with a smile as he picked up a lobster. "When in Nome."

"Isn't the quote when in Rome?" the biker with the large red beard asked.

"Not if you're an Eskimo." The man shrugged and nodded and resumed eating.

ANGEL FLIGHTS

The biker with a patch that read Weasel came back. The man with him was definitely not what Gabe had pictured as someone named Lupe. He looked more Norwegian than Mexican. Gabe grabbed his beer and they moved to another table. Along the way, Gabe motioned for another pitcher and a tub of lobsters.

"Snake, this is Lupe."

The man stuck out his hand, and with the flat accent of someone from Ohio, he smiled. "Glad to meet you. Weasel said you like the king & queen seat I rigged up on his bike." He held up the same kind of seat, but it was just the foam. "I didn't know what color of leather you wanted. We can fit this after dinner, and I can sew up the cover tomorrow morning."

Gabe looked the seat over as the tub of bugs came along with a pitcher of beer. The woman drew two glasses out of her smock and placed them on the table. Weasel took the pitcher out of the tub and poured the beers. The three attacked their lobsters. The seat would wait.

The next morning, Gabe woke up with the finished seat lying beside him. His head was fuzzy, and his vision wasn't much better. He looked around. He was on a cot that was little more than two-by-four construction with a top of boards. The thin mattress felt and sounded like it was stuffed with grass or hay.

He wasn't sure he wanted to know. The shelter, if it were smaller, might be called a cabana. This was the size of a small house, except there were only two walls—if woven sticks and rope could be considered walls.

Gabe sat up. The large open expanse was at the edge of sand that led to the Pacific Ocean thirty yards away. The small surf was what woke him up. He stretched and realized he had not slept that soundly in a long time. He didn't know if it was the beers, bugs, or just the condition of having some time where he didn't have to be thinking about work or who he was supposed to be. He walked out onto the beach and just stood looking at the distant horizon.

"She is as beautiful as she is deadly."

Gabe didn't have to turn to know the speaker was Deaf Mike. He nodded, and then remembered one of the signs Mike had taught him sometime between tubs and pitchers. He raised his fist and made it nod like it was a head nodding yes.

The man came around and made a pair of Vs and then dropped his open hand from his mouth. "Very good." The man hit Gabe's arm softly. "Hearing people seem to learn more the drunker they get. Or maybe it is that deaf people sign slower the drunker they get."

Gabe laughed. "Either way works, yes?"

"Si, Senor."

Gabe turned and motioned at the large cabana.

ANGEL FLIGHTS

"What is this place?"

"I can't hear you unless you look at me."

Gabe blushed and looked at the man and repeated his question.

"It is ours. We bought it and built it."

"You and your wife?"

"No... the Angels. We got tired waking up on the sand. So we built this. Anybody can use it, but on the weekend, it is where we are. We ran some surfers off one year, so word got around and on Friday night, it is swept and clean. We don't know who does it, but it's all ready for us. We do the same on Sunday so whoever sleeps here on Monday, gets the same respect that we got."

"So what about... a toilet?"

Mike laughed a kind of screeching mixed with beating a tin pan with a wooden spoon. He pointed at the cabana. "It's across the street with breakfast."

Gabe laughed when he saw the menu. Pig with eggs, pancakes with pig, pancakes with eggs and pig. There was even a listing for pig with pig. Mike laughed at Gabe's big eyes. "They own a very large pig farm."

Gabe played it safe and ordered the pig burrito with chorizo. When it came, he was wondering why they didn't just wrap a large tortilla across the back of a pig and walk it out. For once, he actually left a few bites of food. Mike was smaller but more experienced and left nothing on the plate. Having nothing better to do at the moment, they slouched in their chairs and sipped at their coffee as they closed their eyes and turned their faces toward the sun.

Sleeping with no walls and eating outside... I could get used to this.

Gabe's mind drifted. There was plenty of room for a small patio or screen porch in his back yard.

13

HOW DID IT GO?

"YEAH, LOIS LANE came by after her shift on Saturday. She had a wad of keys that she likes to drag across the steel pins in my leg. The woman is without mercy. She also taught the nurses here the grand old skill of swizzling the rectal thermometer in the ice water before putting it in. She just forgot to tell them the Vaseline goes on *after* the ice water. That stuff tastes nasty."

Gabe had been holding his ribs since he first woke the other biker up. The man had a lot of pent-up energy from doing nothing. His humor ran from caustic to almost self-deprecating. His favorite seemed to be the abuse he was receiving from the nursing staff.

Gabe had seen the three women at the desk as he passed. He could only imagine what was really going on when the lights were turned down for the night.

"Your extreme suffering is noted. I'll pass it on

to Chet later."

Rabbit sipped on his glass of funny colored ice water. Gabe had dumped part of a half pint of raw mescal on the fresh ice. The man's eyes closed in memories.

As he put the glass down and lay back, his face became serious. "How many total?"

"When we showed up back at the hacienda, there were seven other bikes just leaving."

"San Diego. They drop and pick up earlier. So seven for Dego, and we had... so twenty-three... about average. I've seen the count as high as forty-seven, but I've also seen it as low as four. I don't know how they bunk the girls all in, but they don't even blink when we show up—no matter how many there are."

Gabe was doing the math in his head. "In a way, it sounds like a lot. But then, I also know it probably only represents a small portion of what's out there."

Rabbit nodded his head around the straw. "So how did Sneezy like the new seat?"

"Sleepy. Do they have a Sneezy tattoo?"

"Who cares... it's all for the one weekend... except for us."

Gabe nodded. "I have a feeling we are more branded for life than just a stupid tattoo."

The man pursed his lips and then set down the empty glass. "You're probably right. So... Sleepy?"

"Well, you know the drill. We had come in and

lined up, with the bikes all pointed back out of the gate. We were just standing there when the girls came out. Do they always hug the nurses?" The man nodded. Gabe hazarded a guess. "But we never see the doctors."

"Correct."

Gabe shrugged. "So the girls come out and start pairing up. Sleepy walks over and she had her hand out. She was very serious. So I tossed her the keys."

Rabbit laughed until he started coughing. His face turned red and then purple. Gabe jumped up and ran for the door. The cute tall blonde was already rushing his way. She stepped to Rabbit's side and slapped him hard on the chest. His eyes flew open and the coughing stopped. The wheezing was minimal as he gasped for air.

She stepped to the end of the bed and cranked the head up higher. Turning on Gabe, she poked him in the chest. "Two fingers only. Two. And don't make him laugh or I'll have to put him on a ventilator." She turned to watch the man in the bed. The color was returning to normal, but she still didn't like it.

She reached behind the bed and pulled out some tubing. Placing it at Rabbit's nose, she adjusted the oxygen. She took his pulse and watched him. Leaving, she reminded Gabe about the laughing. Both men chuckled and settled down.

"So she drove back?"

"Nah. But it did shock her. She looked at the new seat and thought a moment. I don't think she gets much in her life that comes easy. I could tell she was touched. She handed me the keys and never said a word the whole way back. I think I felt her either crying or shivering on the way back. I didn't turn around. When we got to Hollywood, she gave me a long hug. Actually, she just kind of hung on me. Then she kissed my cheek and went inside."

Rabbit nodded.

He had carried that kind before.

The sound of the oxygen was soft in the room. The two men sat thinking about life and how it can affect you at the strangest times.

"How was the border?"

Gabe rolled his lips in as he ran his fingers through his hair that was now long enough for the wavy curls to create a sea of waves instead of something that brushed into shape.

"I don't know what it's usually like, but the cars were lined back at least a half a mile. All six of the lanes were only crawling. Mike pointed out a police dog in the door of the office. I guess that's new." Rabbit nodded, thinking. "Mike pointed and spread out his fingers so we split up and fed between all of the lanes and ran up to the border. It still took almost ten minutes."

Gabe shrugged down in the chair, getting comfortable or assuming the position of riding his chopper. "When we all got to the front, we squeezed the cars out and crossed as a mass. Either the border dogs didn't want to deal with us as a group or they recognized us as regulars. Either way, we passed through and headed into Dego."

Rabbit listened and looked for more about the man than the story. "And this coming Friday?"

"I'll have all of my homework done by then, Mommy."

Rabbit chuckled and softly coughed a few times. His hand went up to stop Gabe.

Gabe relaxed. "About the cabana…?"

The man's eyebrows raised and he nodded.

"How cold does it get in the winter?"

A smile washed across the partner's face. "You thinking about packing your girlfriend for warmth?"

"Gertie? Oh, hell no—she sucks heat. She only likes me because I produce heat."

Rabbit laid back—the liquor taking effect. "Don't worry about the winter until the winter gets here. It's the riding in the rain that is the real bitch."

"It must be hard on—"

Rabbit stopped him. "The girls get a bus ride down to the pizza shack, and then they get a frozen Popsicle between their legs. In the rain, you wear greasers—but it's the frozen feet and hands that can test you."

"Greasers?"

"Pants that are one size or so larger—mine have

a zipper sewn down the outside seams. You take lube grease and dirt and rub it into the pants front and sides—everywhere you don't want to get wet. Then you take them to a laundry mat where you will never go again. Burn them in the dryer on high heat for about an hour. When you can clip up the leg ends and fill them with water that only leaks out the back, ungreased part—you're ready."

"January..."

The man nodded softly and then was still. Gabe watched the chest slowly rise and fall. He quietly pulled his leather jacket up off the floor and crept out. He pulled the door most of the way closed behind him.

The blonde looked up as he approached. "How is he?"

"Asleep."

She stood and started walking Gabe to the elevator. "I'll slip him something later. He doesn't sleep enough."

"Thanks... ahh?"

"Lisa. Lisa Taylor. It was Lane—Lois is my aunt."

"How much do you know about Rabbit?"

"Enough. I know that both of you are some of Aunt Lois's Angels."

"And...?"

She stopped and faced Gabe. "I know it all. I can only guess about you... but just being an Angel is enough for me. I've spent my weekends down there. But being married now is what I have to focus on... maybe in a couple of years..."

Gabe looked down shyly. "Thanks."

The woman stepped in and hugged him softly. She whispered, "No... thank you."

As she stepped back, she poked him in the chest. "Only two fingers."

He chuckled as he collapsed around his hands holding his chest. "And no laughing."

"Especially no laughing."

They both laughed as the elevator arrived and Gabe stepped in. "Any idea about how much longer?"

She sobered. "It will probably be the end of September. But it could be the middle of October—if he doesn't behave himself. He will need strong arms for the crutches, or he'll be in a wheelchair for longer."

The doors closed before he could ask about getting back on his chopper.

A few miles later, Gabe was finally digging into a hearty bowl of meaty stew. Chet had even scrounged up some great sourdough rolls he heated in the small countertop oven.

Gabe was exhausted, but he was even hungrier. The last meal was lunch in Mexico. The rice and beans were good, but seemed to go through him like they were air. Only the two modest-sized Machaca burritos had any staying power.

ANGEL FLIGHTS

Most of the bikers knew what was ahead, and lunch had been well after two, but it was now past ten.

"You look like some starving refugee from a starving country." Gabe looked up to watch Chet washing the never-ending flow of glasses. He wasn't really sure how much the man knew about the weekends, so he just nodded.

"I kept meaning to stop for dinner, but every place I passed… just wasn't this." He pointed at the almost empty bowl.

Chet looked at the bowl and the man, and went and ladled out another bowl full. "Here, it will make you sleep like the dead. Even that snake I hear so much about won't wake you."

Gabe looked up and frowned.

"One of the new guys didn't know about her. They went in to do paperwork and have coffee. Next thing you know, this female trainee is screaming and trying to get the snake off her. Her TO was in the can and comes running out with his pants falling down and his weapon drawn."

Gabe drooped one eye. "Was his pistol still holstered?"

They both silently went into fits of laughter. Gabe knew that Chet couldn't wait for some officer to come in so he could add to the story. The abuse of a TO was only rivaled by the joking about or on a new trainee—it was the way of a precinct.

"You do know that Gertie loves women more than she loves me..."

"I do now. And so does Zorro."

The man laughed at the best punchline.

Zorro was now training a female officer.

"Are they really considering putting a female in the field?"

"Oh, hell no—that would be very dangerous. There would never be any prisoners—just bodies. Women think different. Scumbag is a scumbag and a dead one is even better.

"I think they are field certifying her for when they make arrests and need to get a female field-frisked and checked. Things are changing and nobody wants some scumbagette yelling foul because some officer had to check the hard bulge in the front of her dress."

Gabe pinched the bridge of his nose—lack of sleep was fogging his memories. "Didn't Zorro do that once?"

Chet laughed as he remembered the incident. "Oh, hell yes. But that dude was visiting from over Hollywood way. But he still had a bunch of balloons of heroin up his ass. The guy was still screaming rape until the jail doc knocked him out."

Gabe stumbled to his feet. "Chet, it has been grand, but I've got to go get some sleep."

"Say hi to the snake for me. Bring her in for a drink some night."

He nodded at the guys at the bar. "We'll introduce her to the guys and see who will talk to her." The man smiled evilly.

Gabe waved a single fan of his arm. Chet hoped he would make it home all right.

Long day from Mexico.

He went back to scrubbing glasses.

14

SAME OLD SAME OLD

THE WEEKS DRIFTED into months as Gabe rode alone. Drug deals came and went as drug dealers disappeared and new ones took their places. The usual t-shirt under the leather jacket with a cut-off jean jacket was augmented with a denim shirt, and eventually a wool shirt. Under the jeans, he wore long underwear and eventually, his new old greasers with the occasional rains. Gabe got tired of the push-pull circus and finally had the large zippers sewn into the side seams of each leg. This also added a little extra room so he didn't feel like such a mummy.

When the temperature dropped down to bitter cold, Gabe broke down. The frozen feet and hands were too much. He turned to his best expert.

"How is the weather down there?"

"It's going to get up to sixty-four today, Jasper. The locals say they are going to die."

The native Alaskan laughed. "Should I pack my

shorts and come for a visit?"

"I think you would die from the heat, but feel free. I have a spare bedroom. You can share it with my pet snake."

The man lowered his happy voice to almost a growl. "How big is your snake?"

Gabe laughed. "Twice as long as you are tall, and she weighs more than your wife."

"I'll stay here with my polar bear and pet seal."

Both men were conscious of the cost of a long distance phone call. Jasper didn't have clearance to call Gabe back so he got to the point. "Why are you calling your frozen brother?"

"I have a cold problem."

"In your nose?"

"My feet. I'm riding a motorcycle these days. I can keep most of me warm, but it is my feet and hands that get like blocks of ice."

"They are exposed to the wind."

"Well, I have heavy boots and wool socks, but they still get cold after about a half hour or so. Same goes for the hands. I wear ski gloves which are insulated... but after an hour, it feels like I didn't have them on."

"You remember the bladders we put on our feet?"

"Oh, crap... that's what they were?"

"Bladders, gut, stomach... they all work the same. They keep the warm sweat from leaking into your socks. Your socks keep dry, and your feet stay warm. But you have to dry your feet very good every night or you get rust."

"I think you mean fungus."

"That is word. So you go to a butcher and get bladder and put on your feet. You be warm."

"Okay, I'll work on that."

"What else you need? You sound like you are not eating enough blubber."

"Okay, that's probably it. I'll ask the butcher for that, too."

"Okay now. You all fixed up. You call Jasper anytime you have something wrong."

"You're my favorite Shaman, Jasper."

"You my favorite white hunter, Kemosabe. You come back soon, we go hunt Russians again."

"Just as soon as I join back up, buddy."

He hung up. *Blubber and bladders.* A little bit of urp snuck its way up from his stomach.

Not the best memories.

Gabe thought about the bladder and all it was doing. He wandered into his kitchen to find two cops eating lunch while they did their paperwork. He grabbed some coffee and sat down. He was mulling over the bladder problem as he was also looking at what was on the table.

One sandwich was wrapped in wax paper. The bread looked a little dry and curled. His eye fell on the other. The second half lay on top of the plastic

ANGEL FLIGHTS

sandwich bag. He picked it up and took a bite.

"Hey."

"Sorry." Gabe smiled as he chewed. "Do those bags come in larger sizes?"

The cop looked at him with a sneer. "You're a big guy. How big of sandwich did you plan to make?"

Gabe gave him a dead look as he lifted his bare foot and banged it down on the table.

After hitting up the market just before it closed, he headed over to the hospital to see Rabbit, and hopefully a certain tall blonde nurse. She was there.

"I was just about to knock Terry out for the night. How much time you plan to spend with him?"

Gabe leered at her. "Actually, sweet thing, I came to see you."

She leaned back. In Gabe's view, that didn't help matters. "You do know I am married and almost old enough to be your mother…"

He smiled. "Older sister yes—mother… not likely. But, that isn't what I wanted."

"You still want me to knock Terrence out?"

"If you are talking about Rabbit—that can wait. But I just came to visit. But from you, I need some help."

She held her hand out, pointing down the hall. "Have at him. I'll be down in a little bit and knock him out." As he walked away, she called him. "Hey, Snake?"

He turned and she held out her two fingers. He nodded and turned toward the room.

"So your name is Terrence, huh?"

Rabbit just stared at him. Gabe wasn't sure if it was a foul mood or just drugged stupor. "I like Rabbit better—it fits you."

"Just shut up and pour." *Foul mood.*

As he sucked on the straw, his mood lightened. "What's the weather like out there?"

"Getting chilly—but it's the long ride that's the bitch."

"Yeah, that's the one drawback to the whole thing. It gets cold and you freeze." Gabe noticed he was not mentioning the girls. Gabe figured if he was cold, then the girl this last Sunday was frozen. But he hadn't heard one single complaint.

Gabe cleared his throat. "I'm working on keeping the feet and hands warm."

The weathered biker's eyes rose. His lips released the straw. "This I want to hear."

The lack of a cast on the right arm was a huge improvement. His arm was shaky and weak, but he could hold his own glass. He put it down on the bed table. Gabe could see that a couple of minutes had exhausted the strength.

Lisa walked into the room with a syringe already loaded with feel good. "Am I too early?"

Gabe smiled. "If it's going to knock him out right away—yes. He will want to see this. Can you

ANGEL FLIGHTS

get me some surgical gloves, please?"

"Latex gloves? What size?"

He held his hand up and spread his fingers out.

She took the hand and held it as if she was examining it. "You know what they say about a man and the size of his hands..."

"I have very small hands." He smirked.

She reached behind him and opened the cabinet. She looked at the size on the box and then closed the cabinet. "I'll be right back." She hid the syringe under Rabbit's napkin and book.

A couple of minutes later, she returned with a box that was marked Large. "They don't make any sized for shrimp gorillas."

Gabe blew in one and then pulled it on. Rabbit watched with interest. "The latex is waterproof." He looked to Lisa, who nodded. He held up his ski gloves. "These are insulated for very cold air. Even moving air.

"They work great until they stop working. And that happens because the hands sweat. The sweat is soaked up by the insulation. Once the insulation is damp, it stops working."

Lisa snapped her fingers. "So the latex stops the sweat from migrating to the glove, so your hands stay warm."

Rabbit was thinking. "So how do you keep the gloves dry in the rain?"

Gabe peeled the label out and showed him. "The

shell is waterproof."

"Cool. Now, what about the feet?"

Gabe pulled out the long narrow box of food wrap.

"You're going to wrap your feet?"

"Better than letting them freeze. And... one size fits all." He snapped the latex glove off and let it fly at Rabbit."

Rabbit laid back thinking. "Oh god, just shoot me now." He looked over at Lisa. "Oh, Goddess, are you going to shoot me now, or do I have to do it myself?" She nodded and prepped his arm.

He looked at Gabe. "See you Sunday night. Let me know how it goes."

The syringe had barely cleared the man's arm and he was asleep.

"I hope he doesn't become addicted to that."

She pursed her lips. "We have him on it about two or three nights a week. I shoot him only if he's been awake for longer than forty-eight hours. But the dose is about a quarter of what we would normally give. He's so exhausted that it doesn't take much.

"In my opinion, it's more about the racehorse being tied to the wall in the stall than the pain. In fact, I have accidently hit the pins on the cage while he is watching the old Perry Mason reruns—and he doesn't even flinch. He needs to be out of that bed more than anything."

"I couldn't agree more. But yesterday, I went

over to where he's been living. He's on the second floor."

"That won't work, even when they finally cut him loose."

"I'm working on that."

He zipped his jacket over the box of latex gloves. "I'm going to need more if this works."

"If it works, I'll let Aunt Lois know."

He leaned in and kissed her on the cheek. "Thanks."

At home, he put on some thin dress socks and then wrapped his feet. He bundled up and then pulled on some gloves. He fired up the motorcycle as the midnight shift pulled up.

"I just started a fresh tank of fuel, boys. There is also a bunch of fresh tamales in the fridge if you're hungry. The steamer is ready and on the stove."

The two chorused soft thanks. They grabbed their stuff and headed up the dark driveway. Gabe had looked at the thermometer—it was a very nippy forty-nine degrees. With the wind chill of sixty-five, it would be in the low twenties.

A perfect test. He pulled the wool watch cap down over his ears.

A little over an hour later, he pulled into the truck stop in Lancaster. His thighs were cold, but his feet sounded like they were sloshing around in a warm tub. He pulled his gloves off, and they were hot on his frozen smiling face. He thought about his friend up near the Arctic Circle. He had owed him his life then—and he was sure it was going to save some lives now.

The waitress looked at him. "It must be freezing on that chopper."

Gabe held his hand out and she took it. Her eyes flew wide. "Oh, you didn't ride very far."

"Pasadena... and my feet are even warmer."

She looked at the large window. "You must have a heater on that monster."

He showed her the gloves and then pulled up the pant leg to show her the food wrap.

They talked about the cold and riding motorcycles. Finally, she brought him a bowl of soup. It wasn't Chet's—but it was going to have to do. He smiled as he reached into his back pocket and pulled out a beat-up paperback. It had been through a few hands, but everyone had been full of respect. He didn't know what repairing motorcycles had to do with the Zen religion, but he settled in to find out. The temperature outside was stable at forty-one degrees.

15

THE BAD SIDE OF WORK

FEW THINGS DURING the month brought a smile to Gabe's face. A hug from Maria and some special time with Lincoln were the two biggest exceptions. The small boy wasn't forming words yet, but the communication was there—*whatever was on Gabe's plate was Lincoln's to share.*

"You are terrible for letting him do that."

The little guy grabbed a jalapeno pepper and stuck it in his mouth. Neither Gabe nor the boy's mother jumped to remove it.

The first time he did it, it was an experiment on the adults' part to see how he would react. His reaction had them crying with tears of laughter. The kid had squealed and then shoved another and another into his mouth. If it had burned on the way out, he never let on. The kid seemed to be a flow-through firebox. The child was content and burbled as he chewed on the pepper. Maria sat watching him.

ANGEL FLIGHTS

"He gets that from Tio Zorro."

Gabe looked up with a frown. "You don't like hot food?"

Maria blushed. "I love hot Szechuan or even that hot cabbage stuff..."

"Kimchee—it's Korean."

"Yeah, that stuff. Any of the oriental stuff is good, the hotter, the better. But when it comes to Mexican food... Machaca is where I draw the line."

"For your eighteenth birthday, I'll take you to Koreatown. I know a really hot place up an alley. I don't speak Korean, and they don't speak English. They try to burn you out the first time, but I was in the whole way. They have a beef dish that is so good and hot it will make your ears clap."

"Make it my seventeenth birthday next month and we have a deal."

"Zorro will never let you ride on the bike, and I don't have a car."

"You leave Tio to me."

"Find a car and we can take the little boss here." He leaned down and looked at the boy. "What do you think, little man? You want to go burn your ears out in Koreatown?"

There was a whistle from the kitchen. Maria and Gabe looked up. The cook was holding the phone.

Maria became very serious. *Nobody called her.* "Excuse me."

A few minutes later, she came back. She stood

behind Gabe. Her hand played distractedly with his hair that was growing around his scar. "Your hair is growing over the scar really good, senor." She stopped playing with his hair and leaned against his back. She folded her hands on top of his forehead and gently crushed his head back into her breasts. The feeling was soft and comforting, but the breathing was all wrong. Gabe thought about the phone call. Something was wrong.

"Chica... if you don't talk to me... I can't help."

She stood silent, and then gently lowered her head until her chin was on top of her hands. "You're still a cop, right?"

Gabe sighed. He wasn't sure how to answer that question anymore. A year ago, it would have been easy. But now...?

"What do you need done, mi hija?"

She sighed, and the whisper was both serious and impossible. "I need someone killed."

Gabe thought. This was not a frivolous thing like she wanted to kill her brother for being a pest. This was from a far different place.

Gabe turned and spun the other chair around with his foot. He sat her down. "What happened?"

"That was my friend down the street..." She slumped.

"If you don't tell me, I can't help."

She looked up. "Promise me that you will not tell Tio."

ANGEL FLIGHTS

He nodded. "Zorro wears a uniform..." He didn't have to clarify. She knew he was willing to step over a line.

"A friend just brought her sister home. Her sister went... she was pregnant. She won't..." She took in a few deep breaths as she fanned herself with a menu. "She just keeps bleeding. They don't know what to do. I told them to call an ambulance."

Gabe stood. "Where?"

She pointed. "The dark-green house on the left. There is a red Volkswagen in the driveway."

He left the bike and ran. When the ambulance came, he returned.

Gabe could tell Maria had been crying the entire time. An older lady was trying to console her. She was in good hands. He held up a piece of paper as she looked up. "I have his address." She nodded. He mounted his bike and road off.

The area was pure East LA industrial. Few people and the streets and alleyways were lined with trucks, delivery vans, trash, and rotting piles of something. The building Gabe was sitting in front of should have been condemned before it had gone through World War II. The brick façade had gaping holes where one or several bricks had finally just fallen out like rotted teeth. The death trap was only waiting for a good earthquake to knock the legs out of its foundation.

At first, Gabe thought the girl must have given

him a bogus address. Then he saw the Cadillac hiding in the small alley. The car was only a year or two old. Its shine, cost, and polish didn't fit in with the dirt, dust, and rust. Even the cold gray overcast winter sky was more cheerful than the street or neighborhood.

The morning's drizzle had done nothing to clean the abuse and grime. Decades of hard times and destitution had tormented the once heavy-duty rated asphalt—and it was now alligator-skin cobble. The spider work of small standing streams of greasy water in the cracks reflected the wan afternoon lead of the sky. In the middle was a long narrow pond. The rainbow of gasoline on the water tinted the image of the two huddled girls scuttling along the edge of the building. Gabe watched. They could be neighborhood kids taking a shortcut through the old section or they could be passing as a dare. But Gabe knew the truth.

He rose from the chopper, a dark figure backlit by the afternoon light. His movement caused the two across the street to hesitate. Gabe could see the small piece of paper in the one's hand. It was the same as the one in his jacket pocket. He reached into the inside breast pocket. That movement froze the two girls dressed in blue wool jackets and plaid skirts. He knew the school. They weren't in high school yet.

He took out a pen and quickly scribbled the address in Hollywood. He put the pen back as he

ANGEL FLIGHTS

crossed the street. He could see the question on the two small faces. *Run or stay?*

He stopped ten feet away and held out the piece of paper. "I'll trade you."

"What...?"

"I'll trade my address for the one in your hand. The guy on that paper is going to be out of business in a few minutes."

He could see the panic in the one girl's eyes. "Then what?"

"This is your good friend?" He pointed at the other girl.

They both nodded. He guessed they had known each other for most of their lives. He gently took the last steps. With the last, instead of towering over them, he crunched down on one knee. "Look... I know why you're here. But this man just put his last girl in the hospital. We won't know if she lives through the night. He's not a doctor, just a butcher."

The two swallowed in unison.

"Here is an address. It's in Hollywood. You have to be there by three in the afternoon on Friday. You will be back there on Sunday evening. How you get there is up to you—just be there. There is a nice older lady there. She will explain everything to you. Just remember—you will be gone all weekend."

He turned to the friend. "Are you pregnant, too?"

"No." The voice was soft and distant.

"Sweetie, you can drop her off. But you can't come with her." He stuck his hand out to shake. "But here is my promise to you. There will be someone the whole time—that is there to hold her hand." She took his hand cautiously, and Gabe matched the gentleness but with a reassuring grip.

"What is your name?"

"Angel." Gabe let go of her hand.

She smiled.

Gabe turned to the other girl. "Can you be there? And is it going to be a problem to be there the whole weekend?"

She pointed at her friend. "I'll stay with her. We need to study for finals."

"Good. When you talk to that woman, you can tell her how you found out about her. Okay?"

"Okay."

"Now, you need to leave. I don't want you anywhere near here. I'll give you five minutes to get as far away as possible."

They turned and ran. At the corner of the large building, they turned and looked back. They waved and turned around the corner and were gone.

Gabe walked around the other end of the building. There appeared to be only the one door, the rest were large industrial dock doors that rolled up. The docks were about four feet high, same as the back of a large truck. The small regular door was the winner.

Gabe watched the doorjamb as he carefully

opened the door. He had become used to watching doors for booby traps. He didn't think the butcher would try to blow up or kill a potential customer, but he might want to be warned of someone coming. Unfortunately, the striker rod was set so that someone entering couldn't see it until it had moved the bell. Gabe felt the tiny resistance and stopped. He squeezed through the barely opened door.

Reaching up, he held the small set of three bells in his gloved hand. The tongue of the door latch clicked closed. Gabe stood and listened. The sound of a newspaper turning rustled from the open door at the top of the wooden stairs. He could smell the man's cigar.

There was a distinct copper taste in the air. *Blood*. He could hear flies buzzing around in a large room to his right. In the dim light, he could see dozens of large barrels. Gabe guessed at what they contained. The rot of human remains is distinct. That stench was mixed with the rotting wood and whatever the building used to do. As he reached out to ascend the stairs, he was glad he was wearing gloves. The pig upstairs wasn't the cleanest person in the medical world. Gabe could feel a wet slipperiness to the wood railing. He figured he was also lazy and would slide bags down the railing instead of carrying it.

Gabe wanted to take his hand off the railing, but he needed it to steady himself as he kept his feet at the two extreme ends of each step. The belief is that you would be less likely to make an old step squeak. With his size, Gabe knew that a squeaky step would scream like a stuck pig.

The pig wasn't any of the stair treads—it was the last board before the open door. Gabe didn't care.

Gabe had been right about the butcher being a slob and the extreme lack of hygiene. The newspaper collapsed at the sound of the board. The long ash of the large cigar fell onto the paper and then slid down onto the white dress. The woman was fat. The nurse's uniform was covered with old stains as well as new splatters of blood.

Her jowls wobbled as her head snapped around. "Who the hell are you?"

Gabe growled. "Your next appointment..."

Male or female, young or older, skinny or morbidly obese—Gabe was beyond caring or being gentle. He did have the presence to use his open hand when he hit her. The woman was amazingly agile and quick. Gabe revised his estimate of fifty-something down to a healthy forty. The woman kicked him in the crotch.

Luckily, the blow had caught more leg than anything else, but Gabe was sure there would be a bruise there later. After the few seconds of sparring, he realized the woman was fighting for her life, and he was trying to let her live. His MP training took over and all he saw was a uniform trying to hurt him. The rest

ANGEL FLIGHTS

of the fight took only seconds.

Gabe softly closed the front door on his way out. He reached into his pocket and found a few pennies. Pushing hard high up on the door, he caused a gap between the door and the jamb. He stacked three pennies in the gap and forced them down as far as they would go.

He tried the doorknob. The penny jam had frozen the doorknob from turning. It would stop anyone else from casually opening the door.

Several minutes later, Gabe sat at the bar with paperwork spread out in front of him. The coffee was sitting on a coffee ring stained napkin. What had been a bowl of stew was now crusted and long finished.

Zorro walked through the door. He sat down and looked at all the detritus on the bar. "Long day of boring paperwork?"

Gabe looked up and simply exhaled a deep emotional sigh. "I should have gone over to the Palms. At least I would get a little distraction from Lincoln." He looked down the bar where Chet was working hard at rewashing a stack of glasses and trying to look like he was ignoring them. "And Maria is a lot better looking than Chet."

Chet looked up at the sound of his name. "You two need something?"

Gabe waved him down. "Nah, we're good, Chet."

Zorro studied the bartender and then his head ground around to his ex-partner. Nobody was fooling anybody. "So why the phone call?"

Gabe pushed the paperwork into a pile. He hoped he didn't just screw up Chet's bookkeeping.

"Next month, Maria turns seventeen. She wants to go to Koreatown for dinner or lunch. We want your blessing... I don't have a car."

"Borrow one."

"If I knew someone, I would. Then we could take the little man and see how he likes real hot food. But I don't think it's just about the food... I think she wants a ride on the scooter."

Zorro laughed. He had watched the kid eat the peppers. "I don't think anything would affect that kid. He has my stomach." He hung his head. "Look, I'll run it past my sister. It's up to her. Personally, I don't have a problem for a lunch. It would be safer during the day. If you want, I can bring the little man in my car."

"How about we make it a whole family thing? I have something I want to talk to Lito about also."

Zorro frowned.

"Stand down, Tio—he's not in trouble. I want to know how he challenged all those college courses. I think I want to get my degree out of the way."

Zorro smiled knowingly. "Consider it a date. There is a nice place over near the west end. I think the name is Kim or Shim or something. All of the

ANGEL FLIGHTS

writing is in Korean."

"The one that looks like an old house?"

"And painted all red."

"I know the place. I think on Sundays they do an early dinner around two o'clock for the after church people. I'll look into it. Sunday there is a lot less traffic."

They sat silent. Zorro watched the partner he had only had for a short time but had become so much more. Gabe slid him a small piece of paper.

"¿Que es esto?"

"It's an address. You better take serious back up with you. The door is penny jammed."

"What will I find there?"

Gabe shrugged. "Just don't kill the woman. There are other people for that."

Zorro considered the address. "Does this have anything to do with a young girl down at County General fighting for her life?"

Gabe shrugged and sipped at what Zorro knew was an empty cup.

He stood and straightened his tie. He zipped up his uniform jacket. "I guess it's going to be a long night. I'll probably need a coffee break later."

Gabe put down the mug and looked down the bar at Chet schmoozing with one of the regulars. "The light will be on."

16

NEW DOOR?

GABE WOKE UP to the sound of someone breaking into his kitchen. He grabbed his 45 Auto and headed through the bedroom door.

"What the fuck, pendejo? You booby trapping the kitchen now?"

Zorro. Gabe turned and put the pistol back under the pillow. He looked down and decided he better put something on. He grabbed his jeans.

"Damn, Zorro. What time is it?"

"After three. That fucking crime scene went on forever. I finally called the captain and got released. They were just opening drum number one-seventeen. My stomach is old. I just couldn't take any more."

"Jeez… and they were all full?" Gabe started to pour a cup and then put it down. He looked at the clock on the wall—it was only a couple of ticks away from four. He would normally be up in a couple of hours anyway. He knew he wasn't going to get any sleep. He pulled himself a cup and one for Zorro.

The man was collapsed in the one chair looking at the construction.

Gabe put the mug down on the table and took a seat. "I'm bringing Rabbit home in a couple of weeks. He'll be in a wheelchair for a while until he gets the strength back in his arms." He nodded toward the front of the house. "I set up all the weight stuff in the front room. One of the rehab guys over at the VA is going to come by and set up the rest of the stuff."

Zorro started to say something, and then realized that probably anything he could think of—would be four steps behind what was already going on. He closed his mouth and picked up the mug of coffee.

Gabe just watched him. "There is always the bed in the back room. You won't have to share it with Gertie."

"Nah, I'm good. The Cap told me not to come in. He just wants me to check in when I wake up and see if they're finished processing the warehouse. She must have been working out of there for over a decade."

Gabe just wagged his head with a sigh.

"None of the crime scene guys had ever seen anything like it. It gives a whole new meaning to the term slaughterhouse."

Gabe thought. "I think the term you are looking for is charnel house."

"That too." The man sat a moment then got up. "Excuse me." Every cop in El Sereno knew the way to Gabe's bathroom. Gabe hadn't cleaned or stocked the bathroom or kitchen in several months. He never saw anyone bringing anything or cleaning—it just happened. The morning of his birthday, he opened the refrigerator to find a chocolate cupcake with a candle in it.

Who knew that information?

Zorro came back into the kitchen. He was zipping up his jacket and wiping his mouth with the back of his hand. Gabe could smell the trace of vomit. "I think I'm going to go home and see if I can still sleep. Thanks for the talk—I'll talk to my sister." He looked at the missing back wall that was now framed for a large bump out and a hospital-wide door. "He won't fit in the bathroom or the bedroom door."

"First, is this new area and the back door. The rest is next week."

"Who is doing the work?"

"I don't know." They looked at each other. The understanding ran deep. Brother in need.

Zorro nodded and used the old side-door. He stuck his head back in. "The bouquet of her rust-coated hangers shoved up her cunt was a nice touch."

"I'm glad you thought so."

"Are we going to find any fingerprints?"

Gabe held up his hands like a surgeon in scrub-in. "Gloves…"

ANGEL FLIGHTS

Zorro smiled weakly. "Good to know. Good night, partner."

Gabe smiled. "Always, partner." *Always.*

Gabe took a sip and pulled the stack of brochures from Chet's toward him. His thumb found the dividing mark and lifted the top half off. He found the UCLA brochure and opened it to the bookmark.

17

CHANGE OF PLANS

"GOOD MORNING, SWEETHEART." Gabe sat in the lounge chair near the window. The mug of coffee if not good was at least hot.

Rabbit groaned. He rolled over. Gabe noted that he had freedom with the new cast on the leg. "Fuck you." The man smiled—weakly—but smiled.

"Need help getting to the bathroom?"

The man looked up with renewed interest. "Don't fuck with me, asshole... Are you really offering to help me in there—because I'm dying to sit and pinch off a real turd."

Gabe put the mug down and helped Rabbit to the bathroom. As he sat him down, he turned on the water. He leaned over close to Rabbit's ear. "I need to have a person in lock-up whacked."

Rabbit didn't flinch. "Dude?"

"Bitch."

"Find Mike. What day is this?"

ANGEL FLIGHTS

"Thursday."

"Valley carwash, near Cold Water Canyon—get there by two. He does some kind of pick up between two and three. Otherwise, you'll have to look for him out on the circuit tonight. But he never misses the flights."

"She's connected. She'll be out by Monday."

"Is Lisa here?"

"Not until tonight."

"Try Lois over at Mercy—she is probably in the ER. Once an ER junkie, always an ER junkie..."

Gabe heard the growl in the man's gut. "I'll be back in a little bit. Or you can pull that string and get the nurse."

"Go ahead. I'll deal with the nurse."

Gabe pounded lightly on the man's shoulder and left the tiny room. He thought about Lois but figured that was one too many in the trail.

His stomach growled as he reached his bike. He thought about where to go. The Bucket was close, but he figured he could make it over to the Bob's Big Boy in Toluca Lake.

The sun was actually trying to clear away the last clouds for the weekend. It would be cold, but at least not wet.

The freeway had not loaded up yet. Gabe loved the curves on the oldest freeway in the system—The Arroyo Parkway. He took the exit before the park. Winding his way through the streets to the backside of Eagle Rock, he watched the traffic. For some reason the traffic was extremely light, then he remembered it was Thanksgiving.

Crap. The carwash would be closed. And nobody would be hitting The Circuit.

He realized where he was and remembered some work that was a few days old.

He pulled up into the small drive-through dairy. The man came out, but started shaking. "Sna... Snake, I don't have it all. Give me until tomorrow, I promise, I can have it for you then. Please... I have a family."

Gabe left the black wrap-around glasses on. His face was stone. "Mr. Lee, you know how this works. Do you really want me to come back tomorrow? Really? Because if I come back later today, it will be only an arm—but tomorrow..." He looked down at the man's leg.

The man turned ash white. "One minute. You wait... don't go away." He rushed inside. He returned with a fat envelope that Gabe was sure he had already prepared—but was thinking about using some to gamble again in the hope to win enough to pay his debt.

Gabe took the money and stuck it in his jacket. He didn't have to count it. The man knew the punishment for paying short.

"Mr. Lee, which finger do you dial the phone with?"

ANGEL FLIGHTS

The man's right hand shook as he held up his first finger.

He knew what was coming—he had dealt with the Tongs all his life.

In a flash, Gabe grabbed it out of the air and twisted and bent it until there was a wet snap. The man screamed quietly—not wanting to alarm his wife or family inside. Gabe pulled the man across his gas tank. He slapped the man on the side of the head.

He leaned close and growled. "If you ever think to call and gamble again—you remember this, asshole. This is between just you and me. You understand? This has nothing to do with Wong. *Just you and me*. You understand?"

The man nodded as he whimpered.

"I don't think you do." Gabe snapped the second finger. "If you call anyone—and try to place a bet—I will know. I won't come after you. I will wait until that little girl of yours comes to work. Then I am going to tell her all about her father... as I break all of her fingers. She will never play that piano again."

"No, no... I never gamble again."

Gabe slapped the man again. "I wasn't done. You interrupted me. Now there is a penalty. Someday, I will come back. It might be a month. It might be a year or more. When I do, your beautiful wife can ask you why I broke all of her fingers. Now do you understand? When you gamble—it affects everyone in your family."

BAER CHARLTON

He threw the weeping man back to the floor of his store. The man clutched his hand and howled that he would never gamble again.

Gabe drove off.

He believed him.

Mercy was one of the smaller hospitals. That didn't make the emergency room any less busy. Gabe pushed through the doors to the triage area. The medical staff looked up. At the sight of the giant biker, there was no fear on any of the faces. They were just curious as to what would happen next.

Gabe saw the one nurse come out of a curtained room and look over. She stood—watching. Finally, she motioned to him. He had just crossed a line.

She took him into a supply area. Her voice was hard but quiet. "This better be good."

"Two things—there is an add-on for tomorrow. I gave her the address and told her to be there at three."

Lois nodded. "And the other?"

"I need to find Deaf Mike today."

She studied his face. "It's Thanksgiving."

"I just realized that. He won't be making his rounds, and he won't hit the circuit—nobody will."

"It's that important that it can't wait until the weekend?"

"Life and death."

She hesitated for a minute. She reached into her pocket for a piece of paper to write on. Finding nothing, she grabbed a box of bandages. She tore the lid off the box and wrote on the blank inside. "He'll know who gave you this and probably give me the silent treatment for a year. But I don't want to lose him. He and Rabbit are two of my oldest."

"Rabbit is out for several months, so I don't want you to lose Mike. I'll make it right with him. Thanks." He bent and kissed her on the cheek. "Happy Thanksgiving, and I'll see you tomorrow."

"I hope your girl shows up."

"She's scared, but I think she'll be there. I have to warn you—she's not even in high school."

"Oh, Gabe... Take a really good look at them tomorrow. Many... too many of them are not in high school yet."

He realized she knew his real name. He didn't acknowledge it. "Mañana, chica."

She slapped him on the shoulder as he turned. As they came out into the main room, she spoke louder. "Thanks for letting me know, Snake, and try to have a good Thanksgiving."

He waved as he left.

Now for the hard part.

The house wasn't large or even upscale. But it and the neighborhood were anything but depressed.

A few blocks away, Encino became Encino Hills and the elevation was nothing compared to the value of the homes. It was not the kind of address that Gabe had expected of a biker who was a bagman for who knows whom.

Gabe parked on the street. The neighborhood was the sort where everyone still mowed their own lawns, but quietly jealous of the guy with the nicest lawn and garden. Judging by the quick eye tour of the close neighbors, Mike was that guy.

Gabe walked up the perfectly trimmed lawn toward the low-lying ranch style house that was similar to most in the San Fernando Valley. When housing boomed in the forties, orchards and truck farms were plowed under, smoothed out, and paved over. What had once been large farms became whole cities—springing up, seemingly, overnight.

The doorbell didn't seem to work. Gabe heard no bell or chime. He pushed again. Suddenly, the door flew open. Her hair was a wild mess and her apron was dusted with flour. Her hand made the sign that Gabe kind of recognized for *what*. She was obviously very busy and frazzled.

Gabe thought fast… then placed his three fingers over his thumb and bounced his hand off his forehead. He hoped he had gotten the sign right.

The woman laughed. "Close—but more like…" She bounced the M sign off her out-slug butt. "Let me get him." Her voice was crystal clear and he figured she wasn't deaf.

"I'm sorry to interrupt the day."

She turned back, confirming his suspicion. "Dinner isn't for another two hours. You're fine…

who should I tell him...?"

"Snake."

She looked at him for a held moment.

"Angel."

She nodded and turned down the hallway. Gabe thought about stepping in and closing the door, but had a sense that if she hadn't asked...

She came back out of the hallway and without even looking at Gabe, went back into what he assumed was the kitchen. Mike came out frowning, and upon seeing Gabe, waved him in.

"What's up?"

Gabe looked toward the kitchen. Mike understood and waved him back down the hallway. They entered what could have been a bedroom but was an office.

Gabe realized what he was looking at—an office of an accountant. He pictured in his mind what a bagman for a gangster looked like making a pick-up. It would look the same as an accountant picking up paperwork for the week. And, if the guy worked from home... he didn't have to keep set hours or wear a suit and drive a car.

"Figure it out?"

Gabe nodded and struggled with signing the letters—CPA. Mike nodded and pointed at the diploma for a Juris Doctorate—he was a tax lawyer as well. Gabe stood stunned. His mind raced at the thought of what he had come to ask and was now in the presence of another officer of the court.

"Sit down." Mike held his hand out toward a chair by the desk. "If you tracked me down, it must be very important."

Gabe sat with weight. His shoulders sagged. Mike's eyes missed nothing.

"You thought I was just a biker and a criminal."

Gabe nodded. He started to speak, and then closed his mouth. He didn't know where to go with all the new information.

The flat sounding high voice Gabe was getting used to. "First of all, to have found me, and especially my home address, you are either a cop, or Lois told you—or both."

Mike looked up at the door. His wife had two mugs in her hand. "I didn't know how you would take your coffee. Mitchell lives on coffee and I figure you might, too."

Gabe accepted the mug. "Thanks, black is perfect. And today will only happen with a lot of coffee."

The woman looked at him long and hard. "Just get plenty of rest tonight. If you are an Angel, tomorrow will be a long cold day." Gabe nodded in agreement.

Gabe sipped on the coffee as she left. He looked up at Mike and nodded. "Both."

"I figured as much. You ride with Rabbit." The statement spoke volumes. "So what can I do for you?"

"I'm not sure you can... now."

Mike leaned back with his mug. The neatly trimmed hair and beard now made sense. The quick eyes never stopped moving—evaluating. "I got most of that degree while I was in prison for grand theft auto and aggravated assault. I found a little loophole where I didn't have to have a bachelors to go for my law degree."

Gabe frowned. "But if you've served time...?"

"It just means that I can't go to court. I can still file paperwork, and I can represent someone at the IRS office... I just have to use a second to appear in court. Most of the people who graduate with a law degree don't even take the bar exam. I took it and passed the first time. I just wanted to see if I could. The bar still keeps me from going to court other than to represent myself—and I'm not that kind of idiot."

Gabe sipped his coffee and tried to figure out what to do. For once, he was frustrated and at a loss.

"Why don't you just tell me what is going on, and let me figure out how I can help."

"I don't want to put you in jeopardy."

The man laughed. "We run children across international borders to get abortions which are illegal in both countries. We do it without the parents' knowledge, much less permission. Every weekend we are in jeopardy from seven statutes that would send us up the river until we are drooling in our oatmeal and getting pushed around in wheelchairs. What can you add to that?"

"Murder."

Mike sat back. "You, me and anyone else makes it conspiracy—same as every weekend. First-degree murder in California is usually life—out in twenty, maybe less with good behavior. If the person who does the actual killing is an active gang member, it would be tried as aggregated first degree, which carries it over into life without parole or possibly the death penalty—which makes you a special ward of the state in Soledad or the Q for the rest of your life. All except the death penalty applies to what we do fifty sometimes a year."

"It's a woman."

"Same applies."

"She's in county lock-up."

"Makes it easier." He smiled. "What kind of trash needs to be taken out?"

Gabe took a large swallow of coffee and told him. At the mention of the two girls, the man's face turned dark. Gabe knew there had to be some history for what the man dedicated his weekends to. As Gabe described how he had left the woman tied to her butcher's rack and the bouquet of the rustiest of the coat hangers—he had the man laughing.

Mike's wife appeared in the doorway—frowning with a question on her face. Mike wiped the tears from his face and wagged the 'L' sign at her. Gabe realized he would tell her later. This would also make her an accessory to anything that happened. Gabe also understood that this man and wife were a true team—no secrets.

"How long have you been married?"

"Twenty-one years. I was in prison when we got married. She was my court-appointed interpreter. It was love at first sign. I fell in love with her fingers first."

Mike leaned in. "So why the rush?"

"Evidently, she is very connected and will probably get sprung by Monday. The holiday will maybe delay things a bit, but still…"

Mike leaned back and stroked his pursed lips. His eyes wandered over the many large binders stacked along the wall of shelves. "I have many people who owe me favors. I'll figure it out and have the trash taken to the right place tonight."

"Thanks."

They rose. Mike offered his hand. "I'd invite you to dinner, but we have a dozen people showing up and none of them would understand."

Gabe smiled. "I understand… and that's all that counts." As he stuck his hand into the jacket pocket, he remembered. He pulled out some latex gloves. "Your wife cooks, so I know she has some of that plastic food wrap."

The man shrugged and nodded.

"Put on thin socks, and wrap your feet to above

the ankles, then put on your wool socks. It really helps with the cold. Same with the gloves—I have enough for everyone tomorrow."

Gabe headed for the hospital in Pasadena and an early night. The forty thousand in his jacket pocket could wait until the morning.

18

WINTER PLANS

GABE SAT ON the motorcycle in front of the costume shop. It felt strange—he was used to the alley with the other Angels.

He watched the street and every bus that stopped on both sides of the street.

Lois looked out the window. One of the women had called her out asking if she was missing a biker.

"You're going to freeze out there."

Gabe looked back at the door. "If she comes, she needs to see a face she knows."

"You can see both bus stops from here. Come in and stay warm, you're going to need it."

With one last look, he pulled the key out of the chopper and came in. She was right, the view was fine—and warmer.

"Give me your jacket." She held her hand out.

He didn't question her. The heavy leather slid off his shoulders and into his one hand. She took it.

ANGEL FLIGHTS

"Damn, I keep forgetting how heavy these jackets are."

Gabe reached in and pulled the pistol out of the special inside pocket holster. She hesitated and then raised the jacket up and down. "Oh, yes. That makes all the difference in the world." Her eyes rolled tired, up and out.

She passed the jacket to one of the other women. "Sew it on just above his ass... I mean heart." She turned back and smiled sweetly.

"We have something for you guys. It's just a little patch. But it carries everything it is meant to."

"We don't need anything..."

"Shut up. All of you do. Otherwise, you wouldn't be here." She looked across the street. "Is that her?"

Gabe spun around. The girl stood where the bus left her off. She had the little piece of paper in her hand. Her hair was in pigtails and she was still dressed for school.

Lois sagged against him. "Oh. God. She really is that young. Every week, I think I'm ready for this, but then... it's ones like this who show up. It just breaks my heart." She pushed him toward the door. "Go bring the little lamb in like a good Angel."

He stepped out and started walking. The girl saw him. Gabe could tell as her foot turned out she wanted to run. He stopped and held his hand up in greeting. He waved her over. At first, she hesitated, but then crossed the street.

"I almost didn't come."

"I know. It's hard. But I have someone for you to meet. Come on in." He held out his hand, she paused and then took it. He matched his walk to hers.

Lois opened the door. She stuck her hand out to the girl. "Hello, my name is Glenda."

Gabe took the lead. "Glenda, this is... Cinderella. We can call her Cinder."

The girl looked at the two. She was smart enough to understand what was going on. "Glenda the good witch and an angel named Snake." She had remembered the name patch.

Lois nodded, "Except for you, his name is Angel. I'll explain everything when all of the girls are here. But for now, let's get you started." She guided Cinder back through the door leading to the large room where hundreds of costumes hung. Everyone was for a female and was to make them look like they belonged on the back of a chopper. The makeup would do the rest.

The other woman brought Gabe his jacket back. He stood looking at the new patch. It was a pair of elongated wings with a halo hanging on the shoulder of one wing.

"Hey..." Lois snapped her fingers. "I'm talking to you."

"What?"

"You need to be on the road."

ANGEL FLIGHTS

He looked at his watch. "But it's not..."

"Winter program. We have a bus. We haul the girls down and you get them at the gas station in Pacific Beach. There is the pizza place behind, and you can get some chow and warm up. The bus gets there about seven. You go across at night. It's late, but the bus can't split the lanes like you guys can. But the girls are at least warm for most of the way."

Gabe shrugged on his jacket and transferred the pistol back into its holster. "Speaking of which..." He drew out a roll of food wrap and a bag of gloves. "Wrap their feet before they put on the heavy socks. The gloves go on before any other glove. It is amazing how good it works. Even in San Diego, they are going to want the extra warmth."

She looked at him. He bent over and pulled his pants up and wool sock down. "I've been the test bunny and I'm not dead. The wind chill was twenty-one degrees in Lancaster Tuesday night."

She took the supplies and pushed him out the door as three girls timidly snuck in. Gabe figured they weren't there to rent elf costumes. And he knew they wouldn't look so young in a couple of hours.

He mounted and started the engine. With the light holiday traffic, the ride wouldn't take long.

It took only two hours and a few minutes—with only a stop for gas.

As he swung his leg over the bike seat and sloshed his way into the pizza place, he once again was surprised at how well the little bit of plastic worked. A few of the guys were already sitting in the back room. Gabe walked in and set the roll of wrap on the table, as well as the large bag of gloves. There were a couple of jabs in jest from the hardened riders.

"Take your boots off."

"You have a foot fetish, Snake?"

He started on the large guy. He knew the man hated the hot of summer because all he did was sweat. "When you got off to gas up each time… how long did you stamp your feet to get the frozen blocks working again." Everyone laughed and nodded. *They all had.*

"Fuck you. I don't have feet. I have blocks of ice like you."

Gabe sat on the table in front of the man. He grabbed his wrist, and before the man could jerk it back, he held it to his face. Gabe also noticed the man's hands weren't much warmer than his face. He held his hand up to the man's hand.

"What the fuck? How did you keep your hands so warm?"

Gabe reached into his jacket and pulled out the same ski gloves the man had. Then he picked up the bag of latex gloves. He spun around and sat on one of the chairs. "You heard me pull up. I rode down from Hollywood and only stopped in the canyon for gas." He worked off his boot and sock as he talked.

ANGEL FLIGHTS

"I don't have to feel your feet to know they're still frozen."

He lifted his foot onto the table. "Here, take a feel. Wait." He took a bunch of napkins and dried off his foot. "There you go... feel."

The shock on the guy's face had everyone else touching. Three other bikers stomped their way in on blocks of ice, as they were all touching. They turned, somewhat embarrassed.

"Snake, you passed us at Del Mar going like a bat out of hell. You got a jet engine on that wonky bastard bike of yours? What's wrong with your foot?"

"Feel."

The guy touched it and then grabbed it. "What the hell... why is it so hot? Are you sick?"

The fat biker held up the thin film wrap and then pointed at the roll. "We all are going to hotfoot it down to Mexico."

A quiet biker strolled in. He looked at the roll. "It won't be enough. We have thirty-four this trip. I just got off the phone with San Diego. They are trying to rustle up three more local riders."

Gabe grabbed the roll and then went looking for the assistant manager. A few minutes later he came back and banged a log of food wrap on the table. "From now on, he has the girls covered." Gabe didn't have to share that the man's own sister had been one of the first girls.

"Does it matter if you have those thin socks?"

"Not really, but on bare skin the plastic feels slimy and slips around when you walk."

Lizard Larry glanced at his watch. "There's a sporting goods store down the way. I bet they would have those thin socks you wear for tennis."

Gabe and three others offered to go with him. As they were walking out, several other bikes were arriving—Mike was one of them.

He motioned to Gabe. "Done."

"Thanks. We'll be back in a few minutes. Go get warm." Almost all the bikers were stomping their feet as they got off the choppers. Gabe had never really thought about how the feet really just hang out there in the wind, and the blood circulation when you just sit does not bode well.

The four bought every pair of thin adult socks in the store. The cashier and manager were very curious why they needed to go in the back room and find more stock, but the ring up was well worth it. Gabe also bought every thick insulated sock or wool sock as well. A few of the bikers were going to have to make do on the way down.

When they got back, the buses had arrived, and Gabe's extra purchase hadn't truly been needed for the guys. The pizza ovens had made quick work of drying out and warming up the socks that they'd been wearing—and were soaking wet. Gabe didn't want to know about the pizzas. They tasted as good as advertised.

Cinderella gave Gabe a big hug the moment she saw him. She looped her thumb into his center back belt loop and wouldn't let go until he had to go use the toilet. She had already made some friends and that had had a calming quality. *The bus ride...*

Late that night, the guys were sitting around the two large fire pits. The talk was subdued as usual. One of the guys put his boots up on the rocks and watched the last of the flames and glowing embers through the crack between them.

"You need to take the wrap off your feet and dry them out or you will get really nasty jungle rot."

The guy looked over at Gabe. "Did you get it in Nam?"

Gabe shook his head. "No, I got it north of the Arctic Circle on a hunting expedition."

Another voice in the dark asked, "Seal or bear?"

Gabe chuckled. "Bears in a tin can."

The voice cackled softly. "I used to hunt those from under the ice."

Both men knew not to talk about it to any further extent. Gabe couldn't see who it was, but it didn't really matter. Each of the men at the fire had their own secrets—other than the one that they held together.

19

THROUGH THE DOOR

THE MILK TRUCK stood at the curb. It was parked facing the wrong way.

Gabe pulled out the ramp Roscoe had built into the floor. Rabbit untied the chair from the wall and sat poised at the top of the ramp.

"What are you waiting for?"

"We have an audience."

Gabe turned around and looked at all of the small kids on their tricycles and bicycles. They had become his gang. If Gabe was doing anything—they wanted to see. Watching a man on a wheelchair ride down a ramp was going to be high entertainment.

Gabe turned back to face Rabbit. "They're just waiting for you to fall. Don't disappoint them."

The man's lower lip was placed on his upper teeth. Gabe stopped him. "Don't say it."

Gabe saw the grandmother and granddaughter coming across the street. The girl had a bundle in her

ANGEL FLIGHTS

arms. Gabe smiled as they came along side. "Hola Nana y Yolanda." Trying to be polite, he pointed at Rabbit. "Cajones."

The old woman cackled with mirth as she poked at Gabe's crotch. "No, no... estas cajones."

Gabe thought again. "Conejo?"

The girl laughed. "A rabbit? This is a lot of food for your snake, Gabe."

"No, his name is Rabbit."

The older woman leaned back and muttered something to her granddaughter. Yolanda laughed with her.

"What?"

"She said you did a piss-poor job of butchering him."

"Are we finished making fun of the man in the chair?"

Gabe and the young girl turned. "No."

"You're the one who is too scared to come down a little ramp."

Rabbit pushed and was down in a flash. His attempt to steer nosed him straight onto the lawn in front of the waiting kids. His crash didn't disappoint. They all squealed with glee and clapped.

Yolanda laughed. "Your friend is very entertaining."

Gabe looked up from the cherub face hiding in the blanket. He looked over at Rabbit who was now covered with the small gang of children. Gabe shrugged with a crooked smile. "Eh, snake, rabbit, it doesn't seem to matter. They are easily amused."

In the back, Rabbit looked at the large industrial door. "Why does it open outward?"

"The reasons are—it makes it easier for you to open. Also, the wind comes from over there and will blow it against the seals instead of opening a gap—as it would in a regular door. After you get back to walking, I can move the table back into this new large alcove and still use the door to access the back yard."

Gabe opened the door. The fact that the door didn't have a lock on it did not escape him. *Guard snake on duty.*

The bathroom had been enlarged at the expense of the back bedroom. Gabe didn't care. The bathroom easily fit the wheelchair— a walker and crutches would be a breeze. The low curb shower was filled with a pile of green. "Good afternoon, Gertie."

Rabbit stopped and let his eyes run over all of the hardware in what had been a living room. "Either you have started dating a serious health nut, or I'm in the way." He leaned his head back and looked at his friend.

"Neither." Gabe pulled him back into the back bedroom. The bathroom had swallowed the closet and four more feet into what had been a modest room. Along what was left of the one wall, a seven-foot bed had been built in. Having the single-wide bed along the wall left plenty of room for the wheelchair to maneuver—all of the doors were now thirty-eight inches wide.

"If I'm not here, and you need something, just press this button." Gabe showed the man a remote for a garage door.

"And the garage door opens?"

"No, it triggers an alarm. That alarm goes to an answering service that will call the precinct."

"What if it's not an emergency?"

"It doesn't matter—there will probably be a couple of cops on the other side of this wall. Recently they seem to be here night and day. I unscrewed the light in the kitchen—someone replaced the fixture the next day. Even the weights seem to multiply and move around. Either Gertie is getting really strange in her old age, or the place is haunted by cops and Santa's elves."

"Do any of the elves come with a nice set of fun bags?"

"For a guy fresh out of the hospital, you sure are a dirty old man."

"I'll let you know when Gertie is starting to look cute."

"She's already cute."

They heard the old back door open. "¿Hola?"

Gabe frowned. "Si, Nana. Que pasa…?"

"Tamales."

Rabbit's eyebrows shot up with his smile. "Lunch?"

Gabe walked into the kitchen. The woman had a large kettle. Gabe took it and put it on the counter. He had seen the kettle before—he didn't know if it was his or hers. It just always seemed to be full of tamales.

Gabe reached for the coffee can with a slot cut in the lid. The woman protested. 'No, no too... eeh, muchus..."

"Much?"

"Si si si." She smiled and patted his hand and rushed out.

"Now there is a woman I want to give everything to." Gabe looked at Rabbit sitting in the doorway.

Gabe lifted the lid of the kettle and the aroma hit both men. "If I wasn't hungry before, I am now."

The phone on the wall rang. Gabe picked it up. "Hello?"

"Nana heard you like Machaca, so she is making some for dinner. Do you want burritos or tortas?"

Gabe sagged against the counter. "Yolanda, this is too much. She won't take any money, she brings tons of food over..."

The young girl laughed. "Who are you kidding? She highjacks all of the cops that come over. She makes money. It's all good. About dinner, it's my birthday, and so we are coming over for a picnic around your new fire pit."

"I have a fire pit?"

She laughed "Six o'clock. Have the fire going."

Gabe looked at the dead phone. "I guess I have a fire pit."

He walked out the back door followed by Rabbit. They had come in that way, but were so focused on the back door, they hadn't looked deeper in the yard. There was a raised fire pit with an eight-foot wide ring of brick patio all around it. The patio had several heavy-duty chairs that would support an officer and all of their gear. There were even a few wooden Adirondack chairs for lounging on a summer's evening. Rabbit laughed. "Dude, you have a fire pit."

They went over to check it out. As they were looking at the raised pit that was full of sand, two officers walked into the back yard carrying their paperwork.

"What do you think?"

Gabe turned, pointing at the pit. "When did this go in?"

The officers looked at each other. "What, about a week or so ago?"

The one nodded. "But the gas company didn't sign off on it until a few days ago."

Gabe frowned. "Gas? I don't have gas…"

"Sure you do. Your furnace is gas fired, and the new water heater is, too."

"I have a new water heater?"

"Your old one died about a month ago. One of the guys was taking a shower."

"When?"

"It was over one of the weekends... when you were camping up in Big Bear."

Rabbit laughed. "You are so very attentive."

The thin cop snickered and asked, "When did you think was the last time you fed your snake?"

"When she tells me she's hung..." The realization hit him. He hadn't bought any meat for her in months. She was the size that she should be consuming a couple or three full chickens a week.

"She's nothing. I have four snakes of my own. They don't suck down whole chickens... but plenty of mice and such."

"Thanks, guys. Now I really feel like an ass."

"Hey, we all understand. Work can overtake us all sometimes. We're just glad you make the effort to get away on the weekends to that cabin."

Rabbit couldn't resist. "Yeah, Gabe. You should invite everyone up to that cabin some time."

The thin cop held his hands up. "Oh, hell no... I heard there are snakes up there."

"I thought you just said that you have four of your own?"

"I do... but they aren't poisonous or bite."

About an hour later, Gabe got one of the officers to show him about turning on the gas and lighting the fire. One end had a barbecue with separate controls. The guy laughed when Gabe commented that Gertie was going to love it.

Gabe explained by pulling a small steak out of the freezer and grilling it. He fed her the whole steak piece by piece, but rationed the steak sauce. Near the end of the feeding, Yolanda and Nana showed up with sandwiches. Another cop dropped off a bag of marshmallows, chocolate bars and a box of graham crackers.

With their feet up on the rim, and the fire dancing over the sand, Gabe leaned over to Rabbit and quietly confided. "Just like Mexico."

Rabbit harrumphed as his eyes were fixated on the flames, "Just what I was thinking about." He turned and smiled sadly at his partner.

Gabe nudged his arm. "Soon… soon…"

The sky overhead only showed a few stars bright enough to wink through the light of the city. Gabe leaned his head back. His memory of what the sky looks like over the sleepy village of Rosarita filled in the dark areas.

20

THE WORK IS THE WORK

TWO POUNDS IS only ten percent less than a kilogram, but that little percentage is a big thing in the drug trade. Two pounds is thirty-two ounces, about the same as a family size can of raviolis. That can of food doesn't go very far, so that two pounds isn't much. But sometimes, when that two-pound weight is a small chunk of steel with a handle in the middle, it can seem like the world.

Gabe jerked awake to the sound of a strained scream. Gertie, sensing danger, dropped over the edge and slithered for cover under the bed. *Some guard snake she turned out to be.*

Gabe stood naked just inside the dining area as he focused his eyes on the back end of a tight pair of blue nylon running shorts—hovering over a nice set of very long legs.

"Come on, you can do it, Terry. Just give me one more. All the way, honey. Come on, baby.

ANGEL FLIGHTS

You've got this. Almost there…"

The soft voice was seductive, but not enough to overcome the bellowing strain of Rabbit's groaning. The man sounded like he was moving a car all by himself, but Gabe could see the smallest weight in the room.

Gabe looked down and went back into the bedroom to pull some clothes on.

He stood sipping on a mug of coffee as he watched Rabbit get a rubdown on his arms and legs. "How's he doing, Ginger?"

"He has hit twenty curls, three days running, I think if you can find some washers about this size, we could glue a pound of them onto the ends and work him up to the five-pounder." She stood to her full six feet and flexed her lower back by bending back. She had been on the woman's cross-country team for Occidental College ten years before, and still had the stringy muscle mass of that runner. Gabe guessed she must still run a few days a week.

"I'll pick some up."

Gabe focused on his partner. "By the way, asshole… I wasn't going to get up so damn early." He was trying to look serious but the single finger rising from the tiny weight blew that. "Remember we are all going out for Maria's birthday this afternoon. I do hope you have something to wear other than that ratty t-shirt."

"Fuck you… this is my tuxedo you're talking

about."

Even Ginger had to laugh with that one. Gabe hung his head. "Okay, I'll go to a store today." As he turned to get some more coffee, he looked at the cupboards. The doors were closed, even the refrigerator—but he knew they were all full of food, dishes, and anything needed to cook on or eat from—everything was full of stuff he had not shopped for or put there—he hadn't been in any kind of store in a very long time.

As he filled his mug, his eye wandered a couple of feet to the left. *Was the stove new when I moved in?*

He turned at the sound of the back door opening. Two sheriff deputies stood in the doorway. Their arms were full of shopping bags. Gabe didn't recognize either one. His home had become a frat house while he was sleeping. "Good morning, boys."

The redhead stammered. "Are we too early?"

Gabe laughed. He didn't want to know what the secret rules were. "If that's breakfast in those bags, you're right on time."

The two slowly set the bags down.

Gabe attempted to defuse the situation by extending his hand. "Hi, I'm Gabe. You might say I occasionally visit this nut house."

They shook. The redhead, Paul, started trying to find room for the food. The four large cans of coffee he just gave up and stacked on the counter. "We that the living arrangement was changing." He nodded at the larger back door.

Rabbit wheeled through the door followed by Ginger.

"Paul, Pete, this is Mary… er, I mean Rabbit… and his pain mistress, Ginger."

The two deputies almost came to attention with smiles on their faces. Gabe cut them short. "Down, boys. Ginger is attached to a guy that makes even me look tiny."

Ginger sneered, playing along. She looked Gabe up and down, "Very tiny." They all laughed at the jab at Gabe, but the point was taken by the deputies.

As Gabe scrambled a mess of eggs, Paul ran bread through the toaster. "I thought it was a cop who lived here?"

Gabe looked at him. His hair was now flirting with his massive shoulders. The full beard wasn't much shorter. The arms bulged out of the tight t-shirt with a hole down on the side. He didn't feel much like a cop anymore either…

"Oh."

Gabe grabbed some of the money that filled the top drawer of the bureau. *I really need to count this sometime.* Most of the money in the drawer usually went places that were of good use—with December in full roar, he was sure he would pass a few chubby guys in red suits ringing bells. A shirt for Rabbit wouldn't even use a piece of the wad in his hand. For

Gabe and Rabbit, the money in their top drawers was used for other people—to do things—that two tough bikers—could not.

As he reached into the closet to grab his jacket up off the floor, he looked at the three file boxes. It was more of a jogging of the memory—draining large wads of larger bills out of the top drawers and throwing them into the boxes had become more habit than something he thought about. Then there were the large envelopes with stacks of hundreds…

As Gabe walked out the new back door, he looked around the small back yard. Mr. Hirokawa was bent over the line of pink roses. The gentle muttering in Japanese was for the roses' ears only. Gabe stepped back in the door and grabbed the special bag. It was sewn to hold a few dozen fresh cut roses. He stopped at the hose bib and wetted the sponge in the bottom.

The old man looked up and smiled. They bowed and both began cutting roses. Gabe would make a stop at the hospital on his way up to the department store on Colorado Boulevard. The nurses deserved every rose he could pass to them.

After the hospital and shopping, Gabe caught the freeway toward Glendale and the I-5. The traffic was light and he used the open freeway to blow the cobwebs out of his engine as well as his mind. Things had started to get confusing. Doing right—had become complicated. Doing wrong things that enabled him to do right had become too easy. The justification in his mind had become even easier—and none of it sat well. It didn't help that what had started as his personal refuge had become a revolving door of other guys who put on a uniform every day and played by the rules. What he thought of as a frat house mentality was actually those guys also needing a place that was safe for them to have a little peace and quiet. And if that also meant they put in a little work making Gabe's doodles on a napkin into a reality so another cop could have a place to come home—that was the cost. The coffee, food, and maybe a stove... those were extras that helped everyone.

But it didn't bring Gabe peace.

A single yellow Peace Rose was in the bag. Gabe parked in the visitor's parking area. He grabbed the bag off the sissy bar. He stretched as he looked down the length of Mercy Hospital. She wasn't going to be happy with him. But, she wouldn't be alone. He was about to upset a few apple carts, on his way to make applesauce.

The young nurse looked up from the desk. "I think she's in number four."

Gabe nodded. "Anyone in five or six?"

"Six is empty."

He bobbed his head and strolled down the curtained sections. He saw the small plastic number billets that hung down from the ceiling. He stepped into number six and sat down on the stool. He looked out and saw the billet light up. He wasn't sure what he would say, but he needed her to know. He needed her to understand.

Lois looked up at the lit billet and in at the biker slumped sleeping on the stool. Gabe had leaned forward onto the gurney and rested his head on his arms. He was fast asleep. Lois went back to the desk.

"Is he checked in?"

The nurse looked down toward the cubical, and then back at Lois. "No. I just figured he needed to talk to you... why?"

"Because at eleven o'clock in the morning—he is sleeping the sleep of the dead. I just wanted to check that it wasn't more than extreme exhaustion." She thought about just letting him sleep, but they might need the bed.

"Snake? Gabe?" She gently shook his shoulder. He roused—slowly. "What's going on?"

He thought about where he was. His face was furrowed with confusion—and then it cleared. He smiled wanly. "I brought you this." He pulled the rose out of his bag. "It is the first one from my yard. I have twenty-seven bushes, but only one yellow one. The little metal tag on the bush says that it is a Peace rose.

"In the middle ages, a yellow rose that was sent from one king to another was a symbol of friendship and an offering of peace. I need some time. And I want you to know that I will be back, but I can't drive for a little while."

Lois sat down on the gurney and took his hand. "What's going on?"

"I just need to go clear my head for a while. I think I'll go down the inside of Baja and find a little place I can sit with my feet in the sand and watch the sunrise for a while. I'm tired of watching sunsets. In the end, everything turns dark. I think I need some light."

She examined his face and eyes. She could see the pain and exhaustion. "Stay here. I'll be back in a few minutes. Why don't you lie down, I'll turn the light off. We don't need the bed right now, and you need the sleep. I'll come get you in a bit."

He nodded and crawled up onto the bed. He was asleep before she turned off the light. She pulled the curtain anyway.

Gabe sucked on the mug of bad coffee as she unfolded the map. "It's probably easiest if you go out through Riverside and Palm Springs. The crossing at Mexicali is probably a little out of the way, but it's a large crossing."

Her finger drew along a blue line. "But if you take off here, you can cross at Tecate and save about an hour or more. You better fuel up in Tecate. It's a long run down to San Felipe." She pointed on the map. "That is the marine basin for the fishing fleet that works the Sea of Cortez. About a thousand yards further south, right there where I drew the arrow, is Jose and Juanita's place. Just look for a sign that says *No Fish Today*. It's old and faded. Jose's job is to keep you drunk, and Juanita's is to keep poking you and telling you how flacco you are—then feed you until you can't move. The rest is up to you." She folded up the map and handed it to him.

She braced her hand on the side of his face. "I hope you find what it is you are looking for."

He pursed his lips. "It sounds like you have been there yourself."

She knew he wasn't talking about San Felipe. She nodded.

"Did you find what you were looking for?"

She closed one eye and tilted her head as she shrugged the one shoulder. "I thought I had. Things always change."

He nodded and slipped the map into his jacket. She petted the patch of angel wings. "Let these look over you this time."

He stood as he nodded. "I think they will always be with me."

She took his hand for a moment as she stood. Her voice was as soft and distant as the breath of a lover gone in the morning. "Vaya con Dios, amigo."

He smiled, turned, and was gone.

21

HAPPY BIRTHDAY, MARIA

ZORRO LAUGHED AT his niece. She was torn between getting to drive the milk truck and riding on the motorcycle. The motorcycle won out. She leaned into Gabe's back the whole way. Her face rested on his shoulder.

Gabe wasn't so sure that Rabbit was as tender or affectionate with Lincoln in the car seat that was strapped down to the engine cover in the Metro. In fact, Gabe was pretty sure Rabbit was more likely to curl up with Gertie than go near a child. Gabe chuckled quietly.

Maria moved her head to near his ear. "What?"

"I was thinking about Rabbit's face when I suggested he hold Lincoln."

"The man is very afraid of children." She poked him in the ribs. "Don't make fun of him. Kids are scary animals. They look human but don't act like us. They are just mono until... well, with you and

Rabbit, you are still monkeys. But you know how I mean."

Gabe liked the way she mixed Spanish in her sentences without knowing it. She worked hard at not having the stigmatizing speech of the neighborhood she grew up in. She worked hard at keeping her Spanish as well as her English correct. But at times, she stirred things up, and Gabe liked the sound of the stew it made.

Koreatown is a very small area of LA but services a largely hidden population. There were probably more Koreans in Glendale-Burbank area than there were in or around Koreatown. But this was the place—if you wanted the food. If you wanted the real food, then you had to know the alleyways and side streets. Both Gabe and Zorro knew them all. They also knew which to avoid, or which were little more than a front for the casino in the back or the girls upstairs. *Slots and sluts were not just a Korean business.*

What had been a somewhat noisy restaurant when they opened the door became very quiet as they filed in. Gabe leaned forward to Lito's ear. "Dude, I think you scared them." Maria kicked him in the leg.

As a waiter walked past, purposefully ignoring them, Gabe got his attention. "Yaba sayo?"

The man froze and looked at him. Zorro stepped in and quietly asked to speak to Mr. Oh. When the guy remained in front of him, he flashed his badge and said that he was investigating a death where the person had been poisoned by the cook. His voice carried. Seconds later, a man in a starched white shirt came out of the back.

"May I help you?"

Zorro showed his badge. "Either I investigate your cook for poisoning the county health inspector, or we can get a table so we can celebrate my favorite niece's birthday." The man withered under Zorro's glare.

"Of course, right this way." He started toward the back corner near the bathrooms until Rabbit rammed his chair in between two chairs—upsetting the settings and centerpieces on both large tables.

"Damn. I don't fit." Rabbit's voice was loud and full of gravel. "You guys go ahead and eat here, I saw a taco stand about three or five blocks back." He waved at them and backed up. "Go ahead, baby. You can party without your father. I'll be fine."

The owner of the restaurant was mortified. He had wanted to hide the foreigners quietly in the back corner near the bathrooms. Now, if he did not accommodate the man in the wheelchair, he would be shamed. He changed to the large table in the middle—the one with the beautiful flower arrangement in the middle. The one with the little sign that Gabe was certain said *reserved*.

"Maybe this table would be a better table." He

ANGEL FLIGHTS

removed a chair, and then after looking at the size of Rabbit, took out another.

Rabbit's face lit up like an alcoholic on a drinking cruise. "Oh, this will be just perfect." He rolled right up to the table and looked at everyone else. His smile was beaming.

Maria completed the scene as she started to sit. She kissed Rabbit on the top of the head. Turning to Mr. Oh, she sweetly asked, "Do you have a bib for my father? Since he got hit in the head, he has eaten a little messy."

Lito sat quietly with his head lowered. "All of you are embarrassing." He actually held the pose for half a minute—before he started shaking as he quietly laughed.

The dinner was going to be a disaster from the first plate. But Maria took matters in hand. She wiggled her finger at Mr. Oh.

"Yes, miss?"

"Is your cook from Cleveland, Ohio?"

"No, miss. He is from small village in south—in Korea. He is my sister's brother-in-law. What is wrong, miss?"

"Well, we are Mexican. My baby there is just over two years old. His father has been feeding him the hottest peppers I can find—almost all of his life. If his food isn't close to that, he screams and cries and makes a terrible fuss." She put her hand out on the man's shoulder. She nodded at Gabe with Lincoln on his lap.

She lowered her voice and turned her face in toward the man. "Not my baby, but his father—the big guy."

Mr. Oh stood. "I thought you say he is your father…" He realized that he was in the middle of a lot of people who came to eat real Korean food and enjoy themselves. He was out of his league. He left to get the backup pitcher.

The young girl was still in her school uniform. She was about the same age as Maria. "My father asked me to wait on you. He thinks that he doesn't understand."

Maria took a fresh fork and held it up to the girl. "Try the beef."

"What is wrong with it?"

"Please. Try it."

The girl took a bite. She chewed and her hip slowly slid into the attitude of a normal teenager. "Tastes like something the Rotary Club would eat." She picked it up and left.

Seconds later, she was back with a small bowl of kimchee and a fork. She held the fork up to Maria. Maria chewed. Her eyes were locked on the girl. "Better, but not what we came for."

The girl smiled. "My name is Anna. That was the stuff my brother made this morning. It tastes like catsup on white toast."

Maria laughed. "Bingo."

ANGEL FLIGHTS

Anna took the bowl and fork and placed it on another table. "Now we can serve you real food." She smiled at Maria. "How old are you?"

"Seventeen, yesterday—this is my birthday party."

"I turned sixteen last month. I don't know what you ordered, but that isn't what you will be eating." She turned with a smile and almost danced into the kitchen as she sang a song of rapid-fire words and commands. Seconds later, they saw first one then another head peek out of the kitchen at them.

The heat was very different from Mexican food. Everyone had to fan themselves at one time or another. The sinuses were clear and sweat glands were running overtime. The only one who seemed unaffected was Lincoln. He didn't care who was feeding him or whose lap he was sitting on. He was passed not only from Gabe to his mother and great uncle, but even Anna and Mr. Oh had taken a turn. They were both fascinated by feeding hot food to a small child.

Anna sat softly bouncing the little man on her knee. Gabe smiled his lopsided smile. "I wonder how many cultures bounce babies on their knees."

Mr. Oh laughed. "If you were really the father, you would not ask that question. Every father, every mother, every *anyone* who live with baby—uses knee. It keeps the…" He turned to his daughter and rattled off some Korean.

She smirked and rolled her eyes. "It keeps the spit-up away from the shirt." She fanned her hand at her father's shirt as if to hit him. "I did not spit-up on your best shirt. I was a perfect child. It is your son who is the one who does those awful things."

"This is not the proper thing to talk about at dinner table." He reached his hands out. "Now, give me my new manager. We need to talk business."

Gabe watched the interplay of Maria, Anna, Zorro, and Mr. Oh. Lincoln was the binding force that had brought them together and opened up the two cultures to just be friends. The rest of the restaurant was empty. The kitchen staff was sitting where they would have been, eating their late dinner.

Gabe leaned over toward Lito. "What are you doing for the Christmas break?"

"Hanging around the house, I guess."

"How would you like to freeze your ass on a motorcycle and go to San Felipe?"

"What's there?"

"You and me... and some books."

Lito turned his head. "What kind of books?"

"The ones I need to know to finish the last few courses to get my BA."

The kid looked at Maria and Zorro. Gabe thought he could almost smell the burning gears in the kid's mind.

Quietly, the kid did his best imitation of his uncle's deep rumble. "What's really going on?"

ANGEL FLIGHTS

Gabe leaned back and closer. "Well, I thought I'd get you drunk a few times, get you laid a few times and get my lawyer's degree."

The kid blinked a few times. "Can we get some lobster too?"

"We would have to go over to Rosarita Beach for that."

"Okay."

Gabe chuckled softly. *Yeah, why not both?*

22

MEXICO TO STUDY

LITO WIGGLED HIS toes in the sun. The rest of him was in the shade of the cabana. The two cots got moved with the cause of whim. Shade, sun, or stars—Lito had never felt so in control and free before.

They had arrived in San Felipe just before sundown. They had thrown their few things in the cabana, which was little more than a roof and two walls, a few paces from the calm water of the Sea of Cortez. They had ridden back into town to find a restaurant—the last time they moved from the cabana or beach.

The lights from the few signs, and then the light from the chopper's headlight had bound Lito's sight from looking up.

Gabe knew the boy had never been in the desert and, therefore, hadn't really seen the night sky. He had Lito stay in the cabana with his eyes closed while he dragged the beds out onto the sand at the sea's edge.

Guiding the boy with closed eyes, he had him lay down. When he opened his eyes, his world exploded. Gabe was pretty sure the boy hadn't slept a wink all night.

The next day, he never woke up until nearly sundown. They finally started talking over the burritos that Juanita had made. Gabe laughed as the kid tried his first beer.

A few minutes later, Jose returned and held out two bottles of soda—both glass bottles were frosted with years of rebottling. Lito looked at first the Pepsi, and then the orange—he couldn't decide. Jose laughed and laid both down in the kid's lap. The beer he passed over to Gabe.

Drinking warm beer is something Americans find hard to do. The rest of the world simply drinks and wonders what the big deal is about ice.

"How long do we get to stay here?"

Gabe rolled over. Moving the bookmark to his place, he laid it on the hard packed floor. He sat up and looked out at the sea. The water was little more than a giant blue mirror. In the distance was a thin line of darker blue-gray haze that Gabe guessed were mountains—although he didn't remember seeing any on the map.

He turned and looked at the kid who squinted at him with one eye closed. "Depends—what day is it?"

Lito closed his one eye and thought. "Tuesday."

Gabe looked at his watch. "If we can pack in the next ten minutes, we would be just in time for sunset and lobster."

The kid laughed in a high giggle. The only thing for them to pack was a t-shirt rolled in a blanket each. Gabe had enjoyed the child side of the kid that he knew was a lot smarter than he was.

Gabe got up and put the textbook on the stack of six others. A couple of days in Rosarita and they would be back. The books wouldn't move. Nobody else would think to pick up a textbook when they were in San Felipe.

The easiest way for Gabe was to go back to Tijuana, and then down along the cliff to the beach. As they were lazily riding within the speed limit, another motorcycle approached from behind. Out of the corner of Gabe's eye, the large red-skinned Indian chief looked familiar. He smiled as Mike and his wife came alongside.

Gabe made the sign of an L with his thumb and finger and then acted as if he were eating with the thumb pointed at his open mouth. Mike laughed and nodded his left hand as his wife pointed at her boots and waved her gloves. She held up her pinky to her chest, then crossed her arms and ended pointing at Gabe.

Gabe laughed and nodded. Lito leaned forward. "Are they deaf?"

ANGEL FLIGHTS

Gabe laughed and nodded. "Evidently, we all got a hunger for lobster and a sunset. They are friends of mine. Mike is deaf, but his wife can hear."

As they got off the choppers in front of the cabana, the woman didn't take her time to come over and give Gabe a long hug. She finally pulled his head down where she could reach his forehead and gave him a kiss. "The kiss is for being an Angel. The hug is for my feet sloshing around in hot water right now."

She turned to Lito. "Is this your son?"

Gabe laughed as Lito blushed. "This is Lito. He is my tutor so I can finish college."

She stuck her hand out as she realized Gabe didn't know her name. "Hi, I'm Regina, but you can call me Rog—just like in Roger."

Lito bowed as he shook her hand. "Mucho gusto, Senora Rog."

She clapped her hands and laughed. "Oh good… an interpreter."

Lito stepped in and with a loud conspiratorial whisper, "I'll teach you Spanish if you teach me the signs of the deaf."

She reached out and threw her arm over his head—hauling his face into her chest as they turned to cross the street. She looked at Gabe. "Can I adopt him?"

Gabe shrugged. "Why not, I did. He even comes with a great sister with a little boy that will keep you laughing."

The tubs were empty, and the fire was smoldering down to coals. The four sat on the rustic chairs with their bare feet on the large rocks and bricks that ringed the pit. The dim light of the village only obscured the mass of the Milky Way by a fraction.

Regina sat watching the kid, whose head was back as he looked straight up. "Is this the first time you have really seen the stars?"

Gabe snorted that Lito only looked like he was awake. "I brought him down to San Felipe a few days ago. He didn't sleep the first night. I had dragged the bed out onto the sand. He was still awake when the sun came up."

Gabe watched as her face was toward him, but her hands were signing for Mike.

The familiar high-pitched voice was soft. "I remember when my father brought me down here for the first time. I probably didn't sleep much either. San Felipe is nice for stars—but nothing else."

Gabe saw the finger make the question mark.

He nodded toward the sleeping genius. "We don't know what his IQ is, but it's high enough that this last summer, he challenged every class for the four years of high school. The worst he scored on any of the tests was a B. He's over at City College for now, but by June, he will be done and ready to move maybe to UCLA. That is what we are doing here—cramming—me. I have twenty units left for my BA. Then I want to apply to law school. We are hoping I can get into UCLA, so we can be close." He wagged his hand back and forth between him and the kid.

Mike watched the fingers, and then sat back. He grabbed softly at his pursed lips. "I know a few people. What does he want to do with that brain?"

"He wants to be a doctor. A surgeon to be more precise—a nervous head cutter."

The small voice floated from the unmoving head. "Cerebral Neuropathology, repairing the neuron pathways in the brain from perceptual impairment." The kid sat up and looked at Gabe. "Just because I was snoring—a bit, doesn't mean I wasn't listening."

He stood, nodded a goodnight to the other two, and stumbled off to find a cot under the large cabana.

Regina blinked and looked at Gabe. "Does he do that kind of thing much?"

"Talk scary stuff?" Gabe chuckled silently as he nodded and watched the kid stumble then fall onto what Gabe hoped was a cot.

He looked back at the woman. "We've been going over textbooks. I've been cramming, and he has been sleeping the sleep of the dead. But I'll read something—like part of a paragraph out loud and he won't even open his eyes—and start telling me something like—and it goes on to explain that while that is the mythos, the basis is more obscure and oblique... dah dah dah."

Gabe's eyes were scary wide. "That is when I know he has already read these books. Books that I just bought at the UCLA student bookstore that matched the classes I needed."

The two looked over at the loud snoring snort on the other side of her. She smiled. "I think we could all use some sleep." She poked Mike as she stood. "I'll see you three in the morning." She patted the man's foot, and then leaned over and gave him a smooch.

Gabe frowned. "Aren't you staying here?"

She pointed at Mike. "He is. He helped build this cabana. But a girl needs her morning time... and a real bathroom. I stay in the apartment."

"What apartment?"

She realized that he didn't know.

"Over the restaurant—we own all of this. Well, we and the federal government—as much as anyone else owns any land in Mexico. This belonged to my parents. It was all part of the Rancho. That is how we, well, Mike, got involved with the angel flights. My uncle owned the hacienda."

She held out her hand and Mike took it and she pulled. He snuggled into her shoulder still half asleep.

Gabe snorted. "I'll make sure he gets to a cot with a blanket on him."

"Thanks. We'll talk in the morning before we

head back. Pedro is doing up lobster omelets. Goodnight." She turned and was gone—crossing the street.

Gabe hauled on his friend. "Come on, Mike, bedtime."

It didn't matter that the man couldn't hear him—some things are just all physical.

23

NO, WHAT ARE YOU REALLY DOING

GABE STRETCHED OUT his long legs beside the table. Rog stretched out on the other side of the small table as they talked and both watched Mike teach Lito a lot more than just the alphabet.

"He really is that smart."

Gabe snorted softly. "You have no idea. Once we get him into UCLA, I think his goal is to challenge half of the course material on his way to medical school."

"And he is really only fourteen?" She looked over at Gabe.

He nodded. "Fourteen and very scary." Frowning, he watched the boy's signs. They were almost fluid and he was making many that Gabe hadn't learned yet. He leaned over toward Regina. "What are they talking about now?"

She gave him a hard look. "You know it's impolite to eavesdrop."

ANGEL FLIGHTS

He gave her a deadpan look.

"Mike is explaining how we know you and the weekends."

"Oh, shit."

"Oh, shit is right. That kid is already steady with the signing and with what you Angels do. That kid is a lot older than his age."

Gabe sat up and leaned on the table as he stared into his empty mug. "I think that kid did a lot of growing up long before he was supposed to still be a kid. He was only twelve when his sister was raped. Then she was pregnant and now has the cutest kid in the world—which made him an uncle at thirteen. That's a lot for a kid to take in—but you couldn't ask for a better uncle."

Gabe leaned back and held up his mug so the waitress could see. "I think the scary stuff hasn't even happened yet. He challenged the entire four years of high school courses this last summer. If they were to attach a grade to it, he still scored the Honor Society. All he cared about was getting it out of the way so he could start working on college.

"I think the really scary stuff will come when he learns that the cap is off, and he can run as fast as he wants. It's going to take a college with strong intestinal fortitude to keep up with him."

Regina pushed her mug over to get it filled, as well. She looked up at her niece and smiled. Turning toward Gabe as she sipped on the fresh coffee, she glanced over at the topic of their conversation. "What does he really want to do?"

"Just like he said last night—a doctor... seriously... well, actually a surgeon. He wants to do neurosurgery for brain damage or fix things that are wrong in the brain. If you want to know what it really is—ask him, because it's all Greek to me."

She smiled on only one side. "I think that would be more Roman than Greek—Latin to be exact." She sat up and hunched in. "You're right. At thirteen, how does a kid even know about that kind of thing?"

Gabe smiled. "It's how the kid is wired up." He looked at her. "You know how they say you only use maybe a tenth of your mind?" She nodded, and he nodded at the other two. "Have you ever seen anyone learn that much sign language in a couple of hours? That kid is burning up at least half his mind right now. He is completely focused on getting his communication perfect with Mike. Even Mike has stopped speaking out loud."

She frowned and turned her head and watched the conversation. "I hadn't even noticed that. He only does that with me." She watched the conversation as it flowed back and forth. "If I didn't know better, I would say that Lito was deaf from birth, and was raised in a deaf family." She ground her head around with a look of shock. "He is that good."

Gabe raised his eyebrows and smiled. "I told you—scary."

ANGEL FLIGHTS

"And he has applied to UCLA?"

"We both have. I have a few classes left on my BA, and then I want to get my law degree."

She pursed her lips and softly pinched them by stroking them with her fingers. "We know a few people. We'll help."

"I'd appreciate that."

Mike and Regina headed north mid-morning. Gabe and Lito went up to the little cove where nobody cared if you didn't have swim trunks, and they played in the surf. The soak and the sun was the relaxation that Gabe needed. It helped to watch Lito act like a kid, as he tried to bodysurf on the shallow waves.

After a lunch of lobster and clams, they had returned to San Felipe. The long day took its toll and they turned in early. The dark was just starting to turn to black when Gabe heard Lito drag his cot out onto the sand. The idea was appealing, and Gabe followed suit.

The stars were washed across the sky, and Gabe could feel that young kid had something on his mind. In the starlight, he could see the small head moving softly from one constellation to another.

"Why aren't you going to do that Angel thing tomorrow?"

Gabe thought about the time, and where they

were. There might be a letter sitting on one or both of their kitchen tables—from UCLA. There might be a girl that Gabe would have been the right Angel for…

He looked at the belt on Orion as his eyelids closed. There was no real explanation. "Because—I'm here with you—in Mexico."

"But what you guys do—it is important."

"And some weeks there are more bikers than needed."

"And if they don't have enough?"

"Then, I guess the girl comes back the next week."

"But us being here is more important?"

Gabe rolled over and looked at the small dark shape in the dark. Only the starlight created a slim glow of liming on the boy. "It is to me."

Lito rolled over and Gabe assumed he was looking at him. "Studying?"

"That… and spending time with you."

"That's important?"

Gabe thought about how to explain the importance of friendships and family.

"Right now, your life is traveling at only a hundred miles an hour. When you start college, it will start breaking the sound barrier—the days will slip into months, and then years. You will think you took time to hold Lincoln, come to Mexico with me, or have lunch with your uncle—but they will know that it has been months if not years.

"So, for right now... laying on the sand and studying, eating lobster and hanging out in the sunshine is the most important thing that either one of us can be doing. If you hadn't done it, you wouldn't know how. Soon enough, this kind of time will be some of the most important time you can spend."

"With you..."

"No, you little pendejo... with anyone—with your sister and Lincoln. Maybe get your uncle to bring you down. It is the quiet times which you spend with other people that are the most important times in your life.

"Someday, after you have become a doctor, there might be a cute nurse you will want to spend some quiet time with. This is where you bring her. If she can't get into this—sleeping under the stars—then she's not the right one."

The kid snickered.

Gabe growled. "I didn't say now, asshole. I said after you become a doctor, like when you're maybe eighteen or something."

They both rolled onto their backs as they softly chuckled at something that was all too possible. A shooting star raced across toward the south.

Lito's voice was soft and sleepy. "There sure are a lot more stars than I thought there were."

A little later, Gabe thought the kid had drifted off.

"Gabe?"

"Yeah, kid?"

"Thanks for bringing me down here."

Gabe smiled. "I wouldn't have had it any other way, kid. I wouldn't have it any other way."

24

BACK TO WORK

THE MONSOON SEASON began in earnest, and the milk truck got used more and more. Mostly to make lunch runs up to Chet's, but when an engine starts to make funny knocking sounds, the milk truck was the tool to take the bike to Roscoe.

Roscoe looked at Rabbit with his walker. "I think I have an old Brigs & Stratton engine around here that we could rig up to that…"

Rabbit smirked. "Save it, Roscoe. All the cops and Gabe have reamed me with every joke left." He parked the walker against the one wall of the large garage. "I just brought that over for when you're ready for it." His walk wasn't the best, but he was at least walking without assistance. Gabe and he had agreed not to mention the cane in the truck.

"Well, it's good to see you back up this fast." Roscoe slung his leg over the bike and hit the starter. The moment the engine caught and started to run, he turned it off. Bending forward, he looked at the odometer. He leaned back thinking. "Those are some very long and hard miles on her."

Gabe shrugged. "I gotta work."

"It looks like you stuck about two to three-hundred miles a day on her. If I remember right, that speedo came straight out of the box. So those miles are yours. We went through the top end last spring, but this...? She's done. That tinkle is valve-seating problems, but that hum-bump is all bottom-end. I don't think I would even try to save anything out of the gear box."

"But she hardly leaks at all."

"That's because when I built her for Maddie to race, I used silicone caulk instead of the stupid Harley gasket kit. I goo the one side, and then lay a shopping bag onto it. After I smooth it out with my thumb, I trim the paper. Then I goo the other side, and put it together. The paper is the part that comes apart when you need it. But even if it starts to leak, you know it's toast and time to rebuild it. You might know that... if you ever came around enough."

The man threw a rag at Gabe. He pointed at the door to the house and growled. "Honey is in there more weeks than not—crying her eyes out because you never come by and eat her cooking. She's starting to give up and just make me cold gruel and hardtack for meals."

The man was almost yelling.

The door opened quietly, and Honey put her finger to her lips. There was a frying pan in her other hand. As she snuck up on her husband, she smacked him on the butt. Ignoring him, she stepped past him and smiled sweetly. "You two can come in now for apple pie and coffee."

She turned and glared at Roscoe, who was still holding his back pockets. "I'll set your gruel out with the dogs."

They were still laughing when the pie was gone and the coffee was on its second time around.

"I bought a CHP bike last week at the auction. I got it cheap because it had a *noise* in the top end. Funny what a twenty, two tickets to UCLA against USC, and a ping-pong ball in the rocker covers can do to the price. I stepped in at two hundred. Some kid offered three and I added a buck. He knew I was going to buck him until he stopped—so he dropped out on that three."

"You bought a perfectly good Panhead for three hundred?"

"No, I bought a perfectly good Shovelhead that has twenty-eight thousand freeway miles on it—for three-oh-one and the taxes." His smile was hiding a very large canary. He had set them up.

"It has fewer than thirty on it... what happened?"

"It got hit. But you didn't plan on using a stock set of front forks anyway. We can slip that springer on to a new frame and you're good to go. Except now, you have a fresh engine and a soft tail."

Rabbit frowned. "What about me? Mine has some long miles too…"

Roscoe looked at him with a stern daddy look. "You get a '65 Panhead. You're older school, so we're going to use Gabe's frame to keep the profile lower, but I want to stretch it about two inches, to enlarge the oil tank and hide a small radiator to keep it cooler. I can cool Gabe's shovel but getting some new jugs turned with thinner wider roughcast fins. I was thinking about squaring the engine at about ninety-six inches for both of you. They will be high powered, but being square and balanced, they will also run better and longer."

Rabbit was feeling antsy. "About how long?"

"They haven't delivered the bikes to me yet, but I've gone ahead and ordered the parts that I'll need. So I figure about May… so you two need to start thinking about the paint and how big of a gas tank."

The two men didn't have to look at each other to know what was on both of their minds. "The bigger the tank, the better," they voiced in unison.

Roscoe nodded. He had figured as much. He handed Gabe a piece of paper.

"Go see this guy. He has been doing some trick stuff with tanks and frames. He's using a micro-wire on the tanks, which makes a cleaner weld. Who knows—maybe this Littlejohn guy can make you two a pair of slab-tops that hold eight gallons or so."

Rabbit's head rolled over his shoulder as he smiled at Gabe.

LA to Mexico on a single tank of gas.

As the two left in the milk truck, Gabe looked at his watch and then the address. "Let's go do Sylmar after we drop in on this guy. The Fat Man won't care what hour we show up, but we might just catch this guy in his shop."

Later, Rabbit kept turning the raw steel tank over and over in his hands as Gabe drove. "That is amazing. It's the same tunnel, but only an extra couple of inches in stretch and width and we get eight plus gallons. If this guy keeps it up, he's going to make some serious money."

"Speaking of which..."

Rabbit looked back at the two soft-side wide-mouthed duffle bags. They were the same size as a doctor's leather wide-mouth bag, but each of these held twenty kilos of methadrine each. It didn't escape Rabbit that during his absence, Gabe had *grown* the business substantially.

"Yeah, I've been thinking about that. The bikes are one thing—but this old milker is as obvious as a horny bull at a Jewish wedding. I think we need something a little less conspicuous while we are down a bike or two."

"I tried to rent a car the other day, but they required a credit card. I didn't want to leave that kind of paper trail... just in case."

"Who said anything about renting?"

Gabe looked at his partner. He rarely ever thought about the drawer and the wads of bills in it. "What do you think we ought to buy?"

Rabbit leaned back against the door as he watched most of the freeway full of cars whiz by the old slow delivery truck.

"First off, I want something that is fast—very fast. Second, it needs to be able to blend in, something people won't think twice at seeing."

Gabe smiled. "Are you thinking we need to call Roscoe's friend about getting a moonshine runner?"

Rabbit smiled as he shrugged and rolled his eyes. "It does fit the bill..."

That night, Roscoe and Honey both snorted with laughter. Honey hugged Gabe's shoulders as she stood over him pouring him more coffee. "You don't need a moonshine car. You just need a fast Plain Jane. Heck, Mr. Mopar can find you that. He probably even has one stashed somewhere."

Gabe looked at Roscoe.

The man nodded and reached back and grabbed the big black phone off the counter. He dialed from memory. After a minute, there was an answer. "I heard that Ford just bought Dodge and plans to part it out and make Volkswagens."

The all could hear the laughter from the other end of the phone line. Gabe liked this guy already.

BAER CHARLTON

Roscoe listened to some pissing on the side of the barn that seemed to be the usual with whoever he had called. At one point, he quietly put the phone handset down on the table as he turned around and gathered up some scratch paper and a pencil.

He leaned close to the mouthpiece and mumbled, "Sounds good, Dave." He straightened up and smiled as he silently laughed. Finally, he picked up the handset and put it to his ear.

"Listen, Dave... Dave? Listen, I have a guy who is bleeding, and we need to get him to the hospital soon. We don't want to draw attention—so a Goat, Cuda, or Challenger is out. But we need that speed. They also don't want to go the route of a shaker hood. So some kind of grand old lady car—but will whip asses on Colorado Boulevard any Saturday night."

He listened with a few, verbal nods and encouraging *sounds good*. He wrote down 1964 Belvedere, 4-door, radio delete. He underlined the 383 Hemi and positive traction rear end.

"They're nodding, Dave. Do you have your hands on it now?" He nodded. "That's probably out of their price range, but can you drive it by tonight?" He nodded. "Okay, we'll see you in about twenty. I'll let them know." He hung up.

Rabbit was first. "Out of our price range? How much does he want?"

Roscoe's face went blank as he shrugged. "He

didn't say."

Gabe was used to Roscoe. "But you have a good idea how much."

"What he asks for, what he wants, and what he is willing to take for it are probably twenty different prices. Do you want to offer him two grand, and find him towing a piece-of-shit wreck over here? Or do you want to go for a ride that curls your hair, wets your seat, and makes your eyeballs flatten somewhere back behind your ears—and then start the bidding?"

Honey slapped Roscoe along the shoulders. "David has never driven or sold a piece of junk to any of your friends. Dream cars—maybe, but POS's—never."

The car was just as advertised. As it slid to the curb, Gabe and Rabbit thought it was someone going to see a neighbor. But when the big guy with a mass of short curly black hair entered the gate and the dogs barely looked up—they knew this must be Dave. Honey went to the door to let him in and get her hug.

Five minutes later, Roscoe was in the back seat with Rabbit as he poked Gabe in the shoulder. "Go ahead, son. Take the wheel and try her out. You know you have to buy her now. I don't even have to check to know that the last swirly-do down the street got your wood buzzing."

Gabe turned in the seat and looked behind him.

"Do you talk like that with Honey in the car?"

"Who do you think taught me to talk that way? Now grow a pair of balls and try out the pedal."

Dave had pulled up alongside one of the new Camaros on Mission Boulevard—the 327, painted large on the side of the Chevy, looked impressive. Dave let the guy get half a car length ahead across three of the four lanes of the intersection.

The old granny car's back bumper crossed the second line of the crosswalk before the front bumper of the Camaro was halfway through the crosswalk. He nosed the large car into a parking lot as he looked over at Gabe.

"I think she'll do better if you get her a tune-up. I would have, but I've been kind of busy lately."

Twenty more minutes of fun and they were dropping Dave off at his house on the hill. Gabe counted out most of the small folded wad from his front pocket. The large wad in his back pocket wasn't needed.

After talking to Roscoe about what they would have bought up north, both wads would have only been a healthy down payment. Custom-built moonshine cars were as expensive as real racing cars.

As they drove home later, Rabbit eased the car right at the Korean market at the top of their street.

He glanced over at Gabe who was half-asleep. "Let's not get it tuned up for a few weeks."

They both knew the car would be three doors

down within the week. The kid was a wizard in auto shop, and his dad wasn't a bad shade-tree mechanic himself. All it took was the kid to mention that the high school's auto shop had a dyno-tune installed the previous year.

25

SHUTTING THE FAT MAN DOWN

THE LONG GREEN was busy. Both cooks were drawing coffee and ordering food from each other. The larger one glared at Rabbit and Gabe as he set down their second coffee refill. The small restaurant relied on a fast turnover of the morning and lunch clientele. The man leaned in and nodded his head at the workmen standing at the door waiting.

Gabe pulled his hand from his pocket and slid a twenty across the counter. The beefy hand covered the bill and it disappeared in his front pocket. "Your two breakfasts still come to four-twenty." He stood and returned to his grill.

Gabe flipped the paper over and went back to explaining the new breakdown of the meth they were getting from the Fat Man. "When Ramparts had that shoot-out with those guys at the bank, they didn't realize the getaway driver was the big mover in the valley mouth. So all of a sudden, we were double over last fall. Then there was the surf gang who skegged the Barney at Redondo and we filled the gap."

Rabbit frowned. "Skegged a Barney? Who are you and what did you do with my partner?"

"You have no idea, dude. Things are mercurial and you have to pick this shit up really fast or you are like so last year, dude." Gabe laughed.

"Okay, so what now?"

"I think come June, we take out the Fat Man, and then the whole house of cards comes tumbling down for the big sleep."

"With what we picked up just last week, you're talking about well over a few million hits. Even with the city that never sleeps, that has to be an excess."

Gabe looked up and then grabbed his coffee and slurped the last large gulp. He slid down a five and a single and grabbed at Rabbit's shoulder. "Time to go."

A mile down the San Fernando road, Rabbit drew closer alongside as the engines loafed in third gear. Roscoe had been right—the large engines didn't seem to work hard, even though the gearing was skewed towards a faster top-end.

"What was that back there?"

"There was a guy in there that I've seen before. I figured it out. I've seen him on the circuit and a few other places we go. About a month ago, he was at the far end of the bar at Chet's and when I walked in, he left by the back door. I don't know who he is, but being at the Long Green was just too much of a coincidence."

"What's he ride?"

"A car."

"Let me guess... it's black."

"Nope, white." *The car color of choice for federal undercover.*

"Shit."

"That's what I said."

"Let's go talk to Chet."

They downshifted and roared up the on-ramp onto the southbound Golden State Freeway.

Chet flipped the towel over his shoulder. "I don't know him, guys. He started coming in here about a month or so ago. He orders a draft and almost doesn't touch it. I thought it was strange the other day when he ducked out the back while you were coming in the front." He leaned into the bar with his arms spread out and his hands holding backwards. "If I was still on the force, I'd figure out where to lure him in and stand the guy up."

Gabe looked at Rabbit and they both nodded. They knew the perfect place—a late lunch up the hill.

Chet didn't want to know. "How's school going?"

Gabe laughed. "For which student?"

Chet held his finger up and walked away down

the bar. "Get you another there, Frank... Whit?" The two older men shook their heads. Chet picked up a mug and the carafe on the way back.

"Let's start with the kid. Is it true he blew out the entire high school curriculum in just two weeks?"

Rabbit smiled as he adjusted around to face Gabe. He hadn't heard the full story on the kid.

"What two weeks? He took all the tests they could throw at him in six days. It was the two papers that took another three days. To slow him down, they made him type them in the school library. Two nights before, he checked out a book on touch-typing and then practiced at the county library the next afternoon and night. So he was handwriting the first day and typing the second. The kid now types faster than I do—and I'm pretty fast."

He sipped his coffee as he looked at Rabbit and they both snickered.

"What?" Chet knew he just had to ask to be read in on the joke.

Rabbit snorted. "Gabe left the paper he was working on for one of the classes up at Dos Palmas. Maria passed it to Lito, and he not only typed it, but also added all the notations, footnotes, and bibliographies that Gabe hadn't done yet. Gabe was freaking out because he couldn't remember where he had put the thing. When he remembered, they were closed. That Thursday at class, the teacher passed the papers back. Lito had turned it in for him."

Chet chuckled. "What did you get?"

Gabe started laughing and couldn't tell him. He spilled some coffee and wrote the A on the bar.

Finally, they settled down. "So when's he doing his own work…?"

"He's already lined up about a hundred units he wants to challenge. Evidently, the teachers don't like it and pull out like three final exams, and he has the standard time of one test to take all three. He's checking out books right and left, and he keeps doing that evil little laugh of his as he slaps another book closed."

"And how are your studies going?"

"It's not easy getting back in the saddle, but I'm settling in. I spoke to the dean over at the law school, and he said he already had my seat ready for summer session."

Chet frowned. "When did you apply?"

Rabbit closed his eyes as he rolled his eyebrows and head. "That's the point—he didn't."

Gabe looked at Chet through the top of his eyes. "It seems a lot like getting a job as a cop. Evidently, I know someone."

"More like someone knows you."

"That's the other thing. The other day, when Lito and I were in the administration building, one of the admitting gals I've been talking to asked Lito if he was going to sit his MSAT this June."

"But he just started college."

ANGEL FLIGHTS

The two bikers nodded. "Uh-huh, like that ever mattered...?"

Chet leaned back against the back bar. "Oh, Lord... What have we started?"

"Like I said the other day... once you put him in the line, there is nothing in place to throttle him back. Everyone else just has to hold on tight because it's going to be a fast ride."

Chet snorted. "I can see it now. I go in for a rectal exam, and the doc with his finger up my butt still doesn't have hair on his balls yet."

Gabe snorted. "Oh, I can tell you right now he has plenty of hair, and they are stainless steel to go with the big pair that never flinched in Mexico."

Both men gave Gabe that special look.

He held up his hands. "Hey, back off. I'm not that kind of guy. But we were on the beach and these two guys about maybe eighteen or so tried to stick us up. Lito rose up on his elbows and asked the guys in Spanish if they recognized the son of El Presidente... They didn't. He then calmly explained that for every person they could see, there were ten with long range sniper rifles trained on them."

"Yeah, that is some balls. What did they do?"

"They moved on. Lito didn't say any more. He just lay back down and went back to sleep. Not eventually, but like right away."

Rabbit shook his head. "That kid is super smart, too. Did you know he speaks that sign language stuff

Deaf Mike does?"

Gabe looked at him with a dry snort. "On the Monday that we rode down, he didn't know even the sign for a single letter—much less words. On Wednesday, we were bored with San Felipe and rode over to Rosey. On the way, we ran into Mike and his wife Regina. By that night, the kid knew the alphabet and about a hundred words. He spent the morning with Mike, and in the afternoon when they left, Regina said he was almost good enough to interpret a speech. Regina gave me a name in Pasadena. The woman teaches extension classes for PCC. I'm going to take the classes, but I think we might just get her to tutor Lito. I can't keep up with him, but I'm pretty sure he will also be up to teaching Maria, Lincoln, and me as we come along."

Chet shifted. "Why would he want to learn how to talk sign language?"

Gabe put down his mug. "Why would he want to challenge all of the classes for high school? It's the challenge and knowledge. The kid is a sponge, and he's soaking up every bit of information he can find. Besides, it's pretty cool to speak a language that has no sound."

Gabe looked down the bar as a man slid in through the far door. The new choppers hadn't tipped him off as to who was in the bar. Gabe laid his head down before the guy's eyes adjusted to the bar and Rabbit got up and walked out the door. Chet caught the two actions as he pushed off the back bar and turned down the bar. He flipped the towel over his left shoulder.

"What can I get you?"

"Draft." The man slid a couple of bucks across the bar.

Chet poured the beer and cleared his throat. He was between Gabe and the man—blocking the line of sight. As he put the beer down on a coaster, he slid his hand across the bar and snatched up the two bucks for the fifty-cent beer. "Got some fresh pretzels there," he pointed at the bowl of stale snacks he had poured out a few days earlier.

He walked back to the cash register in the middle of the bar. As he rang in the sale, he cleared his throat a second time. Gabe raised his head like he had just woken up. He stared down the bar at the man at the end.

The man hesitated with the beer an inch from his lips. Quietly, he put the beer down and stood. He headed for the bathrooms or the back door. Gabe's guess was the back door.

The man crashed through the back door and looked left toward the end of the building. When he looked right at what was behind the door, the black mass hit him.

Gabe opened the door slowly. The man was on the ground and Rabbit was standing over him with his left foot jammed down on the back of the man's neck—grinding the man's face into the rough asphalt. Rabbit was going through a wallet. He reached under his left armpit and took out another thin wallet. He handed it to Gabe. The badge was FBI.

"There's another in a green Chevy across the street."

They walked back into the bar and took their seats as they continued going through the man's personal wallet. Each item was laid out on the bar. A little over two-thousand in cash—mostly hundreds. His driver's license was from Ohio, but he had a second from Arizona—same photo, but different name. There was a library card that matched the Ohio identity of James Marx. They figured it was his real name.

Chet looked it all over. "What did you do with the guy?"

Rabbit shrugged and mumbled, "He'll be sleeping for a while."

Gabe chuckled. "We figured it wouldn't look right to just leave him there. So we took out the trash."

"You threw him in the dumpster?"

"Nah, that was too easy. We folded him in half and stuffed him in your neighbor's garbage can."

Chet's belly moved quietly up and down. "Head and feet first or ass first?"

"Ass first is too easy, and the image of the lesson doesn't have the staying power."

ANGEL FLIGHTS

"What did you hit him with?"

"That five-gallon can you have back there for grease."

"It's full."

"Yup... and straight to the kisser. I think it broke his nose."

"He'll be out for a while... and then he has to figure out where he is and how to get out." The three laughed when they heard a crash of metal in the back.

"Step one," Chet sipped on his coffee.

A couple of minutes later, they heard the back door open but the guy didn't appear. Rabbit snorted softly. "Vain little fuck—he stopped to check the damage."

Chet reached over and removed the 357 snub-nosed pistol from the array of the man's belongings. "I'll keep this out of harm's way." He stuck it in his pants pocket.

The man walked in from the bathroom in an upright position. White gobs of toilet paper protruded from both nostrils—controlling the bleeding from the shattered nose. He stopped and took a sip from his beer. And then he took a larger swallow. *He knew that his workday was over.*

Rabbit waved him down. "Hey, James, bring your beer and scrawny ass down here. Join the men."

Rabbit leaned toward Gabe. "What do you think—a Marine or Special Forces?"

Gabe snorted. "Marine would still be upside down in the can." He glanced at his watch. "Special Forces would just now be sliming their way through the back door and would engage while leaking blood everywhere." He watched the way the man walked. "I'm guessing about eight to ten in the SEALS."

Rabbit nodded and pointed at the seat that was the third away from him. *Separation in case the guy hadn't cooled down.* "Have a seat, swabbie." The man's head jerked, but he took the seat.

It was Gabe's turn to take over. "Cincinnati or the Columbus office?"

"Toledo. Everyone forgets the best city."

Gabe chuckled. "For barbecue or pizza?"

"Both." The man knew when he was beaten and had cooled down.

"Spatz's over near the college?"

"Hell no. Best of either is under the bridges."

Gabe mooned Rabbit. "Native."

"Born and raised."

Rabbit stepped in. "So you came to the big city to find out how to get your ass handed to you in a can?"

The man was silent as he sipped his beer.

Gabe tried another approach. "So why is a lone Feebie following me around these last few months?"

Rabbit snickered and Gabe gave him a hard look. He looked back at the agent.

"Six."

ANGEL FLIGHTS

"Six?"

"Six months."

Gabe didn't react. "Okay, wasn't sure about the first three. So what is it you want?"

"You have one hell of an operation going on that exceeds state lines... even international borders."

Rabbit sipped his coffee. "Such as? The international thing..."

"You're main supplier or the one we believe is at least one of your main suppliers, is a large gentleman up in Sylmar. He brings in the meth from sweat labs in northern Mexico—the Sonora area, to be exact."

"Why do you think we have other suppliers?"

"The volume you move to your downstream."

"What do you know about our downstream?"

"One is an FBI agent and another is an informant. Between the two, you have exceeded what we expect you would move by what you get from the fat guy."

Gabe was thinking as his fingers stroked his pursed lips. "So why are you telling us this?"

"Because it doesn't matter now—tomorrow before dawn, we start rolling your operation up. By noon, you are out of business."

Gabe looked over at the quiet Chet. He motioned for the phone. Chet pulled the long cord out from behind the counter and set the phone down in front of Gabe, along with a pen and notepad. Gabe dialed.

"Hey Stan... do me a favor. I need the back number for the FBI office in Toledo."

"No, in Ohio... is there really one here, too?"

The agent started to talk and Gabe held his finger up. He cradled the handpiece on his shoulder as he wrote. "Umhum. Yup, got it." He read it back and hung up.

He dialed the number and waited. When a voice answered, he was concise and short. "You have a special agent by the name of James Marx—like the Russian Marx. He works out of your office, and his life now depends on someone who knows him intimately. I will call back in exactly twenty minutes. Have his supervisor there when I call back." He hung up.

James shifted. "It's the middle of the night there. My supervisor is at home sleeping."

"How far away does he live?"

"We all have to be within ten minutes."

"Then you might see the sunrise." Gabe turned. "Chet, can we get three bowls of whatever you cooked up today?"

"Coming right up." The man flipped the towel over his left shoulder and moved down the bar.

As Rabbit broke some more crackers into the chili, he glanced up at the Fed. "So how do you like LA, James?"

"It was good until tonight."

"So what do the feds have on us—other than this alleged drug ring?"

"That's what is so strange. It's like you two don't exist. You two don't even ride bikes that are registered in your names. The registrations go to a cop bike that was crushed three years ago and to a bike that was registered in the racing circuit. In fact, the racer almost held a land speed record for the first woman to break two-hundred miles an hour on a motorcycle."

Gabe smiled at Rabbit. "Must have been a different engine. But that is one ballsy dude, a cop bike?"

Rabbit put his hand over his chest. "I'm crushed."

Gabe pushed his empty bowl over to Chet. "Great as usual, Chet."

"Always happy to serve you, Snake."

"So we saw you at the Long Green this morning, and now you're here. Do you ever think about the places we go?"

The guy was quiet as he wiped his mouth. *He hadn't thought about that—or that it might be telling.*

As Gabe pulled the phone to him, Rabbit leaned forward.

"Just so you know, your partner in the ugly green Chevelle across the street? When he wakes up, he won't be going anywhere. His clothes are in the trunk, but his bracelets are where he can see them."

BAER CHARLTON

He flipped the little cufflink key up onto the bar. They watched the agent blanch. *His bravado was gone.*

"Who am I talking to?" Gabe asked. "Well, Mr. Very Special Agent Thomas, you have sixty seconds to save your agent James Marx's life. Start with his description." He listened for a moment.

"It doesn't matter who I am. You now have fifty seconds, and then we will start on..." He put his hand out and Rabbit handed him the wallet. "A Special Agent screw-up by the name of Robert Chance."

He looked up at Marx. "Really? You took a chance on a guy with that kind of name?"

He turned back to the phone. "Go ahead." He watched out of the corner of his eye as Chet timed the call. When Chet tapped his watch, Gabe hung up. He looked at Rabbit. "It's time to take a couple of tourists out to our favorite spot in the desert."

Rabbit chuckled, Chet walked away with his hands on his ears and Marx turned white. "What did he say...?"

"He said that there was nobody in that office named Marx or Chance. I was mistaken and was probably the target for an elaborate practical joke or a con. And then he hung up."

"No deal. He wouldn't do that. For God's sake, were you talking to Tom Fergeson? I mean, that asshole Weinstein might think this was funny, but if they really got Fergeson out of bed—I mean... he just wouldn't do that. I saved his life, for God's sake. I was his best man at his weddings... I got him laid the night before—each time." The man collapsed on the bar.

Rabbit looked at Gabe with an arched eyebrow.

Gabe winked. "So how many Feebies are invading the LA basin and how do you call them off?"

The guy looked up. One of the plugs in his nose had come loose and blood was oozing down his face. "What do you mean?"

Rabbit stood and reached over the bar to find a towel. He handed it to the man. "Here, clean yourself up while I go get your partner."

Gabe watched the man get a little cleaned up. He knew that this little scene would be a large stick to hold over the agent for as long as he needed. "I'm that this is a standard FBI screw-up and you are the lead on it. So tell me what you plan, and I'll tell you what you are really going to do."

The man kept wiping at his face, which just smeared more blood. He now looked like they had worked him over with a rubber hose. Gabe couldn't stand it anymore. "Go use the bathroom. Pull yourself together before your partner sees you this way."

The man had just disappeared into the bathroom when Rabbit duck walked the other guy in through the front door. Gabe took one look and couldn't stop laughing. The black socks went perfect with the boxer shorts with the little red ants. Gabe had seen them in stores but didn't think anyone would wear them other than as a joke—certainly not on a federal stakeout.

He sighed. "Rabbit, please... I just ate. Please go get his pants and shirt."

Rabbit handcuffed the man to the foot rail of the bar. He looked like he was either washing Gabe's boots with his tongue or was some kind of kinky sex slave. Either way, Gabe thought it just best to ignore the man and hope Rabbit got back with the man's dignity before his partner saw him.

Rabbit was close, but not soon enough.

Gabe and Rabbit listened to a very detailed outline of a screwed up clusterfuck put together by a blind bunch of monkeys that had never been west of the big muddy. They asked a few question, but basically, the activities would end up with many federal agents chasing their hands into each other's backsides, resulting in more than a few dead agents because they had no clue.

Rabbit finally held up his hand for silence. "Okay, so here is how it is going to go down. Tomorrow, you are going to follow us out to the Fat Man's place. Then we will guide you through the day. The following day, you will follow us and take very careful notes. We will review your notes over lunch and debrief you in the evening. Meanwhile, you give that busload of special agents the week off. Trust me—they are going to need the rest. Not this Friday, but

ANGEL FLIGHTS

the following Friday, about dinner time, you will start dismantling our entire network that we show you. Trust me when I say your boys will be going nonstop for at least seventy-two hours. You have no idea how big this is."

The new to the party Agent Ants in His Pants was the first to wonder past the week's events. "What are you going to do?"

"We won't be in town, if that's what you mean."

"No, I meant after we take your business apart."

"We go back to work building a new business—with new people."

Marx poked gently at his nose. The black eyes were starting to swell the eyes shut. "Why are we waiting two weeks? Why don't we just arrest you and take it all down tomorrow?"

Gabe watched the man's face. The one eye actually looked like it was going to cross. He looked at Rabbit. "When I give you the word, you can hit him in the nose one more time. Just before we load them into the ambulance."

He turned back to the two pathetic looking feds. "First of all, you won't be able to see anything for the next couple of days. So we will start this next Monday. By next Thursday, you will have your teams up to speed and ready. The reason for the delay is because you want to do now what we were planning to do but after summer vacation started.

"What happens when the supply chain suddenly

dries up? The market forces the little guys that we weren't seeing before to step up and become our new network. And then... we get to do it all over again."

Chance looked at the two bikers. "Who do you guys think you are?"

Marx jammed his hand onto his partner's arm. "Trust me, you don't want to know." Gabe wasn't sure if the guy could actually see anymore.

"Look, give us where we can reach you, and we'll get in touch on Monday. We need a few days to set everything in motion from our end, and to work-up the paperwork. So take Marx here up to the hospital and we'll get in touch."

As they walked out to the motorcycles quietly laughing, Rabbit punched Gabe in the arm softly.

Gabe laughed harder. *He didn't have to ask to know what Rabbit wanted.*

He started the chopper. It sat higher, but the seats were wider and softer. The rumble was a slightly softer, throatier rumble. The ride was softer, but with the new springs in the front end, the bumps were no longer mushy in the corners. Everything would be broadcast as if it was a rigid front end until the springs were broken in. He remembered the LAPD rider course that Rabbit had gotten him into. He never rode without feeling any and every change, now that he knew what every little bump or twitch meant. He hauled in the kickstand, grabbed the clutch, and then eased the bike out onto Huntington

ANGEL FLIGHTS

Drive.

"Well?"

Gabe tucked his chin in and laughed. Rabbit hated waiting. "The guy in Toledo said that Marx and he went back to the second grade. Marx did save his life—Marx swims and the other guy is now afraid of water. He said Marx is a screw-up in a lot of ways, but he is still his best friend. He said if he didn't start crying about being his best man and all—to just shoot him."

Rabbit was roaring with laughter and weaving a bit. Gabe was glad the guy was in the other lane, instead of sharing the lane as they usually did.

Gabe grew serious. "It gets worse. The guy was very serious. He thinks the head office sent him out here because he would fuck it up. If he does... they will can him. So the guy asked that if we couldn't make sure it came off with Marx the hero..."

Rabbit thought for a few blocks. As they took the left turn through the red light, he looked over at Gabe. "Are you serious? He asked for us to snap a cap on his best friend?"

"He said that if they fired him, he would have nothing left. His marriage lasted for only nine months, so all he has left is the FBI. He said that if he came home and ate his service piece, the ex-wife wouldn't get any support—and it's the guy's sister."

Rabbit still had wide eyes about the sister thing as they parked the bikes in the garage. His voice dropped so the four dark shapes around the fire-pit wouldn't hear. "Do they share the same father?"

Gabe shrugged as he closed the garage doors. "That's when I hung up on the guy."

Rabbit rolled his eyes down and wide. "Hey, boys."

The hands waved, but there were no voices, so they let it go. There was a black and white out front, so they figured there would be one or two officers doing paperwork in the kitchen.

As Gabe opened the old back door, they could hear a female voice. "What the hell is wrong with this dumb snake?"

Gabe smiled at Rabbit and went to defend his girlfriend. The woman was young—maybe high school. The officer was chuckling. She was a ride-along. Gabe leaned in and grabbed Gertie. "Come on, baby. This girl is too young for you." He hefted the snake onto his shoulder and Gertie did the rest by grabbing around his middle. He nuzzled with the football-sized head. "Daddy's little girl hungry? You're getting so skinny. You want some steak?"

The officer looked up from his paperwork. "Just threw some in the freezer about a half hour ago. They should still be ready to go."

"Thanks, Pepper." Gabe opened the freezer door. There were only stacks of steaks. Gabe nodded for Rabbit to look. The two smiled. *It was good to live in the frat house.* Gabe took out a couple. "You two sticking around long enough to join us?"

The redheaded officer looked at the dark haired girl. "Sure." A steak always beat getting back onto the dead streets in the middle of the night.

Gabe flipped out five steaks onto the counter. As he sliced open the clear film of each, he stacked them all on a large platter. "Hey, Ride-Along, how do you like your steak—with or without a snake?" Gabe started laughing and Rabbit slugged him in the shoulder. They both turned laughing to find a solid stone face.

"Dude, your snake is weird, but I like my steak where a good vet can get it back up on its feet."

Chastised, Gabe pursed his lips that slid into a smile. "If you thought her rubbing your leg was weird—wait until you see her eat steak."

"Rubbing my leg was fine. Climbing into my lap was okay... but what is with the snuggling into my neck and hair like it was in heat?"

Gabe pulled on his deadpan face. "She's a lesbian. She especially likes little girls."

The brunette looked Gabe up and down and paused when she got to the snake still wrapped around him like a perpetual scarf. She didn't have to say a word. The blush slowly worked its way up from where the snake crossed his neckline. Gabe turned for the steaks and started out the back door.

"You got a real name, Ride-Along?"

"Connell, Janice Connell."

Gabe didn't want to confuse Gertie or make her decide. He had Janice sit on one side at the corner, and he took the end of the table. Gertie wouldn't have to be fed for the rest of the week. Even Rabbit pushed some of his large steak over for the hundred-pound steak vacuum.

The girl had become fascinated by the large snake. She admitted that small snakes in the garden weren't her favorite thing, but when they get the size of a teenager, the presence changes.

"So what made you want to come do a ride along?"

She popped two more bites into the throat and tapped Gertie on the nose. "This is my third. In June, I graduate, and next fall I start college studying Police Science."

"What do you want to do?"

"Patrol until I can test for Detective."

Gabe scrunched his eyes as he rubbed his hand over his face. He didn't have to look at the clock to know that he had been up for almost twenty-four hours. "Have you heard of any department that has women in the field?"

"LAPD has a couple that just hit the street in team cars, and there is a mandate that just came down from Sacramento allowing the CHP to start testing."

"So which do you want—street or freeways?"

"People."

ANGEL FLIGHTS

Gabe smiled. "No snakes?"

"I can think of only one exception."

"Just don't go kissing her. Her girlfriend is across the street, and I like that woman's tamales."

Gabe gathered the plates as he stood up. Janice took them. "You're bleeding from your eyes. Go get some sleep—I've got this. Thanks for the steak."

"It's not necessarily woman's work."

She chuckled. "I know that, silly." She looked down the table. "That's why I'm going to make Pepper do the washing. I just do the clearing."

Rabbit growled as he also stood and handed his plate to her. "You're going to do just fine on the street. Take shit, but spread it out thin."

She smiled.

26

GETTING READY DOWN MEXICO WAY

IT WAS GABE'S hundredth run down to Mexico. There wasn't a medal or a merit badge waiting. It was just the usual evening of nerves until they reached the hacienda and handed off the girls. Then there would be the dealing with the ache that came from the burned adrenaline that went to no other use than sitting on a motorcycle at speed.

Gabe had taken one of the nurses aside and asked if a certain favor could be taken care of. She nodded and told him to come back the next morning after breakfast. They would squeeze him in before they started the usual day.

The fire in the pit felt good that Saturday night. The sundown was an orange flare across almost invisible clouds. Gabe had spent the day clutching one cold can of beer after another—between his legs and against the small surgical cut with the two stitches.

A few other guys saw the strange behavior, and

silently thumb clasped his hand in brotherhood. They also knew the long ride on Sunday would be memorable.

Rabbit sat down next to him, handing him a fresh cold can. Gabe traded it and Rabbit popped the top on the crotch-warmed one and threw the top into the pit. He drained a few gulps.

"You could have gotten a cold one for you, too."

Rabbit growled as he swung his head about. "I hate cold beer."

Gabe snorted. "Sometimes it feels just right."

They watched the last guy wander off to a cot. There were only seventeen this trip from LA, six more from the south end. They knew it was just a lull. As summer vacation loomed, hormones would take over and the amount of motorcycles needed each week would float back up. They all knew it wasn't just the summer and kids fooling around. There were other dynamics as well.

"How do you want to handle the Ohio boys?"

Rabbit sipped on the warmed can again. "Basically, I think we ought to run it out just the way we laid it out to them. They follow us around and take notes... then next weekend, they get to terrorize the city while we are down here." He rolled his head towards Gabe. "We were going to turn it over to Treasury in June anyway, why not let the kid have some glory so he can go home with his head high for once. We can't take credit for any of it anyway."

"Then what?"

"Well, I'd say it might be time to take a vacation. There is a little motorcycle gathering I heard about up South Dakota way. It's a long ride, but its country I've never seen before. So a little tourist lollygagging would be kind of good, too."

"What's in South Dakota?"

"Beats the hell out of me... Maybe it's just a bunch of bikers scratching their asses and wondering the same thing. It doesn't matter much. I'm going just to get away and look at the countryside."

"Wide open country..."

"Why don't you come along?"

Gabe pulled the beer from his crotch and pulled the tab. "I think I need to start getting serious about law school." He took a long pull on the can and then stared into the soft embers. "There's a guy at the school I sat next to on Tuesday—he's been picking at the class for five years. If he keeps at it, he'll be graduating just before he turns fifty. I don't want to be that guy."

"What's the rush?"

Gabe thought about it. There wasn't really just one thing—it was a bunch of little things that can get lost on their own or become a flood when they get together. Lately he had been feeling like he was standing in a stream that a short time ago was at his ankles but was now tickling his knees.

"Remember that fire-fight at that little bodega...

um... last year?"

Rabbit nodded. "The one in Glassell Park—just off Eagle Rock and Thirtieth?"

"The uniforms shot the hell out of the neighborhood. What had started as a traffic stop became a battle zone."

Rabbit pulled at his upper lip and mustache. "Wasn't there someone... next door..."

"Right, the guy from India with the little restaurant..."

"What about it?"

"The guy still can't do anything with that right arm, and he just sits in the wheelchair. He used to be the breadwinner for the family. They moved here because of him. Now his boy won't go to school because he has to work. The kid is twelve."

Rabbit watched the large ember of what was once a small limb, crumble and tumble down into the ashes. "How do you know that, and what does it have to do with you and law school?"

"I've gone back. I've eaten there and talked to the boy. His mother does the cooking—it's damn good. But his father is a basket case from the bullet that went through his head. It was a 357 Magnum, full metal jacket. The low riders were shooting .22 and .38 caliber pistols. The guy with the rifle had a 30-30."

Rabbit understood the implication of an officer using unauthorized rounds in his service revolver.

Hot loads were one thing—but a jacketed bullet, especially a Magnum, was capable of leaving the area of fire and doing damage to a civilian who was out of the general range of fire.

"What does the city say?"

"They offered them two grand and told them to go away—like back to India."

"So you want to help immigrants?"

Gabe thought for a moment while he calmed. He knew that he couldn't really explain it, but on the surface, that was what it looked like. His face cleared.

"Remember about four or five years ago there was that cop who was gunned down on Spring Street...?"

"Stopped the bank robbers..."

Gabe nodded. "The city wailed and beat its chest. The young widow and boy were shown in every news cycle for days. The mayor stood there on television and told her that *we take care of our own.*"

"They were setting up some kind of scholarship fund or something for the kid..."

"Yeah... well, that and the big death benefit for an on-duty death."

"Right, so she's set up. What about it?"

"Her name came up in class. She's on welfare. The state is saying she got a death benefit, and the kid has some fat scholarship so they don't want to pay her welfare."

ANGEL FLIGHTS

Rabbit lowered his eyes. "So what really happened?"

"The scholarship was nothing more than a few thousand bucks thrown into the widow and orphan's fund. The insurance has refused to pay because the officer was transitioning in his own vehicle, and therefore, technically, wasn't on duty at the time—even though he was in the middle of his shift."

"So she's broke."

Gabe nodded. "She is so broke she has to go to the free clinic for health care, and is volunteering at the law library to qualify for the free aid law services—but if it goes to trial, and you know it will—they take away the lawyers because she would be suing the city and the law center's charter prohibits them from taking her case."

"So what do you want to do?"

"I don't know exactly what I want to do… right now. But I do know this—there are plenty of people out there getting screwed. I don't want to be one of the screws. I want to be one of the helpers."

Rabbit sat quietly watching the embers. "Let's take a serious look at what's in the drawer when we get back."

"What about the boxes?"

Rabbit frowned and glanced over. "Oh… crap…" He had forgotten about the boxes

Gabe started coughing as he choked from seeing Rabbit's face.

Then Rabbit's eyes opened wide in remembrance. "I think there is a duffel bag or two... in my closet..."

Sunday afternoon, the nurse took Gabe aside. She handed him a few small packets the size of his hand. "Hold them like this. Then snap it in half."

Gabe could feel something fragile break in the pack.

"Now wiggle it like this."

As Gabe followed the motion, the pack became cold—just like it said on the pack. She smiled and didn't have to tell him what they were for. He gave her a hug.

Turning he looked for the dirty blonde. "Puff... time to ride."

The girl hugged a couple of other girls that were with the guys Gabe recognized as being from San Diego. She turned and headed for the bike. Gabe put his hand on the nurse's shoulder. "Thanks again... for everything you all do."

"We'll see you Friday night." She waved at everyone leaving.

Gabe legged onto the bike and started the engine. He and the blonde put on their shades together as if they had been an item for years. The nurse smiled.

Gabe turned to Rabbit and nodded. Rabbit led them out. Mike took up the drag position of the seventeen bikes headed for LA. The border was the next

ANGEL FLIGHTS

stop, and hopefully not a full stop. The evening was mild and refreshing. A light breeze was blowing in from the coast and smelled nice. Things couldn't be better.

The border was jammed.

"What do you think?" Gabe could tell they were still at least a mile from the crossing. To run the lines with this many bikes, for that long of time, would certainly draw attention.

"The next crossing over is the one they watch too much. This is the only one for a hundred miles we are safe on." Rabbit weighed the circumstances.

"I think the Federales will be glad to see us go. It's the US boys that could be the bottleneck." He turned and made a sign in the air with his pinky and thumb out to the sides of his fist. The hand moved back and forth.

Gabe could hear Mike's big Panhead coming up through the traffic. As the man wove into the packed cars, he ticked his head up.

Rabbit didn't talk, he just echoed the nod but toward the traffic and border crossing in the distance. The deaf man took the bike out of gear and weighed his two hands up and down.

Rabbit patted his forehead, and Mike responded by rolling his head and shrugging. He held his left palm up and split his right hand through the two middle fingers.

Gabe figured he meant to just go ahead and

see—not to run the gate.

Rabbit turned. "He thinks to just balls it up and see what happens. They've never really stopped us before, and it's not like this is their first time to see us…"

"It just feels… off."

"Maybe something happened, but it's not us."

Gabe clunked the bike into gear and slowly started rolling between the cars. "I sure hope not."

The sunlight was turning soft orange as the line of bikes made it to the front. The tourists didn't want any trouble and stopped to let the bikes go first. The Mexican guards just fanned them across.

The American held out his hand and Gabe eased to a stop with the bike in neutral.

"Do you have anything to declare?" The six dreaded little words that tightened every tourist's gut.

Gabe reached into his pocket and laid one of the cold packs on the gas tank. He thumbed the cylinder and then shook it.

Reaching down with his right hand, he pulled the now warm one from under his crotch and handed it to the patrolman.

"Don't get into a bar fight with a guy who likes to kick you in the nuts."

The guy smiled. "You two are from LA, aren't you?" The guy was motioning with his finger between Gabe and Rabbit.

ANGEL FLIGHTS

Gabe's hand moved back to the clutch and throttle. He was ready to run for it. The patrolman's stance was relaxed, instead of on-guard.

Rabbit was also ready. "Who wants to know?"

The guy held up his index finger. Gabe could feel the girl, called Puff, tighten her legs against his hips. She didn't like it either.

The border guard looked towards the small office. "Hey, sergeant—you have that note for Snake and Rabbit handy?"

The man dipped his head and ducked back into the office. Rabbit gently pulled his clutch in and his leg rose until his boot hovered over the shifter.

Gabe matched him, and he could feel the tension transmitting back down the rest of the bikers.

The seconds were like hours.

The officer finally came out with a small piece of paper in his hand. It was pink. Gabe recognized the official note from a pad. He didn't have to look to that the bold type on the top read *While You Were Out*.

He handed it to Rabbit who read it and passed it to Gabe.

"Fat Man dead. Call soon as back. Ohio."

Gabe and Rabbit exchanged knowing but relieved glances. Gabe shoved it in his pocket and looked up at the officer.

"Thanks."

He let out the clutch and seventeen bikes roared

into California in fewer seconds.

Gabe felt the girl shift forward.

"We need to stop at a gas station or something. I think I peed my pants."

Every tank was full since Rosarita, but when Gabe made the sign for gas, nobody rode on.

27

FAT MAN IS DEAD

"WHY DON'T YOU guys come on over for a steak tomorrow night, and we can talk." Gabe gave them the address and hung up.

Rabbit stood in the open door of the refrigerator. "Do you think they know how to read a map?"

"If they don't... Gertie gets their steak. Speaking of the lady of the house...?"

"I saw her out in the back trying to make nice with that ride-along girl. I think she was trying to sneak up her skirt."

"That girl needs to wear pants. She just did a ride-along a couple of weeks or so..."

"Last week. She is wearing pants." He turned. "And... she's here with Zorro."

"Oh, shit."

"That's what you get for parking out front."

Gabe reached around and pulled a beer out of the fridge. "We need a bigger garage."

ANGEL FLIGHTS

Rabbit stuck his head into the commercial stainless steel refrigerator that had somehow appeared over the weekend. He opened the other door to find the freezer side stacked with packages of meat. "Speaking of bigger... is it just me or does this room make this fridge look fat?"

Gabe looked where the now missing cupboards had hung over a much smaller residential refrigerator. He opened the back door. "I don't even ask anymore. And with something like that—I damn sure don't want to know where it came from."

"What about the electric bill? This monster has to—"

"What electric... or gas bill? I haven't seen one for well over a year. I keep waiting for them to cut us off—but it never happens."

Zorro looked up from the fire pit where the barbecue was now burning hot. "The new fridge? Chet got it for you."

"Shut up, Zorro... that is more than I wanted to know. Janet or something... Janice."

The girl blushed only slightly. "Let's just keep it at Jan."

Gabe sat down, "Works for me. Is my old partner behaving?"

She looked over. "Zorro has been... um... interesting." She smiled and winked at Gabe.

Gabe looked at Zorro. "I thought you were on permanent days... what are you doing on swing?"

"Not swing. This is the end of the day, and we… I… thought it would be nice to swing by for dinner. Today I have dined the young lady at all the right places and shown her the sights."

Gabe looked at Jan. "I'm assuming he took you up the hill to meet his niece and grandnephew?"

"Maria is really nice, but that little scamp stole my heart."

Gabe opened his eyes big. "Lito was there, too?"

Zorro laughed. "Nah, he was down at the college talking to a couple of people. We'll save that kid for some other time."

Jan laughed. "Maria told me about her brother. Is it true that you two are going to UCLA together? I mean, isn't he like only fourteen?"

Gabe nodded. "And he will probably be done with his undergraduate work and still be younger than sixteen. The medical school has already provisionally saved him a seat."

The back door swung open and Rabbit came out with a large platter stacked with steaks.

"Someone just keep that glutton away from the steaks until I get mine…"

The girl laughed as Gertie raised her head up from the girl's lap and watched Rabbit. "You mean this little girl?"

Rabbit laughed. "No, I mean Zorro."

The steaks had been surprisingly good. Gabe still did not want to know how they had appeared.

ANGEL FLIGHTS

Jan sat stroking the flat football head lying on the table next to her. The last scraps of gristle or trim had gone down the live garbage disposal. She looked back up to Rabbit. "Honor Society, but I missed being Valedictorian by at least three people. Our school is very competitive, but I have been involved with more of my interests than the bits and pieces needed to get the speaker spot."

"Did you want the honor?" Gabe took up the plates. Jan knew better than to move.

"Actually, I think my parents would have liked the honor more than I would. Having to build a speech that nobody really listens to, and never remembers anyway, would have taken time that I can better spend working on my future career."

Rabbit smiled and sipped on his second beer. "Like hanging out with the old fart."

Zorro's face was a silent protest, but then he started laughing.

"I don't know about other ride-along participants, but I'd rather pull one of the older training officers than the young guys who they don't let near the real streets. But then, I see this as more of a pre-training or schooling. In school, they will tell me one thing. And then I have to unlearn the books to learn the streets. It's bad enough that the deck is already stacked against a woman."

"Is that a whine about it not being fair?"

Jan held her hands up. "Not in the least. My

mother would have been a meter maid at best. Or some drudge secretary in a uniform. But at least now, I get a shot at being a real officer on the streets. Maybe one day, they will actually see us as just another officer and we will be in a car alone."

Zorro pushed his index finger along a perceived crack in the antique walnut table. He looked up at Rabbit. "See what I've been putting up with all day?"

Gabe came back in. "Jeez, Zorro, you suffered so much today."

Zorro snorted and looked at Jan. "Not hardly—I'd take her as a trainee today, just the way she is. Listening to her today made me feel like I wanted to be twenty all over again."

Rabbit pointed backward with the large knife he was picking at his thumb with. "Watch him."

Zorro glared. "My god, you have a dirty mind, Rabbit." He turned back toward Gabe. "When I started on the force, I was where she is talking now. I was the only Mexican on an all-white force. They weren't even sure I had the brains to drive a car."

The guys were laughing and then saw that he was serious.

Zorro nodded. "That's right. I was always the right-hand seat—last to the party. When an opening came up at Ramparts, I jumped for it. It was a hotbed of shit—nobody wanted to move into the broken down part of town. They still don't—so I got it. Then there was another Mexican and finally a black and an Asian. Things were slow, but they changed."

He held his hand out toward the high school girl. "Now, it is their time. And that is why I would like to be a single strip and watch it all happen. I saw ours. I'd like to be around long enough to see them get everything she's talking about."

They all laughed as she whined a common wail. "I wanna be a sergeant."

***

The morning was one of those crisp air rarities that the LA basin occasionally coughed up. Instead of the cloyed air of rancid, rotting vegetation that marked the older neighborhoods, Gabe thought it smelt as if someone had stuck the air in a refrigerator just long enough to freshen it. As the choppers rolled down Mission Blvd to meet up with Valley, he knew the nice smell would only last for a short time.

A city bus slowly slid by belching half-burned diesel as they came to a stop at the light. Gabe's eyes seared slightly. The clean part of the morning was over.

As they took off, the bus pulled away from the curb. The large elongated blue-black cloud wavered like a snake behind. Gabe twisted the throttle and Rabbit followed suit. They blinked, as they passed the bus, and then let the throttles go. As they passed the turn that would take them to Boyle Heights, a black and white rolled out. Gabe glanced at his speedometer as the siren squawked once.

"Shit." Rabbit slowly braked and headed for the driveway into a large parking lot. They shut off the motors as the black and white slowly nosed into the parking area.

Zorro's window was down. His elbow was out. He was alone. He eased around so he or they were not looking into the sun.

Gabe and Rabbit both knew that something was on Zorro's mind, but it would normally take some time to get past the shit-shooting.

Gabe cut it short. "We're on a tight time schedule here, Zorro."

Zorro leaned back into the seat. He was going to still take his time. "I had a nice time last night."

"Get to the point, Don."

The man's face showed only the slightest twitch of irritation. "I didn't want to mention it last night with Jan there... but there is a shitload of federal crap kickers in town."

"FBI..."

"And then some." The man lowered his dark glasses. "Word on the street is that some politician wants to clean up the streets, and today is the day." He was referring more to the figurative now than that exact day.

"We're aware of what's going on, Don." Gabe

wanted to stress the working relation, not the more relaxed usual nickname

"Gabe, I'm just warning you. You two need to head for a hole somewhere. These assholes start shooting, one biker looks like any other biker. To them, a scumbag is a scumbag, and a dead scumbag is one that doesn't talk or have to be explained."

Rabbit glanced at his watch. He looked down the wide boulevard at the traffic that was building. "Gabe, we don't have time for this. Don, if it makes you feel better, come on over tonight for dinner. Right now, we have to go to work."

He fired up the chopper and started for the street. Gabe nodded at Zorro and followed. They roared down the large four-lane toward their first stop ten minutes away. They knew if they didn't set things in motion today—tomorrow would never come.

The machine shop never seemed to change. Every week they were there, and it seemed like Werner was working on the same small part... one after another. Even the plans never moved—they just gathered more coffee rings.

"Que pasa, Werner?"

The machinist didn't even look up. "Nada fucking thing, Rabbit." His focus was fully on the tiny drill hardly moving in the tiny block of metal. "Grab some coffee. I'll be with you in about ten minutes."

The two bikers looked at each other with

frowns. Shrugging, Gabe walked off to the break room.

Sitting at the table were the FBI agents, Marx and Chance. Gabe sized up the gray suits and Midwest haircuts against what their boss had shared earlier that morning. He strolled nonchalantly to the coffeemaker and blew out a mug. His back was to the two while he poured. "Didn't want to wait until dinner?"

"When Special Agent Werner told us that he was sitting on eight kilograms of pure methadrine that he had cut for you two—we decided it would be best to be involved in today's activities instead a possible stand-up tonight."

Gabe only smiled a little smile. *Werner had lied—there was a total of eighty kilos that he had cut five different ways, and into three-hundred and sixty different packets. Special Agent Werner wanted to retire.*

Gabe took a sip and turned around. Thankfully, neither man had been stupid enough to pull a weapon. Gabe nodded. "Okay, but this is the way it's going down. You follow until we give you the signal by patting the top of our head like this." He showed them—a large sweeping, dramatic reach that became a triple pat. "That is your cue to pull over and wait. You are not to get within even two blocks of any of the drops. You got that?"

"That's not the deal."

ANGEL FLIGHTS

"Then we are done. Enjoy your ride home to Ohio. Hope you like your small town junior sheriff slash dog catcher and divorce."

Manx started to rise. "Now wait a min—"

"Fuck you. This is the way it is." Gabe watched as Rabbit entered with his weapon down by his side. Gabe continued. "This isn't some six-month candy-ass panty raid. We've been on this for over five years. Bringing all of this together was delicate, hard, and dangerous work. At any moment, we could have been killed. Rabbit damn near was.

"You *tried* to do background on us. You know how solid our cover is. You never even got a whiff of Treasury or Rabbit's CIA connection. This town is loaded with every single alphabet soup that you can think of. I'd tell you about three more—but then Rabbit would have to shoot the two of you, Werner, and me. You two are total fuck-ups back home. If you even stopped to think about it, someone thought you might learn from the masters. So they sent you here—now." Gabe's finger pounded firmly into the Special Agent's chest—driving him back into his chair.

"In another month, this would all be done and gone. You would be picking up road kill on the south end of Toledo. But we need to be the ghosts that we are. We have a couple of other cities to clean up before we clean up some shit in Congress. Therefore, now that you have tried to fuck it up—we have a change of plans. It is now time for you to choose one of three doors." He held up three fingers and counted them off.

"Door one, you get up, say goodbye and go home. Door two, you do exactly as we tell you, and you follow the plan exactly, you do not question Werner or us, and you stay out of the way with no addendums. You keep your eyes buried in the newspaper today, and you go home a hero."

Chance cleared his throat. "And door number three?"

Rabbit's voice rumbled from the door. "We have a favorite spot to show you—out in the Mojave Desert." Gabe noticed Werner was standing close behind Rabbit. The man cycled the pump on the shotgun. Both of the Midwest screw-ups blanched.

Marx's croak was almost a squeak. "Door number two. The newspaper looked interesting today."

Gabe watched Werner smile as he turned back to his machining.

"Okay, so here is how today will go down. You can stay here... or just go get some time by the pool at that fancy hotel, you are staying in. We don't care.

"We are going to be in and out all day long. We have several deliveries, and we can't take loads for more than one or two buyers at a time. We have over fifty-some keys to dump today, and our bikes go places your car can't. We don't have time to hand-hold you two. So, if you cause Werner any prob-

ANGEL FLIGHTS

lems—he will shoot you—then we'll bury you tonight. I suggest you head for your hotel or sit quietly in here." Gabe pointed to the full coffee maker. "There is plenty of good coffee."

"We talked to Ferguson this morning and he assigned a few details that need to be staked out. You two will get the full details this evening at your hotel. We'll see how the day goes and if you behave."

Marx did not want to seem the total pushover. "We'll just hang out here and see how it goes."

"Fine, but just remember, when you go out there to the bathroom, Werner gets very jumpy on days like this. So be quiet and stay in here or go home."

"Got it."

Gabe put down the empty cup. He and Rabbit walked out to where Werner was placing some parts in a box. "Ja, I get jumpy." The man smiled.

Gabe looked at the stuff in the box. "Aircraft parts?"

"Experimental. I get huge bucks for keeping my mouth shut. Today is the end—I box them up and get paid."

Gabe gave the man a deadpan look. "The weight you told Manx is about a large retirement away from reality. Where did you want to go?"

"I have ten banks that will wire the money to the Caymans. It will be there for less than a day."

"You know that tomorrow there needs to be no more Werner."

BAER CHARLTON

He pointed at the machined parts. "This was all I was trying to finish."

"What about getting paid for those?"

"Swiss account. It doesn't stay there either."

"So, you weren't planning on sticking around until June anyway...?"

Werner smiled. "There is always the party that is worth sticking around for."

Rabbit stuck his hand out. "You've been a good man to know."

"Rabbit, you need to get out of the business—both businesses. You still have your humanity, and you are a good person. Find something good to do that takes care of Rabbit."

"Looking into just that, Werner."

Gabe scuffed his feet. "Let's get some product moved."

"Werner, you'll need to be the bagman while we run. When you have yours stashed, we'll cut you loose."

"Works for me. While you are out, and once they are gone, I can run to the banks. Most have branches close by." He turned to the large table with drawers under it. He lifted the tabletop from the back end. There was a large area behind the drawers. "Here is your first three drops."

The men looked down into the cavity and pulled up the duffle bags. Each had a tag with a number. They knew the system of where and who each six-digit number represented.

"Over the weekend, I processed all of what you brought me before the Fat Man was killed. With what was left over from before, that brought you up to a full hundred kilos to break down. I put in some extra where I thought it was deserved—like up on the hill. You will need to really hustle because you will be making drops to everyone." The two bikers nodded in understanding.

The day had begun.

Rabbit looked over the numbers, and then put them back in a selected order. Six bags were in a stack and four more were set to one side. "Let's leave those for later. Set up the forty-fives next. They are close by, so the idiot twins won't think we ran on them. Then follow with the nine straight threes. After that, we can run the two seventy-sevens and the six seventy-fours in one take. By that time, I think they will be bored and gone. I want to haul the heavies down after one but before the traffic starts to load. Set the forty-one and forty-two first for the final then just run the line through the fifties. By that time, you will be gone and we're on our own. About lunch, we'll give you the information packet to give to them when you leave, or if they have gone already, we'll just drop it at their hotel. As for the bag, just break it in half. We're good with that."

They both looked for Gabe's approval. Gabe nodded and squeezed the guy's shoulder. They all knew that the day's bag would be well over a million dollars each.

Werner put his hand out. "My only regret is that we won't know where to share a drink one day."

Rabbit thought about that. "You know that huge statue in Brazil?" *It was a neutral country with no extradition.*

The man nodded. "The one on a mountain?" He stretched his arms out.

"That's the one. How about Christmas day at noon, in..." he turned and looked at the Harleys, "1974?"

They shook.

Rabbit and Gabe rode away with the first run. Werner listened to the sound of the motorcycles as he packed the last of the boxes. The stack wasn't impressive. Six rather smallish boxes—but they represented so much more. Werner smiled and turned. Now to keep the two Ohio boys entertained just enough to make them bored.

28

DELIVER AS IF YOUR LIFE DEPENDS ON IT

THE STRAIGHTEST SHOT for the first long delivery was some little-used industrial back roads that wound through the old manufacturing and finally, the oil fields. Even though time was of the essence, with a little over two hundred pounds of contraband, and no badges or legal documents to back them up, the boys rode casually at the speed limit.

The road through the oil fields rolled over the central area of southwest LA and finally let them out near LAX. PSA's 707s and Flying Tigers Constellations and Pole Cats were a constant scream overhead as they rode directly under the landing pattern. Neither of the men tried to talk. They had made this run every week for over a year. Each had their own thoughts to deal with. The day started out wrong, and it would take some doing to make it right.

The blonde in the tight jeans and work shirt tied up under her large chest never said a word. She handed them the large envelope and took the black trash bag Rabbit had pulled out of the duffle. She slung it into her own duffle and kicked her Triumph into life. With a nod, she was gone. Gabe and Rabbit both knew she was one of the few who would escape the next day's dragnet.

There had never been much talking with her. Gabe remembered the first small bag. The woman had brought a guy who had tested it in his own nose. With his thumb pushed against his nose, tears in his eyes, and stomping his foot against the pain—he had silently nodded. The business had grown rapidly from that first pound to the fifty pounds of today. Tomorrow she would be looking for a new supplier—or go out of business for a while.

At the next stop, Gabe grabbed the whole bag. They walked along the side of the large warehouse. The large building was a controlled customs warehouse. They entered the small door in the back. The counter separated them from the two guards. Both had Browning Hi-power 9mm pistols strapped high on their hips. The men looked like serious military—except for the soft middles. *Something a crisp military haircut cannot hide.*

The two guards looked up and nodded. Rabbit stayed watching the two as Gabe stepped through the door into a secured space. He looked at the wide-open truck doors and nobody around. He snorted softly at the idea of this being a highly secured warehouse. He turned into the inner office as the man looked up.

"Got some time for coffee?"

"Nah, we're trying to make the county line for a clam chowder lunch."

The man pushed down on the handle of the large safe that was unlocked. Reaching into the steel box, he removed four large tan envelopes and flipped them onto the desk where Gabe was stacking the five large packages taped up in black plastic garbage bags.

Gabe placed the envelopes of money into his bag and turned. "See you next week."

He knew the man saluted him with the Cub Scout two-finger salute, as he started putting the hundred pounds of drugs away in his safe. Gabe was sure the man would still leave the safe unlocked—unsecure was his nature. *Tomorrow that would be his downfall, and half of the freight handlers would struggle to stay awake as they worked their usual overtime.*

The third stop was a fast stop. The mechanic at the car rental came out of the dark garage. As he walked, he pulled the fat envelope out of the back of his pants from under his shirt. He reached into Rabbit's bag and removed the three boxes that were marked as brakes for Plymouths and replaced them with the envelope. Gabe and Rabbit watched as the man walked back into the garage and tossed the boxes onto a shelf in plain sight. Someone else had set up the drop, and not a single word of hello had ever been exchanged. They knew there wasn't a single Plymouth car in this fleet of rentals. The boxes would never be touched except by the person who knew what was inside. *That would be the job for the team of Feds sitting across the street that set up the night before.*

Werner was parking his car as they pulled up. Gabe and Rabbit noticed the stack of boxes was gone from near the door. The man was smiling. Gabe put his arm around the smaller man's shoulders and asked quietly, "All taken care of?"

The man nodded. "They transferred it while I was there. The bank even gave me the confirmation chit. It's already moved and that account is closed. I'm good."

The Ohio crew came out of the office. "What took you two so long?"

Rabbit growled. "This is why we didn't want you dragging along today. Everything is timed, and that includes us having a nice breakfast on the beach watching almost naked girls. Now get back in your fucking hole or go home. We have work to do, and you're not part of it." He moved his jacket back with his hand to show the automatic. "Unless you want to become all we do today."

Manx grabbed Chance and they went back into the office.

Gabe reached into the large green steel toolbox and took out the black bags. He passed the one to Rabbit. "We'll be back in about an hour. In case you're still out, where are the next ones?"

"The rest of the morning stuff will all fit in the workbench. I'll stack them with the numbers up. The afternoon runs I'll put in the green toolbox."

"Great, we'll see you in an hour."

Traffic kept them a little longer.

The motorcycles could have wound in and out of any traffic, but they were forced to sit and wait for one of the more interesting pick-ups that they had raked into their net over the year. A little research had turned up the buyer wasn't a sting operation. He was just a sergeant who was overweight, couldn't run the mandatory obstacle course anymore, barely could shoot the combat course and knew that he would never make it to retirement age. He needed a backdoor. Providing pep pills to fellow officers was his back door.

One of the automatic pill press machines Werner had built in his shop was dedicated exclusively to the service of this man. Werner mixed a full kilo into almost a hundred pounds of talcum powder, chalk, and baby milk formula. Gabe and Rabbit figured the

ANGEL FLIGHTS

way the sergeant was buying the pills, cops across the city were eating them like candy—even though they were twice as strong as what they made for the afternoon deliveries. *Why give the criminals and gangs the edge?*

The black and white rolled up. They were in the top parking lot of Dodger stadium and a few blocks away from where the sergeant had arranged for Rabbit and Gabe to take the motorcycle-riding course.

"Hey, Whale…"

"Rabbit, Snake, how's your day going?"

"Just working the shift." They walked toward the open trunk with the large duffle bags. Each bag weighed over a hundred pounds. "We gave you about ten percent extra… make it last."

"Are you two going to be in town for the shit storm that hits this weekend?" The man handed them a medium duffle back. It also had the fast slide band that fit down over the sissy bars. He closed and leaned on the trunk. They could see he was tired and hurting.

"Our job is done. How about you?"

"This will all be cash by midnight. There is a redeye that has my name on it. I'm toast, boys."

Gabe softened. "We're going to miss you, Whale. I want to also thank you for the training on the bikes."

The man waved the thanks down. "It was nothing. I'm glad you found it a help. Too many take the course and still hit the streets and screw it all up. As for you two... I owe my little time of retirement to you." He looked out at the brown air that hung and stopped the panoramic vision at the closer high towers of downtown. "At least I don't have to spend it here."

Rabbit kicked at the asphalt. "Any idea where?"

"Yeah. There are some cabins up in the Alberta area—Jasper Park. When I was just a shave-tail, there was a movie filmed up there. Marilyn Monroe. I worked some studio security on my vacation. I fell in love with the place. Even then, I knew that I didn't want to die on some oil-stained street in central LA. If I got to choose, it would be sitting in an Adirondack chair sipping some good Canadian whiskey."

"No fishing pole?"

The man laughed. "I hate fishing. I hate golf." He grabbed his large gut with both hands. "I like sitting and drinking. It's what's killing me, but I'll damn sure be happy when I get where I end up."

Gabe slung his leg over the chopper and stuck out his hand. "It's been good, sir. You don't have to worry about tomorrow..." He waved his finger at the trunk and the bag. "This is one that they don't know about."

"Trust me, son. They know. They just don't know whom or how high it really is. I'm just the bagman, and now I'm going to go park my car and walk away. I suggest you two do the same."

ANGEL FLIGHTS

"Sarge," Rabbit quietly stuck his hand out, "thank you for everything you have ever done for me."

"Terry, of any of us, it's you who needs to get out. I don't even remember what you looked like or what you were like in uniform. You have been under too deep and too long. Hell, son, I don't even know if you're still a cop undercover—or just a drug pushing biker. When I was your TO, you were like a son to me. I'd like to think you will get out of this all right."

"Whale, you need to trust your training. I knew my exit the day I turned in the blue and got on a bike. I'll be just fine. I know that movie you worked on. I think I even know where those cabins are. I'll come find you if I come north."

"I'd like that, son. I truly would." He pinched the snot off the end of his nose. "It would mean a lot to me."

"Then consider it done, sir."

"Don't call me sir, I work for—"

Rabbit laughed. "No, you don't. You're done. I'll see you soon."

"I'll keep a bottle full for you."

The old man wiped at the sides of his eyes as he watched the two motorcycles float their way down the enormous parking lot. He turned to his patrol car. *One more stop and then the airport.*

Gabe and Rabbit stopped at the house to drop

off two large duffle bags filled with fat envelopes. The thought the feds would try to raid the house wasn't even a hiccup. There seemed to always be at least a few cops, if not sheriffs, or CHP around at any one time. There was no lost love between the locals and the feds. The locals would jump at the chance to shoot a breaking and entering—it would be a righteous shooting with no investigation.

They stood at the closet looking at the five banker boxes that were already there. Both knew the bills in each box were bound and stacked tight—all hundreds. Rabbit's closet was a mirror image—even down to a few duffle bags.

"How much college did you say you wanted?"

Gabe flattened his lips into duck lips and buzzed them. His eyes were large. "I guess I haven't been paying attention lately." He looked at his friend. "How big was that fishing boat you wanted?"

They both laughed at the old stereotype as Rabbit threw the duffle bags in on top of the boxes. "We'll worry about it later."

The ride down to the Navy yard was short by miles, but long in that they took city streets the entire way. The rough old highway was something they both would not miss. Passing the smell of bacon, sausage, and whatever else was coming from the

Dean plant was another thing. They both liked the small amounts that they had for breakfast, but when you render hundreds of tons a day, the neighborhood air drips with the reek of hog fat.

As they got south of the stench, Gabe yelled at Rabbit. "We are taking the freeway back. I don't even care if it's the 605 and forty miles out of our way. I do not want to ever smell like this again."

Rabbit gave him a thumbs-up.

The machinist mate was waiting as they pulled up. "You two are late."

Rabbit gave him a hard look and pulled the clutch back in, stomped on the shifter, and started to roll.

"Wait." The guy held up his hands. "I didn't mean it that way. It just means I'm late punching in, and I can't go stash the… well, I'll just be late."

Gabe looked at the medium-sized bulging dark blue duffle bag. He got off the bike and pulled the large, heavy black bag off his sissy bar. He dropped it on the ground just before Rabbit's hit the same spot. One hundred one-kilogram packages of pills and five kilos of powder that was ten percent pure. They knew that with the huge push in Vietnam, the Navy Yard had been pushing overtime for at least a couple of years. A hundred dollar jar of a thousand pills could go a long time—or be used-up in a week or so of long overtime.

Gabe took the blue bag and strapped it to the sissy bar. The straps barely fit around the unyielding contents of the bag. As much as they had wanted to see the cocky machinist mate get his due, Gabe and

Rabbit had talked over what it would do to the whole yard. A grenade or a B-52 strike would be more humane, but not so patriotic. They decided to just let it go.

Rabbit kicked his chopper into gear and then glanced over at the man struggling with the bags. "Make it last—we won't be back."

He dumped the clutch and shot off as the man's face dropped open. Gabe caught the look and smiled as he followed his partner. He was sure there would be some kind of retribution taken out on the guy for the sudden cut-off.

But that was not their problem.

They decided to have dinner at a little place in San Gabriel that Gabe had found the year before. The Italian food was amazing, but the people who owned it were even more so. Mama's chin barely cleared Gabe's belt buckle when she hugged him. Her husband, Michael, wasn't much taller.

As they pulled up, the garlic and tomato smell made their stomachs remember it had been a long day.

Rabbit ran across the street for a bottle of red wine while Gabe got hugged for bringing Mama a fresh eggplant. Neither of the men liked eggplant, but they dutifully ate the few slices she would fry parmesan style.

Rabbit swished the wine around in his water glass. The restaurant couldn't get a liquor license so it was BYOB, and Michael served it in the water glasses so they didn't have any wine stuff that the health inspector would see.

"So what was your quick take on what's in the closet and on the bikes?"

Gabe kind of knew what was stacked tight and neat in the heavy boxes. Combined with the day's take, and what pocket change was in each of the large bureau drawers—he did some fast calculating, "About four, maybe four and a half each?"

Rabbit's closed one eye. "Is your math right?"

"Probably even north of that."

"We are talking million here—not hundred-thousand…"

Gabe nodded. "Now that I think about it… the boxes might have even that much. How many boxes are in your closet?"

"Five, maybe six… and a few bags."

"How much did you stash in that bank in Mexico?"

"A little over eight-hundred."

"I've got a couple of other banks down there. We need to figure on taking some more down tomorrow."

"If it's all hundreds, I figured out a way to make half mill look like a bedroll. "

"Tomorrow morning, we need to find a couple of bank boxes here as well. You'll need access for schooling."

"Whose?"

Rabbit smiled. "Lito's going to need a bunch. And I have an idea for a little business venture."

Gabe swallowed the last of the piece of bread that had finished wiping the plate. "What about you?"

"I have stuff already out of the country. I haven't figured out what I want to do next, but I know it has nothing to do with what I've been doing the last ten years of my life. For now, that drawer has more than anything I need. Seeing how expensive food and stuff is at the house…"

They laughed as Michael came with two containers of spumoni ice cream. There was a lit candle in each. Mama was with him.

As Michael put the ice cream on the table and straightened up, he put his arm around her shoulders as she grabbed him.

"It's not our birthdays."

"No," the small man with the pencil-line mustache smiled. "It is our fiftieth anniversary."

Gabe looked around the room. It was late and they were the last customers. "Then get two more glasses and we can drink a toast."

Michael turned and took two from one of the tables already set up for the next day.

As Rabbit poured the last of the wine into the four glasses, he glanced up. "So how did you two meet?"

ANGEL FLIGHTS

"It was on the ferry between Messina and Scilla."

They drank a toast, and then Mama went back to the kitchen for her fresh batch of marinara sauce, as Michael pulled up a chair. Turning it backwards, he straddled it as he sat down.

Gabe and Rabbit knew it would be a late night— and they did not care.

29

ROMEO AND JULIET

"IT WAS A marriage classico." The small man sighed. "She was Italian, and I was Sicilian. But, for us, it didn't matter. We knew at first sight.

"She was standing at the railing, a girl of thirteen. I was the wise old man of fourteen. We eventually started talking, but we had to be secret about it—she was always with an aunt."

"A chaperone."

He pointed at Gabe. "Exactly. But, luckily for us, her aunt liked one of the sailors, as well as his wine." He winked. "So with the hour of sailing, we got to hold hands and talk.

"By the time she was fourteen, we knew. We had a little money, and I borrowed a little more, and one morning, we slipped away and took the train to Rome. We had hoped to be married before anyone could stop us. But that was not to be. We chanced to see one of her uncles and a cousin—with guns. I didn't have to see to know that someone from my family would also not want us to marry. So we begged a bit and took another train to Venitza. From there we got jobs on a small fishing boat as cook and deck hand."

"Did you know anything about fishing?"

"No. But Maria knew cooking and their last cook—they had cut up for bait because he kept poisoning them. I was at least trainable. Actually, I ended up driving the boat. I understood the map, and I was sober when it came time to dock—instead of hit the dock." He drove his fist into his open hand as he laughed.

"One day, we saw one of my cousins. So we took a job on a ship that ran up into the Black Sea and Russia. It turned out the two families found out and soon we were running across Russia, but Russia..." He shrugged.

Gabe realized the time frame the man was talking about. "Either the Revolution or World War One..."

Michael nodded. "Smart boy. I lost an uncle and two cousins during the war from freezing. Maria lost two." He held up his fingers.

Rabbit held up the empty bottle. Michael shook his head. *The liquor store had already closed.* The Italian smiled, held up a finger and left. A minute later, the kid from the liquor store came in, set down another bottle, and left. Michael came out of the back with the corkscrew. "Where was I? Oh, yes." He opened and poured the three glasses full.

"We got swept up in the rush to make armies. I was too small to hold a rifle, and I told them I was only twelve and Maria was eleven—but we knew how to cook. That was enough and the next thing we knew, we were on our way to Poland. That was a very nasty winter. There were months we didn't have a bath. Food was even scarcer."

Gabe frowned. "Months... no bathing...?"

Michael held up his glass. "A glass of wine is a phone call away. We assume a restaurant will be open and we have clean clothes in the closet. But there was a time when none of that existed—for many people—not just Maria and me, but for millions of people."

He looked at Gabe. "What is the longest you have gone wearing the same clothes and not washing them? A week?"

Gabe held up his two fingers. Rabbit only smiled.

"So you have no idea what it means to wear your underwear until it rots into just sand. How thick wool pants become pounded to clay. There are people in this world who have a bath in a river in the spring. Those were the kind of people that we rode with. When we finally washed our clothes, we were in heaven. But in the winter, in Poland—any water is just ice. So we cooked and kept our heads down. In

ANGEL FLIGHTS

the early spring, we were south of Gdansk. I had traded some extra bread for a compass, and when we lucked across a small village, we scavenged for clothes. We were lucky. We fit the small clothes of kids. The soldiers fought over threadbare coats. One night we snuck out of the camp. By the light of the stars and a few matches, we made our way north to Gdansk. We would have stayed there for the rest of the war."

Gabe poured some more wine. "Did they find you there, too?"

"The spring of 1919." Mama came around the end of the low wall. "My uncle was a persistent man. He was a detective for the Carabinieri. He was good at finding people."

Michael pointed toward the kitchen. She nodded with her eyes closed and patted his leg as she sat down and offered out her glass.

Rabbit took the gist of the story. "So, the war was over, and you two are on the run again... from Poland."

"Si. So we turn to the sea again. This time France—but we know to keep moving. So we go west to Spain."

Gabe held up his hand. "Wait. So you two have been on the run for... um, four years. Are you married yet?" He holds up his hands as he starts to do the math working back from 1970.

Maria smiles and shakes her head no. She pats

Michael's thigh lovingly. "No. We would have to post banns and to do so..."

"So you're living in sin?"

Michael's face was mock horror as Maria quietly giggled. "We had a marriage mantello—same bed, but with a blanket, a mantello, between us. I was still pure."

Michael nodded. "It was not so easy, but we were good Catholic kids. We knew it had to be right."

"Finally, we ended in a small town on the coast of northern Spain. It was a simple fishing village with a bar, which also served tapas in the afternoon. It was what passed for a restaurant in those days. Even with the war, there was money or something to be traded."

Maria smiled. "Except for virtue."

The three men raised their glasses.

Rabbit prodded. "And they still found you."

Michael put up his hand. "Almost."

"One day, a couple of men came in. They sat and talked with the owner. All of them kept watching me as I cleaned. Finally, the owner called us over. He told me the men had just come from a village thirty kilometers away. There were men looking for a young Italian couple. He asked if we knew about it.

"The man had taken us in. He made room for us in the hayloft of his barn. He gave us work. I could not lie to this man. So I told him the truth. It was a

ANGEL FLIGHTS

big risk." Michael held out his hands in supplication.

"He asked if we had ever done anything that would make us impure. We told him no. He asked why we had never married in all of those years. So we explained about how dangerous it would be to post the banns and stay somewhere that long." He poured a little more wine, took a sip, and continued.

"He sent his son to fetch the priest. When the priest arrived, he told him a short version. The priest again asked if we had done anything that God would not look kindly on. I told him only that I had stabbed a soldier who was trying to molest Maria. He said that I was only doing God's work by protecting a virgin.

"He said the circumstances demanded he waive the banns, and the wedding happened that evening. The whole village was there." The two Italians sat back with warm smiles—remembering the day.

"After the wedding and feast, the entire town escorted us to a small shack on the edge of town. They made us stop a few yards away. Four men dragged two dead pigs into the shack. As the men rushed out of the shack, fire engulfed it.

"The women of the village pulled black shawls over their heads and began to wail and weep. We had never seen anything like it. They were pounding their chests. The men began to cry as well. It was the saddest thing we had ever seen. We turned to the restaurant owner for an answer. He pulled us away to the docks."

Michael leaned forward and his voice lowered—as if sharing a great secret.

"He told us a sad story about how a young couple had been hounded from their homeland by their own families—intent upon killing them for simply being in love. Romeo and Juliet had not endured the suffering these two had. The families chased them across all of Europe and a war. And then, when they had finally found a tiny bit of peace—they had been married by the village priest."

Maria finished for Michael. "But... happiness was not their destiny." She frowned dramatically and waved her open hand back and forth as if to erase. "On their wedding night, in their nuptial bower—the lantern had tipped over and they had burned to death."

Gabe and Rabbit both had horrified faces. "That is horrible... but such a great story. But did it work?"

Michael nodded. "The owner gave us money and had arranged for us to be smuggled to Canada. Eventually, we made our way into America and became citizens.

"We had a restaurant in Chicago. In the early 1950s, we had the biggest banquet hall, and so it was the place to hold a large dinner. One night, with a large party, I went to check on things. One of the customers recognized me and fainted. He was one of my cousins." Maria's eyes grew big as if it was she were the cousin who thought he was seeing a ghost.

"After we revived him and convinced him that we were alive, he told us what had happened. The men had shown up the next day. The coals were too hot to poke through, but the women were still at the fire wailing in pain and sorrow. Each time a man tried to tell them the story, he too would break down. By the time they had the whole story, they too were crying.

"What we could not know was that after Russia, the two families had grown accustomed to each other. They were trying to bring us home and tell us that we were forgiven and to let us marry. Since that time, many of the family have married back and forth. At first, they called it a Romeo and Juliet marriage—but after Spain, they call it the Michael and Maria. But now we call it for the love of pigs."

The four chuckled. Maria put her glass down. "One of our nieces and her new husband went to find the village." Michael laughed and went into the back. He returned with a photograph.

The two newlyweds were standing behind a statue of two pigs. They were mirroring the love-struck faces of the pigs leaning into each other. The plaque was not in Spanish. Gabe looked up. "Gli Amanti?"

"It is Italian for The Lovers."

Gabe looked again and then dropped his hand. "Wow."

BAER CHARLTON

Rabbit raised his glass. "Here is to fifty years of wow—and the best love story ever."

The little village of San Gabriel was dark except for the cheerful golden light that spilled from the large picture window at the front of the tiny restaurant named Mama B's. The night was still. Soft, happy sounds, as well as the smell of homemade marinara sauce made with love, came from the open door long after the closing time of ten o'clock.

30

CRICKET

THE LATE NIGHT hadn't affected the need to take care of serious business on Friday morning. Rabbit and Gabe filled their jackets and a small duffle bag each, and then headed their own ways to find banks and safe deposit boxes.

By one o'clock, the closets contained two boxes each. Even with all hundreds, only part of one box could go south with them. They taped envelopes to their bodies, fed Gertie and went off for a late lunch.

"Where is my little man?" Gabe roared as he stepped into the restaurant.

He could hear the tiny slapping of the flat shoes as Lincoln came out of the back. He grabbed the squealing kid and swung him up toward the ceiling. There were already a few shoe marks on the surface. The diaper marks never showed.

"He just ate. You're going to make him throw up."

ANGEL FLIGHTS

Gabe tucked the giggling kid under his arm like a football. "Who just ate?"

Maria shook her head. "You are all just a bunch of kids."

Rabbit pulled Lincoln out of Gabe's arm from the back. "Jet Jockey!"

The squeal even made his mother laugh. The two funniest uncles were here to visit Lincoln.

Gabe stepped over to Maria. "Where's your brother?"

"At the house," She nodded across the street.

"Call him and tell him to get over here fast."

"What's up?" She looked at him seriously.

He pointed and then turned back to his partner. "And we need whatever Pepe wants to make us for lunch."

"Jet Jockey!!"

Gabe watched as Lito looked both ways and then ran across the street. He jumped the low wall instead of running the extra eight feet to the opening. "What's up?"

Gabe took him into the back room. "How much short do you think the scholarship is going to be for you to be a surgeon? Not just a doctor, but the whole show?"

The kid grew serious. He knew that this wasn't just about him doing a math trick for a party.

"Probably about eighty to a hundred grand... Why?"

Gabe pulled two large, fat envelopes out of his jacket. "You need to get a safe deposit box for these. We can discuss it later. If you can't get a ride in the next hour, you call your uncle at the precinct. That needs to be off the street by three this afternoon."

The kid looked at the envelopes his hands were barely able to grip. He could guess at what was in them. He was smart.

"Is this dirty?"

Gabe weighed his answer. "Everything is dirty to one degree or another—just don't lick it. You need to use it, and do good from it. You got that?"

"I'll have to call Tio."

Gabe reached past the kid and started dialing the phone on the wall.

"Stan, Gabe. I need Zorro code two at the top of the hill. He'll be tied up for an hour or so."

He listened, "Thanks, Stan," and hung up.

"You had lunch yet?" The kid shook his head.

Gabe took the two envelopes and turned the kid around. There was no way they would fit in the kid's small pockets. He pulled the tucked in white shirt out and shoved the envelopes halfway down into his pants. He fluffed the shirt over the kid's new butt. He slapped the envelopes and pushed the kid back into the dining room. Leaning into the kitchen had told Pepe that Lito was also eating .

Ten minutes later, the black and white pulled up across the street. Gabe pushed down on Lito's shoulder. "Finish your lunch, Flaco. You need food to study hard." He met Zorro on the sidewalk.

"You need to take Lito to a bank. Not one you bank at. He needs a safe deposit box. Probably a medium will do. He has some trophies and collectibles that are very valuable and he lives in a bad neighborhood—whatever gets him a box today. Don't ask questions. Just get it done in the next hour."

Zorro examined his friends face. "The city is blowing up right now."

"I know. It's going to be fine. Lito has nothing to do with all this. We'll talk when this all settles down, okay?"

"Sure. You know me. I've got your back."

"Especially when it comes to this family."

Zorro nodded with a wan smile. He looked around Gabe and they both turned to see Lito coming out of the restaurant. Gabe noticed he was walking only a little funny getting used to the extra beans in his burrito.

Zorro frowned. "Tuck in your…"

Gabe stopped him with his hand. "He likes it with the tails out. It's a thing he's going through." He gave the uncle a hard look.

Zorro sighed as he rolled his eyes. Gabe turned to the kid and pulled some money out of his pocket. He pulled a couple of hundreds out of the middle. The kid's eyes got huge. "Get as many years as this will pay for—probably three or four. Ask if they have a special rate for paying for five. If the math works out, get Zorro to cover the rest. I'll pay him back."

Gabe turned and muttered only for Zorro. "Watch over him."

Zorro patted Gabe on the patch with the wings and halo. "Like a guardian angel."

Rabbit came to the door. "You want to finish this or are we out?"

Gabe knew the next meal might be late in Mexico. "Give me a couple of minutes."

"We've got time."

There were only nine bikes lined up in the alley. Gabe pulled in and parked next to the polished red Indian Chief. He looked at the fresh engine. Mike had missed a few weeks as he worked finding parts for the old bike. Gabe figured it was one of the most babied bikes in the LA basin, and knowing Mike, probably had a half million miles on it.

"Good to see you two." The high squeaky voice was all Gabe needed. He signed the sign for same.

"How do you like the new engine?"

"Looks like the old one."

"The old one was only eighty-inches. I liked how yours responds and got the mechanic to build me ninety-six."

"Is it squared?"

"No, it's round…" The man frowned. *Maybe he hadn't understood the question.*

ANGEL FLIGHTS

"No, squared. Is the stroke the same as the bore?" Gabe used just general hand shapes instead of signs to describe the engine terms.

"Oh, oh, yes. He also balanced everything. This bitch is so smooth it makes the other one feel like it was a John Deere or something."

Rabbit nodded up the alley. "Where is everyone?"

"Lois already cut five of the guys loose. They had a bunch of girls not show up because they are afraid of something. There are cops everywhere running around like they are looking for something—but don't know what."

"Yeah, we noticed that, too."

Rabbit put his index knuckles in his front pockets. His hands were always ready. "Do we have a count yet?"

Mike held up his hand with the index finger up and then flicked it down to his thumb held out. *Eleven*.

The door opened and Lois stepped out. The men shuffled in with varied greetings for the woman from a kiss on the cheek to a quick hug.

There were no new angels this trip.

The men lined up in a loose arc of what was normally a lot more.

Lois stepped to her usual place. Gabe had long notice that there was no more paint on the concrete where Lois walked each week.

She slowly turned and looked around. "Some of you have heard this speech a hundred times. And I want to thank you for that opportunity and your help. Just to remind you about what we are here for…" She looked at Mike and signed as she greeted him. "Good to have you back, Angel." He nodded.

"A few years ago, some very special courageous doctors and nurses got tired of seeing young girls of all sorts of ages coming into their emergency rooms. The girls were usually hemorrhaging, bleeding, as a result of a visit to a butcher up a back alley. They were desperate to terminate what was growing inside of them. We make no judgments about why they come to us. They are in need, and we don't turn them away. If they found us, they are desperate. How desperate you may ask? They usually have no other avenue.

"There are no hard statistics as of yet, but the street numbers go like this. Eighty percent of the girls has been sexually assaulted by either their own fathers, brothers, or a trusted uncle. Usually, this has been going on for years. These girls come from poor families, middle-income families, and wealthy families. Child molestation, incest, and pedophilia have no defining boundaries. It happens in white, colored, Mexican, Asian, and every other kind of people you can think of. So, if you have any hint of judgment you might pass on these young girls, you can leave now. Any questions?"

ANGEL FLIGHTS

She slowly turned, as she looked everyone in the eye. All were solemn, quiet, and shaking their heads.

Lois turned toward the inside door. She nodded and the woman standing there opened the door.

The parade was the usual selection of hard-bitten biker women that looked between twenty-five and thirty. They filed out and formed a mirroring semi-circle to the bikers.

Lois looked at the woman by the door. The woman nodded.

Lois looked at the girls that now looked like what was referred on the street as 'ol' lady' or 'biker bitch.' She sized up each girl. They were all playing the role of not only their lives but also the man who was transporting her. Their safety was in each other's hands.

"Here are the rules. You will choose your Angel. No Angel will choose you. You will show them your name tattoo on your arm. By Sunday, that tattoo will have been washed off." She pointed over her shoulder at the men. "Every one of these men is named Angel—no matter what a patch on their chest may say. Their name is Angel. Go ahead, say hello now."

The line of girls chorused, "Hello, Angel."

"Great. In a few minutes, you will choose your Angel. This is your Angel for the duration of the weekend. If something was to happen, you only have to remember that one name. Any other Angel will also help you. Now, just as your name isn't Mickey, or Sneezy, or Jiminy Cricket, their name isn't Angel. You will use these names and that is all you are to know about each other. DO NOT TALK about anything personal. You can enjoy the sunset, talk about how bad the traffic is, maybe even comment on how you can smell the ocean as you pass it. But you will not talk about anything personal. Do I make myself clear?"

She walked along the line of girls. They all nodded obediently.

"After you choose your Angel, you will leave here. You will get on the motorcycles and your next stop, other than for gas, will be in Mexico. You will be let off in a courtyard of the home you will be at for the weekend. On Sunday afternoon, about this time, your angels will return to pick you up. The border crossing will be busy with a lot of tourists coming home.

"You will say nothing at any time during the crossing. This is the most dangerous part of this whole weekend. You will literally have your Angel's life in your hands for this entire time. You must play your part to perfection. If you have any doubts, pretend to be very sleepy and just nod your way through the process. Any questions?"

There were none.

"Okay, without talking, choose your Angel."

As usual, the girls had been visually sizing up the guys. For most, it was the first time they had gotten any choice about anything male. Finally, the first one broke ranks and the girls shuffled towards their choice. The men knew the routine—they just stood there until they were chosen. The first contact was usually the Angel resting his hand on her shoulder as they waited for Lois to cut them loose.

"Everybody good? Great. Safe journey everyone. We'll see you Sunday night."

The alley became deafening with the choppers. Mike had broken the group into two sets—five and six. The six would take the inland Empire route down through Temecula, and the five would do the 60 to Brea Canyon and on down to the I-5 to San Diego.

The inland group all had longer reach on their tanks and so Rabbit and Gabe led the other four. Everyone wound through the rush hour city streets to their preferred entrance onto the freeway for their destination. Gabe and Rabbit were looking for the faster I-10, chunked off large steps east and south by winding through first the outer reaches of Hollywood, then the faster boulevards that crisscrossed the eastern LA basin.

As they passed through Pomona, the girl behind Gabe had not even so much as made a chirp. Gabe chuckled at his joke as he thought about the tattoo that he hadn't gotten before. He had packed a couple of Sleepys, a Cinderella or three, four Docs that he could recall, a Peter Pan, enough Mickeys and Minnies to qualify as an infestation. A few weeks before he had gotten Goofy, and Rabbit had pulled a Pluto—but this trip was his first Jiminy Cricket. At least he could call her Cricket—he drew the line at calling anyone Goofy, and Rabbit had admitted that Pluto was just wrong.

The names were from all the Saturday cartoons. Almost every redhead Gabe had carried had opted for Woody the Woodpecker. Rabbit had gotten a tall gal once who had flashed Foghorn Leghorn. She had quietly leaned in and said, "I'm horny, but you can call me Foggy."

Gabe had gotten Bullwinkle down to Rocky. They had carried birds, dogs, cats, mice, and even several Olive Oils. One roly-poly gal had pulled up her sleeve to reveal Yogi Bear's sidekick. It was during the heat of summer and her shirt was unbuttoned to a point where the name Booboo applied. Some of the girls had proved playful in a way that made it obvious they were only being that way to cover up how scared they really were. The names came and went, but one thing Gabe and Rabbit knew was consistent—the girls they brought down were not the same that they took home. The experience changed all of them.

On the turn south of Riverside, they pulled into the large Atomic Gas station. The girls had reported back several weeks before that the toilets were clean. Everyone cycled through as tanks were filled and bladders emptied. The next stop would be Mexico. Rabbit checked his watch.

"We on time?"

Rabbit shook his head. "Traffic was lighter than I thought. Even with taking the highway instead of the freeway, we're still going to be early."

"What about taking the pass back over to the I-5?"

The other biker named Sandy had been listening. "We could also pass through the east crossing. It wouldn't take any time in the crossing, but the highway west sweeps far south and comes back up to connect from down San Felipe way. It should eat up most of that hour. Then we could just ride a little slower going out to the hacienda."

Rabbit looked at Gabe.

"That's the way we came when I brought Lito down. I wanted to see at least one alternative. It's a small crossing, and mostly they get the trucks coming up from Sonora. So, yeah, I think it would work. Otherwise, we would have to stop for dinner somewhere at the north end of San Diego."

Rabbit noticed the last of the girls coming out of the bathrooms. He was the last to get in so he decided. "Okay, but I've never been through there, Sandy, so why don't you take the lead with Snake and take us on across. Now I have to see a man about a horse." He strolled over to the bathrooms.

Later, Gabe glanced at his watch and looked over to Sandy and Rabbit. Rabbit looked at his watch and smiled. As they started out of the gate, the pack of five was just arriving. Mike waved. They would save him a tub of lobsters.

The tubs were taken back. The shells had long been burned to ash in the pit. Rabbit was nursing his second beer as he watched the early moon set into the ocean. He didn't really speak to anyone, just mused with his own observation. "Sunsets are things of beauty, but nobody pays attention to the cold crystalline beauty of a full moon sliding into the sea."

A female voice answered. "It is like an ice cube—slipping into a hot drink—only to disappear." Regina came over and knelt down next to Rabbit and Gabe. Her voice became quiet. "Do you two know who brought Jiminy Cricket down?"

Gabe turned in his chair. "I did. What's wrong?"

"They called. She's not doing well. They might need you to ride tonight or early tomorrow morning."

Gabe gave her the half-full beer. She nodded as she stood. She squeezed his shoulder. "Get some sleep. I'll come get you if they call."

"Thanks, Rog." Gabe looked at Rabbit. Getting shot or beat up or even stabbed was something the two faced every day. They pulled their pants on without a second thought about it. It was all part of their strange job. But this... this was an innocent—a civilian. Usually one who never asked for the situation. This was all different—and it affected the two big men down to their cores.

"Ever have this happen?"

"I've known of a few—but none of mine." Rabbit was silent for a long time. And then his voice was more of an exhausted sigh. "They are so young. I saw the one you got. She's very scared."

"I thought she was crying a couple of times, but when I checked the mirrors, her jaw was just locked. Her face was hard as stone."

"Did she say anything to you?"

"Not a word. Not in Hollywood, not on the bike. It's like she's a robot or something."

"You get those sometimes. I always wonder if they don't go home, and sometime down the road, they just lose it and pack it all in… or end up in a hospital because they didn't succeed."

Gabe poked the stick at the embers. "In Adak, we had this corporal who just couldn't handle the dark. At the middle of the day, for the four hours that there was any sun on the edge of the world, he would sit at the end of the runway. We kind of knew, but you never really expect people to take their own lives. But then one day, the guy put a Kabar to his chest and leaned against a crate. To make sure, he had his Colt to his temple."

Rabbit pictured the desperation the guy must have had. "Did it work?"

Gabe shook his head slowly. "The knife slipped and skidded along the ribs when the gun went off. The guy's hand was at the wrong angle and the bullet zipped around the skull under the skin. The guy had the pistol so hard against his head, the expanding gas cloud had hit the skull, and the only place for the gas to expand was between the skull and skin. It lifted the entire skin-balloon off and made it three sizes too big for the skull."

Rabbit was sitting up. "Did he live?"

"They rushed him into surgery, but the guy was very mechanical and a few nights later, he figured out how to get what he wanted. He took the leads from his monitor and plugged them straight into the wall socket."

Rabbit fell back. "That is determination."

Gabe stood. "I've never looked at life or how I do things the same way. I'm going to get some sleep. In the morning, I might not have a chance to get to a bank, so I'll leave my extra bed roll with you if that's okay."

Rabbit pursed his lips and stood. "Sure, I'll just open it with a numbered and keyed box. That way you can come get it next week or so and move it wherever you want."

The embers glowed red and gently illuminated the two men.

Gabe stuck his hand out. "It's been an amazing career and adventure with you. Thank you for being who you are and having me along in everything."

"I used to think I was better as the lone bull. But it has been better with you along." He chuckled and waved his left hand, "Gertie.... Eeah..."

They laughed and then went searching for an empty cot.

31

RUN

ACROSS THE DESERT, there was a thin glow. The line of hot gold had yet to slice the earth from the sky. Mike closed the screen door quietly. He couldn't hear it, but he knew the sound would be loud in the early morning with nothing moving but a few waves. The early seabirds would be waking but not moving.

"Gabe," he shook the man who shuddered and rolled. "I can't see your mouth." He waved his hand to follow.

As they crossed the small street, he explained with his fist to his ear like a phone. "She's making you some breakfast. You can get a shower."

They climbed the stairs, and Gabe paused to look at the flat Pacific Ocean. The calm gray water blended seamlessly with the gray sky. He stepped into the apartment.

A large coffee mug met his hands as he walked

ANGEL FLIGHTS

in. "Good morning, sunshine. Get a shower—breakfast will be ready in about ten minutes. I hope you like stinky old lobster." She smiled and kissed him on the cheek as her hand pointed the way toward the bathroom.

"What did they say?" Gabe mopped at the little bits of food on the plate with a piece of tortilla.

"They did her surgery about seven last night, but she keeps hemorrhaging. They are afraid she might also have some internal problems as well. She hadn't told them she had been in pain for the last couple of weeks. So they want to get her up to one of the clinics to do more exams, and if she needs surgery, a hospital in north San Diego is easier to explain than one down here."

"Does someone have a map or something?"

"The doctor left last night and will meet you this morning in Mission Valley. Everything is easy to find, and then you can follow him up to the clinic."

"What about…?"

Regina put her hand on his shoulder. "Look—that is all I know. I shouldn't even know that much—but I do. You just need to get up there, and they will explain the rest. We can talk next weekend when you two come back down."

"You're staying here?"

"Dude, I'm on vacation for three weeks. This is my time of year to pork out on fat bugs and tortillas. Besides, I get to visit all of my family down here."

Gabe thought a moment. "Could... would you hold something for me?"

"Of course..."

Gabe ran out to his bike and pulled the fat bedroll off his front forks. He checked to make sure that nothing had come loose to expose the large package concealed inside.

"Got a closet I can throw this in?"

Mike and Regina looked at the strange, large blanket-roll. They knew it looked more like three or four large blankets rolled together. Mike turned and cleared the small lace runner and a few religious statues off a large old wooden buffet. He pulled out two drawers slightly, and then the top center drawer. Reaching in upside down, his finger pushed. With his other hand, he raised the top of the buffet. Behind the top shorter drawers was a space large enough to hide a small person.

The man smiled. "It is very old and sometimes in the old west, there was a need to hide things."

Gabe stuck the bedroll in and Mike closed the top. Gabe could hear the softest of clicks. He was sure the entire locking system was wood.

"Thank you." He shook the smaller man's hand.

Regina stepped in for a hug. "Vaya con Dios, but ride like the devil."

Gabe nodded and left.

The silence was the kind that only came from thick walls of stone or adobe. The hacienda was

ANGEL FLIGHTS

adobe. As Gabe rode through the large gate, the noise of his motorcycle seemed to be sucked into the tall walls—never to be given back.

The nurse waited calmly near the front door, her hands clasped. She waited as Gabe parked the chopper and turned it off. As he swung his leg over the seat, she turned and started through the door. *She was all business.*

The giant front door closed with the dull boom of a feeling more than a sound. Gabe thought of castles as he was guided down the hall. "She wants to meet you first."

"I brought her down yesterday on the bike."

The nurse didn't stop walking, merely turned, and gave him a look that silenced him. He couldn't remember his mother ever giving him a look like it—but it had his mother written all over it. He kept his mouth shut and followed.

A young girl lay in the hospital bed. She was propped up by several pillows. She belonged in a pediatric ward somewhere—not in an abortion clinic in Mexico.

"Hello, Angel."

"Hello, Cricket." He didn't know if he should stick his hand out or not. She raised hers and took the lead.

"I apologize for not talking at all on the ride down. I don't even think I thanked you last night."

"It's okay. Not every girl talks. Some talk too

much. It all equals out, and it is what it needs to be. But for now, we need to get you back north. "

"My name is—"

"Cricket." He cut her off. "Where is the makeup?" He turned to the nurse.

"It's over here. They usually do their own…"

It was his turn to be all business. "She will need all of her strength to just stay on the back of the bike. And we need to leave as soon as we can. You get her clothes, and I'll do her makeup." He took the tray of makeup from her.

Gabe sat on the bed. He looked at the face that looked younger than Lito. *Babies.* He took the dark eyeliner pencil and drew in her eyes heavily like the cholo girls. Next came the brown shadow. The whole face got a smear of foundation, and then some blush and finally powder. He rubbed the powder. "You need it jammed into the foundation so the wind doesn't blow it into your eyes. It doesn't feel good." He smiled at her. "Or so I've been told."

She chuckled softly.

"What about those false eyelashes?"

"They blew off. Or we started too early to remember—with that roaring hangover."

He looked at the clothes that the nurse laid on the end of the bed. He turned. "Do you have any extra stuff… like maybe a watch cap or something? We need to cover that hair. It's too nice."

A moment later, the nurse returned with a Navy

wool cap. "Perfect." Gabe pulled it down on the girl's head and then shoved the shoulder length hair up into it. He stood back. The transformation wasn't great, but at this hour of the morning, it was going to work just fine. "It's going to have to work. Remember, you have a hangover, and if they so much as slow us down, start to act like you might throw up."

The nurse pinched the bridge of her nose. She was trying not to laugh. She could imagine the poor border guard who held up his hand. This girl might just give him more than a try at throwing up.

She pushed on Gabe's shoulder. "You go wait out by the bike. We'll pad her up and bring her out." She picked up the hand-drawn map. "You can study this. The car is a blue Buick Electra. But you'll be the only people in the parking lot at this hour."

The sleepy border guard had his coffee mug in one and just jerked his other thumb over his shoulder as he took a sip. There were almost no cars at that hour.

The nurse had been right. The blue car was the only one in the giant shopping center's parking lot. In the distance, a single truck with a vacuum on it was circling around and around. The man was leaning against the car. As they pulled up, he stood.

"How are you doing, Cricket? You want to ride in the car?"

"No... The wind and air feels good." Gabe and the doctor could tell she was fading fast from the loss of blood.

The doctor looked at Gabe. "We're about fifteen minutes away."

Gabe growled. "Make it ten." He adjusted Cricket's jean jacket so she was bound to the sissy bar.

The man nodded.

Gabe was afraid the guy had never broken a law before in his life. But, as they raced up the on-ramp, he remembered what kind of laws this guy broke every weekend. A speeding ticket was nothing to this guy. *They were there in nine.*

Gabe slid off the bike and took one look at the slumped Cricket. Her arms hung at her side, and her head was flopped to her one shoulder. As she started to fall, Gabe grabbed his arms under her and scooped her off the bike. The doctor rushed to the door and held it open.

"This way." The doc led the way down the short hall. The two nurses looked up.

"Room three." The nurse followed Gabe. "On the bed."

Gabe draped the girl on the bed and before his arms were out, the boots and hat were off. As he stepped back, the pants and jacket followed. He turned and left. He figured one more breath and he would be looking at the naked girl.

He stood outside the room listening to the commotion. "Start drip of glucose and another of saline.

ANGEL FLIGHTS

Where is the blood? We're bringing it to temperature now. BP is 90 over 52. Heart rate is 62 but thready. Elevate her feet. Cook some blankets in the autoclave, I want her warm."

A nurse came down the hall carrying two units of blood. She didn't even look up at Gabe. He finally just walked over to the one nurse at the desk.

She looked up. She had seen the same look before. She pointed down another hallway. "Take it to the end, turn right, and all the way down. The coffee is about twenty minutes old."

Gabe sat more stunned than thinking. Everything before had been a clean drive down, drop them off, pick them up, and drive north. He had never really thought about them much. Not like Maria. But then... he had shaken her hand. It was not her name, but it was her name. She, forever in his mind, would be Cricket. A human being—a very young girl. As he hid her real face, he had realized just how young she must really be.

Younger than Maria was.

The doctor walked into the small break room. At first, he hesitated at waking the very large man. Courtesy and understanding that it had been the adrenalin that had knocked the biker out overrode his caution. He sat down and gently shook Gabe's knee.

"Wha...?"

"It okay. I just wanted you to know that we are going to transport her to the hospital. I can't do the right surgery here. She is showing signs of peritonitis, and we need to go in within the hour. We were able to stabilize her, but she has a lot of inflammation and has lost a lot of blood." He rested his hand on Gabe's knee. "The ride this morning... you probably... no, you did, most definitely, save her life."

"Can I see her?"

"Sure, she's awake. She's groggy but awake. The ambulance will be here in a couple of minutes."

Gabe walked into the room. The face looked even smaller. Someone had removed the makeup.

He stopped at the side of the bed. "Hey?"

"Angel." She tried to move her hand.

He took it in both of his. "You're going to be just fine. They are taking you to the hospital. You are one very sick girl—but they are good, and you will be able to go surfing again soon enough."

The voice was soft. "I don't surf. But I want to learn how to sail a boat."

"You'll do that soon enough. There is lots of time."

The nurse touched Gabe's arm. "The ambulance is here."

"Angel?" The voice was half panic.

"Yeah, Cricket."

"Stay with me."

Gabe looked at the doctor.

"You can't ride in the ambulance—it's a clean environment. But you can follow."

ANGEL FLIGHTS

He turned back to the girl. "I'll be right behind you, kid."

Gabe backed out of the way but maintained eye contact with the small girl. The ambulance team transferred her to their gurney and hurried out the door. Gabe followed and didn't get on the bike until he had waved to her and they closed the doors. The hospital was only a five-minute ride away.

32

STAY

THE YOUNG NURSE stopped in the hall winding her finger in around her dark ponytail as she watched and thought. The huge, gruff-looking biker was sitting in the room with the little girl. Except for meals and a few breaks, he never left her room. For three nights, he had slept in the lounge chair. All he asked for was a blanket—which he then gently laid over the girl.

She shook her head as she reached the nurse's station. The older nurse looked up. "The biker?"

"Yeah... he never says much to anyone. But he's in there and he listens to the girl. I don't think he talks much, but it's weird. He's always there for her."

The third nurse turned in her chair from where she had been filling in paperwork. "Like he's her guardian angel?"

"Yeah, like that." The nurse continued stroking

her hair—first one hand and then the other. "The other day she was sleeping. I thought he was asleep also—but when she cried out in her sleep... he was wide awake and stood up. He put his hand on her arm and she calmed down."

The oldest of the three leaned back in her chair. "You two don't really pay attention much, do you?"

"What do you mean by that?" The young blonde took offense.

"Did you ever stop to talk to him?"

"He says hello... but no, he doesn't really talk."

"If you talked to him for even a minute, you would notice an old worn-out patch. It's a large rectangle just over his heart. It's a pair of angel's wings with a halo hanging on one of the wings."

"What do you think it means?"

The woman shrugged. "I don't know—I'm just saying that he has an interesting patch—that I've never seen before. And, when I worked in the emergency rooms up in LA—we saw a lot of patches."

The three nurses looked down the hall at the door to room 412. They were lost in their own thoughts and questions.

Curtains filtered the hard afternoon sunlight. Gabe thought it was the kindest light for the young girl. The pale freckles were not even enough to call her freckled. The dark brown hair was spread in lazy waves on the pillow, but where the sunlight glowed through a wave, the base deep red showed. Gabe pictured her in the sunshine with a ponytail. He had a hard time picturing her with a smile. For some reason, there was just too much sadness about her.

He watched as the sheet rose and fell. She was sleeping again. Her face would flatten out and relax as she slept. Whatever was grinding into her soul was at rest while she was. He waited for the rhythm to become paced. Her hand softly slid out of his as she rolled over, her lips softly smacking as she wet them in her sleep.

Gabe rose and tiptoed out of the room—keeping the steel slugs in his boots from striking the floor. He turned toward the elevators.

The voice was soft from behind him. "Sir?"

He turned to find the blonde nurse. His head nodded up in acknowledgment.

She pointed at the angel patch. "I noticed the patch before. What is it for?"

He thought about the last couple of years. He thought about his relationship with Rabbit, their work and friendship, and how the bond had grown. Images of getting to know Mike and finally meeting Regina—and them taking Lito under their wings. Finally, he thought of the years of bringing girls south and returning with women, and then there were the last few days with a tiny girl named Cricket.

"A gift." He turned and walked away.

"But...?" The nurse stood with her fist on her hip.

ANGEL FLIGHTS

The afternoon was giving way to the evening. Gabe sat slouched in the chair with his feet up on the bed. Cricket had giggled when he first did it. It had only taken minutes before the relaxed man had fallen asleep. Now, the two were eating little tubs of orange sherbet.

Gabe pulled the spoon from his sucking lips. "This would be a lot better with chocolate sauce on it."

"Oh my," The girl held her spoon and cup as she fell back into the pillows with closed eyes. "Chocolate." She sighed.

Gabe watched her with a frown. "How often do you have chocolate?"

She busied herself with the sherbet. "Oh... occasionally."

"Does it... affect you?"

"Do I like it? Sure—who doesn't?"

"But that's not what we are talking about, is it?" Gabe put his empty cup and spoon on the stand. "You don't get it at home... do you?"

She shook her head as she scraped the bottom of the cup. Her concentration was diligently focused—avoiding Gabe and answering. It was the first insight Gabe had gotten confirmation as to the kind of life this little girl lived in. If her eating chocolate was restricted—what else was controlled?

He got up and left the room. She watched him go. Her face froze as her hands began to tremble.

The trembling migrated to her lower lip. A single tear leaked out of her left eye. She wiped it away as she returned to the empty cup—determined to not cry—to find one last drop that escaped her previous efforts. She could hear her father's voice—*die before you cry.*

She could hear her father's voice in a lot of ways. None of them was reassuring.

She looked up. Gabe was standing there with four more cups of sherbet. As she smiled and took one of the cups, he placed two on the stand and opened the other. He traded with Cricket.

As he started to sit down, he suddenly stood as if he had sat on something. He looked at the seat. With his left hand, he reached around to his back pocket. His hand returned with a chocolate bar. He tossed it on the blanket where her lap was. "I think you dropped something."

She stared at the bar. She knew this was all hers. The voice was little more than the chirp of her nickname. "Thank you, Angel." She looked up. "Would you like some?"

"All yours, kid. Milk chocolate gives me gas something fierce. You wouldn't want to ride behind me if I ate milk chocolate. Why, I've had truckers who were behind me—pull off the road and wait until the air cleared."

Gabe had hoped for a laugh, but he settled for the wan smile. "You are so silly."

ANGEL FLIGHTS

He bowed with a swept arm for flare. "I will take that as a high compliment."

As Gabe finally sat, he stuck the first spoonful of sherbet into his mouth. "So do they have you cut up frogs and stuff at that school?"

"We saw a movie about them doing that... once. I don't know if I could do that... I mean, what's the point?"

Gabe frowned as he thought. *To learn about where the organs are? Maybe just to see if you are able to cut into a dead animal—kind of like cutting up the turkey for Thanksgiving.*

"So if there is ever a need for a frog doctor...?"

Can a young girl actually be this serious all the time? Gabe scratched his head as he started on the second cup of sherbet. "So you would rather just jump in and start cutting up a human cadaver?"

"Cada... a what?"

"Cadaver—a dead body."

She sat blinking. Gabe wasn't sure what she was processing. He knew she was in some kind of private school—probably parochial—based on the lack of science classes. Her knowledge of some areas was stellar, but in other basic areas, she kept faltering with little or no knowledge.

"What kind of school would have dead bodies to cut up? I mean other than if you were studying to be a doctor..."

Gabe had heard the shoes before he saw the

nurse.

"Good evening. I just need to take your..." She looked at the small wooden spoon hanging in the young girl's mouth. She looked over at Gabe and the matched wood in his mouth. Gabe was smiling sheepishly. The nurse didn't skip a beat. She looked at the chart for temperature and shook the thermometer. She stuck it in her own mouth as she strapped the cuff on Cricket's arm and took the rest of the girl's vitals.

Pulling the thermometer from her own mouth, she looked at it. She raised the chart and entered the data. She winked at Cricket.

"Keep this up, young lady, and we'll have to throw you out and make you go home." Not getting the smile she was looking for, she turned on Gabe. "As for you... I need to go get the other thermometer."

Still not getting any reaction from the girl, she turned to leave.

Gabe moved. "What was the first cadaver you had your hands in?"

The nurse turned. That was eight more words than she had heard come out of the man's mouth before. "Probably the frog we cut up in seventh grade. Why?"

"We were talking about poking around in cadavers."

"Human?"

Gabe nodded. "Any and all."

The woman returned to the end of the bed. "In high school, I already knew I wanted to be a nurse, so I took a few biology classes. We had snakes, a rabbit, and even a cat."

Cricket pulled the spoon from her mouth. "How does that prepare you for learning about the human body?"

"In college, I had an anatomy professor who had once been told that all that animal stuff wasn't of any use. So, by the time, I got there, it was normal for the class to be working on a human cadaver as well as a pig, a goat, and a sheep."

"Why?"

"Because... so much of it *is* the same." She put the chart down on the end of the bed. "The liver in all four are almost the same. In fact, back near the turn of the century, there was a type of goat that was bred to be used just for liver transplants. There is an island in a large lake near where I grew up that used to raise them. When word got out to the public, instead of seeing the miracle of being so close to that animal, people raised hell and the practice was stopped—even though the liver was a perfect match for any blood type. The sheep hearts, as well as ones from a primate like a chimpanzee or a baboon, are a perfect match for ours as well. Some day we will figure out the right place and be able to save a lot more people—unless the mechanical heart beats it to it."

She watched the girl. "You're pretty quiet. Either this is a bit much for you, or you have an interest in medicine..."

Cricket waved the wooden spoon and then put it in the cup before setting it on the stand. "What was it like sticking your hands in a human body? I mean, it used to be a person..."

"It still is a person. My first body is still walking around. I opted for the Navy to become a nurse. The service has a warped sense of how to do things. Well... I guess it makes sense from a guy sense of things." She put her hand up in a stop motion at Gabe.

He pulled his mouth back. "They sent you to Vietnam for your training by fire?"

She nodded. "I was only there for forty hours before they put me in the operations tent. I didn't even know how to give a shot or start an IV, and they had me mopping out bleeding guts. Somewhere during that time, the surgeon guided my hands down to an artery. It was so full of holes that it was pumping out half of what was going through it. He told me to put my hand around it to stop some of the bleeding, but not to stop the flow. If he clamped it—it would have stopped the flow and the man would have died."

"But he lived."

She nodded. "Later in medical school, I had

teachers that said I was lying. They had gotten their education from a book. That doc in Vietnam wasn't even a doctor—he was a Navy corpsman. He had little training more than I would have had as a nurse—probably less. We were busy as wasps in a windstorm. Nobody asked if the guy cutting them up was a doc or a corpsman. Just save their lives and get them home or back in the jungle."

Gabe shifted. "Quite the corpsman."

The nurse's face drifted to another time. "He was quite the teacher, too. I learned more about real medicine than I did getting my RN. He is why I've applied to medical school. I want to be a surgeon... or at least a doctor."

Cricket was pensive. "So sticking your hand in that man's guts changed your life?"

The nurse glanced at her watch. "The short answer is... maybe... well, probably in a way. The long answer would take hours, and a few beers to explain. Let's just say, I'm glad I met him and in the circumstances that we worked together."

She turned. "Now I have others to attend to."

Cricket lay back and gazed at the ceiling. "Wow."

Gabe wanted to hear the long story.

The soft lights of the city sparkled through the black of the window that reflected only the one small light over the bed. The two had played a couple of hours of gin but had lost interest. Cricket lay looking at the dark window—her back toward Gabe. Gabe sat looking at the sliver of skin where the hospital gown didn't close. He thought his thumb probably wouldn't fit between her spine and her shoulder blade. He thought about why they were here... and how small she was. *So young.*

"Why do you do it?"

Gabe looked up at her head. Her body hadn't moved. He wasn't even sure she had spoken.

"Do what?"

The small body was silent. Gabe was now sure that she was asleep and hadn't spoken.

She rolled over. There was wetness about her eyelashes. "Care... Be an Angel?"

Gabe's mouth opened... and then slowly closed. It was something he had thought about but had never asked himself that direct question. *Why?*

She watched his face. His eyes weren't focused and he was squirming mentally. "I didn't mean to pry..."

He held his hand up and then looked up. "It wasn't prying... It's just that I had never really thought about it before." He shifted and pulled his feet down off the bed. "I started..." He cleared his throat. "You met my partner..."

"The one with a patch that says Rabbit?"

He nodded. "He was in... Oh, hell... He was in a bad fight. He ended up in the hospital for a long time. He asked me to take his place in the flights. I showed up, Lois said okay, and I did my first ride. The next week kind of turned into a couple of months… which turned into…" His voiced drifted off as he realized how many years, how many trips, and what that really meant in terms of girls that needed their help.

"Years…?"

He refocused as he nodded. "Years."

"That's a lot of caring…"

"That's a lot of young girls that had nowhere else to turn." He sat up. "In the Marines, I saw guys who got to a place where they didn't know what to do… Some girls find themselves in that same place, and then they end up in the same grassy area. I guess I do it because I hope if I care and do this little thing, like take a weekend in Mexico, you girls don't end up in Forest Lawn with a little stone plaque with two dates on it…"

"And maybe we will know that there is someone out there… even if we don't know who they really are, who—"

Gabe nodded. "Cared."

Cricket rolled back onto her back. Her eyes danced about the tiny holes in the ceiling tiles, as if she were looking for a pattern that made sense. Her eyelids slid closed, and with a soft sigh, she rolled over to face the window. Moments later, Gabe could tell by the soft, steady rise and fall of the one shoulder that she was quietly asleep.

A while later, an older nurse peeked in. A moment later, she returned with a blanket and gently placed it over the large man's body. She turned off the light and left.

As she pulled the door to block most of the hall light, she heard a soft, "Thanks." She smiled and returned to her paperwork at the desk.

Thursday morning was slightly overcast with fog. The going would be slow up the coast, so Gabe opted for taking the inland route. In Riverside, he decided to stop for lunch. For years, he had heard of the Mission Inn, so they searched around and found the old hotel.

The two of them stood gaping at the grand entrance. The hotel had been made in the style of the California missions but had traces of the later mission or Arts and Crafts style. Everything was substantial and dark wood. The overhead timbers were exposed, rough-hewn, dark, and massive.

"Wow."

Gabe smiled. "That was exactly what I was thinking."

"When was it built?"

"Mr. Miller started this section of addition in 1903, young lady."

Gabe and Cricket turned to find a very prim and proper elderly lady standing behind them. From the woven straw hat to the low heels, she was a pageant of soft powder blue.

The woman stuck out her soft, gloved hand to Cricket first. "Daisy, Daisy Portbury. My Mark worked a short time for Mr. Miller when we first landed here in 1921."

Cricket shook her hand. They were almost the same height. "Amel... er... Cricket. So pleased to meet you, Mrs. Port...um..."

The woman put her white gloved hand on Cricket's shoulder. "I'll tell you what... you be Cricket, and I'll be Daisy." She turned and extended her hand toward Gabe.

Gabe shook with a smile. "Gabe, Gabriel Street... Are you here for lunch?" He ignored Cricket's look at his exposing his real name.

"Once a month... My Mark used to bring me, so I now come for tea in his memory."

"If you care to, we would be honored to have you join us. I for one would like to hear more about this glorious place."

The lady pursed her lips, as she looked the large man up and down. "Normally, a proper lady would decline such a brash offer from one of you motorcycle types. But having ridden Nortons, Indians, and Harley Davidsons in my day, I can't think of better company." She wrapped her arms around Cricket's arm. "And you come accompanied with a delightful companion as well."

She turned Cricket and started her toward the hostess station. "Now, dear, tell me something dreadfully wonderful about your companion before we sit down. I already saw the majestic black stallion parked at the curb."

Cricket smiled slightly as she glanced back at Gabe. "I think he has a sweet tooth for orange sherbet with chocolate sauce on top."

The woman chuckled. "How wickedly naughty of him... I think he might have to corrupt us later."

The small bowls were scoured clean except traces of orange or brown. Gabe sipped on coffee as the two ladies sipped on proper tea. Gabe had relaxed and enjoyed the tales the woman had been telling them of her time in the Royal Dispatch, riding Norton motorcycles in the Great War, and then serving on Indians and Harleys at March Field during the second war.

Gabe put down his cup and wiped his mouth. "But I still don't understand why the king couldn't knight your husband. After all, he had saved the Queen from a dreadful swim in the Thames."

"Oh, he could—if Mark would only divorce me. You see it was my family that was the problem. We had been the Royals in North Umberland—that had all the bastards by Edward. Unfortunately, when he took the throne, we were still in the family business of running arms into Scotland and stealing cattle on the way out. You just can't have the king of England related to cattle knickers, now can you?"

Gabe smiled... *doing good by doing bad*. "So he made him a social ambassador to Riverside..."

"So we could join the rest of my family here. My Mark didn't have any family of his own by then—other than me."

Cricket poured the two some more hot tea that the waitress had just brought. "What does a social ambassador do?"

"Not a thing, dear. It doesn't exist. It was merely a way for the king to reward my Mark for all of his service to the crown and country, and grant him a stipend that would see us through our last years. But it did need a little help, so Mark and I have done what we could along the way. Now, I also have a little coming in with Social Security to help."

Gabe glanced at his watch. "I hate to be the bearer of bad news, but for us, it is getting late and we have a long way to ride."

"Well, this has been a delightful change from my usual solitary tea. If you are ever this way again... on the first Thursday of the month... I would love to reciprocate."

Gabe stood as he handed the folder to the waitress. "If I am out this way, I would be honored to repeat the experience."

Daisy looked at Cricket. "And what about you, my dear?"

Gabe started. "Oh, we're—"

Cricket cut him off. "I can't think of a better way to have a lunch." She reached over and hugged the frail looking woman… and then helped readjust the woven straw hat.

They stood by the chopper as they watched the woman get on the city bus. Gabe turned to Cricket. "That was a nice thing you did. But I'm not sure giving her hope…"

Cricket squinted as she looked up at the large man. "How hard is it to remember the first Thursday of every month?"

Gabe wasn't going to argue. He thought about everything that he and this girl had talked about, and yet had not talked about. He fished a battered old card out of his wallet. "Look, if you ever need help, you call this number. The person who answers is the desk sergeant. There are two guys named Stan, and one named Gordo."

"Fatso?"

"His name is Gordon, he's skinny, but everyone calls him Gordo. Anyway, just tell them you need to get ahold of Gabe. They'll usually know where I am."

She studied the card. "Gabe Street." He nodded, she had remembered. "They will know where you are unless it's the weekend, and then I know where you are."

"Yeah, something like that."

"So you're a cop or something." She looked up and at the patch over his left pocket.

ANGEL FLIGHTS

Gabe thought. "Angel."

She smirked. "Or a Snake…"

He snorted and turned toward the chopper.

She nodded and stuck the card in her pocket. Her memories of the letters on each number on a phone dial were clear—the number was easy to remember—it spelled the two words 'for help.' *They both knew the rules had been thrown in the gutter.*

The rest of the ride was quiet. The traffic was mostly light until they got close to Hollywood.

They got off of the motorcycle in front of the costume shop. As they walked toward the door, Cricket stopped him. She didn't look him in the face, just his chest. Her hand was flat on the center as if she could feel his heart. She paused a moment, and then hugged him. She hung with desperation. Gabe expected her to start crying. She only held on as he folded his arms over her back. Finally, he pushed his head down and softly kissed the top of her head.

She let go but held her hand on his chest—stopping him there. She patted his chest once, and then held her hand there for the span of a few heartbeats. Her hand fell reluctantly, and she turned. He stood and watched the young woman walk into the store alone.

That is a lot of growing up in only a week.

The glass door closed and the reflections were of the cars passing on the street. Gabe turned and looked far down the street. It was still early enough.

BAER CHARLTON

He rode out to the produce market. They were closing, but the older Italian farmer looked in his boxes and found two good-looking eggplants. Gabe needed a little vino, a little garlic, and a lot of Mama B's. He would stop on the way home and pick up a chicken for Gertie.

33

STUDENTS

FRIDAY AND THE alley pounded with a full run of motorcycles. The load was heavy and the alley was full.

Gabe walked down the line as he thought about the past few years without Rabbit in the run, or by his side. He understood the years of being undercover had taken their toll—but he still missed the big guy.

He waved his arm and pointed the large, full-dressed classic red motorcycle. "Mike is your lead on this. He will take you over the high line and down the 605 to the 5. Stay packed up, you have four new riders. So, you new guys, stay in the saddle. At speed, we keep within four car lengths. Your first stop for fuel will be in Orange County. Is there anyone who doesn't have a full tank from a few miles away?" They all shook their heads. "Okay, Mike, lead them out." He waved his arm to point out to the street.

The next group sat waiting. "Sandy, you only have six, so run them straight out to Riverside and take them over the small crossing." He looked at the other five. "Does anyone have a problem of running for a hundred miles?" Most smirked and patted their larger tanks. "Great. Sandy, we'll see you in the heat." They pounded each other's fists and the man eased his crew out.

Gabe addressed his group. "Is there anyone who has a problem with a hundred miles?" They all shook their heads. Most who were invited to be Angels had larger tanks—either stock five gallons or custom larger. A hundred miles was out of the range of a three-gallon slim tank, and a biker running a peanut or Sportster tank wasn't someone with calluses on their butts anyway.

"We will be dropping down through East LA. At a certain point, I will be able to see what I need to know if we are taking the 10 or rerouting to the 60. Stay tight, but don't run a red light. We don't need a cop pulling you over for a ticket today. If you don't make a light, we will know and pull over. I don't want to lose any of you sheep. Ride careful, and keep your heads about you. Let's have a great evening."

Gabe checked his book bag on his forks and slung his leg over. "You good, Snow?"

The girl nodded. The smile was slight, but it was there.

Gabe didn't know why, but he always liked the last run of summer. The air was fresh, it was a race to the border against the sun going down, and the smog was light enough that when they hit Riverside, he could smell the orange orchards. His fuel stops were in Corona, then the sleepy town of Poway just north of San Diego.

Two nights later, as he put the chopper away in the garage, he heard another motorcycle coming up the street. He waited. The bike slowed and then turned in and chuffed up the driveway. The bike was stock. Under the helmet, the face was clean-shaven. With the large goggles, Gabe didn't recognize the rider.

Rabbit eased the full dressed bike into the small space left.

The steaks were cooked and eaten at the fire pit.

Rabbit pointed at the trees that were along the back of the small lot. "I recognized what I think is a mixed tree of grapefruit, orange and lemon. But the other three I was stumped on."

Gabe pointed to each in turn. "A Russian Fig that is supposed to bear fruit all year, a black avocado, and a Japanese pear grafted onto a quince trunk."

"What's a quince?"

"It is some kind of fruit from Turkey, which nobody eats, so they graft other stuff onto the trunk. It also is supposed to dwarf the pear so it won't get more than about eight feet tall, but produce as much as it would if it was sixteen or twenty."

"Wow, look at mister gardener here."

"Nah, the kid next door just tells me what his dad plants."

"Well, I like what you've done to the place... which is about nothing."

"Things have been about the same around here. School pretty much consumes my time... other than the weekends."

"How's that going?"

"I take my books and get some studying done on Saturday and Sunday morning. The guys respect it and give me my peace and quiet. Mike and Regina gave me a key to the apartment, so in the evenings, I can go up there where there is light and cram for finals. What about you? You dropped off the face of the earth. Someone weed-whacked your face and you drive an old man's bike."

Rabbit snorted. "Don't be badmouthing the dresser. Those bags can hold a lot of stuff when you're on the road."

He scooted down in the chair and put his feet up on the rock wall around the pit. "After I buried Whale, I didn't really know what to do." His hand flopped out as he pointed his finger at Gabe. "Don't let me forget, I have documents for your Swiss bank account, as well as your Canadian accounts. Whale didn't have any family—except for us."

"Good, tuition went up again this year." Gabe chuckled.

"How's Lito doing?"

"He started medical school last fall and is driving his study group nuts because he needs a ride everywhere."

"How are his grades?"

"I don't know if he will ever be challenged enough. He's still pulling a four point zero."

"Good… we need more doctors."

"So where were you this last year?"

"Mostly, I went north from Jasper. I wintered over in the Yukon and gold mined."

"Get anything?"

Rabbit pulled a thumb-sized nugget out of his pocket. Gabe whistled low as he looked it over. "Yeah, impressive, huh? It cost me just over two grand in Dawson. I thought if I rubbed it on the walls of the mine, it might attract some of its friends. No such luck."

He put the stone away. "So with things getting warm, I went over to look at Alaska. They're getting ready to put in that pipeline, but that seemed a lot like real work so I made my way down here."

"So now what?"

"Do I still have a room?"

"Sure, Gertie sleeps with me every night, so she won't even bother you. Oh, and the sandbox got bigger." He pointed at the medium-sized doggie door.

ANGEL FLIGHTS

She likes using the grass instead—even in the winter. But, if it's really cold, I have to watch her. She can get out here, but she gets too cold, and I have to come carry her back into the warm house."

"So maybe I'll just hang out around LA for a while and see what is going on while I look for what I want to do with my life."

Gabe held his beer out and they clinked bottoms. "Welcome home."

Life at the police frat house pretty much was always the same. Even with Rabbit back, the officers floated in and out, Gertie got plenty of attention, and the front weight room had returned to a living room that now had a substantial library of law books. Rabbit noted Gabe's consumption of alcohol was only around him, so he stopped also—except the occasional half beer with Chet.

Chet polished one glass after another. "So how's Gabe doing?"

"Doesn't he stop in?"

The man put the one glass in the cooler and turned to the next. He glanced down the bar and measured what was left in each of the five glasses. He turned back to Rabbit. "At first, it was about once a week like the old days, and then it was down to once a month... I think the last time he was in... the Dodgers were winning."

BAER CHARLTON

"How are they doing now?" Rabbit broke off some of the roll, dipped it in the stew, and stuck it in his mouth.

Chet shrugged lazily. "Who cares—Tommy is getting old and fat and cares more about his restaurant than he does the pennant. So screw them. I'd rather watch the Padres."

"San Diego?"

Chet snorted. "Nah, San Gabriel High. Either them or the Roosevelt Rough Riders."

"Cheaper seats and more fun—but how are their hot dogs?"

Chet laughed. He hadn't been to a school game since he was in school. "Probably better than mine." He bent over and put away the last glass. He flipped the towel over his shoulder. "So... Europe, eh?"

"Everyone talks about taking the Grand Tour, and other than Mexico and Canada, I've never gone out of the country. How about you?"

"I'm pretty much like most guys. Mexico to drink, whore, and fish... then there was the little vacation Uncle Sam sent me on in Korea. Other than that—nada. Don't even have an interest in going up to Canada. I hate flying, and that is just too far to drive.

"Speaking of which, I saw the new bike—very nice."

"Speaking of driving a long way... I bought it off a guy in Fairbanks and rode it back."

ANGEL FLIGHTS

"I thought the road is all dirt."

"The AlCan is. But the road to the harbor is okay." He smiled. "I took the ferry down to the north end of Vancouver Island and rode the rest of the way. Some very pretty country up there."

Chet moved down the bar to refill the rocks glass under the wavering finger. *He should cut the guy off, but he only has a block to walk home.* "So, why didn't you drag Gabe in with you tonight?"

"He has a night class tonight. In fact, I think they both do." He sipped on the coffee.

"Lito is how old now?"

"Turned sixteen this last month."

"Driving?"

"He never took the time to learn. Zorro said that when he pulled his head up to breathe, he would teach him on the training course before he lets him drive with the idiots on the street."

Chet wandered back as he moved the towel over the shiny metal of the back bar. He flipped the towel on the floor and then over his shoulder. "That's a great guy Zorro. He's another one who almost never comes in."

Rabbit stared at the towel and wondered how it was that the shirt never seemed to be damp under the towel that was constantly there. He was ignoring Chet's angst about not seeing old cop buddies.

The man had made a decision when he first bought the bar, and never put in the ubiquitous red-light dome or any other paraphernalia that marked the place as a cop bar. He had watched too many of his buddies over the years drinking themselves to death or out of a job. The bar's sign stayed unchanged as the Duck Dive. Rabbit wasn't even sure the man had even told anyone he had bought the bar. He looked down the line of five at the bar and was confident that none was retired cops of any order.

A regular doesn't have to say much for a bartender to know a lot about the person. When you go from figuring things out on the street to pouring booze and cleaning glasses—you spend your day figuring out your clientele. Chet knew his people. There were just enough to keep the place open, to keep him busy and away from taking the lead retirement that too many his age took. He knew that when he dropped, he would probably have a towel and glass in his hands. It wasn't exciting, but it suited him.

Across the LA basin, night classes were just letting out. Lito pulled his books together and stacked them on top of the three yellow legal pads he had been taking notes on. He carefully lifted the whole into his book bag.

"You do know that when you ride on that motorcycle, the covers of the books become scuffed and they slide out of alignment."

ANGEL FLIGHTS

Lito looked up into the eyes of a blonde student. Her powder blue eyes sparkled as she smiled at him, teasing the young man. Her attention made him nervous. He knew he was not in her league, and certainly not anywhere near her age. "The seven-point-six-four degree of alteration is within acceptable parameters."

She smiled broadly. "Hmm, true dork—deflects with a higher degree of absolutes to assure the conversation stays away from grounding anywhere near having coffee—much less getting to know your new study partner and lab buddy."

Lito blushed. "I already have a study group..."

She shook her head, "No you don't. They fired you. They're meeting right now over at the math bar for drinks. You no longer have a study group—same as me." She stuck her hand out. "Patricia Weinstein, everyone calls me Pit. I don't care if it means that they wish I would crawl into one, or if it's because I'm kind of like a pit bull dog. When I get my teeth into something I like, I don't give up."

He took her hand. It was warmer than he thought it would be. "Rafael, Rafael Garcia... but everyone calls me Lito. Why did your group fire you?"

She shrugged. "Same as you. I'm guessing you challenged most of the undergrad classes, and now at nineteen, you're the youngest medical student UCLA ever had. They got threatened."

"All."

"All what?"

"Well, almost all of the classes... and you are right. At sixteen, I'm the youngest ever. There was a kid that started up at Stanford at fourteen."

She sat on one of the desks. "But at sixteen, you would still be in high school."

Lito smirked. "High school was almost two long weeks of tests during the summer two years ago."

"All four years in two weeks?"

He nodded. "How much did you challenge?" He was pretty sure he now had her number as well.

"About a year's worth of high school, but a lot of the undergrad stuff. Did they give you a score?"

Lito scuffed his foot on the floor. "Yeah, pretty much a three-ninety-seven for both."

"What did you get on your MSAT?"

"I didn't. They had my seat waiting and didn't make me take it. You?"

"I took it, but I was sick with the flu so I only got the third highest score ever." She also was rocking her leg back and forth. The conversation had gotten to the point they both recognized it was beyond establishing that they were the different ones, and they could either walk away and go it alone or team up.

"What's your downfall?"

"I always have trouble with anatomical stuff..."

Lito smiled. "I can help you with that. My struggle is the nervous diagnostics."

"That is my focus. I want to be a neurosurgeon."

"Same here…"

The large double doors at the top of the amphitheater banged open. The large biker clomped down the steep steps. The look on his face was passive, but his presence was foreboding. The girl hugged her books tighter to her chest.

"Did you get her phone number yet?"

Lito blushed. "I think we were just getting to that." He turned. "When do you want to get together and study?"

She glanced at Gabe and then back at Lito. She knew they were together, but she hadn't been so close to the large man. With him being up the stairs, he appeared even larger.

Gabe stuck his hand out. "Hi, I'm Gabe, Lito's uncle."

She squeaked. "Pit."

Lito snorted softly. "Her name is Patricia, but people call her Pit… like the center of a good peach."

The girl blushed even harder. Gabe chuckled. "When do you want to get with the genius here?"

"How about tomorrow afternoon…?"

"No can do. He doesn't drive, and I won't be around to bring him."

She turned to the kid. "I have a car. I can come to you."

Lito pulled out one of the yellow pads and tore

off a page of notes. He flipped it over and wrote the address of the restaurant down as well as the phone number. He handed it to her. "Come for lunch… and be very hungry."

She looked at the address and city. She turned a little pale.

Gabe cleared his throat. "It's actually a very nice neighborhood. He grew up right across the street and his sister runs the place."

She folded the paper and stuck it in her purse. "Then it's a date." She and Lito both blushed as the implications of her words settled in.

Gabe growled. "I think it's time to leave before things get misconstrued." He waved Lito up the stairs. "It was nice meeting you, Pit. I look forward to your influence on Lito. He's deathly afraid I'll turn him into an axe murderer, a biker, or a lawyer."

Her mouth opened, then she skipped a few steps to catch up with Lito—where it felt safe. Gabe chuckled softly behind his smile. *Aww, the kid met someone that he can actually relate to.*

34

I'M LEAVING—BUT FIRST

"OH, NOW THIS is Rabbit food." Rabbit smiled as he rubbed his hands together. The burrito was so big it was already breaking apart. He closed his eyes as he inhaled the aroma of the spiced pork.

Maria leaned against his shoulder. "Estúpido... that is what you get for going away for so long." She poked him in the ribs. "Flaco. You have no meat in the locker, no junk in you trunk. You stay around and I feed you right."

He laughed. "Yeah, I've seen el Gordo Zorro." He ducked as the hand swung. Zorro was thinner than he was, but Rabbit knew the man could eat and burn it up just sitting in the patrol car.

"Where you been?" Maria sank into a chair. Rabbit could see she was tired. Even though the restaurant was small, there was just her and the cook to handle the occasional crowd and half of their business was take-out.

ANGEL FLIGHTS

"I was up in Canada gold mining."

She looked at him for a long moment and then sat back and laughed. "You are so full of shit, Rabbit. You would freeze in Canada. They have real snow and ice up there. No... really, where were you?"

Rabbit pulled the nugget out of his pocket and laid it on the table in front of her. "I saved this one just for you. I thought it looked like a rabbit's foot—maybe it will bring you good luck."

Her eyes were huge. "This is fake..." She lifted it. "Holy mother of God..." She looked up at the man who was sitting more serious than she had ever seen him before. "You really dug this up?"

He nodded. "It was an old mine. I lived in it all winter to stay warm. You have no idea just how cold it gets up there above the Arctic Circle. We put up a tent just inside of the tunnel and vented the stovepipe to the outside. I think we cut the limbs off of every dead tree for a mile around. I don't ever want to go back."

"But you hit gold..."

He nodded. "Me—and three other guys. They gave me half of what we had mined over the winter, and I walked away. There are easier, better ways to make a living."

She pushed the large nugget across the table. He pushed it back. "No, I really did keep that one for you."

"It's too much."

He shook his head. "No... it's not enough. I need you to do something for me."

She eyed him. "What?" She tried to growl like her uncle or Gabe. It came out more like a Chihuahua than anything threatening.

Rabbit chuckled. "Oh, you are so very vicious. Lincoln better behave or else."

"Lincoln best behave anyway. What do you want?"

"I want you to find someone that you can trust. I want you to find another cook and at least a part-time waitress. Just because you're Mexican and Pepe is illegal doesn't mean you have to work seven days a week for ten hours a day."

"It is how the owner is."

He rolled forward and put his hand on hers. "No, that is how the old owner was. The new owner is telling you to hire some help. Hire some of the neighborhood kids that need the money and help."

She studied his eyes—searching. "New owner?"

He smiled softly. "New owner... It was final yesterday."

"But he no tell me."

"I told him that if he ever came up the hill again, I would have his legs broken." She could see he was serious.

"So what I do?"

"You've been running the place all along. We'll

ANGEL FLIGHTS

figure out what to do about the checkbook and deposits and stuff, but for now, you are the manager. Hire a waitress and someone for Pepe to train."

"But he is..."

"A wetback? Si. But I have already contacted a lawyer to get that changed. For now, we can get him a work visa, but eventually, he will need a green card. I don't want any problems with any kind of law. I don't need it—you don't need it. Está bien?"

She was breathy from being hit by the news. "Si, is okay."

"There is another thing."

She opened her face dramatically because she could see the twinkle returning to his eyes. "More? Now what?"

"I'm going away for a while."

She laughed. "To prison?"

Rabbit laughed until he choked. *It would all work out.*

Later that night, the two men waited for the two cops to go inside. Gabe's lap was full of snake. Her head lay in the crook of his neck. Gabe could tell she was asleep. "So what did you tell her?"

"The truth—I'm going to Europe. If I thought she would come with me and bring the squirt, I'd take her along and maybe never come back."

"Did you tell her that you love her?"

"What are you... nuts? Do you have any idea what she must view me as? I'm thirty-seven, for

God's sake." He did the math. "I'm old enough to be her father."

"So you're just going to keep running away from her, and maybe she might someday figure out that she can't have you and move on…"

"What am I supposed to do?"

Gabe wagged his head and gazed at the low flames. "Why don't you go to Europe? Maybe you'll find a Countess on the Riviera, who is pining away for a beat-up old biker who might come along and sweep her off her feet before arthritis disables him, and she just has to settle for a laconic tap of your cane or walker. Right before your false teeth fall out of your drooling mouth."

"Funny guy."

"You know, when I first met you, I thought you had to have the biggest pair they cast in solid steel. But now, I find that they are small, and you had them made in papier-mâché."

"Fuck you."

"Piñata balls." Gabe started laughing. Gertie woke up and gave him a disgusted look before sliding down and going in the house. Then that made Rabbit laugh. The two friends sat laughing at their situations that resulted in them sitting in a backyard—together—and alone.

35

WE'RE OUT OF A JOB ANYWAY.

MEXICO HAD BEEN quiet and warm. The same couldn't be said of LA. The last hour had been a grind through the kind of traffic that forgets how to drive in the rain. The song doesn't even begin to explain about the rain in southern California.

There is no drizzle or light rain. Gabe groused, *hell there isn't even a hard rain—there is only where someone opens the fire hydrant in the sky.*

Even with applying water repellent to their jackets, the leather was soaked before they were north of San Juan Capistrano.

For the next sixty miles, Gabe weighed either slopping it home to a hot bath or stopping and finding a warm motel to dry off. It wasn't until he knew he was only twenty minutes from home that he remembered he could buy a whole motel. It wasn't about the money—he just wanted to be home.

He was glad the girls were riding back in the

ANGEL FLIGHTS

bus. It hadn't been the plan, but someone had looked at the weather moving in and sent the bus down. It had just started to rain as they got to the parking lot. The bikers hadn't even turned off their bikes. Most would make it at least to the next fuel stop, and some would just make it home. As they made it to the I-5 and I-405 split in Orange County, the groups had fractured.

As the remaining smaller groups hit the 605, they broke into every man for himself. Nobody cared. Getting home safe was the only goal.

Finally, Gabe lay in the warm water. He was thinking about adding more hot water when Gertie slid over the rim of the tub. She snuggled in the warm water with her face near his. Her tongue flicked out and into his nose. He laughed. "Yes, I'll get dressed and make us some steaks."

As he toweled off Gertie, and then himself, he heard the back door open. He never even thought about the door anymore.

While studying for finals, he had kept a small tick-list of the guys who used the house. Some used the cabana that was set up for the weights next to the garage, but everyone came through the kitchen to get coffee. His tally had expanded to eight precincts, three departments, and two fire crews.

Gabe pulled on a pair of cut-off shorts and a t-shirt. Padding barefoot, he followed Gertie through the hall and the dining room. She stopped at the kitchen door and coiled. He had only seen her stack her mass once, and that was when the K-9 didn't stand a chance—it was a dog and on her turf. The pride of the officer, immediately upon seeing the snake towering at almost five feet and ready to strike—had squatted, and flooded the floor with urine and shit as he let out the worst whine a ninety pound German Shepard could—he sounded like a poodle who had lost its toy.

The officer blushed almost purple as he dragged his dog from the house—never to return again. Gertie had thought it was so disgusting that she had not crossed that part of the kitchen floor for almost a year.

Gabe used everything to clean the spot.

Some things are simply marked in the mind forever.

Gabe looked over Gertie's head. With a total body length of over fourteen feet, she had no problem raising her head to look any regular officer in the eyes. Especially, when that officer had a plate with a steak on it—cooked perfectly to her liking—already cooked.

The man sat turned in the chair. His right hand rested on his weapon. His arm said ready, but Gabe was reading the fear in the face.

"Jesus, Manx... it's the suit. Slowly stand up and take off the jacket."

The man was slow and deliberate. Gabe wasn't

sure how long he could keep a straight face.

"Shit. That didn't do it. Carefully throw it out the door."

"It's raining out there..."

"A little rain on that stupid gray suit or piss her off. It's your choice." The man carefully opened the door and threw the jacket out on the lawn. Gabe was sure there was a large mud puddle out there somewhere.

"Not enough. She's knotting up the lower tail. Quick—the pants." The man complied.

"She's still knotting..." The man's shoes and socks were followed by his pants. Only the federal wallet and pistol lay on the table. The man stood crouched to run in only his red briefs and old man sleeveless undershirt. Gabe was tempted.

Just then, two of the older South Pasadena detectives walked in the old back door on the side of the house. They looked at the federal agent standing like a statue either farting or shitting his pants. The older one smiled at Gabe. "Hey, Gabe, I picked up some chickens for Gertie." He put the shopping bag down on the counter, stepped over, and took Gertie by the chin. He leaned over and kissed the top of her head.

Manx stood as he stared at the two detectives dressed in gray suits similar to his.

Gabe shrugged and stepped into the kitchen. "Huh. Must have just been the stench of Fed in the room." The two detectives and Gabe stood facing away from the pasty-white federal agent standing almost naked. The three shoulders did nothing to hide the laughter.

Gertie figured that whoever the new guy was, he was no threat. She moved to the exposed side of the counter, and using the counter and refrigerator as pressure walls, climbed onto the counter to find out what was in the shopping bag. The detective took the one chicken from her and removed the plastic bag. Holding it out, he smiled as she opened her mouth, and then covered the large hen. By the time he had unwrapped the next one, she was ready. The third one took an extra minute for her to adjust.

Manx sat with his soaked, grimy suit in his hand. He watched the last two whole chickens disappear. "That's the secret? Bribe her with food?"

The other detective turned. "Oh, hell no. If she doesn't like you, she will stand you up and you better be making tracks fast." He backhanded his partner's back. "Remember that little Asian officer from Parker Center?"

The detective looked up as if he had remembered details. "He had spilled soy sauce down his front?" He turned around and smiled at Manx. "Poor guy didn't stand a chance. He was just the right size. But to the guy's credit—it did take her three weeks to digest that guy. Those Sam Brown belts and all the shit they carry... that is a lot of hard stuff to shit out."

Manx had heard enough. He slid down in his chair and held his hand casually to his mouth. His eyes rolled in Gabe's direction. The look was pure boredom or lack of tolerance.

Eventually, the two jokers left. Gabe loaned Manx a t-shirt and a pair of shorts one of the officers had left. He didn't tell him it was one of the female meter maids. As they sat sipping coffee in the quiet, Gabe nodded at the Fed.

"You're a little far from home—again."

The man studied Gabe. Finally, he reached under the table where he had placed a briefcase. He pulled a modest file out of the case. "I could use your help."

"I don't do that stuff anymore."

The man placed his hand on the folder. "How do you think you did on your final exams?"

Gabe calculated the man. "Fine."

Manx let slip the tiniest hint of a smile at one corner of his mouth. "Two B-pluses, and the rest A's."

Gabe thought about how the man could know what he got on tests that he had taken only a few days before. "What will I get on my bar exam?"

He slid the folder around for Gabe to look at. "You won't be taking it. You'll be busy."

Gabe opened the folder and looked at the three mug shots. He pointed at the guy in the middle.

"This one is dead."

Manx slowly ground his head back and forth. "You killed his brother—the meek one."

"There was nothing meek about that asshole. He's the one who fucked Rabbit up."

Manx leisurely blinked. "Like I said, he was the meek one of the triplets. His brother Raymond was out of the Chicago area. It's rumored that he has the blood of seven on his hands." The man shifted. "And, when I say hands, I mean he doesn't like using any weapons other than his hands."

"You said—*was* out of Chicago..."

"That's right. He has been here about three months. The empire you two built up in meth—he is building in heroin, opium and hash—but a lot bigger. Word on the street says he is moving about a half-mill a week already."

"And the other brother?"

"Sister—family business... she's serving time in Mississippi for drugs, and five homicides that they could prove. One was her husband on their wedding night and two of his bodyguards. Her weapons of choice are brass knuckles and any blade that is handy. Louisiana is still looking at about twenty unsolved murders that they think she's good for."

"So why now?"

"Why now what?"

"Three years we don't hear from you. You don't write, you don't call, and you missed my birthday—

you didn't even send me flowers..."

"You sent me back to Ohio with weight. You were right. I needed to learn from a master."

Gabe leaned over and looked under the table.

"Fuck you... I didn't say I learned everything. But what I did learn was that with certain people, you can't catch them by playing fair or by the rules."

"So you came out for another lesson?"

"I asked to be transferred out here."

"I'm not looking for a job."

Manx leaned over and pulled another very thin folder out of his case. He opened the folder and turned it around. There was a column of long numbers. They were broken out by country.

He looked up at Manx.

"Right now they are just numbers. I know you don't recognize all of the numbers, but Rabbit would recognize some of them, and Special Agent Werner would recognize the rest. This isn't all of it, but it would be enough to get the attention of the other two."

"So what do you want—Rabbit to come back? I don't know where he is."

"He's in the south of France right now. I don't think he's going to like breaking up with his girlfriend, but when he finds out she's with the KGB, I think they will be done. We don't have an extradition treaty from Brazil, but Israel has been very good getting people out of there. But Werner has done very well at learning Portuguese, and he may have a new family that he can enjoy his old age with. So, no, I don't want to upset those apple carts. Although... Rabbit might come back on his own—I think he is getting bored with floating around Europe."

"So if I work for you, I get to keep my accounts and my freedom."

The man held his hands up. "Whoa, this is not blackmail. I just wanted you to know who or what kind of person I have become. After all, I did learn from a couple of masters."

"I still don't want to work for the FBI."

"I, or we, get that. So what we want you to be is a very knowledgeable special investigator attached to the US Attorney General's office here in LA—pretty much, what you used to do—but without the drug connection."

"But I'm kind of busy already."

"Yeah, well, maybe not for long." He pulled a three-page brief out of the folder. He glanced at it and then handed it to Gabe. He got up and grabbed Gabe's mug and took the two to the counter and re-filled them.

"Does this mean what I think it means?"

"Yes. The Supreme Court will hand down their decision on Roe vs. Wade in the next month or so—probably right after the first of the year. There will be a small split—but only so the dissenting opinions can leave the door open for the states to weigh in on the third trimester… Soon, your little trips to Mexico will be only for the beer and lobster."

"How can you know that?" Gabe looked up from the brief and took the offered mug.

"Welcome to the big times, Gabe. Welcome to the *very* big times."

36

THE GAME REMAINS THE SAME

THE DUCK DIVE had never been so full. Valentine's Day just seemed like the best day to celebrate. Some might suspect what the real celebration was, but didn't care. The rest were only concerned that a chapter in their lives could now be closed.

The regulars at the bar were confused by the noise and the number of people. But the fact that Chet wasn't picking up any money off the bar was making it okay. The other fact was that their glasses seemed to keep refilling on their own.

Chet leaned over as he refilled the three coffee mugs. "I don't know who your friends are, but you can come bring them by anytime."

Gabe laughed. "I could tell you who they are, but then…"

"I know, I know—you'd have to shoot me."

Rabbit laughed. "No, we'd have to go get you tattooed."

ANGEL FLIGHTS

Chet laughed. He just waved it down and then pointed at the one in the middle. "Just bring the pretty lady by instead."

Lois winked. "Chet, if you weren't married, I would come by on my own."

The man walked off to put down the non-paying coffee and start pouring some more beer.

Gabe leaned over. "His wife passed away about ten years ago. When it comes to Chet—what you see is pretty much what you get."

Lois thought about that. "Sometimes, Gabe—that is enough." She sipped on her mug as she watched the bartender.

"Where were you when you saw the news?"

"Monaco. I had to get the concierge at the hotel to translate. He went one better. He sent the bellhop out to get the New York Times. The kid didn't understand what he did to get a hundred dollar bill as a tip, but the truth was, the biggest Franc note I had was a ten—which is about a buck ten."

Lois leaned back as she sipped on her coffee. Her eyes sparkled as they passed over all of the bikers she could still get ahold of. Everyone wore an Angel patch. Some were fresher than others. None less deserved than any other. These were her boys, her men, her Angels. "Best damn Wednesday night ever." She held her mug up.

The other two mugs clinked from both sides. Rabbit growled. "I wouldn't have missed this for the world."

"Speaking of the world…?"

"I'm going back. Interpol made me an offer I couldn't refuse."

Gabe buried his face in his mug held by both hands. "Special Investigator to the Solicitor General?"

Gabe watched the crowd as he sipped on his coffee. He thought about having Chet freshen up the Bushmills in it. He didn't have to look to know that Rabbit was staring at him with a shocked face. He'd tell him later about the jobs while they sat by the fire.

The scarves were the only needed addition beyond the fire pit to keep warm. The shots of tequila also helped. Gabe knew Gertie was buried under the electric blanket and would be nice and toasty warm when he finally crawled into bed.

"And you were going to tell me about Mr. Screw-up when?"

"Hey, you show up in the middle of the night, and things have been kind of non-stop today."

Rabbit shook from the sip of tequila. He smiled at Gabe. "That Lincoln is growing like a weed."

Gabe smiled. "And your investment?"

Rabbit shrugged. "It's all good. I don't need it to make me any money, just not lose money either. I check in with the bookkeeper every couple of weeks. Maria is doing pretty well. Word has gotten around and the neighborhood comes out to eat at the place that has provided some of the kids some work and training. Did you know she had even done some catering?"

Gabe nodded. "One of the guys transferred to Parker Center, so the Captain and Zorro had her cater his going away party. I think that neighborhood is going to be crawling with cops like this place is."

"Hola. Senior Gabe?"

Gabe chuckled. "Ready for some midnight tamales?" He laid his head back and called out. "Nana, bien aquí."

Yolanda giggled as she came around the corner. Rabbit jumped up, and Gabe followed. "Hey there, little one. Long time no see."

The young woman rushed into Gabe's embrace. She turned and hugged Rabbit. "Damn, it is good to see both of you. I miss the neighborhood."

"Hey, it was you who moved away, not us."

"Ay! I know, I know. Some days I think about moving back. When Eddie is away on maneuvers, the base becomes too empty. The moms who stick around, I don't want to be around. Girls these days don't cook or sew. They just want to lie on the couch and watch Match Game or old Lucy shows."

"Is that where the Marine is—maneuvers?"

"He's up north in the mountains. It's called the cold weather training station, but everyone calls it blue balls and ass."

"How long?"

"Until the end of March or something."

The men looked at each other and smiled. "Time to come home."

"I brought a bunch of the baby's stuff, and I have plenty still here. So maybe I'll stay here for a while."

"That would be nice." Gabe gave her a side hug with his arm around her shoulders.

She slapped playfully at him. "Stop, you distracted me. Nana made tamales."

The two men laughed as Rabbit turned off the fire pit. "Of course she did."

37

SAVING CRICKET

GABE KNEW THE ins and outs of who was or wasn't on duty at three in the morning. He kept the bike at only seventy down Valley Boulevard. He whipped through the winder onto the Golden State as he headed for the Santa Monica Freeway. He thought about how strange and similar the freeways were to his life. The federal government numbered the highways and freeways, and then the State let the city or county of Los Angeles name the freeways. So if you were an Angelino, you knew the names. If you only lived in the city, you knew the numbers. If you were from somewhere else—it was all just confusing.

By the numbers, he would use the 5-10-405. By the names, he would use Golden State, Santa Monica, and San Diego. To some, he was Gabe, to others Snake, but for tonight, he was once again Angel.

He took the off-ramp. The light was blinking red, he rolled through at forty and wound up the engine as the buildings fell away and the rolling hills of the oil fields took over. He held the speedometer needle between the two zeros of the hundred. If any officer was sleeping in the fields, or doing his night's paperwork, the bike would come and go with little more than a look-up of the officer's head. The dark avenger streaked through the desolate land populated by untiring oil well pumps, bobbing their heads like giant praying mantises in the night.

The black bike's flames flashed on and off as Gabe rode down the wide boulevard. He passed the biker bar that was neutral territory—except for the occasional personal dispute. A bike was parked out front for the night—gathering a wet sheen of morning dew. Gabe knew, on days like these, the damp would be just a dry film by the time the sun crested over the San Gabriel Mountains. Late summer in Southern California sucked every bit of moisture from the living and the inanimate.

Gabe saw the large unlit yellow shell. He surged the chopper and then let it coast the last half block. As he nosed up into the gas station's large apron, he saw the black and white with the two officers getting out. He glanced back at the station and found the dark phone booth.

As he swung his leg over the seat, he saw the dark form rise in the booth. The door cracked in the middle as Cricket began to open the door. Gabe put his gloved hand up to stop her. She froze.

Gabe took his gloves off and laid them on the gas tank. Walking around the front of the bike, he approached the two cops. It did not escape his notice that both of their right hands were either on or near their weapons. His smile was friendly and his hand was out and almost palm up as he approached the last steps.

"Special Investigator for the US Attorney General, Gabe Street... I want to thank you guys for watching out for my girl." He shook their hands.

The older cop, probably the training officer, grumped. "Kind of an unusual request in the middle of the night..."

Gabe smiled. "But you had paperwork to get done anyway—right?"

The cop smiled. Gabe had just showed his badge.

Gabe pointed at the man's shirt. "Let me borrow your pen a moment." He turned to show his hand and the back of his pants. He took out his wallet. Removing a couple of cards, he shoved it back.

Gabe took the pen and using the cruiser's front hood as a desk, wrote his address on the back of his cards. He returned the pen and held out the two cards. "The coffee is always on, and there is no lock on the back doors. There is more food in the fridge than a precinct, other than Ramparts, can eat in one sitting. Everything is fair game. Anyone there can explain how to turn on the gas fire pit or the barbecue."

He smiled. "Oh, and the lady of the house is about fourteen feet long, and if you want to bribe her, bring a couple of fresh whole chickens. She loves her steak barbecued with steak sauce, but she'll only take it when I'm there. Beyond that, she has free run of the house and yard. If you shoot her or abuse her—even the vultures will never find your body."

They put the cards away muttering soft thanks. Gabe doubted he would ever see either of them, but stranger things had a way of happening—and it was good protocol to extend the offer. *Besides, what is a couple more cops hanging out at the frat house?*

As the cops left, Gabe walked over to the phone booth. The girl shot out of the door and wrapped herself around his middle. If she had grown two inches in the past four years, he would have been surprised. The hair was longer, and the body didn't feel quite as sack-of-bones—she was filling out into becoming a woman. He cradled her head in his chest as her body quaked from the sobbing.

"I'm sorry, I'm sorry…"

Gabe patted her back and softly stroked her hair. "Shh, shh, shh… I'm here…"

Once they had both settled down, Gabe knew they needed time alone to finally talk. He remembered where there was a small, all-night coffee shop out on the coast.

BAER CHARLTON

The pre-dawn filled the café with surfers, whose only concern was waiting for the light to see the waves. The café's front wall seemed to be made from old school long-gun surfboards with various chunks missing and manufactured shark bite marks. The newer, smaller, surfboards leaned against the old.

Gabe guided Cricket toward the corner booth near the window so he could watch the bike. There were four young blonds in the Mexican serape-cloth hooded sweatshirt that surfers up and down the coast favored. He cleared his throat as he looked at his watch.

The kid in the corner with a dozen hairs on his chin looked up and his pale blue eyes grew big. "Dude. Like, we were just headed out." He brought his leg up and shoved the other kid off the bench with his foot. The four scrambled to be anywhere the giant biker wasn't.

Gabe snapped up the check and shoved it in the kid's chest. "Don't forget to pay your tab. And make sure you tip the same amount or more." He looked back at the frazzled waitress at the end of her shift. His head ground back around and looked at the ticket. It was for three coffees and one tea. Gabe knew they had been roosting in the booth for at least an hour. "How much cash do you have?"

Gabe plucked the two fives out of his hand and took back the ticket. The kid started to protest the ten dollars for a one-dollar tab. He shut his mouth and he left.

As the waitress came out from behind the counter to chase the surfers, Gabe stuck his hand out with the money and ticket. He noticed the rest of the surfers were adding large tips to the small change they had originally placed on their tickets.

Gabe smiled at the waitress. "We'll start with two coffees and a couple of menus, please."

Gabe sipped on his coffee as he watched Cricket carefully measure out the half spoonful of sugar and then two spoonsful of creamer. He realized she was of that age where every calorie was counted.

"So what happened?"

Cricket stirred her coffee ritualistically as she looked out the window. "It was my fault."

Gabe growled. "Bullshit. What happened?"

Her eyes snapped back, but her face followed slowly behind. She sagged slightly. "My best friend, I thought, brought me down to celebrate my birthday. We went to the beach, and then were going to have some dinner and be home by curfew."

Gabe waited.

The young woman collapsed and folded back against the booth. Her gaze moved to outside the window and the night before. "We had a fight. It was stupid really. I was wrong to stick my nose in..."

"What about?"

The waitress came over smoothing out her

apron. "Do we know what we want?"

Gabe pointed at Cricket. The girl looked up and down the menu and then folded it closed. "I'll have some wheat toast—dry."

Gabe snorted. He had watched her eat orange sherbet. He looked up at the waitress. "What would you have if you had been up all night?"

The waitress smirked—knowing. She pointed at the biscuits and sausage gravy. "I'd probably have a side of two over easy so the yolk can mix with the gravy."

Gabe closed his menu. "Great, that's what she's having. I'll have the side of wheat toast."

The waitress laughed at Cricket's reaction. She looked at Gabe. "What do you want with that toast?"

"Breaker omelet, hold the hash browns. They give me gas."

The waitress then remembered where she had seen the biker before. "Did you want your usual canned peaches instead?"

Gabe smiled. It had been a few years, but a waitress remembers.

He turned back to Cricket. "What was the fight about?"

Cricket mentally sorted through what had just happened and got back to her and her girlfriend. "She was thinking about finally putting out."

"Putting what out?"

Cricket's eyes bulged with exasperation. "You

know, for an Angel, you sure are dense. She is going to have sex with her boyfriend."

Suddenly, everything clicked. He realized she was talking about sex, but not adult sex. He squinted. "Which birthday?"

"Seventeenth."

"How old is she?"

"Sixteen. She'll be seventeen in January."

"Let me guess—her boyfriend has been carrying a condom around for the last year."

She snorted. "If he even has one."

"So what happened?"

"She went to the bathroom. When I went looking, she had left me—and the bill."

"Where was the restaurant?"

"Somewhere down here near the beach."

"Why didn't you call someone?"

"I did." She growled as she sank in the booth. "I called almost everybody in my church youth group. But everyone, who had sworn they would help me to the ends of the earth—was either having dinner, studying, or it was passed their curfew."

"Why didn't you call your folks?"

Cricket leaned forward and starting eating very industriously.

Gabe reached over and gently lifted her chin. "If you won't talk to me—I can't help."

"My mother doesn't drive..."

"Why?"

Cricket sat dead.

Gabe softened. "Why?"

She took in a deep breath and let it out slowly. "Because... she's drunk—she wrecked two cars that I know of. She just stays home."

"What about your father?"

The look on her face told him everything.

"What did he say?"

"I was out past my curfew and good girls are home in bed by that time..." She stalled.

"What else?" He asked softly.

"That if I was going to be a slut... then I was no longer his daughter and don't come home."

Gabe controlled his anger. "What time was that?"

"A quarter after ten."

"Where were you?"

"I don't know... I had already started walking."

"Did you know how to get... where do you live anyway?"

"South border of Pasadena, near Cal Tech..."

Gabe sat back. He wasn't sure if he wanted to tackle the next question. "Was he the father of your...?"

The voice was smaller than a mouse but roared in his mind. "Yes."

They sat, sifting through their thoughts.

"When did he start?"

"Touching me?" The dam had broken and now

she was just mad. "I don't remember when he didn't put me to bed and rub me. I guess I was about nine when his fingers became other parts. Then he started sleeping with me—at least for the first part of the night."

"Where was your mother?" Gabe was incredulous.

"Usually, she was passed out on the couch—drunk. First thing daddy would do when he came home was mix her a large martini. With dinner, she would have another one or two, and after dinner she switches to just vodka in a juice glass."

Gabe pushed the last of the omelet away. He had lost his appetite. "You called me at three. What did you do for five hours?"

"I tried to call a few more... from church... and then just started walking when I ran out of dimes."

Gabe thought about her father. "How serious do you think he was about you...?"

She cut him off. "I don't want to go back." He could tell this was not a little girl tantrum. This was a woman drawing the line.

"Okay... then what do you want to do?"

"I don't know. I'm broke. Everyone I thought was a friend—isn't. Everyone I thought was..." She slumped. Her arms lay beside her. Gabe watched as she started to cry and then stopped. She muttered something and then sucked her lower lip into her mouth and bit down firm—holding it in place.

"What did you just say?"

She didn't answer.

"Cricket...?"

"I said—*die before you cry.*"

Gabe had heard the saying before—in the military—not out of the mouth of a small girl. "He taught you that..." She nodded.

He looked at his empty mug. Turning, he held it up and the waitress nodded. He glanced at his watch. They had been there for over two hours.

Gabe apologized to the waitress. "I'm sorry we're camping..."

She put her hand on his shoulder as she poured. "Honey, you take all the time you need. I was off a half hour ago, but the day girl didn't show up. It's not the first time. I don't care. I don't get to see a big brother talk to a little sister enough. It just doesn't happen anymore."

She turned to Cricket, who was now frowning at her. "Honey, I don't know what the problem is, but you have a brother who loves you and will help you see it through. You understand, honey?"

"He's not my brother."

"Then what is he?"

"My Angel..."

"Then, sweetie, you are truly one of the blessed ones." As she turned, she patted Gabe's shoulder.

Gabe sipped the hot coffee. "So what do you want to do... with your life... not just now."

She shrugged against the exhaustion. "I've thought about being a doctor ever since we talked about cutting the frog and people up."

Gabe smiled with a snort. He had forgotten about the conversation. "So?"

"I want to help people... I'm just not sure about the blood and stuff."

"There are a lot of doctors that almost never see blood. A family doctor sees sick people, but if someone really cuts themselves—they go to the emergency room. A dermatologist never sees blood, but they help a lot of kids with zits."

He saw a small smile.

"A radiologist only sees the X-rays. I can take you to a hospital right now and introduce you to several people who help people in need—and don't deal with blood."

"Okay."

"Okay what?" Gabe had forgotten how fast her mind could shift.

"Take me there."

He froze. He had been talking metaphorically, but she wanted to go physically. He knew it was a test, but his mind cleared. He glanced at his watch. "We can't go until evening—what do you want to do until then?"

"Sleep."

Now he was stuck. He thought about a motel—and how that would look. He thought about Maria—

and how that might also look. He had no choice.

"How do you feel about snakes?"

"What kind?"

"Big."

"How big is big?"

"Bigger than me."

"Does it bite?"

He shook his head.

"Is it dangerous?"

"About as dangerous as a Cocker Spaniel… But she really likes girls."

"What color?"

Gabe laughed. "That matters?"

"It might."

"Green, dark green. She's a boa constrictor."

"Is she in a cage?"

"Never. Her cage is the house and yard. She could cross the street, but the kids come to her, so why make the effort."

"Kids? Like as in little kids that could be food?"

Gabe nodded.

"So she snuggles?"

Gabe nodded.

Cricket snorted. "And she likes girls?"

Gabe protested. "She likes me, too. She sleeps with me. I feed her." He quirked his mouth and shrugged his face.

She laughed. It was the first time Gabe had seen even a real smile.

ANGEL FLIGHTS

"So if you take me home, I can sleep, but only if I share a bed with a giant snake?" Gabe made the face again.

She laughed. "This I've got to see. We can go to the hospital later."

Gabe sat at his desk making phone calls. Finally, he got through to the person he knew could help him. He explained the situation in detail. The coffee in his mug ran out. He heard a couple of guys coming in the back door.

"Excuse me a moment, sir." He put his hand over the receiver. "Whoever just came in the kitchen—I'm on the phone, but I need a coffee refill, please."

Zorro stuck his head around the corner. Seeing the mug, he came and retrieved it.

"Sorry about that, sir. I needed to play traffic cop for a second. So, as I was saying, I have firsthand knowledge that if she returns home, she will be sexually molested, raped or her life may be in danger."

He listened as Zorro put the mug down and sat. Gabe wrote on the legal pad. "Yes, sir. I believe that is exactly what she wants." He underlined a few words for Zorro. "No, sir. She doesn't need child services. She turned seventeen last night."

Gabe sat back and listened.

"Sir, if it makes things easier, I would take that legal position. I can go wake her and you can ask her yourself..."

"Yes, sir. She was walking around all night. She called me at three o'clock this morning—we've been talking ever since. I just put her to bed about an hour ago... she's sleeping with my roommate, and I think that is more protection than a regular guard dog."

"No, sir. You heard wrong. Gertie is about a hundred-fifty pounds now."

"Eight o'clock tomorrow morning would be just fine, sir. We'll see you in your chambers."

"Thank you, sir—we'll see you then." He hung up the phone.

Gabe looked at Zorro. "What?"

"You have an underage girl sleeping in this house?"

"She's sleeping with Gertie."

"Oh, yes. That makes it sooo much betterer."

"How much do you really want to know?"

"Dios mios. I'm going to need coffee for this, aren't I?"

"Si." Gabe frowned. "Who came in with you?"

"Solimento. A couple of shave tails were leaving as I came in. There are a bunch of bags on the counter.

Gabe rubbed his face with both hands. "I'm afraid to go look. Every week I have to go give food away. This frat house is out of control."

"I'll say... a snake that runs the place, and now a child in your bed."

ANGEL FLIGHTS

"She's not in my..." He remembered where Cricket was. "Oh, never mind." He got up and took the coffee mug into the kitchen to survey the damage. After putting the food away, and taking two forty-pound bags of corn meal across the street along with twenty pounds of homemade jerky, the two men relaxed by the fire pit as they split a steak. Gabe watched a police helicopter a mile away.

"So now what... you become her new daddy?"

"Don't make it sound dirty—and the title is guardian, not daddy."

"Well, it just looks dirty. You're old enough to be her daddy... and you bring her home..."

Gabe cut him off. "What is it that you really want to say, Don? Just spit it out. For the last hour, you have had that look like you ate something bad or you really needed to take a large shit."

"Maria."

"What about her?"

"Exactly—what about her?"

Gabe put his face into his hand. "Cripe." He looked up. "Don't start that shit on me. Lito tried that crap four years ago. It didn't work then and it..."

"And she still feels the same way."

"What...?"

Zorro just shook his head. "My God, you are the most stupid pendejo I have ever known. She fell hard for you the minute you picked up Lincoln as a baby."

"He's a cute kid." Gabe rose up on one arm in

defense.

Zorro snarled. "And he is attached to my niece."

"Do you guys yell at each other like this all the time?" They turned to see Cricket coming out the back door. "Because if you do... I don't want to live here." She sat down. Zorro eyed the Trustee jumpsuit.

Gabe took a deep breath. "No, no, we don't. Usually, I hit him, and he pulls his gun and shoots me in the leg. After a while, with arguments of extreme stupidity, I don't have a leg to stand on."

Zorro glared at Gabe and leaned over and extended his hand. His voice was soft and gracious, "Hi, I'm Don Diego Garcia, everyone that matters..." he gave Gabe a mean look then turned back with a smile, "...calls me Zorro." They shook hands.

"Amelia Burns but anyone I think is important knows me as Cricket." She waved her finger back and forth. "And, you two are...?"

Gabe growled. "He wants to be my uncle."

Cricket chuckled. "And the problem with that is...?"

"I'd have to marry his niece."

Cricket pulled her feet up onto the chair and wrapped her arms around her knees. "Gabe, if you don't talk to me... I can't help you."

Zorro roared and almost fell out of the chair laughing. He slapped Gabe on the chest as he started coughing, and pointed back and forth from Gabe to the girl. Gabe waited it out. He had been laughed at before. Zorro's face was slowly coming back from purple—even in the dark.

"Gabe?" Cricket blinked.

"It's complicated."

"Explain complicated."

"She's only twenty-one."

"Do you love her?"

Zorro now became silent. This little girl was cutting straight to the point. Zorro knew his niece well. He also knew that he wouldn't want to be a male in a house with these two women.

"Do you?" Cricket drummed her fingers on the arm of the chair. Gertie slithered up into her lap. The football-sized head found her neck and settled back to sleep.

Gabe nodded.

"I'm sorry, I must be deaf... you said what?"

"Yes."

"Have you told her?"

"No."

"When should your new seventeen-year-old daughter tell her for you?"

Gabe's face turned white.

Zorro chuckled again. "Oh pendejo, you are so very screwed now."

38

WHERE TO NOW?

THE EMERGENCY ROOM was busy. Gabe had never thought about how busy an emergency room could get on a Thursday night. Even without stabbings or shootings, Mercy was a busy place.

As Gabe and Cricket walked in, one of the nurses came out of the back. He recognized Gabe from the few times he had been in. He waved. After he had called a patient, he stepped over to Gabe. "We're really busy tonight, but I'll let her know you're here."

"Thanks." Gabe directed Cricket over to part of the waiting room where there were fewer people.

They had been sitting for over an hour when a woman and two kids came rushing in. "My husband just got brunged here by an ambulance. He named Jerome. Jerome Hayward."

Everyone in the waiting areas now knew her business. The nurse was trying to help her quietly, but the woman was not quiet. "You not understand! I needs to see my man."

The nurse stood with her hands outstretched. The woman became even more agitated. "I can *not* leave my babies. Someone gonna *steal* my babies.

Gabe had seen similar circumstances on the street. It was the kind of situation he eventually hoped to mitigate. The woman became more agitated. Gabe suddenly realized he was watching Cricket approach the woman. She stopped in front of the children and started talking to them. Soon she was speaking with the woman, and the woman was calming down. Cricket pointed at Gabe, and then they were all walking over to him.

"You a cop, like she say?"

Gabe stood nodding. "I'm a Special Investigator for the US Attorney General's Office."

The woman waved her hand. "Fuck dat. Is you a cop?"

"Yes, ma'am."

"And she be yo daughter?"

"Yes, ma'am."

"And I can trust you? You ain't gonna run off with my babies?"

"We'll be right here."

Cricket led the kids into the corner where there were some magazines. She grabbed one and began softly reading to the children. Soon they had stopped looking at every noise near the door where their mother had gone and were engrossed in the story Cricket was making up about the models in the Cosmopolitan magazine. Gabe wondered what she could do with the Road and Track that he was bored with.

The doors swung open. A nurse in blue scrubs came out. Gabe was dozing until he heard Cricket take a sharp breath. His head snapped over to where Cricket was with the two children.

He felt his foot being kicked. "Hey, Sleeping Beauty..." Gabe stumbled to his feet. He wrapped Lois in his arms. It had only been a couple of weeks, but she was so good to see.

Lois pushed him away, and then pulled him back for a quick hug. She buried her face in his chest. "I think that young lady is one of our girls."

Gabe laughed. "Lois, meet Cricket. You can call her Amelia Burns today, but tomorrow, she gets to decide what she wants for a name. Cricket, you never knew her name, but this is Lois Lane."

The young woman rose. Her eyes were filled with tears. She stepped over as the two children, who didn't know what was going on, watched. Cricket reached out her hand, and then thought better and just hugged. Lois joined her as they hugged and cried. Cricket whispered at the side of her head. "Thank you, thank you. I can never thank you enough."

Finally, they sat down and Cricket introduced Donovan and Aretha.

ANGEL FLIGHTS

Gabe explained about the woman.

"He's headed for surgery now. He was at the wrong end of a gun." She was slowly shaking her head as she talked. She and Gabe both knew that a body can only have so many holes, and then they can't plug them.

Cricket understood. "We can stay as long as we are needed."

Lois put her hand out to Cricket's knee in the jumpsuit. "Thanks." She turned back to Gabe. "You really know how to dress your girls up... at least we put jeans on them."

Gabe gave her a screwy face look. Lois apologized. "Sorry, it's just a screwy night. We don't usually have the shootings, but here he is. We also have a guy that was found on the side of the road up on the Angeles Crest. His motorcycle crashed into the side of the mountain, but that doesn't explain the guy's condition."

"What's wrong?"

"Well, maybe it would be something you would see in Canada or Alaska. The guy's temperature is around eighty-eight. He should be dead..."

"He has exposure. It's really called hypothermia."

"You know about this?"

"Four years in Adak, Alaska... of course, I know about this. I almost died of it."

Lois jumped up as she pulled him up. "Cricket,

are you okay here? Gabe needs to come be an Angel."

"Sure..."

Lois spun him around. "Our doctors treat sunstroke and stuff. We don't know anything about this stuff. How the hell could he have hypothermia... it was fifty-some degrees up there."

"Not when the wind chill is fifty miles an hour. That would put it somewhere near twenty degrees or lower."

They banged through the double doors.

When they finally came back out again, there was a pink glow in the parking lot. Gabe looked out as Lois gently shook Cricket awake. *This all-nighter stuff had better be stopping soon.*

"The woman's sister or something came and got them about midnight. They had to sedate her. She was hysterical and it was scaring the kids. I guess her husband didn't make it."

Lois hugged the young woman. "We try to save them, but not all of them make it."

Cricket looked up at Gabe. "How about your guy?"

Gabe shrugged. "He'll live to ride another day. But I think he's learned his lesson about riding in the cold. He didn't even have long underwear on. They think they are in sunny Southern California, but when it gets cold, and then they get on a motorcycle—surprise—they freeze to death." He turned to

ANGEL FLIGHTS

Lois. "That was why we did the food wrapping on the feet and the latex gloves before the ski gloves. Some of the guys told some real horror stories about those three-hour rides in the winter."

"So where to from here?"

Gabe looked at his watch. "In a little more than two hours, she has a date to talk with a Superior Court judge in his chambers. They get to work it out as to what she wants. After that, we'll play it by ear according to what she decides."

"I'm not going back."

"And that is exactly what the judge wants to hear. Today is the day you get to decide what you want with your new life. Nobody else has any control—it is all up to you."

"Anything?"

Gabe nodded.

"What if I want to change my name?"

Gabe nodded. "Anything."

"What if I want my name to be Cricket Street?"

Gabe stopped nodding. His smile froze.

Lois laughed. "Oh, my. The man is speechless."

Gabe swallowed. "How do you mean that?"

"I want to come live with you. I don't ever want to go back to my parents."

Gabe took in some extra air. "I mean, what sort of relationship?"

Cricket laughed and gently punched him in the chest. "Silly old Snake... you're too old for me. Besides, polygamy is illegal in California, and you have to deal with that other woman. Of course, you may never get to sleep with Gertie again... as long as she stops pushing me out of the bed. Did you know she's a blanket hog?"

Gabe laughed. "Yes, she is. But then she can't keep them warm, so she comes for you next."

Lois held her hands out. "Stop. Let me get this straight... you don't want to marry Gabe because he is too old, but he is already married to someone else, and..." she shook her head, "who is Gertie?"

Gabe and Cricket laughed and said at the same time, "The snake."

Lois frowned. "Oh God... Someone better take me to breakfast and explain all of this."

39

WHAT DO YOU WANT?

GABE SAT ON the bench as he looked down the long hall. He glanced at his watch. *8:43 a.m.*

The Clerk had come and taken Cricket just after eight, and now Gabe had to just sit. At least he had tapped plenty of coffee over breakfast. Lois was fun to be around. He hoped she stopped in to visit with Chet more.

After sorting out all of the females in his life, Gabe wasn't sure that Lois would ever even drive down the block after having Cricket describe sleeping with a snake that outweighed her and was long enough to wrap around the bed. Although the idea of police floating through the place night and day intrigued her—she wanted to know if there were any Angels.

Gabe glanced at his watch again. *Two minutes had passed.*

In his chambers, the judge and Cricket sat in

ANGEL FLIGHTS

comfortable chairs. The judge wanted her to be comfortable and asked where she wanted to sit. She had asked where he would sit if he were going to read a good but long story.

The man was glad he had cleared his morning. He was finding the story was not simple, and the solution was even more of a conundrum—but with simple overtones. His notes had long become a laundry list of what needed to happen. He sat quietly listening to the inner workings of a horror story, the likes of which, by the time it reached his ears, was usually boiled down to sterile mundane legal terms and facts. Long ago, the grizzly details of the cases that came before him had been blanched and cleaned by lower courts until there was no more emotion. His life had become a parade of words that had little attachment to hearts, minds, or lives. His exposure to the street level of life was more distant than if he were watching *Ironside* on the television.

The judge frowned. "Wait." He looked at his notes. From years on the bench, his hand took notes seemingly by its own volition. He looked at what he had been writing. "Let's go back to Mexico..."

"I'd rather not."

He smiled softly and hoped it looked more like compassion than laughter. "I understand... well, I'd like to think I understand. But..." He looked down again. "In 1970—how did you get to Mexico?"

She thought about the answer. Her memories

scrolled like motorcycles on the freeway—racing alongside the ocean in the late afternoon sun. The memory was like the weather—sunny, but not that warm. She could feel the size and strength of the man between her knees. There was a solid feel from the man she had only met an hour or so before—if anything were to happen, she was behind his protective shield.

Her eyes drooped closed as she leaned back against the comfort of the large leather chair that was so secure—much like the backrest on the chopper had been. If only that thirteen-year old had known how things would progress to this day—she wouldn't have been so afraid.

"Amelia?"

Her eyes flew open. There was a man sitting there in front of her. They were in a very powerful, richly appointed office... Her heart raced, and then she remembered that this was not her father. She remembered she was now safe. Because of a man... and now, it was her turn to protect him.

"I hitched a ride."

With his experience dealing with far better professional liars, the judge knew the answer wasn't right—or at least not the whole answer. But it was an answer he could work with.

"How did you know about the place in Mexico?"

She snorted softly. "Same way your secretary

probably knows about the lawyer on the other side of the building having an affair with the cleaning lady, who is actually an illegal alien working with a bogus social security card and driver's license. People talk, and around schools, girls talk—a lot."

The side of the man's mouth turned up. He really liked this girl. "Is there a lawyer in the Public Defender's office having an affair?"

Cricket sat with a dead face. Her eyes studied the man. She knew he was powerful, but she had grown accustomed to her father having that kind of power, but also flawed.

She spoke quieter, but with no less strength. "I find it interesting that you want to know about an affair—which is titillating, but you don't want to hear or see if anything is going on that is illegal in the building."

He understood that it was not this building or house that she was talking about.

"So let's talk about your father."

"What do you want to know?"

"You said that he molested you—for how long?"

"I don't remember a time when he wasn't touching me, or putting me to bed."

"When did—"

"Did he start having sex with me?" The judge pushed out his hand in uncomfortable acknowledgment.

BAER CHARLTON

She realized that she was on the firmer ground here. "It's okay to talk about it, to say the words. I'm not going to break. That happened a long time ago. It happens when you find out your good friend sleeps in pajamas, but only her mother has ever seen her without any clothes. It happens when you find out all of your friends in the fifth grade have no idea what a penis is, but you know what it tastes like, or how many holes your own father can fit it into—because he has been preparing you for it all of your life. It happens when a boy takes your hand at age eleven—a boy you think of as nice—but when he leans over at lunch to kiss you on the cheek—you start screaming. Breaking happens in little ways. Having your father stick his penis in your vagina or butt before you have your first period..."

She stopped and sighed. "It's not a big break. By then, it is just another one of the small breaks—the cracks that happen. You lay there while he grunts and tells you how pretty you are, how he loves his pretty little girl, and when you don't know any better—you think it is normal.

"He tells you how pretty you are—yet all the while he is doing the worst possible thing a father can do to his daughter. Or at least, it was what I thought back then."

"Until you got pregnant..."

She flattened her lips and sighed out a raspberry. "That was just another break or crack. By the time I was eleven, I had already found the right books in the Pasadena main library. I knew that I would get pregnant. I knew about eggs and sperm and what happens when they get together on the right... or wrong time."

"What I didn't know, at thirteen, was how the sperm got to the eggs. I thought it didn't matter if he was in my butt, or I was sucking him or if he was screwing me in my vagina. If I had known, maybe I would have done things a little differently back then—but then, I wouldn't have met..."

The judge shifted uncomfortably. He was used to socially acceptable conversations, and this had become an important conversation—but not one he had expected to hear coming from a seventeen-year-old girl. Especially one dressed in what appeared to be the same attire that some of the defendants wore in his court.

"Let's talk about Mr. Street for a moment..."

"What do you *need* to know?"

The emphasis on the word *need* did not escape the judge's notice. He thought about his questions.

"How long have you known him?"

"Four years."

"Where did you meet him?"

"You don't need to know that."

He put down his pen. He thought about some of the lawyers he knew. She would beat them to a pulp if she ever became a lawyer. "Okay, give me some idea that I can work with."

"Up an alley in Hollywood—it was a pleasant afternoon near Hollywood and Vine."

"Did you share a soda?" He referenced Marilynn Monroe being discovered.

"The orange sherbet came later." *Touché.*

"What does he do?"

She thought about what he meant and what he did for her. But she knew the man only wanted the conventional answers. Things he could write in his notes. Answers that would fit in little boxes so they were easily filed away—*where do you file the job of an Angel?*

"He is a detective or something for the Attorney General." Cricket fluttered her fingers in a fiddle of dismissal.

"Do you know what a Special Investigator for the US Attorney General's Office does?"

She smirked. Now she knew that Gabe had only found a name and phone number—they had never met.

"I don't think Gabe fits into that suit or model of what you think he does. Yes, he is an investigator—but I think once you meet him, you are going to have to change how you think about what the job is or means.

She shifted, and turned in the large chair. "Look." Her legs came up and tucked under her. "The next thing you want to know is the only thing that is important. You want to know why I want to be emancipated, and why I want Gabe as my guardian or father—whichever we have to do."

"Which do you want?"

She breathed gently as her eyes searched for the right answer in the pattern of the threadbare Persian rug. The pattern was a twisting set of vines that led away and then back. There were many vines, but there was always the cohesive overall pattern. She thought about how she felt on the back of the motorcycle. She felt the solidness of them talking when she was only a scared girl in the hospital, and then again in the café at the beach. Her mouth drew back and her face warmed as she thought about the otherworldliness of sleeping with a snake that could kill you—but you knew she only wanted to be as close to you and your smell as she could get. She thought about what it would be like in the coming years.

She looked up into the kind eyes of the man who was waiting patiently—the only man who could help her decide her fate—and grant her what she wanted.

"What I want..." She squeaked. She cleared her throat, swallowing the rising lump. "When I'm fifty..." Her eyes filled with tears. She bit her lip and wiped at her eyes. "I want to still call him daddy... or any other name of endearment I can make up." She wiped her eyes and then drew the sleeve of the jumpsuit along her nose as she sniffed. "But, if all I can get is a guardian for now, that will be enough. What's in my heart will never change.

"All of my life, until last night, I had a father. My teachers and friends saw him and thought I was a lucky girl to have such a parent. They had no idea what it was to live your life where you are tied so completely to a monster... A monster that is so powerful nobody can see it—they only see the man.

"Four years ago, I was at the end result of that hell. In the turn of events, I met the kind of person who would carry you out of hell with their last breath. If it meant taking a bullet like the Secret Service is supposed to do for the President—he would do it. I only had to look in his eyes to know that. Would he take a bullet or go that far for any of the other girls? I don't know... but I do know with all of my heart he would for me.

"Four years ago, I almost died. Gabe scooped me up, strapped me to the back of his motorcycle, and at the risk of going to jail for the rest of his life, brought me to safety from Mexico. But he didn't just make sure I was safe and then disappear. He stayed with me. I'm sure now it broke every rule the hospital had, but he never left my side.

"When they wheeled me into surgery—his face was the last I saw. When I woke up—he was sitting by the bed—holding my hand. Every night, he was there watching over me, protecting me. In the middle of the night, I would wake up—he was there. His eyes were open. If I asked for some orange sherbet—he went and brought it back. When they released me, he brought me home to LA. He never even asked my name.

"We weren't supposed to know who the other person really was. But before he let me go, he gave me his card and told me how to get in touch with him. He trusted me with his life. My own father hadn't trusted me to be out past my curfew. Gabe made sure I was alive and well. My own father had only cared if his sex toy was home when he wanted to play his sick games.

"When I was alone and in need, down at the beach, my father called me a slut and told me not to come home. I was stuck there because I was left there by someone who I had thought for years was my best friend. One by one, my entire church group turned their back on me because it was inconvenient—because *I* was inconvenient. My own father wouldn't come to my rescue because it was inconvenient—so he threw me away.

"I then made two collect calls. Nobody asked why... They just helped. Gabe made sure I was safe—and that a cop car would stand by until he got there. He never asked why because, in his mind—it didn't matter."

She shifted in the seat and took a deep breath and let the air out slowly. "So your question is—how do I know. How do I know what a real father is like?

How do I know what kind of person Gabe is? How do I know if I will be safe with a man who I have spent less than a week with? How do I know if this is what I really want?" The judge gently nodded.

"Because... of the father I had for seventeen years."

The judge looked down at his notes. He couldn't trust his voice to talk. He took his time.

He took a deep breath and stood. Walking around his desk, he thoughtfully eased into his desk chair. He swiveled around and pulled a book from the wall of library behind his desk. Cricket had wondered if they were even real, or more importantly if the man had read any of them. She thought about the large library her father had in their home. She had never seen a book in the man's hands. She understood the trappings of power and perception.

The judge wrote a couple of notes on a fresh pad.

He looked up. "We also have a very difficult legal problem to take care of. This is one I would not be involved with, but it would be more of a local issue."

"My father..."

The judge nodded. "Your father. What we have are crimes against statutes, as well as religious crimes, and crimes against nature. And from what you say, he won't be an easy target. Powerful, well-known public figures never are. In order to take him down, it will entail you being dragged through some of the worst mud and gutters that society can muster. You will be portrayed as mentally deranged—that you suffer from flights of fantasy of a deviate sexual nature..."

She growled as she leaned forward. "Anything the LA Times dares to print—can't even come close to the reality of what he did. Society doesn't talk about these monsters because they can't handle a life that lets them exist. We have pretty names like pedophile and molesting because people in your world can't deal with things like old men fucking little girls who aren't in high school yet. There are laws against sodomy. Society, if it even whispers about it—thinks it is about one man fucking another in the ass as the Bible describes it. However, they would never talk about a father doing that to his little girl or boy—but that is the real hell of this society. We don't talk about things that make us uncomfortable, and so we have a scion of the community—who does it for fifteen or sixteen years—and gets away with it. Queers, who want to have sex because they actually love each other, are breaking the law if they are caught. But people like my father..." She shifted and put her feet down. "I'm sorry. I get a little—"

"It's okay. We're not talking about the price of gas and how that impacts the price of food or milk. We are talking about a very real problem, and for you, it is very close and raw. But what I am saying is that as viewed through the law and how things are prosecuted... the burden of proof and the kind of investigation—"

She held up her hand to stop him. She stood and placed her hand out again. She went and opened the large old door. She wondered if all the doors in the building were as heavy and thick, or if this one was bulletproof. She walked through the anteroom as she ignored the two legal assistants. She opened the other door and leaned out into the hallway. "Angel?"

Gabe looked up.

"It's your turn at bat."

As Gabe followed Cricket and his body filled the large doorway into the judge's chambers, the judge looked up from his desk. His eyes got only fractionally larger as his understanding bloomed fully.

He stood and put his hand out and it was consumed by the larger man's hand. The shake was warm and reassuring. If the judge had any doubts before, they were instantly banished.

As they sat, the judge looked down at his notes. "I want to apologize for making you wait this long," he looked at Cricket, "but we had a lot of territory to cover. I think we have come to an understanding and a meeting of the minds, and so I only have a few questions to cover."

Gabe glanced over at Cricket. If he had any problem about waiting for almost three hours, they

ANGEL FLIGHTS

all disappeared with the smooth, calm look on her face. She reached over and took his hand.

Gabe faced the judge. "Shoot."

"Are you financially prepared to take her on?"

Gabe had already covered this in his mind as he paced the hall. "I own my current home outright. I plan to buy another house outright. I have no student debt, and I have been putting another young man through medical school. I have personal assets that are more than adequate to put her through as much schooling she might want or need—with or without any help from scholarships.

"I work as a Special Investigator attached to the US Attorney General's Office—"

The judge interjected as he looked at the hair, beard and biker attire, "I would say more like a Very Special Investigator."

Gabe smiled and nodded. His uniform of the day was no suit. "I'm a GS-25 but in January, I'll be taking over a certain task force that carries a new standing. Because of what I bring to the game, things are more than a little unusual, and I'll be bumped to a thirty-two and a supervisor position."

The man nodded. He placed a small check next to the first question.

"You mentioned that you own your home but are buying another..."

"The house I have now is only a two bedroom. It worked fine up until now..." He didn't feel the need to mention Rabbit and the several dozen officers that wandered in and out. "But as it is now, she has to share the bed with the family pet. So a larger house would be in order."

The judge glanced at the small framed picture of his Golden Retriever with a duck in its mouth on his desk. His eyebrows rose in interest. "What kind of dog?"

Gabe tread safely. "It's not."

Cricket laughed. "I told you my life is one that doesn't fit with society's ideals. Gertie is about fourteen feet of the prettiest green that an Amazon Boa Constrictor can be. She's a little pudgy, but if you want to come over and tell her she needs to be on a diet—be our guest." She waited for the shock to settle in.

The judge thought about the information that he had dismissed because it didn't make sense. He then remembered something else, and how very few large snakes were slithering around the LA area—especially ones that were given freedom to roam. "Do you live in...?"

"El Sereno."

"I think you might know my old partner—he owns a bar now."

"Chet gave me your name and number."

"So this isn't about making more room for her—"

"No, sir. And it's not about having the forty or

fifty officers at every hour of the day in and out of the house. It has to do with the rest of my life. I think I'm supposed to go ask a young lady to marry me this afternoon or this evening. She has a son that I wouldn't mind also calling mine. So you see... I'm kind of in the middle of a family explosion."

The judge adjusted all of his information to merge with the new information. He skipped a couple of questions that were now frivolous and almost nonsense. His pen stopped at the last question.

He looked up. "Father or Guardian?"

Gabe looked at Cricket. He could tell she was holding her breath. "If she will have me, I'd rather be a father. You see, I can't have any children of my own, and if I had the pick of the litter, I'd take the one with the five freckles on the nose."

He was rewarded with her blushing as her breath exploded. Her breath seemed to propel the small body out of the chair to around his neck. Not even Gertie had ever squeezed him that tight.

Gabe squawked from the stranglehold. "I understand that adoption can take a year or more, but by then, she'll be eighteen..."

The judge smirked as he tapped his pen lightly on the notepad. "Most of that time is spent doing a lot of background investigations... I think you cops call it butt sniffing. But when the compelling evidence is presented in such a way that even a Superior Court Judge can see the light... it can be done in a few hours."

Gabe pulled away from Cricket and gave her a goofy questioning look. She nodded. They both turned and nodded at the judge.

The judge smiled. "Father it is. I'll have the clerk draw up the papers and have them ready this afternoon. We will have you sign the emancipation papers first, and while my clerk takes them downstairs to file, we can sign the adoption papers. We can't file them at the same time, so we need at least a thirty-minute delay in the filings."

He reached over and buzzed the intercom.

"Sir?"

"David, when can we have them back this afternoon to sign and file some papers, say about a one hour slot?"

"Sir, Judge Barker took over your afternoon so we can fit it in whenever you want."

"Come on in, and we'll get the information you need to work up the paperwork."

Gabe held up a finger. "We'll need one other thing…"

"What?"

"She'll need a passport very soon. I'll be taking her and maybe the family to Brazil for Christmas."

"That is a State Department thing. After we have everything done, you can take it to your boss. I'm sure Thomas is very handy when it comes to things like that."

ANGEL FLIGHTS

As they all rose, the judge looked again at the trustee jumpsuit and the penny loafers. They just didn't go with the long brown hair and cute face.

"Um, Gabe?"

"Yes, sir?"

The judge nodded towards Cricket. "I think maybe you might find a little time soon to let the trustee off for good behavior—and maybe find some more appropriate clothes?"

"Yeah, Dad." She gently slugged him on the arm.

Gabe rolled his eyes. "Working on it, sir. We'll see you about two?"

The law clerk nodded.

"That should work just fine."

40

WILL YOU?

THE AFTERNOON SUN had gone from golden light in the window to deep shadow. The judge reached over and turned on his desk lamp. The soft glow of the green glass top of the antique reading lamp cast muted shadows on the dark walls. The three softly talking about the future, traffic, motorcycles, and sailing—could have been the image of conspirators plotting clandestine dealings. The weight of what they were actually doing did not escape any of them.

As the conversation on sailing wound to the end of any of their knowledge, the judge looked to Cricket as he stood. "My dear, could you give me a few minutes with Ga... your new daddy?" He smiled. He liked the glow that came to her face by him using her term for father."

She nodded as she stood. As she passed behind Gabe, she bent and kissed him on the top of the head.

ANGEL FLIGHTS

"Be an Angel."

The judge waited for the heavy door to close. "You're going to have your hands full with that one."

"I know. But I think she's just wound tight right now." He waited for the judge to sit. The judge took the seat that Cricket had just vacated.

"While you two were off trying to find some new clothes and have lunch, I made some phone calls."

"About…?"

"You… and her father, *the* Mr. Burns…"

"What did Chet have to say?"

The man chuckled. "I talked to more than just Chet. But he did steer my other phone calls."

Gabe waited the man out. He could tell the man was still trying to put it all together.

"I think you would have an easier time proving the man on the grassy knoll than you will be in trying to take down Burns. His law practice has become the least of his income, power, or influence. I think that if the man wanted to, he could snap his fingers, and come New Year's Day, there would be no parade down Colorado Boulevard."

"Are you saying that we just roll over and give up?"

"No, I just wanted you to know what you are up against. The man wields enormous power. People think Beverly Hills is the throne of power in Southern California, but it is only the visual social trappings of the power of Hollywood. Before the movies, it was just a nice place to live on the hill. The movie moguls and stars made it. It was close, and there was still raw land to build the mansions they could afford. The house Cricket grew up in pre-dates Charlie Chaplin. The power along the ridge overlooking San Marino is more than Beverly Hills, Hollywood, and Brentwood combined. The stuffed suits of Pasadena built the Miracle Mile on Wilshire Boulevard to keep the filth of their money away from their tennis courts and cement ponds.

"What I'm saying is—if you go at this man head on—you will lose. Cricket will lose. This man will mount a force in his left hand that could take away everything you hold dear. It is the old evil kind of thing where you don't kill the man—you kill his family, burn and salt his fields, and sink his ships—and leave him standing on the shore watching the entire destruction."

Gabe sat quietly for a few moments. In his head, he heard a very short conversation one night in the dark of a cabana by the summer sea. He chuckled. Then he laughed—because it was so true.

"What could be so funny?"

Gabe gave the man a very toothy smile. "There are many ways to kill a man—utterly destroy him—and yet leave him untouched."

"Go on…"

ANGEL FLIGHTS

"Let me ask you a very serious question, but imagine we are sitting in your men's club. The room is packed with all of your longtime friends and associates. Your power is invested in not who you know, but who knows you."

"Yes...?"

"You're married?"

"Yes."

"Does your wife know that you still fuck sheep?"

The man's mouth opened... and then just hung there.

Gabe solidified the gelatin the man's mind had become. "You're thinking how you can't answer the question either way—damned if you do and damned if you don't. However—you're forgetting you are in that room. Just as fast as your mind is racing... so are theirs. The next thing to move will be their tongues. You and I both know this isn't true... but perception—that is everything. And all power is founded on perception. *All power*."

The judge smiled and leaned back into the chair. "Keep me posted."

Dad and daughter walked out of the court building and across the street to the parking structure. Gabe looked at the baggy jumpsuit. "What kind of clothes...? Hell, I don't even know where to take you shopping." Their midday foray in downtown Los Angeles had been a bust—except for lunch.

BAER CHARLTON

She grabbed his arm. "I do. And you even know how to get there."

Gabe pulled up in front of the costume shop. They were both laughing. "You know I can afford something, anything new..."

"I don't know any store that carries what I need or want right now." She pulled on his arm, laughing. "Come on, daddy."

Gabe growled in her face. "Just remember you are never too old or too big to be turned over someone's knee."

She laughed and danced away. Gabe was amazed. He had struggled for almost a week to get her to even smile—and now...

Gabe sat waiting. He didn't recognize the ladies who were working the shop. Cricket didn't either. She tried to tell them about how four years before the store had supplied the jeans and gear for her to look like a biker—but she only got blank stares. So Cricket was on her own as she searched the racks for what she needed.

Cricket turned in front of the tri-mirror. The jeans looked a couple of years old, and the cut-off jean jacket over her leather jacket was a great match for Gabe's. "It's not perfect, but it will do for now."

Gabe pointed at the penny loafers.

She rolled her lips in puffs. "Yeah, they aren't what I would want, and they don't have anything I like—that fits."

ANGEL FLIGHTS

"What do you want?"

"Boots. But those big clunky things you wear look fine on you, but I need something a little more fitted—like a cowboy boot or something."

Gabe stood and swept his arm as he did a deep, dramatic bow. "As you wish." He stood, and with a smile said, "I even know how to get there."

Twenty minutes later, they pulled up at a small store. Cricket got off with her face screwed up into a twisted frown. "Nudie's? What kind of place is named Nudie's?" She turned laughing. "Can you even take me into this place with a straight face?"

Gabe smiled. "I think they were in business when Roy Rogers and Dale Evans were your age. They make some of the best cowboy boots in the world."

Once inside, Cricket gawped at the leather goods throughout the store. She was carefully stroking the fine carving on a saddle when Gabe walked up. "Makes you almost want to get a pony, huh?"

Cricket looked at all of the hanging decorative parade quality tack. "I already have a pony. But none of this would fit—it would all just slide right off her." She turned with an evil smile. "But I'm going to ride her all night long tonight. She damn near crushed me last night."

Gabe wasn't thinking as he turned and mused. "Yeah, she likes to be on top."

Cricket stopped and started trying to muffle her

laugh.

He spun around and stuck his face in hers. He growled in his best imitation of a scary voice. "Behave."

It only made her laugh harder. *Parenting was not going to be easy.*

Thirty minutes later, they were climbing on the bike. Her new boots looked as worn and old as Gabe's. The fit was almost perfect, and they had been made for a movie that ended up not being made. Cricket had been reading a brochure of theirs and told them that she would be back to get a pair measured and matched to her feet when she stopped growing. Pedro had turned to Gabe and asked if he had stopped growing. Cricket laughed and said that he had stopped growing—he just had not grown up yet.

Turning her over his knee was sounding more and more like an option.

Filing all of the paperwork had taken longer than they had thought. By the time the clerk returned with the last of the conformed copies, it was four o'clock. Lunch had been good, but now at six o'clock, Gabe and Cricket were hungry.

Gabe thought about going up the hill—but he wasn't sure if he wanted to become a father and ask Maria the big question all on the same day. He looked at his new daughter as they stood by the motorcycle. He had braided her hair back for her. It exposed her face and made her look even younger. Not as young as the small girl in the hospital, but just younger. It made him think about another young girl—a girl who had taken the hand of her boyfriend a lifetime ago.

"Do you like eggplant?"

"It's not orange sherbet... but it's okay. How is it cooked?"

Gabe smiled softly. "With a lot of love." *Kind of like today.*

41

WELL?

GABE LAUGHED AS he listened to the commotion in the other bedroom. He spread his arms and legs luxuriously across the entire bed. The sheets and blanket were flat, and all his. The hundred plus pound snake was not draped all over him.

He felt the end of the bed sink and the antique frame creak under the weight of the large snake. His solitary moment was over.

"Did the little girl throw you out? That is what you get when you hog all of the blankets." The football head, with black slits set in gold pools for eyes, glared at Gabe as the body quickly gathered around his body heat.

Cricket stood in the doorway. Her thin legs stuck out of the bottom of one of Gabe's t-shirts. The hem was just below her knees. "The blanket stealing I can handle. That was *not* what she was doing. She brought a dead something into the bed and tried to

ANGEL FLIGHTS

feed me with it. It was gross."

"That was my fault." A giant of a man stood behind her.

"Eep!" She jumped and retreated to the safety of the bed, snake, and Gabe.

Gabe laughed. "Hello, Rabbit. I heard you might be getting bored with Europe. How's the KGB?"

The man growled. "Too close for comfort." The man frowned. "How did you...?"

His face lit up and he pointed at Cricket. "Hey, I know you. Um..." He snapped his fingers several times then pointed at Gabe. "She was the only one..."

Gabe was laughing at his friend trying to sort through well over a few hundred girls that they had transported. But his friend was correct—there had only been one Jiminy Cricket.

"Rabbit, I'd like you to meet Cricket Street."

The man's face dropped open. "But... but she's only..."

"My daughter."

Rabbit froze, slowly closing his mouth. Three times, he held up his finger to say something. Finally, he closed his eyes and took a deep breath. Opening his eyes, he sighed. "Oh hell, this is going to require coffee..." He turned on his heel. As he turned the corner, he called back. "You're in my bed."

Gabe snorted. "My house."

The shaggy head peeked back around the corner.

"Oh, yeah... there is that."

Gabe smiled at his daughter. "Give me two minutes at the toilet, and then you can have the shower." He bounded out of bed.

"Don't forget to put the seat down."

His head was the last to disappear into the room. "Seat never goes up."

A few minutes later, she found the sign behind the toilet.

IF you are reading this, you are standing up and splattering on areas where our snake crawls with her bare skin. Please respect her delicate nature, her health, and the health of the many small children who live to pet her—AND SIT THE FUCK DOWN. Or be prepared to clean the whole house. Thank you, the management.

Rabbit stood looking in the refrigerator. "What do you feel like for breakfast?"

Gabe kicked him in the butt with the side of his foot. "The Long Green."

Rabbit stood with a silly smile. "Perfect... On the freeway—or in the riverbed?"

"Please. I'm a family man now."

Cricket howled, hooted, screamed, and laughed the entire way up the concrete riverbed. The guys kept it under a hundred—for most of the way.

In front of the long, low white diner, Cricket growled in her best imitation of Gabe, "You know I want a bike of my own now—don't you?"

"We will have to talk to your mother if I marry her."

Rabbit's head snapped up. "You're getting married?"

Cricket laughed. "He's trying to grow the balls to find out."

Rabbit pointed at her with a frown. "Where did you find this one?"

They fed through the door into the diner. "I think the egg cracked, and out she popped—snapping, biting, and snarling."

Gabe stepped over to the counter and quietly laid down a fifty. "This is going to take a while. Where do you want us?"

The slender cook turned toward the end of the long counter. "Mike, Stan—these people want your seats." The two men looked up and took in the bookends of tall, muscular, and shaggy bikers. The dishes were pushed back and the men were standing before the cook had whipped the fifty off the counter—it disappeared into his pants pocket.

Rabbit cracked his knuckles over his fifth or sixth mug of coffee. "I haven't broken any legs lately..."

Cricket smiled, but Gabe cut her off. "The last thing I want anyone to do is touch him. Even poking him gently with your finger would go to the superior court under the heading of assault with the intent to do bodily harm. On top of that, there are three of us talking about this, so it would also carry a conspiracy charge on top. So bare minimum, we all go away for twenty years with no parole—just to start."

Rabbit pointed at Cricket. "She's a minor."

"Stanton vs. California, 1962—she would be tried as an adult because she was conspiring with adults… even if one of them acts like a child."

Rabbit gulped the last of the coffee. "So what was all that about you getting married?"

Cricket reached over and rolled Gabe's wrist so she could look at the watch. She laughed. "Don't you want to talk about this over lunch?"

Rabbit glanced at his watch and snorted. "Yeah, and I know just the place."

He covered his mug with his hand as the cook reached to fill it. Standing he threw a pair of twenties on the counter. They disappeared as the mugs were bunched in his hand. "You three have a great day, y'hear?"

They took their time enjoying the weak sunshine as they rolled south down San Fernando Road. Rabbit patted the large tank on the full dress bike, so they nosed into the Atomic station. Gabe looked at the large sign that read 'EVEN.' He knew his license plate ended in a five, and he was looking at the seven on Rabbit's bike. He snorted softly as he removed the cap and began to fill his tank. The attendant never even glanced at the plates. Gabe knew he hardly paid attention to the plates on cars and trucks—a sale

ANGEL FLIGHTS

was a sale, and Atomic never ran out of gas. Gabe couldn't even remember there being any lines to speak of, even at the height of the crazy summer. They just kept pumping.

To Gabe, it seemed like a day of straight eating. He knew he needed to slow down. Maria shifted on his leg as they watched Lincoln show Cricket all about serving guests on the patio. The new gas heaters had extended the summer's business of people who wanted to sit outside in the sun. The gentle fingers played absentmindedly with Gabe's hair.

Rabbit was behind them going over the books. "Wow, do you realize that you tripled the labor bill, but almost doubled the business for a net profit increase of sixty-three percent? Those are crazy numbers."

She looked back. "What, Jefe, you wanted me to run the business in the dirt?"

Gabe snorted. "Ground—not dirt."

"What's the difference?"

"The ground is at the bottom, but dirt is everywhere."

"It better not be." She pulled his ear up and looked in as she started giggling.

The door was pulled open and Lincoln ran in. "Mama, mama, Kick-it wants to be a doctor like Tio Lito."

Maria looked up at the young girl. She liked the kindness she saw in the eyes. She could tell the young girl had actually liked spending time with Lincoln—not just allowing her and Gabe to talk about what hadn't been said all of the last years. "Is that right?"

She nodded. "Yes... well... probably. I know that I want to help people."

"You know it is very expensive, this school?" Maria wrapped her hand around Gabe's head and covered his mouth.

Cricket could see the sparkle in the other young woman's eyes. "I'm a straight A student. I figure I can get scholarships when I finish my last year of high school."

Maria finally laughed. "We don't finish high school in this family."

Gabe closed his eyes as he laughed softly. He had seen the car pull up across the street. Zorro and Lito were climbing out.

"But your older brother finished high school—he's at college in medical school."

"My *little* brother never took a single class in high school. You can ask him yourself." She held out her hand as Lito walked through the door.

Cricket turned. The boy was her age. He was not the older man that she had envisioned. "But you..."

Gabe laughed as he broke loose. "Are only seventeen? Is that what you were going to say?" He turned to Lito and Zorro. "Lito, Zorro, may I present Cricket Street—my daughter. Sweetie, this is Lito, and his uncle and my former partner, Don Diego Garcia—Zorro to those that matter—who you met the other night."

The men shook her hand. "If you are only seventeen... how are you in college? Wait... you have to have a Bachelor's degree before you can..."

Gabe cleared his throat. "First, let them in the door before you attack. And second, you need to ask the questions in the right order, because this is the boy... er... man, who is going to show you how to do what he did."

Lito and Cricket were sitting across the room at their own table talking about school. The real estate agent had shown up and Rabbit went with them to look at the big pink house down the street. Zorro sat with Gabe as Maria came and went with the customers.

"So what did she say?"

"We're going to work on it. There is no real hurry, but we are looking at the big pink house. I think the way it sits on that larger lot, and that tiny empty lot next door, we can probably do some additions with even a small apartment for when Rabbit is in town."

"So what would you do about the house in Stockton?"

"Cricket and I will stay there for now. Maria just wants me to start spending more time here—act like a real suitor." He smiled. "But if we can expand the pink house—that will also take some time before we can all move in."

"And then the Stockton house?"

"You mean the frat house?" Gabe laughed. "I think we could go away for months, and nobody would notice, except the neighbors. But, no, I'll always keep the house. I think maybe I will probably just leave it as my office so I don't bring home any of the work."

"So does that new position mean you have to clean up, cut the hair and beard?"

Maria came by and suddenly wrapped her arms and hands around the hair and beard. She scowled at Zorro. "You hush... I like his Jesus hair and beard."

Gabe shrugged and ducked his lips. *Who knew?*

42

THE NECKLACE

GABE AND CRICKET sat in the back booth of the diner. The booth, at one time, had been where the mayor of Pasadena received large envelopes and then handed out smaller envelopes of cash. Every cop in Pasadena knew the restaurant and the story of the large booth. Gabe had chosen the booth for that very reason.

Gabe was in the corner, watching down the long restaurant at the street through the front windows. He could imagine the mayor, those many years before, taking advantage of the same view. The darkness of the long room, with its dark wood paneling and high ceiling, made the windows—from the street—mirrors. He watched as the two black and whites pulled up. One parked north, and the other south. *The Pincer, prepared to chase either way.*

Gabe had not planned to get up. But when he saw one of the cops, he was pretty sure what the nametag would say. It would have been rude for him not to stand.

As they approached in the standard swagger that came from the new load of heavy gear that went with the uniforms, Gabe could read the shiny brass plate. "This is a very pleasant surprise, Officer Connell."

Cricket's head turned at the sound of a familiar name. "Janice?"

Jan's head snapped to take in the young girl. "Amelia?"

Cricket pulled herself out of the booth, and then was baffled at the protocol of the uniform. Jan led the way and hugged her anyway.

"You two know each other?"

Jan smiled. "For years. We go to the same church just over here on Lake. Our parents have been friends since before we were born, I think." She looked down at the young girl she had her arm draped across. "We were in the church youth group together."

Gabe growled softly. "Oh, this could be awkward."

Jan picked up on the tone and look on his face. She looked around at her partner and the other two. "Maybe you better read us in on what is happening, and then we can all decide."

Cricket shifted around and sat between Gabe and Jan. The other three officers, even with a booth made for six, found that with the bullet vests, and other things hanging on the vests, and Sam Brown belts, the third opted to grab a chair and sit at the end.

Gabe bought whatever they wanted for breakfast. The coffee helped with the minds that were having a hard time understanding the new reality about someone they all thought they knew. Three of the four attended the same church.

Jan pushed her empty cup forward. "So you don't want us to do anything—just be there."

"Exactly." Gabe put his mug down. "My take on this, and those in the real know is if anyone touches him, he will unleash holy hell. But if we pull this off correctly, there is nothing he can do."

The officer with the slight gray at the temple cleared his throat. "So first, we are going to the house and just stand around while she goes and gets her stuff…"

Cricket nodded. "There is only one thing in that house that I would ever want—it is a locket my grandmother gave to me when I was twelve. It has a picture of her and me in it."

The man nodded. "And then we follow you up to the church."

Gabe cleared up what the man was really asking. "I want you there at the house so the neighbors don't say she broke into the house or anything. They see the uniforms, and in their minds, it is all on the up and up. If it makes you feel better, you or Jan can go in with Cricket."

The man held up his hands with the palms out.

"The tough part is going to be at the church..."

Jan growled as she patted Cricket on the thigh. "No, it's not." She looked at Cricket. "You weren't the only girl he touched inappropriately."

The other younger cop with the still-pink cheeks growled and mumbled. "It wasn't just little girls that Mr. Burns was touching." Silently, the other five digested the subtle information. They all knew rape was never about sex... it was about power of another being.

They stood and left as Gabe handed the older blonde waitress some money. "Thanks, Kathy."

"Anytime, Gabe—it was good to see this old booth used for bringing down the corrupt and powerful, instead of the other way around. And we expect to see you and your new daughter here more often."

Gabe gave her a quick side hug and kissed her on top of the head—*a head that held over fifty years of the darkest secrets of Pasadena.*

Services were underway. The priest had just administered the sacrament and was putting away the containers. The altar boys were scurrying about their duties as they all prepared for the next part.

The large double doors at the back of the sanctuary were thrown open and banged against the walls. The priest spun about to see who would dare to interrupt his service.

The small steel slugs buried into the heels of Gabe's boots sounded like medium firecrackers, or the fire of small caliber pistols, as they struck the stone floor. The two looked like a parody of a showdown at the OK Corral. The rough street clothes presented no less of a sinister visage as they stomped down the center aisle.

The priest squinted. The girl looked familiar, but he couldn't place her. As they got closer, his eyes widened and he looked at the pew with only two people sitting in it. The man looked up, seemingly from private prayer or dozing. He examined the priest's face and aberrant behavior. Seeing the priest looking back down the church, Mr. Burns turned to face the last steps of a large man—and his daughter. He scowled at the street tramp clothing.

"How dare you come in here like that—"

Gabe's voice was controlled volcanic heat. "No. How dare you, sir?"

The man looked about and then saw the four police officers as they circled behind the giant biker and his daughter. One of the officers... the female looked very familiar. Then he realized who she was.

He held his finger up, pointing at Jan. "You! You dare come in this church, this house of God—"

Gabe cut him off. "You have no right to point a finger. You are not pure here. You have no piety here."

The man half rose. "Who are you to tell me—"

"I, sir, am your worst nightmare." Gabe's voice rocketed off the stone walls of the cathedral. Even the half deaf could hear exactly what was being said. "I am the avenging angel, and I know all of your sins."

The man's face was almost purple. "You. Know. Nothing."

Gabe pulled Cricket forward. He realized Mrs. Burns had yet to look up. Gabe was sure more than a few ounces of liquor had something to do with that.

"Look at this girl." He raised his voice. "YOU, Mrs. Burns. Look at the woman that was once your daughter. The daughter you never put to bed because you were too drunk. This is your last chance to look at her." The woman shrunk in on herself.

"Mother?"

The woman shriveled and shook as if Cricket had just beaten her.

"How dare you speak to my wife?"

"You call that a wife? She is the woman you spurned in favor of your daughter. You stopped sleeping with your wife the minute you could move your little girl into a real bed instead of a crib. That is the woman you no longer touched, you just got her drunker until she wouldn't get in the way of you molesting and eventually having intercourse with your own flesh and blood. She was only for you to trot out and show off that you had a marriage. Meanwhile, you touched and played with the naked body of a small child until you could train her to accommodate your every sick whim and lust."

The priest had made his way to the confrontation, but Jan put her hand on the man's chest. He looked at her—pleading that she would tell him that what was happening wasn't real or true. Jan just shook her head and mouthed the words— *It's all true.*

The once powerful man twisted away from the words.

Cricket found her voice. "That's right. What he has said is all true. You molested me every single night, until the other night when I called for your help because I was out after curfew, stuck at the beach with no money to get home... and you called me a slut. You told me never to come home. You told me that you would never have a slut living under your roof. It was my seventeenth birthday. For seventeen years—you made me your personal slut. Well, now... I'm free. You have a slut free home. You got what you wanted—a house where there is no slut.

"Nobody to lie on the floor—while you take them in the ass.

"Nobody to dress up in pretty pink—so they can suck you.

"Nobody to let you screw them while they are

dressed in their school clothes, and then have you force them to wear the same clothes the next day—so the nuns can smell your semen on the skirt.

"Nobody to make play your twisted sick sexual games because they won't tell anyone."

Cricket took a deep breath. "Well, Father, I'll tell you what. Starting today, I won't tell another soul because, from this moment forward, you are dead to me. Whoever you thought was your daughter never existed, doesn't exist, and never will. As for spreading the word about your sick little shit, and your tiny penis—I don't have to." She stood straight and stuck her arm out pointing as she slowly turned. "They will do it for me. These great friends of yours—the ones whose daughters and sons you touched in ways that only someone who had been there can tell. Yes, all of those children you touched, groped, molested... they will now know that they can speak up, they can speak out, and they can destroy you with total impunity."

Carefully, a young man stood in the middle of the congregation. He cleared his throat. "I'm..." He cleared it again and stood straighter and spoke louder. "I'm sorry. I didn't know, Amelia. I thought I was the only one."

Slowly, as the congregation and priest watched in horror—many of the youth rose. Some were close enough to reach out and take each other's hands. Some wept silently.

One young girl rose. Her eyes were wet, but all could sense the iron pouring down into her spine. She lifted her chin. "No more."

Cricket turned about, looking at all who were standing. Gabe saw no tears in her eyes, only steel. Cold... hard... steel. She looked at Jan. "We're done here." She turned and walked up the long aisle. The church was silent, except for the beginning of whispers. Gabe and the four cops followed. Their eyes were only on the young woman ahead.

The Avenging Angel with truth as her sword.

As they neared the door, Jan mumbled to the older cop. "It looks like there might be a need for an investigation or something here."

The older cop glanced back over his shoulder at the people standing. He looked back at Jan and smirked sadly. "I think the investigation is done. Now it is time for retribution and justice of a more biblical proportion."

43

RIO

HIGH UPON A mountain named Corcovado there stands a large statue of Christ the Redeemer. He stands with his arms outspread looking out across the sea. The people standing at the base of the hundred-foot tall statue are tiny in comparison. The statue overlooks all of Rio and represents the Christianity of Brazil.

It is one of the most recognizable statues in the world.

Gabe teased Cricket. "Why in the world would a guy stand like that? His arms must be really tired."

She poked him in the belly as she hung at his side so she could look up. "He is holding his arms wide like that so you can see how much I love you."

Gabe couldn't answer, so he just hugged her harder.

"Vocês percorreram um caminho longo, senhor."

ANGEL FLIGHTS

Gabe turned them around to face the familiar voice. The man stood there with his wife and four children. "Werner, your Spanish is getting worse."

"But I think my Portuguese is getting better." His wife smiled and nodded. "Where is Rabbit?"

"Just taking in the sights, Werner."

The man turned to see Rabbit walking with a small boy. Maria and Lito bracketed Zorro as they all came up the path.

Werner smiled. "In Brazil, we have a saying that happy news is best shared over a meal."

Gabe laughed. "I think we need to go find a feast."

Rabbit and Zorro were echoes. "I'll drink to that."

The End
OR maybe just the beginning

OTHER BOOKS BY BAER CHARLTON

The Very Littlest Dragon

Stoneheart
(Pulitzer Nominee 2015)

Southside Hooker Series
Death on a Dime – Book One
Night Vision – Book Two
Unbidden Garden – Book Three

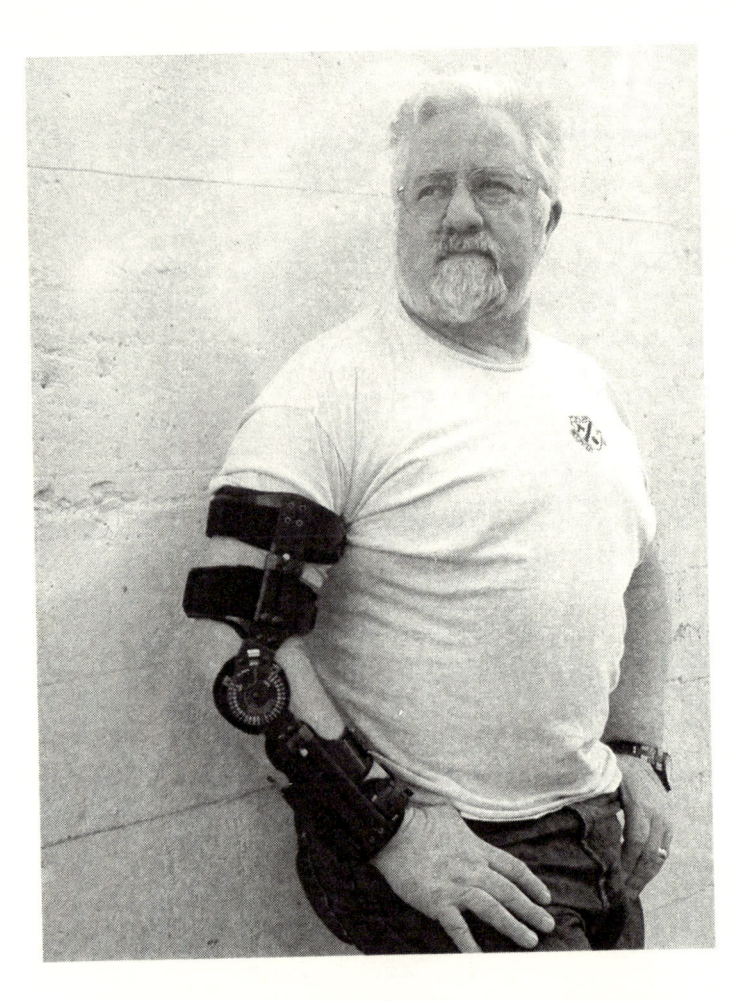

BAER CHARLTON, AUTHOR

ABOUT THE AUTHOR

Baer Charlton graduated from UC Irvine with a degree in Social Anthropology, monkeyed around for a while, and then preceded onward with a life of global travel, multi-disciplinary adventure, and meeting the memorable array of characters he would come to describe in his writing. He has ridden things with gears, engines, and sails and made things with wood, leather, and metal. He has been stitched back together more times than the average hockey team; his long-suffering wife and an assortment of cats and dogs have nursed him back to health after each surgery.

Baer knows a lot about many things in this world. History flows through his veins and pours out of him at the slightest provocation. Do not ask him what you may think is a simple question, unless you have the time to hear a fascinating story.

You can find more about Baer at his website.
www.baercharlton.com

CPSIA information can be obtained
at www.ICGtesting.com
Printed in the USA
FSOW01n2302191015
12359FS

9 780984 966677